M.A. MOLLENKOPF

The Graviscape

Unexpected Expedition

To my wonderful family and friends – I'm so grateful that each of you afforded me the space and encouragement to explore the creative art of storytelling. Thank you.

Contents

Chapter 1: On Mars

What they suddenly wanted done was just impossible.

With no less than fifteen strangers staring right at me, I dipped my head, looking down at the ground and then slowly shook my head from side to side, trying to figure out how to make this work.

"Okay, okay, let me consider this for a second," I said as I raised my head and pasted on a fake smile for the bureaucrats.

I stepped away from the table toward Sarah and whispered a question to her. She looked up as if the answer was in the sky, then back down to me and murmured a seriously long, exception-filled response. I let out a low whistle thinking about what she'd said.

"I think we can make it without help from the tug," I whispered.

I looked over at Huang, who had a solemn look on his face, so I gave him a grin and moved my eyebrows up and down a couple of times.

"Huang, what are we looking at here, four or five?" Huang looked at me and I saw the slightest smile appear on his face.

"Roger, sir, this is looking to be at least a five-WTFs-per-hour event," Huang replied quietly.

I smiled more fully at Huang and Sarah to give them a reassuring look as we continued quietly exchanging thoughts until a crisp, but shrill voice crackled from the speaker in the center of the table.

"Captain Murray!" the sharp male voice said, "you will report on time with the required complement of personnel and cargo or face disciplinary actions consistent with the policies you are violating."

"But sir," I retorted, "It's not safe to try and pull all this together and meet the space tug timeline. I just need a couple more days to get everything organized—"

"Listen Dave," the voice started again in a softer tone, "I don't mean to be unreasonable, but the senior agency leadership has received several reports concerning you and your crew.... And, well, the reports imply that you are horsing around and not tending to your assigned missions—so the order has come down from the Ops director—get your missions done and get back here on schedule. Earth Prime station out."

Everyone around the table turned their heads in unison to look at me with a reasonably judgmental look in their eyes as my face started to flush in embarrassment.

Well crap, that sure seemed final.

"Sir, that's just not true," I retorted back into the speaker using my best super-deep tough-guy voice even though I knew it was going to take about twenty minutes to get a response.

In fact, these long-range conversations always seemed to be one-sided because of the propagation delay of sending a signal from Mars to Earth, which took about ten minutes, then another ten to receive the response.

Anytime HQ said "Out" at the end of a transmission, that pretty much ended the conversation.

I looked at the faces around the table, and, despite the sidebar conversations, I noted several staffers and military personnel collecting their papers and documents with intent to leave the meeting room now that the conversation appeared to be over.

I got the feeling that no one believed in me.

Well, regardless of everyone else in the room, I really wanted my crew to believe in me. But that's been a tough road to travel because of some of my decisions, especially the decisions made under pressure that didn't turn out so well.

Anyway, one man was looking at me with strong intensity, like I'd done something to offend him. I think his name was Max, I don't know where I remember him from but yes, Max was his name. As I was contemplating Max, four people moved my way from the other side of the room, appearing to approach for what I hoped was a conversation and not a confrontation.

I recognized them as part of the Agency base-engineering team. Good people and innovative thinkers. You have to be creative in order to be stationed on Mars and handle the wide variety of challenges they encounter each day.

Leading this foursome was a person named William Castle, a man in his forties wearing a brown Agency engineer uniform. He strode right up to me and started a conversation. "Dave, I'm sorry about this. I don't know what reports they are talking about; we haven't sent them anything."

"No worries, Billy, I'm sure there's some sort of misunderstanding at the root here. We've worked out a plan that I think will work if you and your team can help us with a few details. Do you still have those container pushers?"

"Yes...I think so. They are pretty old, you know. If my memory is right, we have about thirty of them. I think using them in this situation would be tricky. Getting that many super-heavy lifts sequenced just right will require a lot more time than I think you have.

"You may not recall but those are the older leader-follower type that operate in a chain with one leader engine and four to ten follower freight cars."

I smiled uncomfortably as I tried to control the anxiety that was creeping up and replied, "Billy, I've got a strategy that will work. Can we go over to your ops facility to discuss the plan? I mean, can we go right now as I don't have a lot of wiggle room in the schedule."

Billy nodded up and down in what looked like a firm yes and said, "A plan huh? Okay, roger that, we are heading that way right now—will see you there, Dave."

I reached out to Billy and gave him an appreciative, strong handshake and said, "Thank you Billy; I owe you one."

Billy looked at me with the broad grin that he gets when he's trying to be funny and said, "Hell, Dave, that's more like eight or ten that you owe me. I'm not sure if this is doable, but I'll withhold my 'expert' analysis until we hear your plan."

With that, Billy and his associates walked out of the room while Sarah,

Huang and I collected our papers and tablet computers and prepared to follow them to the engineering ops center.

After a couple of solid hours of analysis and planning in the Agency station engineering main conference room, we started feeling a little bit better about our plan. Sidebar conversations continued as the Mars station chief Gerrard came into the room in his dress uniform, which was decorated with a pin and few insignias that indicated he was a very experienced, senior civilian leader in the Space Colonization Agency.

Gerrard owns a small but important chunk of Mars station, and he'd be held responsible if we created a major disaster trying to get the cargo and related items off Mars and back to Earth station.

Gerrard looked around the room, spotted me, then walked quickly to the table where Billy, Sarah, and I were working through final plans. Billy and I stood as he approached.

"Captain Murray, I see you've once again managed to make your unpreparedness an emergency for my organization to deal with."

I looked around at the assembled team, feeling a rather severe sinking feeling developing in the pit of my stomach, so I faked a smile and prepared my deepest, calmest tough-guy voice. "Chief Gerrard, hello, it's good to see you again. And I do understand your view, but there are other issues that we've not been able to highlight up to this point."

Now Isaac Gerrard and I came up together in the Agency, and he moved fast. It was warranted, as he is brilliant, if not a bit too by-the-book for my tastes, but a good friend nonetheless. He'd treat me, my team, and this situation in a professional way, and I was fairly sure that the Agency was leaning on him as well.

"Okay Captain, let's hear it, what are the issues?"

"We'll have to talk in private sir as there are security concerns related to the issues."

The Agency chief looked at Billy, then over to Sarah, finally refocusing back on me. "Okay, let's go to my office, just you and me."

I looked around at the team and focused on Sarah. Sarah Maxwell is the *Algonquin*'s Chief of Navigation and Sensors: Computer Science Track. She's young, but she's a smart, trusted leader, and most importantly, third in command. I asked her to finalize the sequencing of events because getting it right was important for success, and I knew she could handle getting it done.

A few minutes later I found myself seated across the desk from Chief Gerrard as we sat alone in his office.

"Alright, Dave, let's hear it. What are the complicating issues?"

Now I addressed him as "sir" because he was senior to me, and that's the protocol for the Agency. That's just how our system works, but I must admit, I was surprised at his rather aggressive interaction with me given how long we'd known each other. I wondered if something else was bothering him. "Sir, there's been a rather vicious outbreak of Snale pox in the hydroponics district...." Snale pox was a water-borne virus discovered by a researcher named Dr. Randal Snale just after we started colonizing Mars. Snale pox grows in algae that sometimes leaks into water or food supplies and could easily spread to take out a lot of people in a short time span.

Gerrard sat up straighter, immediately concerned. "Damn. Is it under control? What is the spread ratio?"

"Sir, the full details are classified," I said and saw Gerrard wince slightly. "They've managed to isolate the sections of algae, moss, plants, and employees so spreading has been neutralized. Several employees remain hospitalized but most concerning ...." I had to think about what I was about to reveal because I was not supposed to do so, but I felt he deserved and needed to know. "There have been eleven deaths."

Gerrard suddenly looked sullen and peered off into the distance over my shoulder. And with a deep breath, he replied. "Dave, my wife has not been home in two days. She's been isolated over in the military barracks with several of her coworkers, and they've been very tight-lipped about whatever situation is going down. I knew something really bad must have happened if they were keeping the details from me. This is not good." Gerrard paused and rubbed his eyes, then exhaled slowly. "Okay, so what's the mission, and how can we help?"

I thought about the stress he must be feeling regarding his wife, probably more than he was letting on. An idea popped into my head about how to set him at ease. I pulled the tablet computer out of my cargo pocket and looked through the data.

"Sir, I see a Catherine Gerrard on the list at the military barracks. As of 2100 yesterday, she has reportedly experienced no symptoms, and I believe that's where they are holding folks that were not exposed to the sections of plants where the Snale pox was found."

Gerrard turned back to meet my eyes. He perked up a bit and said, "Thank you, Dave, I appreciate you sharing that information."

He knew I must have been sharing sensitive info. His eyes contracted just a millimeter as he said, "What about our food and water, any risk to the supply chain you can share?"

I looked down at the tablet, scrolling through the data pretending to read it as I thought about how to provide insights without revealing classified information. The agency wanted to handle this carefully and restricted access to nearly all the information. *Well crap. There's no way for me to do that.*

"Sir, there's been a significant effort to trace the origin of many key supplies, and luckily most of the contaminated food and water has been successfully recalled or is in the process of being returned. Most colonists will not know how close we came to a disaster of epic proportions. So, this is why we are in a bit of a spot."

Chief Gerrard glanced around the room, then looked back at me. "What's the whole story here, Dave? HQ calls me out of the blue and says that you have been here screwing off and have failed to get priority cargo loaded for transport. Transport that will miss the scheduled cargo tug back to Earth, and, I guess, miss some timeline that's not been mentioned. Dave, they indicated it was because of negligence. I told them that was uncharacteristic of you, but I never got a response or any details. The lack of response is puzzling. Have you made any new enemies back at HQ who you can think of?"

I thought about that for a moment. My mind shifted immediately to the run-in I'd had with that jackass, Max. But that had happened here, and it seemed unlikely that he would be linked up with anyone who mattered back at HQ. My brain raced. *Max is tight with that Agency geologist, Sasha Rairkov. She's a major pain and could have something to do with this.* "Well, sir, I did have a run-in with one of the geologists that works for Dr. Rairkov, guy named Max Randolf, but I can't imagine they would send secret reports about me back to Earth as our run-in seemed to be focused as much on the company I was keeping as some research effort he was working on," I said with a perplexed look.

Gerrard nodded and looked as though he was contemplating something. "Okay, I'll look into it quietly, Dave. Can you share some of the mission background?"

"Yes, sir. The short version is... we were on route to Outpost Yankee when we received a flash notification. So we immediately diverted within laser range of the nearest message buoy and downloaded our traffic including the sensitive flash message." I moved around a bit in my seat but kept my eyes locked on Gerrard's eyes, and he nodded as I spoke. "The message diverted us here to take part in the Snale pox response action as *Big Al* has a superb medical facility and staff. After arriving, we focused on the affected districts, working on the hydroponics systems and eradicating the Snale pox virus across the colony's footprint, including performing supply chain analysis. Then, out of the blue I get this Agency request to load and deliver one hundred tons of important cargo back to Earth."

"You're saying it was a request, not an order?"

"Right, and I thought it very odd, but it just said priority-2 cargo transport request. Since it wasn't an order, I decided I didn't have to accept it. I made the decision to decline it, but did not respond with an official reclama. I figured the leadership back on Earth knew that I was dealing with the classified Snale pox issue, so I ignored the request. Then I got called to the carpet late last night which led to the session this morning over at the Colony HQ." I sucked in a deep breath and continued. "We are packaging samples of the algae, moss, and other plants, along with the virus for transport, and we obviously want to get that right, so there's not been a lot of time to get rock-transport plans calculated in. Now... I did stop by to see a couple of ladies, and on one of those engagements, while at dinner, the guy I'd mentioned before, Max, he and I got in a pushing contest, but after that he disappeared."

The look on Gerrard's face told me he was mentally assembling the situation. "So now I have to get all the virus-related packages stowed and secure plus figure out how to get one hundred tons of frigging rocks off the planet so that we can catch the inbound tugs in about twelve hours to transport everything back to Earth."

I saw Chief Gerrard make a few notes on his tablet before he looked up at me. "What is the difference in time to Earth if you miss the tugs?"

Without looking at my tablet I told him, "The tugs will have the cargo and Snale pox samples to Earth's logistics perimeter in 21 days. But I can take them directly from Mars Colony to Earth Prime Station in thirty days. So if you add the time it takes to get from the logistics automation perimeter to Earth Station, which is about six additional days depending on the level of traffic already in the line, we'd make it there three days later than the automated logistics system could get it there. Plus, my team could be conducting analysis of the Snale pox genetics and exchanging them with scientists back on Earth the whole way home."

"Hmmm, I should think the Agency would go for that set of tradeoffs. Three days for direct transport. What about your op to Yankee?"

"They've redirected the *Liberty* to handle that visit. They don't have the size or surgical staff that the *Algonquin*'s got, but they do have more modern medical and engineering capability to meet the mission."

"Yes, *Big Al* is quite a capable colony support ship; too bad it's being decommissioned," Gerrard said.

I raised my chin just a millimeter or two before fake-smiling hard and replying, "We'll see, sir, if that happens. *Big Al* has been up for decommissioning three times during my term as Captain, and each time I've managed to push the timeline."

"I see," Gerrard grinned at how hard I'd worked, angling to keep the mighty *Algonquin* in action. "When do you need to leave orbit to make it back to Earth on your own?"

I didn't need to consult my tablet to reply, "We need to depart from Mars in twenty-eight hours. So we'll be hustling to get the cargo up to *Algonquin* now that we have a plan. By the way, I really appreciate Billy and the team's

CHAPTER 1: ON MARS

help. We couldn't do any of this without it, so thank you for that."

I could see Gerrard now realized how much of a time crunch we were under, and he smiled and stood up from his chair. He put out his hand. "Dave, we'll do what we can to get you out of here as soon as possible. If you need anything, call me directly. I'll let you know what I find out about this 'request' to transport the cargo."

I stood and shook his hand heartily, then hurried back to the conference room. On my way, I submitted an urgent request to have Carrol Gerrard moved to the priority list for screening, and, hopefully, for her to be returned to duty status shortly thereafter. *The Chief has too much responsibility to be alone here,* I thought.

Back in the conference room, I went over the final details of using our cargo tether to yank the cargo into space to make sure we all understood what we were going to do. "Our glorified space hook should be able to pull this much weight up to the *Algonquin* if we can boost it high enough into Mars's light atmosphere with the initial push; we've done this sort of thing before on planets and moons where the gravity is low, just not quite to this size and scale. To make this work, the *Algonquin* goes into low orbit, and, essentially, unreels a really long tether that has specialized vertical and lateral control hardware every few hundred kilometers. Attached at the bottom end of the tether is a specially designed hook, and a tiny aerospace ship to guide the hooking mechanism toward the target cargo."

I paused to look around the room, but I could see they were all with me, so I continued. "The big idea is to use cheaper, unmanned rockets attached to big cargo boxes called 'pushers' to get the cargo off the surface to a certain elevation in the atmosphere. Then we catch the cargo with the hook and pull it toward the *Algonquin*. The pushers are not piloted, so there's a lot less risk to human life."

We all shook hands and departed the conference room heading in our different directions to execute our assigned tasks.

An hour later I arrived out at the pusher launch point, which was the Mars colony's perimeter. We conducted all automated launches off the planet at that location to avoid risk to the massive colony complex if something failed or went wrong. We packed the cargo containers, wired them up and used wheeled drones to push them outside into the launch area. "Alright Sasha, this is the last crate of cargo, right?" I stated as definitively as possible, trying hard to be congenial, because Dr. Sasha Rairkov is a very reactive person, and I was hoping she would respond with a yes.

"Yes Captain. By the way, you are aware of the urgency to get this material back to Earth, right?"

I wonder if she knows about me getting called to the carpet by the agency ops director? "Roger Sasha, I'm tracking the critical timeline. Although it doesn't make much sense to me to risk life and limb to get a bunch of rocks back to Earth. I'm not sure who would make such a request to the Agency, because it's an inherently risky maneuver." I was probing for more details.

Sasha stopped what she was working on, removed her gloves, stood with one hand on her hip, and looked at me for a few milliseconds before she finally replied. "If you are asking if I spoke to headquarters, the answer is yes." Sasha let that sink in, and then she said, "I told them that... that you—Captain Dave Murray and his crew—were distracted by other missions and uhh, 'visits.' I need this material back on Earth as soon as possible."

Sasha raised her fingers making air quotes around the word "visits," which meant she was cognizant of my visits with a lady friend in the colony complex. That, coupled with the fact that she'd called home to Earth station to gripe about me and my team, pissed me off. "Well that was a cheapjack thing to do; why didn't you just explain to me the urgency of this issue?" I said with annoyance.

"I tried several times," Sasha began, ready to rant at me, just as her pet goon, Max, sidled up to our conversation.

"You mean you had your associate, Max here, bother me with this when I was having dinner with a friend. You know, I have many other roles on this mission that you are not aware of. Sometimes, things we think are important are not so important in the grand scheme of things. Hell, I'd like to find the person that invented round shoelaces and kick their asses on general principle, but that doesn't mean something so petty is going to happen."

I was looking at Max then, with a "just try it" smile on my face. Sasha started in on her priority list again, and Max just stood there, adding in what he felt were key points to support her argument, and the whole thing was starting to draw the attention of several folks working on the launch process.

Damn, I hate talking to her. I stood there as she railed on, stonewalling. She was brilliant, there was no doubt, but it was hard to look past that mean, ugly attitude to try and build any sort of relationship. I continued to be unresponsive, and she finally stormed off in a huff, Max trailing behind her. That was okay by me; I had work to do anyway.

We conducted the final cargo transport coordination meeting, then I headed back to my ship so we could employ the space hook and get this cargo loaded and get on our way.

On my way back to my transport ship, I stopped in at the colony shoppette to grab a few essentials as requested by the crew, and I also had to get peanut butter for me because I do have a thing for it, so for me, it's an essential. Yes, that's what I said, rich, nutty peanut butter. It's a well-known colonist staple, but most non-colonists don't realize that peanut butter sits by itself at the top of the colonist food pyramid... more or less. Then I headed back to the spaceport where our dinghy, *Ranger-1*, was parked. Huang Fei was sitting in the pilot's seat in a video teleconference with engineers aboard the *Algonquin* and the Mars station.

Huang, a superb young leader and an outstanding pilot, looked in my direction, giving me the okay sign to tell me everything on the conference was proceeding as anticipated. I gave him a thumbs up and headed to the back of the dinghy to hide... err safely store the peanut... err... *important crew supplies.*

The *Ranger-1* is quite the nifty little aero-spaceship that enables a multi-person crew to get from space to planet side and back, quickly using the latest in advanced, but small-engine, tech. After I had stored the precious cargo, I went back to Huang, who had completed his call. "All right Huang, how many WTFs per hour are we looking at now for this crazy cargo mission?" I asked with a big grin on my face.

Huang returned my broad grin, then pretended to be serious for a moment saying, "Zero, sir. I have a feeling this will go very smoothly."

I smiled back. "Holy moly, zero? That would be something Huang!" We discussed a few notes resulting from the coordination with various points of contact involved, and, after checking in with the *Algonquin*, we decided it was time to bug out.

An hour later I was back on *Big Al* working through cargo storage plans with the crew while Zane, the *Algonquin*'s deputy commander and executive officer (XO) worked on the plan to hook the cargo from Mars's light atmosphere.

I thought about Huang's prediction of zero WTFs per hour but... my inner monologue was counting WTFs per hour at around the range of ten to twenty. *Gotta think positive,* I told myself, trying to control the apprehension twisting my gut. *Especially in front of the crew.*

Zane and Mickey, the ship's co-lead engineer, verbally jousted about the space tether's ability to withstand the strain of such a large load and debated whether or not to supplement the lift by using the older, less advanced space crane from the heavily modified Mars moon, Phobos to perform the initial catch.

I'd never bet against Mick; he's the best mechanical engineer in the Agency. Miguel Romero, Mickey for short, is the one engineer you want on your ship if the going gets tough. And let me tell you, in space, the going is always tough. Zane and Mick opted against using the Phobos station crane, as it was better suited to shuttling lighter weight material, like people, between the surface of Mars and low orbit. Also, the complexity of maneuvering Phobos station at this late hour added too much additional operational complexity, as Phobos was mostly a small military station and not well equipped for this sort of work.

"Sir," Zane's voice crackled over my wrist-mounted computer, the Femto-Com. "Priority message from Mars Colony HQ, if you didn't see it. It requires your response. Something about the tug is all I can see in the subject line."

I raised my forearm to read the message and replied, "Roger Zane, I acknowledged their message. It was a notification that the tug was being taken offline for maintenance as there was damage to the main tug engine. There will be a navigation hazard notification coming in soon, so they are just letting us know."

Zane's face popped onto my FemtoCom. "Sir, did you say a tug suffered damage? The very same tug we were supposed to rendezvous with to ship this cargo back to Earth?"

"Roger Zane, that's what it said. Very odd, as those tugs are really tough buggers."

I could see Zane look down for a moment, then back up at me as he replied, "Wow, so I guess our renegade decision worked out for the best after all."

I smiled back at Zane and said, "Yep, I think we are on the right path for getting both missions accomplished." I wondered if Zane had thought my plan would fail. *I need to work on building trust with the crew, especially Zane.* Zane and I chatted for a bit as the time for launching the cargo from Mars approached.

The ship and crew were ready. Well, as ready as we could be to catch a hundred tons of rock being shot at us from the surface of Mars. "Sir, if we miss hooking those containers, there's going to be a huge mess to clean up on Mars. The colony security channels are really buzzing with activity, hope it's not focused on us."

I thought about Zane's comment and quickly replied, "Naawww, I'm sure there's other issues to sort out down there. Besides, this is going to work flawlessly, I'm certain of it," I lied.

My stomach started twisting up just thinking about the catastrophe that would occur if we screwed this up. Given my past mistakes, a blunder of this magnitude would end my career. *They'd probably put Zane in charge immediately. No, I've got to think positively, this will work,* I told myself. *And when it does, I'll buy back some respect from the crew.* Nearly everyone was counting on us to execute flawlessly.

Zane looked back toward me and gave me a smile and a thumbs up.

"All right Zane, time to saddle up. Let's get Huang checked in and ready," I said, grinning at Zane as I got cowboy reference in.

A short while later, showtime came with the *Algonquin* moving into position, and Huang maneuvering the space hook several hundred kilometers below in what passed for an atmosphere, by piloting the fantastically delicate hook ship, making last-minute path adjustments. I was fidgeting in my command cubicle on *Algonquin*'s flight deck, with Zane and the rest of the crew on watch in their shallow cubes—they were in front of me but positioned slightly lower.

It's ironic that nearly every manned deck on the ship looked like a 1990s multi-level cube farm where everyone sat together, yet were afforded some privacy if desired by raising their cube walls and sitting versus standing. The actual purpose of the movable cube walls was to provide radiation shielding and run oxygen, water, and other conduits to each person during long emergency sessions. In the early days of colonizing the solar system, the cumulative effects of radiation over long-term space travel caused significant health problems and resulted in retrofitting each deck with more granular, redundant radiation protection.

"Huang, remember the abort criteria, if the torsion rating exceeds 8.6, we abort—period, full stop," Zane smoothly restated for what seemed like the tenth time. Crap, we were all tense; the whole event seemed to be moving at a glacial pace.

"Yes, sir, tracking 8.6 on the torsion meter," Huang calmly restated.

I could see Zane was worried about Huang flying that hook ship as it wasn't much of a ship at all, just a seat strapped to an awful lot of engines, a couple of wings, and a long protruding yet massive hooking mechanism all straddled by a pilot in a full space suit riding along.

A few minutes later, Mars Colony Base Ops started broadcasting that the cargo pushers had lifted off and sent out subsequent trajectory measurements in hundreds of meters. Zane coordinated activity between Mars, Huang, and Alex Singh, the second of two *Algonquin* pilots who was also a computer systems engineer. Mars slowly rotated into position while Huang maneuvered to get the hook into the right spot.

Everyone was watching the holographic event model that depicted Mars, *Big Al*, the hook ship, and of course, the star attraction, the cargo, as it lifted from Mars thanks to those massive pushers. *Big Al* had to have just the right amount of forward velocity to drag the cargo up into space without snapping the tether, so Alex was constantly making calculated thruster changes to reduce the probability that a tether-snapping amount of torque would build as the lift went down.

The cargo looked like a string of boxes hung below the massive pusher engine that did most of the pulling, bringing the boxes into the higher regions of Mars's atmosphere. Each of the cargo containers did have sufficient thrust to get their boxes off the ground, but they were small and designed to wear out quickly, allowing the pusher engine to take over and remove the slack in the cables that connected the cargo boxes.

We all watched the holographic display tensely as Huang's hook ship came up behind the pusher engine. As he approached, he carefully adjusted his course and speed to match the engine's. "Almost there..." Zane said over the comms link. "Almost there..." once again, as Zane narrated his internal monologue for the rest of us.

Huang's voice broke in, "*Algonquin*, this is *Hitcher1*, I'm in position, permission to hook? I say again, *Algonquin*, this is *Hitcher1*, I'm in position, requesting permission to hook the cargo."

"It looks good to me. Zane, Sarah, Alex, do you see any issues?" Zane then Sarah, and finally Alex all replied stating there were no detectable anomalies, and that Huang should execute the hook.

"Okay, let's do it. *Hitcher1*, *Hitcher1*, this is *Algonquin*; you are cleared to hook the cargo. Execute, execute, execute," I said as clearly as possible, knowing that despite microphones in his helmet, Huang was buffeting in Mars's atmosphere so he couldn't hear as clearly as he'd like.

A few seconds later Huang successfully hooked the cargo, slowly ascending from the surface of Mars. Huang blurted out, "Got it! Wow, that took a lot longer than expected. *Algonquin* this is *Hitcher1*, the cargo is hooked." His excitement caught me off guard, but we were all happy the hard part had finally been completed.

Minutes ticked by as Mars Base Operations Engineers, Zane, and Huang, coordinated the cargo's ascension from Mars's light atmosphere. "Huang, what is the torsion reading?" Zane calmly barked as the *Algonquin*'s forward momentum increased, and the slack started popping out of the tether.

"It's 6.6 and rising fast sir. I'm not liking this—7.2 now," Huang stated with concern grinding into his voice. Mickey commented to Zane that the velocity numbers looked right on and that the tether's smart controls should be able to handle the load.

A sudden snap jolted Huang's little ship as a large portion of slack snapped out of the *Algonquin's* tether, despite the built-in controls to prevent this type of event from occurring. "Huang, disconnect now, now, now, now!" Zane yelled over the microphone.

"Zane, what's happening?" I said, while the milliseconds spent waiting for a response seemed like hours.

"Sir, the tether's built-in controls are having a difficult time balancing the twisting and tension as the *Algonquin* pulls out of orbit; the weight is right at the edge of being too much... and we really need Huang to disconnect as there will likely be more tether snaps. Also, I'm pretty sure that snap hurt the hook ship and potentially Huang himself. That ship's not designed for significant cargo adjustments, remote piloting, or pilot protection. Besides, there's not much he can do down there now that the cargo is hooked. We'd originally planned for Huang to stay snapped to the cargo and tether so he could help mediate any severe motion, but it's too late for that now, only the tether's lateral controls can do that work for us."

"Huang, are you okay?... Huang!" I yelled over the radio—no response. I started mentally working through the list of things that could have gone wrong with Huang when suddenly a series of alarms went off on the *Algonquin*. Mars Colony Ops broadcast loud buzzing sounds with a computer voiced narrative repeatedly stating: "Proximity Alert, inbound spacecraft trajectory too near the *Algonquin*."

What the hell is going on? I thought. *Well, I guess that's one WTF.*

I mentally backgrounded the Huang hook ship and cargo situation and started working on the proximity alert. I looked over to the XO's cube, "Zane, what ship is getting too close? I don't have a visual; what's the NavRadar show?"

Zane glanced at me, an alarmed expression on his face. "Sir, two inbound moving targets, no ID signals being emitted, and they are coming in freaking fast and from the IR sensor it looks like they are executing a massive burn to slow down."

Oh crap indeed. The chances of two ships coming in this fast and having some sort of ID signal emitter failure at the same time was nearly impossible. This likely meant pirates. Not the fun, storybook pirates of ole, modern vicious pirates that steal, kill, and generally destroy anything or anyone that gets between them and their prey.

"Mars Ops 3, we've got visitors up here. Need support ASAP!" Zane called out with noticeable strain in his voice.

Two very long minutes after Zane repeated the warning, the Ops Officer at Mars Station finally replied, "Roger *Algonquin*, we've dispatched two *SkyLarks* from Phobos Station, ETA twenty-six minutes," the ops officer from Mars Station responded.

I looked over at Zane and Alex who both looked back at me. "Crap, we'll be dead in twenty-six minutes! Zane we need to—"

"Sir, I suppose now is a bad time to mention that I took the coils out of the rail gun for maintenance and have not had time to reassemble the weapon," Alex said with both courage and a moderate amount of cracking in his voice.

Under my breath I quietly said, "Crap," and then aloud I blurted out, "Mick, you've got to get that railgun reassembled, like minutes okay?" I barked into the ship's intercom.

"I'm on it, Dave," came the rapid reply from Mickey.

"Zane, where are the two bogeys headed?" I barked.

Zane rapidly scanned multiple screens and the holographic display. "Sir, pick up the events trace in the Holo Map. I'm sending you the trajectory estimates," Zane replied.

I quickly flipped on the Holo Map's events trace display which showed Mars, Phobos station, the *Algonquin* and tether. "Okay, okay... looks like they are after the cargo, one ship to whack us and the other ship to tow the cargo away I'm guessing," I replied.

"Sir, I'd say we need to execute evasive action plan Charlie then accelerate away," Alex offered.

Zane quickly cut in, "We can't go evasive Charlie as we'd likely lose the tether and cargo, and we can't risk dropping those rocks on Mars station. Sir, recommend evasive Alpha+, that will make it hard for their rail guns to target us while hopefully not jerking the cargo and tether around too much."

Thinking for a millisecond, I shot back, "Roger that, Zane, execute Alpha+! Mick, what's the deal with that rail gun?"

After what seemed like a long minute Mickey replied, "Sir, the rail gun will take hours to fix; it's not helping us in this fight."

"Okay that's two WTFs people; lets try to avoid getting to three," I said as I thought through courses of action, "Okay, plan C it is. Zane, you have command; I'm taking *Ranger-1* out to protect the Algonquin as best I can. Please try and get a hold of Huang; I'm worried something serious is wrong down there."

Zane, Alex, and Sarah all looked back towards me truly shocked. "Sir, *Ranger 1* has no weapons. How are you going to defend *Algonquin*?"

"Well, if I have to I will ram the attackers as carefully as possible to keep them away from *Algonquin* and to try to protect Huang. I'll figure out the details on the way."

Zane checked some instruments and looked at me. "Uhhh, sir, I'm probably the better selection to take *Ranger-1* out—"

I cut him off. "Roger, totally agree if this were a different situation. I'd send you but I'm a much better pilot than you," I lied with a smile. Zane looked back at me with that quiet understanding he had, and I jumped up and hurriedly traversed the ship's inner core. I made my way to the docking bays where I found *Ranger-1* right where Huang, Sarah, and I had left it earlier.

I realized every second counted, as the pirate ships streaked toward us, and I needed to get moving. I hopped into a transport quality space suit and then into *Ranger-1,* backed the ship away from the *Algonquin,* and began maneuvering.

I had done a fair amount of flying with *Ranger-1*, so this part was no problem. I scanned the instrument panel and asked the NavComp to populate the NAV Holo Map with the ships in the vicinity of *Ranger-1*. The computer complied, and I saw the two bogeys on screen tagged as unresponsive ships, noted as *Moving Target Indicators 3 and 4* respectively. I then looked up, and out the overhead portal in the direction I'd expected them to be. There I could easily see them both firing retros hard to try and slow down from the crazy speed they had put on in order to attack us with surprise. The bigger one was heading toward the tethered cargo, and the smaller one was heading toward the *Algonquin.*

I did a couple of calculations to figure out how I could be in position to ram the ship headed toward *Algonquin* and started thinking about Huang again, but there was no time for that, and I needed to get moving. "NavComp! Mark MTI-3 as bogey 1 and MTI-4 as bogey 2 and plot an interdiction path to MTI-4 prior to 3811354892 EPS standard time." The NavComp dutifully plotted the course and warned me of the extreme stress my body would encounter trying to accelerate to that location in spacetime.

No sooner did I click the "I Acknowledge Risk" button and *Ranger-1* freaking' took off! I always enjoyed flying *Ranger-1* because the overhead canopy portal allowed the pilot to see a full 180-degree view of the sky, and it was always beautiful to see the stars this way. In this case, however, I felt like *Ranger-1* was an evil giant, trying to crap me out of its exhaust pipe using acceleration as a crapping mechanism. "Ahhhhhhhhh!" I screamed into the radio to no one in particular. "This truly is going to be a four or five WTFs-per-hour event!" I blurted out for no apparent reason. I nearly blacked out as I focused on the Holo Map. Finally, the acceleration backed off, and I could see MTI-4's trajectory changing course on the Holo Map as the NavComp adjusted its trajectory based on real-time sensor readings of its flight path.

I looked around the cabin and tried to get myself into a position where I could ram the attacking ship and eject through the emergency escape hatch just before impact. Just then, I noticed two new signals on the Holo Map. The NavComp recognized them as Skylark-3 and 4 from Phobos station.

Damn! Those guys must have really pushed the limits to get here this quickly.

A voice came over the comms link from Skylark-3, "*Ranger-1* please abort current course! We've launched a field of railgun munitions that will pretty much destroy your fancy little ship if it continues on its current flight plan."

Okay dokey, better turn now... say, I'm trying to do something brave here... I thought. "Acknowledged SkyLark-3, really appreciate the effort you must have committed to get here; we certainly owe you one," I said, feeling better about the situation. "NavComp, return to the *Algonquin*: best, safe speed," I said. The NavComp acknowledged the command and started to comply.

Crap, I think I left part of my ass back there after the initial rush to intercept MTI-4. "And NavComp, please be sure to avoid the railgun munition field emitted by the Skylark-3 and Skylark-4." *Ranger-1*'s NavComp AI dutifully contacted *Algonquin*'s orchestration AI, which relayed a munitions field trajectory report from Phobos station's orchestration AI, so that it could calculate and execute an avoidance maneuver along the path back to *Algonquin*. Fifteen sweat-drenched minutes later, I made it back to the *Algonquin* in one piece, and after reaching the bridge, I asked Zane what was going on and if Huang was okay. Zane laid out the events as they occurred, with the Skylarks running off one of the Pirate ships and severely damaging the larger one, taking it in tow back to Phobos station.

Man, those pilots are bold. Huang was back on board the *Algonquin,* and the hook ship was tethered for repairs outside the maintenance portal on the ship's port side. Huang's comms had been knocked out by the snapping motion of the tether, but, thankfully, he was okay.

We conducted an extended after-action review to identify and work through remaining issues that needed to be addressed prior to planetary departure but overall we were in good shape—and wouldn't you know it, Mickey managed to get the rail gun working again.

What a day, I thought, *just another day in the Space Colonization Agency I suppose. Oh well, at least the hard parts are done. It should be smooth sailing from here.* We'd reeled in the cargo from Mars, picked up a few people from Phobos Station, and started organizing the crazy amount of cargo in preparation for tomorrow's trip back to Earth.

The doctors started looking at the latest Snale virus data, and after talking with Gerrard, I found out that the pirates went after the tugs first, which is what precipitated the earlier report. Pirates were on the prowl for something, we all agreed. I posited that they somehow knew about this high-priority cargo, and Gerrard thought it was a possibility.

We were overwhelmed with cargo and ended up mounting some of the sub-containers outside the ship to the external docking points as there was just no room left in the internal cargo bays.

Dinner in the galley that night was indeed fun. "Captain…" Zane started, "just what exactly did you intend to do with *Ranger-1* and the pirate ships?" he smirked.

I looked around the table as everyone looked back at me, and I described how my plan was to try to give them a more difficult target to shoot at, and, if I had to, I would have rammed them to keep them from damaging the tether or boarding the *Algonquin*, ejecting myself at the last possible moment. "No matter the situation, I never give up, but, as you know, I do reserve the right to cuss the entire time," I said with a lilt of humor in my voice. From there, the conversation descended into humorous jabs at me by the senior crew members as the junior members looked on trying to judge how much of the conversation was in fun, and how much was serious.

"Flying the hook ship was complicated, exhilarating and terrifying all at the same time," Huang said as he relayed how events unfolded for him while the crew and I listened. Huang used his hands to simulate how he flew to hook the cargo as he told the story. "The tether was easy to shift around which made me a little overconfident. I was not expecting the strong snap that stunned me when the slack came out of the cargo tether. The snapping motion scared the absolute crap out of me and knocked out my comms. Luckily, I was able to stay conscious enough to disconnect and recover." Huang looked around at the crew as he told the story. He finally looked at me to gauge my reaction, so I responded with a wide grin. "Well done Huang, you are a superb pilot with nerves of absolute steel. I love your optimism too as I recall you estimated this would be a zero-WTFs-per-hour operation! Very optimistic thinking Huang; very optimistic."

Just then our stunningly beautiful, Agency-contract surgeon, Abby, walked slowly toward my table, and she smiled as she sat down across from me. *Damn, she's beautiful: tall, blond hair, and glowing blue eyes.*

"Hello, sir, just wanted to let you know I completed all the surgical consults here on Mars and Phobos Station."

"Err, hi Abby, that's great to hear; they really needed your expertise, and you didn't let them down," I replied with my best low, tough guy voice accompanied by an attentive but restrained smile. I tried to look uninterested as she spoke, but I could tell she sensed that she was a bit of an outsider from the regular crew, so I shifted my attention to her more fully. "How many surgeries did you manage to fit in this tour?" I asked.

"Seventy-seven, and all recovered well, except for two patients who had multiple complicating factors. And, they were older and quite fragile. *Algonquin*'s MedBay really is world class; it's great we are able to bring advanced medical help to the colonies."

We chatted about the virus, the challenges with medical care, and the people we encountered in our missions. Abby seemed pretty happy with how things had concluded. She smiled at me, then got up from the table, noticing someone float-walking by that she wanted to talk to, but she looked back at me, and we locked eyes for just a millisecond longer than normal. Then she calmly smiled and said, "It was good to see you, Dave. Let's talk again later," and then she walked away with purpose.

My inner monologue started. *You lost an opportunity there. Abby is into you. Well crap.*

Okay, calm down. Abby has a lot of work to do. You'll see her later. It's difficult to get access to critical or urgent medical treatment out here so I'm glad the Agency regularly rotates these doctors, surgeons, and other specialists to help keep the apparatus that is the Space Colonization Agency—commonly known as the SCA—moving materials and building and fostering colonies. But it can get lonely. It's generally frowned upon for a ship's captain to carry on in a romantic relationship with a member of the permanent crew. However, relationships with rotational staff, like medical or scientific specialists becomes the best chance at having a meaningful relationship given all the time away. And Abby. Well, we've had a few off-duty hours together playing chess and talking. I really liked her. I was just thinking that maybe she liked me too...

I ended up eating more than I needed, and then I headed back to the bridge to check on Zane and the team. All was well there, so I checked out of active status for the evening giving Alex command for the off-shift so Zane and I could get some rest. I headed back to my cabin, cleaned up a bit and strapped myself into bed.

At first, as tired as I was, my mind kept replaying the brief conversation with Abby, wondering how I could have done better, and wondering if any of the crew noticed us talking. It was ridiculous how much I was thinking about it. Thankfully I finally managed to calm my mind and get to sleep.

Chapter 2: Potholes in Space

Early the next morning, I made the rounds through the ship, checking in on the crew, and then I spent some time with Dr. Roth and the medical staff. Dr. Roth had turned out to be a great friend and mentor over the years. He was always a superb source of advice and reassurance for many things and has a penchant for straight talk.

We discussed the Snale pox analysis, and how his folks were making progress in developing a vaccine for this genetic variant despite the colony on Mars having adequately contained the nasty bug. It was great to be able to talk to the staff to thank them for all their efforts back on Mars and say how grateful I was that we got the cargo and people onboard, just in time for making a sprint back to Earth Station. After the official discussions, Doc and I shifted over into his private office for a few minutes. "I tell ya, Doc, yesterday was one for the books. If we can get all this cargo organized and back to Earth Station on time, I'm going to give the entire crew four days off at the station."

Doc smiled, "Nice idea, and I think there's still a lot of 'ifs' that need to line up in your favor before I'd suggest you give the whole crew four days off at the same time. Besides, we still have to negotiate the whole decommissioning situation, and if we end up being late, well that could cause us a lot of trouble."

"Not to worry, Doc, I've been working on the fleet modernization chief, and she's uh, well she's starting to see things my way," I replied.

Doc gave a wry grin and replied, "Ahh yes, the venerable Director Stephanie Ward, sure, she'd be the right person to work on to help keep the *Algonquin* in active status. She seems a little too young for your... coordination, Dave."

"Doc, it's not like that, nothing romantic although she's very pretty and genetic therapy has me looking younger and younger all the time. Some ladies like a more seasoned man. Just using my experience as a ship's captain to influence her."

That got a snicker from Dr. Roth as he motioned for me to shoo away saying, "All right, time for you to move on, I don't want to hear about your 'influence' operations." He used air quotes around the word influence.

I smiled and picked up my tablet and coffee bottle and said, "See you later Doc; have a good morning," and floated out of the medical bay doors toward the main corridor that connects to all the internal cargo bays. I started verifying cargo types, amounts, and locations while validating container ledgers.

We had to get the cargo reorganized. It was as if we had just thrown it all in a box to be sorted out later. When you get to the destination, unorganized cargo can be a pain to unload, and that can take a lot more time and effort, making the logistics folks give you a poor rating when they have to organize your mess for distribution.

And, as captain it was my responsibility to make sure we had all the cargo that Mars station said was transported aboard, and given all the friction with Sasha and Headquarters, I wanted to verify ledgers myself. *Yep, this was going to be a fantastic day of tedious but satisfying small tasks.*

A few long hours later I headed back to the bridge to check in with Zane and the crew. "Thanks for the update, Zane, I'm going to head into the conference room, I've got a meeting with Dr. Rairkov and Mr. Randolf in about fifteen minutes, and I want to prep a bit now that we have the cargo mapping under control, but let me know if the herd gets spooked," I said with a wry grin as he shook his head back and forth at yet another cowboy reference. Zane's parents were, no kidding, cowboys back on Earth. They had a massive ranch in Montana, and on the Big Island of Hawaii. They really enjoyed the western cowboy culture, and they named their son Zane, after the famous author, Zane Grey, who wrote cowboy adventure novels back in the 1800s. So anytime I could get a cowboy reference in on Zane, I did so, as it reminded him of home, his parents, and generally nice things. Oh, it may have annoyed him too, occasionally, but overall, I hoped that invoked pleasant thoughts for him.

About twenty minutes later, I heard Zane say, "He's in the conference room, go ahead on in."

Max Randolf, AKA Mr. Tough Guy, and Dr. Sasha Rairkov floated into the room and strapped in around the conference room table.

"Dr. Rairkov, we've got all your…" *What was it she was bitching about? Oh, that's right, the ore.* "Your ore accounted for on board the *Algonquin.* Just like I said, you may be a couple of days late, but I doubt it will be more than forty-eight to seventy-two hours after processing your ore through the logistics network."

"Captain, yes, we are aware of the schedule, and would like to request that you organize the ore so that we can push it immediately into the logistics network as soon as we arrive." She smiled as she continued with what looked like a forced smile, "We are not accustomed to working under such difficult circumstances to do our jobs, so I think that we've been too… aggressive in working with some of the staff."

What the heck. Is this some sort of half-assed apology? Better avoid it for now, stay focused on the mission, I told myself.

"Uhh, I understand. Yes, we still have some reorganization work to do, but it should be completed before we get back to Earth."

"You ass…" broke in Max. I turned my head to look at him in annoyance while he scowled at me, "She just apologized, and that's the best response you have?"

"Look, Max, calm down. That didn't seem like an apology to me, but it doesn't really matter; I mean, we are reorganizing the carg—"

Max cut me off. Yet again.

"You are just as your Psych profile painted you: an incompetent coward that can't handle the true stress of leadership or making hard decisions."

What the hell, my profile says that? And how'd he get my profile? Damn it, Crystal. My ship's psychiatrist must have given it to them either inadvertently or on purpose. *But why would she do that?*

My stomach started to twist with stress, but none of it was warranted.

"Look, calm down. Everything's going to work out roughly on time; what the hell is your problem with me anyhow? What did I do to you?"

I looked back at Sasha and said, "What is with this guy? My crew and I are busting our humps to help you get your precious ore back so you can study it."

Sasha's face turned red with irritation as she replied, "Look Captain, I don't want anything else to go wrong here. Your absurd plan to get the cargo off Mars worked, and while I'm surprised, it did, in fact, work, I still think we should have departed weeks ago while you were skulking around on the Mars colony, wasting time, not doing your job, and pushing the departure into a crisis instead of handling it properly."

My stomach was twisting up pretty good at this point. Man, I hate confrontations and arguments, as they cause my face to flush, my stomach to churn, and my heart to race uncontrollably. "For the record Sasha and Max, I was... *am* under classified orders to lead the Snale pox response plan on Mars..." Sasha looked at Max and then back to me, the look on her face indicating she didn't know about that. "My crew and I were working pretty long hours to coordinate and execute the response plan. And, *you're welcome*—the Snale pox crisis is fully under control and only took about seventeen long, hard days of 'skulking' to get that way. Please, take some time and go visit with Dr. Roth in the MedBay, he can give you all the details you need."

Sasha's look settled a bit as she turned her head to look at Max and then back at me as she replied solemnly, "Captain, I...I was unaware. Okay, that explains quite a bit." She paused and then continued, "Regarding the uhm. The other topic. I think you may have had an... engagement with one of Max's... friends. A Ms. Teresa Concepcion."

What? It took a few seconds for me to put it all together. *I had a date with Max's girl on Mars? What, that doesn't make sense. Why wouldn't he... or she say something.* I started to have a flashback to the restaurant the night Max came to the table where Teresa and I were enjoying a casual, non-romantic meal. I didn't put it together then because Max caught me off guard and mostly talked angrily about the ore, and how I needed to get my priorities right. *Crap, she could have mentioned that he was her boyfriend or something.*

I was so stunned; it took several seconds of contemplation before I could think about replying to them. Before I could respond, Max said, "Teresa Concepcion Randolph," with an incredibly icy voice, an angry-looking face, and a lot of emphasis on the word *Randolph*.

Well crap.

My heart was pounding, stomach twisting into a pretzel while my face flushed red—*Probably bright red by now,* I thought. I looked at Max, then back toward Sasha and said, "Look...."

Suddenly, the ship felt like it had hit a massive pothole in space. Ker—Woompf! All power went out. Yes, all power, including battery power, apparently. It was completely dark, and the ship's sudden motion slammed my face against the conference table.

"Owww!" I said to no one in particular. I heard shouts and exclamations of shock from the bridge as I tried to gather myself. I unstrapped myself and immediately banged my head on the ceiling as I tried to get out of the conference room, feeling my way to the bridge.

"Zane, Sarah..." I said as I floated into the bridge area.

"Dave," Zane replied, "we're in a bad spot here. Nothing is responding; it's like we struck something, but we didn't. I'm not sure what's going on."

Sarah chimed in, "Oooh. I banged my head on my workstation, *crap.* Hold on. Right. Nothing's working here."

Huang replied in sequence, "Okay, I don't know what's going on, but something's wet in here. I'm feeling droplets of moisture."

Sarah jumped back in, "Okay, hold on, I'm going really old school... going to try and reset some manual breakers in the conduit cabinet if I can find it... Found it."

I noticed a slight hue of light from above. I looked up at the windows in the commander's starport and floated up to see the faint bluish-brown hue shining in through the windows which were generally never used except to pass time looking out at the stars. *Hmmm*, I thought.

No Stars.

I started to panic a little—that little twist in my stomach was beginning to kick in. *Yes, that's odd. I didn't see anything normal out the windows.*

No twinkling stars. There was nothing but a soft bluish-brown light glowing in all directions. "It looks like we are in some type of... of weird, blueish-brown colored debris field or something," I said.

A few minutes passed and finally the emergency battery power came online, providing limited but welcome light and power. I could see blood droplets floating around in the bridge area. "Huang, you've got a cut on the side of your head," Sarah said.

Huang started feeling around for the cut with his right hand. "Ahhh, that would explain the liquid droplets," Huang replied.

Zane said, "I got it, we'll turn on the atmospheric hyper filter to get these droplets out of the air. Mickey, you guys okay down there? You are the only ones with no status response on the team status board."

"Captain Murray," said Sasha from the conference room. "Max is injured and unconscious."

I looked at Zane and said, "I got this one. Get the ship back into shape as best you can and get anyone injured like Huang down to MedBay." Zane nodded in agreement as I grabbed a cloth napkin off my workstation and floated my way back into the conference room.

In the dim light of the conference room I could see Sasha hunkered over Max, who was face down on the table and bleeding from what appeared to be his head. "Sasha, let's take a look," I said as I gently pulled Max up off the table, turning him slightly so I could see his face. "Oh, that's a nasty gash, Max," I continued as I looked over at Sasha.

"Ya know, I didn't know who she was," I said, looking at a worried Sasha. I put the napkin over Max's wound to put pressure on it, hoping to slow down the bleeding. Max started moaning and started moving around a little trying to gather himself. "Here Max, put your hand here, and let's get you down to MedBay and let the doctor take a look at you." I took a moment to look right at Sasha, dead in her eye, and then I smiled gently. She smiled back, and I moved to grab Max under one arm and gently shifted him around and pulled him out of the conference room, then on a careful float-walking path to MedBay.

29

"Doc, I've got a customer for you," I said as I pulled Max into the MedBay. Nurse Gina and Riley took him into the triage room and strapped him in as Doc sidled up to me. "Damn, Dave, what the heck was that? That damn near knocked my skin off."

I looked up at Doc and realized he looked shaken up, which was pretty unusual for the normally rock-solid doctor.

"Sorry about that, Doc; trust me, that was not planned. Hey, are *you* okay? You are looking a little green around the gills."

Doc broke eye contact, which troubled me a little, and he said, "I'm alright, just feeling a little off, probably just all the action."

"Okay," I replied, "I'm heading back to the bridge, will check back in with you shortly."

Doc gave me a forced smile, "Alright Captain, will see you shortly. We'll get everyone all patched up and back into the game as soon as we can. If any serious injuries are discovered, I'll let you and Zane know immediately."

"Thanks Doc, you're the man," I said as I floated into the corridor.

The next twenty-four hours consisted of several meetings and sync sessions where the crew and I tried to figure out a way to get away from this part of space. The reactor couldn't operate without emanating radiation that was leaking through the shielding for some reason. This was unusual and was freaking Mickey, Maria, and the rest of the engineering staff out. This meant we were basically living on battery power until we could stop the radiation leak. If we limited use of the battery system to just the basics, such as processing the ship's air and basic heat, we estimated that we had about ten days of battery power.

Doc and the medical staff got everyone patched up and back into business, but he privately reported to the senior staff that he was not feeling well and was going to put Nurse Gina in in charge of the MedBay.

Nurse Gina was actually a Bio Life Sciences PhD., but everyone called her Nurse Gina because she was a nurse first, before becoming a physician's assistant and then a Bio Life Sciences PhD. She spends a lot of time studying problems that crop up on our missions, like the Snale pox outbreak. She is an exceptionally talented woman who really enjoys working with Doc and his son, and now intern, Riley.

So, I know MedBay is in good hands with Gina but, I've never seen Doc step down, so I was worried about him. I made a mental note to ask Gina for some private feedback after tomorrow morning's staff huddle.

On the second day, we tried blindly firing the maneuver thrusters to get out of the bluish brown crud and try to get back on track to Earth. Unfortunately, nothing seemed to work, and we were clearly not able to move out or away despite trying various maneuvers.

Well crap.

The crew was starting to get frustrated with our current situation: living off batteries without reactor power makes it really cold in the ship. Making matters worse, Dr. Roth's condition had worsened, and he was strapped into a bed in MedBay. Gina was officially starting to get worried about Doc, and asked Abby to help her figure out what was going on.

I sat down with Mickey and Maria in engineering to discuss how to raise the temperature in the ship. It was getting bone-chillingly cold, and experience told me crews could handle it for a day or two but if it continued unabated, folks would start getting easily irritated—unfortunately, they would get sick too.

After our mid-day staff huddle—where very little got accomplished as our situation hadn't changed much—I thought it would be a good time to circulate around the ship and try to brighten the crew's day a little. The idea was to try to use humor and goodwill to head off any unnecessary friction. I stopped by the galley to pick up a tray full of muffins that our culinary specialist, Monte made from scratch. "Monte, how are they looking?" I said as I floated into the Galley.

"Hey Captain, yep, they are sitting right here about to get wrapped. I really appreciate you authorizing me to fire up the ovens; I think this is just what the crew needs—a little TLC." Monte said as he smiled broadly, clearly proud of his handiwork. Monte had already posted four hot water, coffee, and tea stations around the ship so folks could get a warm drink pouch once in a while.

"Excellent Monte, you know, sometimes muffins are mission critical," I said with a lilt of humor in my voice.

Monte nodded his head in agreement and replied, "Like now."

I smiled and nodded, and we chatted about his day and how he and the team had been doing in the galley while he finished wrapping the muffins. Monte was the only full-time cook so all the other crew members took turns helping with kitchen staff duty so he wouldn't be overwhelmed.

Damn those muffins smell good. Looking and sniffing... I couldn't take it any longer, the smell of those wonderful muffins was taking over my brain. "Say, Monte, it's probably my duty as Captain to, you know, test the muffins."

Monte looked at me with a surprised smile and said, "Oh, I'm sorry Captain, here." He turned to hand me a really large muffin from the rack of the ones already wrapped. "I made this one first to test the ingredients. It's just like the others from a blend and consistency perspective. You go ahead and give it a try and let me know what you think."

I couldn't take my eyes off the muffin. The whole damned galley smelled wonderful with light scents of pumpkin, cinnamon and yes, peanut butter. Finally, I forced my eyes over to look at Monte. I was grinning with muffin lust and said, "All righty then, let's have a taste." *Mmmmmm, so delicious.* "Perfect Monte, Mmmm, just perfect," I said as I savored the muffin. Monte looked at me and was smiling so hard he was nearly bursting with pride.

Monte finished up two more trays of muffins, and I patted him on the back and thanked him for his efforts to help the crew feel a touch better about things. "Okay Monte, I'll head to MedBay and start handing out muffins and work my way to the bridge, and you head to engineering. Will see you somewhere along the way," I said smiling broadly. Monte nodded as he removed his cooking apron and grabbed the other tray of warm muffins. I headed out the door and maneuvered straight for our wonderful medical facility—*Man on a mission,* I thought. A mission to share some positivity via muffin magic!

"Ladies..." I said as I floated into the MedBay to check in on the medical staff, and Doc in particular, "... I've brought some special snacks from Monte, our own culinary rock star. I call this a Monte special." I continued smiling as I handed out the peanut butter pumpkin cinnamon muffins, wrapped carefully to reveal the dessert's beauty but safe for weightless enjoyment by humans.

Both Gina and Abby took one, although Abby immediately wedged hers into a pack of things strapped to the MedBay workstation, where she apparently had been working. Abby smiled but was focused intently on her tablet computer that was no doubt populated with Doc's data. Gina looked a little harried but smiled back at me and bit into her muffin.

As she chewed it a bit she said, "Mmmm, this is wonderful Captain, thank you. Oh, peanut butter... goodness the peanut butter flavor is pretty strong."

On the bed between us, Doc's fatigued voice wearily broke in, "Gina, I swear if we gave Dave an MRI today, I'm pretty sure we'd find that he's made from about half peanut butter."

I smiled down at Doc strapped into his bed as Gina and Abby floated on opposite sides. "Howdy Doc, how are you feeling today?" I said smiling as big as I could while looking Doc straight in the eye.

Doc was quick to respond, "Feeling okay, Dave, although a tad worse than... well than yesterday. Nice of you to bring by some muffins. I'm not up for one right now, but perhaps later," Doc replied, a bit out of breath and sweating.

"Okay Doc. Well try to get feeling better, we are all really worried about you, and want to have our lovable medical curmudgeon back as soon as we can have him," I said with a smile, and Doc chuckled.

Abby broke in with a beautiful broad smile and said, "He's not a curmudgeon, he doesn't come to the meetings."

I smiled over at her. *Damn she has a wonderful smile. Hell, she's beautiful when she frowns. Whoa, Dave*, I told myself. *Look Away! You are staring at her too long.* Thank goodness, Gina saved me. "Uh, Captain, we are starting to see evidence of some kind of over-exposure symptoms with Dr. Roth. Very similar to low-dose radiation poisoning. Could be related to his numerous implants."

I snapped back to reality and looked at Nurse Gina. "Okay, well can we start treating for radiation poisoning?" I asked.

Abby drew my attention again with, "Well sir, we don't have the right mix of modern drugs aboard to test with, but we do have some colony stimulating drugs that we think will stabilize his bone marrow. Gina is putting her PhD to work by trying to make a more advanced drug that will help him excrete irradiated cells if she can get a good understanding of the radiation type." I looked over at Gina. She had a direct, solemn look that still carried a smile.

"It's going to take some time Dave, but I'm working it as hard as I can."

My stomach twisted with that familiar feeling of concern and self-induced stress. I must have been looking at Gina too long, with the 1,000-meter stare of concern, because Abby gently touched my left forearm, snapping me back to now.

"Captain," Abby said, "we'll keep you up to date on this."

As I looked at Abby's beautiful face, I saw her quickly nod her head toward Doc. I got her intent in a millisecond. Pay attention to the sick person in the room and don't get all doom and gloomy.

I looked back down at Doc and said, "Doc, did you see the updated stats on that all-star Cincinnati pitcher, Hans Fletcher? I mean, holy cow, he's got more strike-outs than the rest of the Reds' pitching staff. I still don't think he's worth a $62 million contract; he's just not that good," I said shifting the discussion to a topic of passion for Doc—baseball. That got Doc talking.

"Like hell, Dave, they ought to be paying him twice that amount. His curve ball can't be hit by ninety percent of the league. Do you know what kind of advantage it is to have that kind of talent in a starting pitcher these days?"

Doc and I both grew up watching the Cincinnati Reds Baseball team, and though he's fifteen years older than me, we still have a lot in common, and fond memories of watching those home games. I grew up in western Indiana while Doc came up in eastern Ohio which always gave us a lot of things to talk about. We both came from small farm communities where we learned life lessons and grew up within the same kind of culture.

Our baseball conversation kept going, and it seemed to have perked up Dr. Roth pretty well. Gina and Abby looked happy about his increased energy as Doc got animated about some of the baseball stats. Gina asked Doc's son, Riley, to take the tray of muffins along the route I'd planned, mostly to get him out of the MedBay as a break from being worked up about his father's worsening condition.

Overall, the crew appreciated Monte's cooking efforts and even the delivery. I did take a little criticism from Sarah, Maria, Zane, and Mickey over the strong peanut butter influence in the muffins. Yep, Monte expertly threw me right under the bus stating that, "The Captain gets to select the deserts, that's why there are always many peanut butter–related dishes aboard the *Algonquin*."

I pushed back saying, "Peanut butter is good for you, and since we don't have anyone with an allergy, what's the harm?"

Besides which, I don't want to end my life knowing I could have had another bite of peanut butter.

On day five I really could sense everyone's stress. The cold and the uncertainty were taking a heavy toll. *We have to try something.* After a little planning and coordination, we tried to fire one of the main engines to push us out of wherever we were now stuck. This turned out to be *a really short test* because our main engines use a lot of electricity to generate propulsion, and we were running on battery power, so we didn't have much to spare for running up the engines. This is usually okay when our reactors are running, as they can generate one hundred times the needed power for the engines. *Big Al*'s design was power first (reactors), engines second, and tether box third. Over time we added a world-class infirmary in the MedBay while expanding the cargo bays to make *Big Al* a space RV that could go anywhere, at any time, and handle nearly any task with the right crew complement.

Maria, our co-chief of engineering, figured out a way to temporarily shield us from the reactor, so that we could actually run the reactor to recharge the ship's batteries. We might even be able to run the reactor constantly at a low output level thanks to her innovative shielding solution. Maria used the computer to design a sort of layered shielding blanket that took about three hours to print using the ObjectForge.

This, too, was a gamble, because printing the material was costly in terms of power. Everything seemed to cost power. It was cold and we'd already lowered the ship's ambient temperature to thirty-three degrees. That's the lowest setting Gina would allow. From there we'd have to put everyone in suits, and living in bulky suits... well, that gets old quick. Everything is difficult when you are in a hard-shell suit. Peeing, eating, even physical contact with other people... well its abysmal to do for any length of time. It's funny, the agency learned long ago how important hugs are in space travel. Mandatory contact like hugs, handshakes and fist bumps are required for space flight and have been for over fifty years. Humans need contact as its critical to maintaining crew morale. Difficult to do in the thick suits.

We were really lucky to have Maria as our co-chief engineer as her abilities nested and overlapped with Mickey's in a particularly effective way. I had to give up two lower-class positions to have both of them on the staff, but that trade has paid for itself multiple times in the past couple of years. Hell, it was Mickey's idea to offer her a co-chief position, as she recently had graduated from the Agency's engineering academy. Mickey had been in contact with her and knew how innovative she was. He told me we could leverage her expertise to graft newer tech onto the *Algonquin*'s old hull and thus keep *Big Al* around longer.

Anyway, Sarah pointed out how risky our full engine test really was: since most of our gauges and sensors are totally inoperative. We could have unknowingly traveled deeper into this place we were stuck in or fail to detect an asteroid or an explosive condition in the propulsion system. After careful consideration, we decided to pause further main engine testing until we could be surer of our situational variables. We were getting increasingly desperate to move the ship out of this screwed up part of space... *Gotta keep working on the problem. We have to be careful not to do something catastrophically wrong.* I've seen my share of catastrophes in space. They never get better. They only get worse.

On the positive side, the team's analysis indicated the bluish brown hue being emitted from the ship's hull was some hybrid form of Cherenkov radiation. This discovery also helped Gina identify a potential treatment for Dr. Roth.

The radiation that was bathing the *Algonquin* was also affecting Doc's skin and nervous system. Doc's body was riddled with advanced sensors, so removal of some, or all, of them would take a significant effort. At every skin embedded sensor location, radiation burns were starting to appear. However,

Gina and Abby were considering how to remove the larger sensors. Especially in Doc's head and the relay junctions along his spine where damage was likely affecting his nervous system.

Doc thought the combination of his cybernetic sensor system and gene treatment was helping him fight the apparent radiation sickness.

I still didn't understand how his cybernetic sensor system worked, but it was supposedly limited compared to regular human sensor organs, such as ears and eyes. He said that he built in an aggressive innate immune signal to his sensors and cybernetic architecture to ensure the body would properly respond to a range of dangerous situations. Doc was getting worse and I think Gina and Abby are right to fully consider all courses of action.

Chapter 3: We are Where?

On the morning of the sixth day, the ship seemed to run into that same space pothole, as we heard and felt the now somewhat familiar Ker—Woompf sound that coincided with the strong physical jolt that shook everything in the ship.

All this was followed by a slightly less frightening, but still anxiety invoking, system-wide power loss. Let me tell you... when all power stops working, to include everyone's wrist computer, well, it's time to freaking panic, as there are few conditions where that much power should be disrupted.

I thought things were already bad. It's interesting how situations always have the capacity to get worse. The two main reactors remained offline but started leaking badly... again. Fortunately, all the recent focus on the reactors paid off as the engineering team swung into action to remedy the situation and fix the damn reactors before things could get out of hand.

Other damage to the ship turned out to be a little worse than last time. We lost one of the secondary cargo bays, and the hook ship, as they snapped completely off the ship docking points, resulting in a serious hull leak.

The high-gain antennae array was oddly sheared off and missing, and several crew members were injured during the bump. Doc was injured the worst; he suffered a nasty concussion because he happened to be floating just above his bed on a short tether that Gina put in place to give him freedom to move around a bit. Being strapped into bed so long isn't healthy for anyone. As the report goes, he was bleeding profusely, but his son, Riley, sprang into action to stop the bleeding and save his father's life.

Riley was one of two interns on the *Algonquin*, and it was no coincidence that he was onboard, as Doc planned to retire in the next year or two as the *Algonquin*'s senior medical officer. Riley hoped his internship would eventually lead to a permanent medical position with the agency. It's difficult to get selected for key positions without good experience. Long internships are the preferred method of capturing experience for future agency personnel and mission specialists.

Riley was a good kid and was understandably distraught when his father's head was injured during the rough bump. I temporarily reassigned him as direct support to the medical team as Abby and Gina indicated Doc's situation was deteriorating.

Thankfully the hull breach was a quick repair job by the crew, enabling Mickey and Maria to focus on the remaining infrastructure and instrumentation repairs.

Overall, the situation was quickly improved, and best of all, we were finally free from the weird, bluish-brown field effect. We could see the stars again!

Zane and Sarah were having a devil of a time trying to figure out where we were, but it was good to see them collaborating vociferously. I could see tons of positive energy in crew behavior across the ship. The Cherenkov radiation dropped off, and systems were returning to normal.

I took a moment to peer out through the commander's skyport at the top of the bridge. Seeing the starfield is something I love dearly. It's always beautiful to see the planets, moons, and stars, and... this time, I immediately noticed that the stars didn't seem to line up correctly—at all. I looked all around from the window portals and well, I didn't see much that looked familiar.

No Earth, no Mars, no Sun, no nothing. Now I'd experienced this sort of thing before in a simulator test back on Earth—the longest four hours of my life. I eventually passed the simulation test by adjusting the model's registration points and re-computing several times. Sarah and Alex had tried to accomplish the same feat several million times aided by the ship's computer. So far, all attempts had been unsuccessful, no matter how radically they altered the model's registration points. No joy.

Well crap.

We were floating along in space while assessing which direction to head toward to begin our trek back to Earth. Dr. Roth's condition had worsened and it was causing a fair amount of emotional pain for me as I tried to stay focused. Thankfully, Huang has managed to stay upbeat for all of us.

"All right, sir, things are looking up... probably scaling back to be only a one or two WTF-per-hour day ahead of us," Huang said as he energetically worked through all his duties down in the pilot's seat.

Overall, everyone was excited that we were finally out of the bluish brown space and now we could get back on track to Earth. It was great to see nearly the entire crew energized and thinking positively.

Chapter 4: The Meeting

The operations update meeting started off normally: "Okay, team, let's go through ship and crew status." I said as we started running through the status of ship systems and crew status, especially the items aligned to our key lines of effort.

"Well, the engines check out now that we can use the gauges and sensors, the plasma pressure was a concern, but we've fabricated a manifold patch that's within original specs," piped Mickey, gulping as he swallowed the last of his coffee. "I recommend we capture the cargo bay while it's still nearby, it seems to be relatively intact, and we can do that with maneuvering thrusters only."

"Okay Mickey, good call... Zane, see if you can lasso that cargo bay, worse case we can tow it back to Earth with our tether cable if the external mount points are too damaged," I said.

Sarah said, "We still can't pinpoint where we are, and therefore have no idea which direction to go now that the engines check out." More than a noticeable amount of frustration was present in Sarah's voice, and explicitly depicted on her normally smiling face.

I could see and feel her emotional strain as we all listened to her report. She was close to the edge, and I wanted to reach out but I dared not, now was not the time. I made a mental note to pull her aside later and see if I could help her deal with the stress of this seemingly unsolvable puzzle.

I fondly remember when I first met Sarah. She was notified of her assignment to my ship, and within twelve hours had tracked me down in the middle of the night to ask a question about the *Algonquin*'s new fuel-system controller. *Yikes, what a nerd*, I mused, as I smiled and went back to sleep.

"Chuck's condition hasn't really changed," said Gina glumly snapping me back into the moment.

The meeting started to get tense. Our inability to understand our present location was causing overwhelming tension as the reality of our grim situation started to set in.

I needed to say something impactful and prophetic here. *Maybe try for inspirational, yep, that's it,* I thought.

"Okay, team, let's hold it together. Solving hard problems is the greatest mark of courage that humanity can wield, so let's work on the problems here a little at a time. I'm certain we'll get ourselves back on track." I said using my lowest, calm voice, with my brow furrowed.

Before anyone could really respond, warning alarms began sounding from the flight deck.

"That's the collision alarm. An object is coming in fast!" Sarah barked as she jumped up and headed to her navigator's cube just in front of the captain's cube. She quickly analyzed the limited sensor data feeds and merged them into the ships common operating picture which was immediately presented on the Holo Map display.

After looking at the Holo Map and seeing the inbound indicator moving *real* fast, I hit the intercom. "Emergency folks, everyone grab a hold of something solid, were about to collide with something coming in hard and fast."

Several seconds later, no crashing collision had occurred. Just the incessant intersection of numerous sensors and collision alarm tones which had mostly maxed out into a single, solid tone. Whatever it was, it was within the collision alarm's closest range, which means it should have been right next to, if not on top of, the *Algonquin*.

"Electrical systems are fluctuating again," Zane commented.

The cameras were not working so I floated to the top of the flight deck and looked through the commander's portal: a circular observation point with multiple windows pointed in many directions affording a broad view around *Big Al*.

"Holy crap! It's a ship of some kind... massive, definitely not recognizable from standard hull types I can readily identify. Maybe... maybe it's a Viking pirate ship!" I exclaimed to no one in particular.

Zane chimed in with, "It's scanning us, sir."

What the hell? How'd Zane know that? "Zane, what do you mean?" I barked with as much calm dignity as possible.

"Sir, the backup sensor array is being flooded with electromagnetic radiation in uniform, stepping wavelengths. I'm taking the sensors offline. Its amplitude is massively strong," Zane replied with a little hesitation in his voice.

"Okay, thanks Zane. Man, this is a big freaking ship. I've never seen anything like it. Its engines look like they are all over the place and green." Alex was seated in the flight engineer position and was already analyzing sensor data. "Alex, any patterns in these emissions Zane is seeing?"

"Not especially, sir, but I'll need some time to analyze; it's possibly some form of generic communication, but it would have to be very simple as there's no detectable modulation."

"Or like I said, it's just a scan," smirked Zane wryly in Alex's direction.

Alex looked a little worried and responded, "It could be the Viking pirates. I've heard a tactic they often employ is to flood a targeted vessel's sensor arrays to overload and incapacitate the associated equipment."

The massive, spider-shaped vessel seemed unknown in design to me, but I've been fooled before by pirates. Pirates have been known to heavily modify freighters, essentially turning them into battleships. A key issue in this case, however, was the size. This thing was huge; it dwarfed the *Algonquin* as it was more than 1800 meters in length with no discernible features or sensor arrays in the logical positions. Although given the situation, I'm thinking it was probably Not a simple, repurposed freighter.

"Zane, are you reading anything else from the sensors...? Spectrograph? IR? Beam scanner?"

"I'm not making sense out of these readings, sir; it's going to take a little time," Zane responded.

A few seconds went by. "Well, it looks like you'll have time; they're reaching out to capture us with some type of arresting gear," I quipped.

"Are you sure?" Sarah asked.

"Well it's that, or they're about to frisk us." Sarah didn't respond to my comment, but I saw a small smile cross her face for the first time in several days. It was a welcome sight.

"Zane, release that cargo bay you lassoed. Its oversized, unwieldy mass could cause complications if they do grab onto us and decide to jerk us around. Let's start prepping for condition red as well." I ordered.

"Acknowledged on both, sir; the cargo bay has been released."

After locking on to the *Algonquin* with what amounted to a rather sophisticated-looking tethered claw, the massive ship began accelerating. I pondered our situation as Alex and the rest of the crew began frantically analyzing various sensor readings and securing multiple internal ship sections.

After many quiet minutes and multiple unanswered questions publicly posed by several crew members, I blurted out an obvious question, "Zane, any planets or systems nearby?"

"I...I can't really tell, sir. Sir, we are really accelerating though." Typically, Zane prided himself in his thorough knowledge of the ship's disposition and surrounding situational awareness, but his ambiguous response was coated with the same uncertain feeling that struck us all. Who were the operators of this spacecraft, and what was going to be our next step; should we resist now? Or later? Or at all? Should we fire thrusters and attempt to maneuver away?

Like most ships in the Argus class, we were not a well-armed starship and possessed no Marine Infantry soldiers on this particular voyage from Mars to Earth. We had a railgun, basic small arms, and some old mining explosives that we should have turned in long ago.

Sarah commented, "Sir, we've really increased velocity... systematic and steady acceleration."

A few minutes went by as we all looked at sensor screens, and one another when we could manage the time. Sarah broke the silence with a very worried look on her face. "We are really moving now, sir; my estimate is we're traveling in the neighborhood of 220,000 Kps." Sarah's voice cracked with the stress of uncertainty.

Well, that got everyone's attention—every crew member within earshot craned their necks around to look at Sarah. "220,000 Kilometers per second? Wow, that's pretty fast... it's approaching... are you sure?" I asked.

Now typically, I know better than to publicly second-guess one of Sarah's estimates.

Crap.

"Captain, the formula is fairly basic; I'm reflecting a sounding laser off the cargo bay we left behind. Would you like me to review the formula with you?" Sarah retorted with an increasing lilt of aggravation in her voice.

"Okay, okay, let's try this again; does anyone have any concrete information that can help us here?" I announced, cutting Sarah off before she could get going further.

If we were back on Earth in the velvety, green hills of Indiana I could have heard crickets chirping over the zero responses I received. I looked around and no one wanted to offer any thoughts. Who could blame them given all the stress we'd been through the last few days? I figured giving folks some space would be best. "All right folks let's huddle in two hours, that'll be best-guess time, and we'll sort out our next steps," I said into the ship's intercom.

So there we were, lost in an unidentified part of space, being towed at half the speed of light by a freakishly large pirate, or perhaps even alien, vessel.... I needed to sort through this, but unfortunately, there were no easy answers to anything this week. At least not yet. *Perhaps getting off the bridge for a few minutes and talking with Doc would help provide me with some perspective. Perhaps just being in the room with him will help me think through this strange situation. Yes, that's it.* So I told Zane I was going to get some air and departed the bridge. I float-walked down to the MedBay, stopping along the way to reassure a couple of folks I encountered. When I got to Doc's bed, I noticed Gina was strapped in the bed next to him, and she was sleeping so deeply she was snoring. "Ahem... Gina," I said as quietly as I could. I didn't want to scare her.

Gina moved and stretched her arms as she replied, "Apologies, sir, I must have fallen asleep for a few minutes. Err... we've been testing different treatment options for Dr. Roth."

"No sweat Gina, I understand, we all need to give our brains a break, especially given our situation. A little rest might help you think of something important. Why don't you just take a break, get a shower, or get some warm food. I'll call Abby and stick around until she can come down and watch over Chuck for a stretch.

"Yes, sir, I could use a change in scenery. It might get my brain functioning properly again." Gina nodded, smiled weakly, and floated out of the MedBay.

I sat down, pouch of coffee in hand, and started talking to my unconscious old friend. I told him about the situation and asked for his advice knowing that he couldn't respond.

Meanwhile, back at Earth Station, the Agency struggled with the *Algonquin*'s disappearance. "Ray, Jake, what do we know?" said Logan, the Agency's operations officer, "the President wants an update and the Administrator wants the situation brief updated ASAP."

Ray responded, "We don't know much more except that the *Algonquin* seems to have vanished thirty hours after departing Mars station, based on the station's telemetry. As of about an hour ago, no debris has been found, and there are two Merlin-class explorers searching for her.

"There was an attempted pirate incursion during the Cargo loadout on Mars, but they performed a thorough sweep of the area and no other pirate ships have been detected."

"Anything from the plasma trail analysis? That old ship should leave quite a trail," quipped Logan.

"Nothing conclusive, sir," piped Ray. "The trail disappears some 360,000 kilometers from Mars station. It's as if they just disappeared."

"Research, do you guys have anything new?"

Jake, the senior astrophysicist piped up hesitantly, "Yes. After surveying the search quadrant with the Newton array we've noticed several violent energy bursts with no obvious sources. Also a few anomalous events were detected in the area where the *Algonquin* should have been."

"What do you mean anomalous events?" Logan replied.

"Well," Jake began, "we've noticed a rather high number of temporal gravitational lensing events, or TGLEs as we've called them. Normally, we detect, and chart, massive gravity sinks because they bend light originating from distant objects like galaxies and appear to warp the view."

Jake shuffled some papers before continuing. "We're calling them events because they seem to be very small and appear to last mere hours to days, whereas normal gravity sinks never appear in *our* solar system, but when found elsewhere, they are reasonably perpetual. We really stumbled onto their discovery due to the high-resolution scans of the *Algonquin* search area."

"Okay, scope this for me; what does it mean? Is it related to the loss of the *Algonquin*?"

"We're not sure, so we're setting up a better method of studying the TGLE's using several radio telescope arrays so we can figure out what's causing them and get more data."

"Okay, I understand. Theoretically, if one of these TGLEs appeared in the *Algonquin*'s path... what would have happened?" asked Logan.

As if time had frozen solid, Jake looked around at everyone standing in the huddle; he exhaled and responded with, "We don't really know. But currently, we assess the field effects are being caused by an unknown type of nano-sized black hole, which would essentially crush the *Algonquin* into a singularity. The *Algonquin* could never have detected it, as there would be no sensor impulse responses reflected from the singularity, and there would be virtually no matter remaining from the *Algonquin* to be found. But again, we don't really know what's going on here. The TGLEs do seem to correspond with the high energy bursts timewise."

The look on everyone's faces suddenly grew quite solemn as they considered the probability of Jake's supposition. Finally, Logan grabbed control of the meeting. "All right, well I suppose it's a theory worth considering. We'll scale back the details until we have a better read and update the leadership on what we know. Jake, I'll need another update in twenty-four hours in my office, and Ray, join us please."

Chapter 5: A New Puzzle

I surveyed Doc's unresponsive body. I couldn't help but think of all the marvelous, official, and unofficial things Doc had contributed to the Agency. Heck, significant contributions to society itself for that matter. Dr. Charles "Chuck" Roth was a leader in the medical research field, and more importantly, he was the bridge between two major physiological camps trying to improve and extend human life—the cybernetics and the cloner groups.

It was recognized early on that humans would need longer productive lifespans as we began the difficult task of colonizing our solar system. Scientists and doctors had long known how to connect, electromechanically, into the human brain, and subsequently were able to create moderately effective prosthetics on a broad scale.

Conversely, cloning turned out to be a lot more complicated, after it was proven that behavior could be manipulated by tampering with genetic information... a point the Bong Cha crime syndicate clearly illustrated to the world.

Over a forty-five–year period, the Bong Cha syndicate had successfully cloned and replaced hundreds of key international government personnel at all levels, hoping to literally take over the world at a time of their choosing. Luckily, their vicious plot was exposed before it could be executed. Not by a security researcher or scientist, but, ironically, by a scorned lover and former employee of their cover cloning company. The resultant auditing and scrutiny of any cloning operation became an enormous cost. A burden that few companies could take on.

Being so highly regulated, one would think that black-market cloning would be very profitable, but it's not really very prolific... probably due to the severe punishment that's involved. Death or lifetime imprisonment without the possibility of parole for all involved. A heavy price indeed for tampering with the code of life.

After about ten minutes of solid contemplation with an unresponsive Doc, I paged Abby. A few minutes later she float-walked into the MedBay with Alex, our resident computer expert, in tow. I stopped talking to Chuck and stood up glancing at my wrist computer to see if our status with the pirates had changed. Nope, nothing new.

"How is he?" Abby asked.

"Status seems unchanged," I responded as I shifted my position to make way for Abby.

"Let's have a look," Abby said as she beamed with that fantastically beautiful smile. She grabbed a couple of instruments and began examining Doc.

Abby was brilliant and intriguing. As I watched her work I remembered that she mentioned some previous experience with this sort of situation, but highlighted that she's not a neurobiologist by any means. Working with Nurse Gina was helping her think outside the box with Doc's situation.

Looking over toward Alex, I smiled lightly and said, "Alex, what brings you down here?"

"Sir, a combination of security preps, stretching my legs and following up on the odd RF emissions from our encounter. I wanted to let you know there's no discernible communication in the emissions from the super-sized, spider-looking ship. Also, the emissions have stopped, so the XO thinks they've got what they were looking for or have decided to stop trying in the case it was a communications attempt. I've got several of the wideband, RF emissions recorded, so I'm going to continue analyzing various aspects to see if I missed anything."

"Okay, thanks Alex, please watch for any hidden signals that could be used by pirates to gain command and control of our ship." I replied.

"Okay sir, will do... Oh, and that geologist, Sasha, and her team of merry men we picked up on Mars, well she is pretty upset about us leaving the cargo bay behind. She's pestering the XO pretty intensely, and I think he's had about enough from her."

Perfect. That Sasha is a boatload of trouble waiting to make port. And I thought we were starting to get along better now. I could feel myself imperceptibly grimace. I caught myself and then smiled gently at Alex. "Okay Alex, I'll jump into the situation shortly."

Alex nodded, glanced at Doc solemnly, and then left the infirmary. Doc had a pretty broad following for a ship's senior medical officer.

On our last mission, Doc taught Alex sign language because Alex's latest love interest on Enceladus Station was deaf and Alex wanted to impress her by conversing with her by sign.

Normally human anomalies, such as being deaf or blind, would be genetically treated and eliminated on Earth, but many children born on the smaller, remote colonies are not as fortunate. Most colonies and outposts lack access to sophisticated medical facilities.

"No change," Abby somberly replied, "the doctor is still in a coma, but his neuro scan shows slight improvement, that's a positive sign. Gina's cyclic neural chemical treatment seems to be working."

That was good news. I know Abby and Gina had been working together on that for the past several days. That little bit of good news brightened my mood and moved my stress-meter down a notch. "Thanks Abby; Nurse Gina should be back shortly, please give me a yell if his condition changes," I said as I began floating out of the MedBay.

I decided now was a good time to engage Sasha about the cargo, so I went to the guest quarters, but "Sasha the Great" was not around. I thought of her as 'Sasha the Great' because she's positively brilliant, beautiful, irritating and annoys me with her self-preoccupation—all at once.

Zane met my eyes upon my arrival to the bridge with five quick words: "She's in the galley, sir."

I smiled lightly and asked for a status report.

"No real changes, sir; we've been underway for a couple of hours, same velocity and direction. There've been no signs from the tow ship, and Sarah thinks she's identified Canis Major and the constellation Orion. She'll provide an update after confirming a few more details as scheduled." Zane smiled with a pep of energy.

"Okay, thank you Zane, I'll be back in a few minutes." Sarah didn't even break her analytic gaze; she focused sternly on her workstation, fingers whirling over the keyboard and analytic graphics flashing across her displays. She appeared to have a look of shock or disbelief on her face which unsettled me a bit.

Chapter 6: Accounting Problem

Sasha immediately began running her mouth as I floated into the galley and strapped myself into a chair across from her and a seemingly subdued Max. "Captain, as I tried to explain during our briefing on Mars, I represent the Agency's Tech Acquisition Division and—"

I immediately cut her off. "Sasha, I realize your ore is urgently required for business on Earth. I further realize you work for very powerful people within the Agency, and I *was* listening on Mars, but as you can see we're being towed about the galaxy by some unknown people for an unknown purpose. So if you'll just calm down and let us do our jobs, I think you'll find things will go much, much more smoothly." Sasha was really wound up and kept talking as if I hadn't said a word.

"Open your eyes captain; we are not being towed by some alien race; it's merely a sophisticated kidnapping being carried out by the Viking Raiders! They easily possess the technology, and you need to act now to recover my ore! It's taken me two years to acquire the ore from deposits deep within Mars. It has properties that are unlike any other naturally occurring—" Sasha was cut off by an intercom klaxon followed by a broadcast from the flight deck:

"Captain, please come to the bridge; we've begun decelerating, and we're seeing some activity from the tow ship," said Zane over the intercom.

Thank God.

Conversations with Sasha always seemed to end with her yelling at me. I supposed I could avoid that this time. "I've got to get back upstairs. Just relax, we'll recover the cargo bay; have a little faith, will ya?!" I exclaimed at her in exasperation, knowing full well that we'd likely never see that cargo shell again. I had empathy for Sasha; I really did: the time and effort, the disruption to her life and work, but it wasn't the top concern in my mind. I wanted us all to stay alive first. I left Sasha in the galley and sprinted back to the flight deck just in time to see Zane stick his head into the view portal. "Zane, Sarah, Alex... what's going on?"

Sarah started in, "We're decelerating rapidly, sir; we're also approaching what appears to be a small solar system with at least eight planets. I think we are about six hours away at present rate of deceleration. Here are images from the sensors; as you can see there are a large number of dis-similarly shaped energy blooms, which we assess are spaceships of unfamiliar design in vicinity of the sixth planet."

"What's this bright blob?" I asked.

"I'm not sure sir, but its signature resembles a very large space station," Sarah responded, switching the display to hi-res sensor image mode. "And as you can see it's not in orbit of the third planet, which means it's nothing like what we've got in our solar system captain."

Holy crap, I found myself thinking, *is it possible that these really are aliens? Or is this just another elaborate pirate trick being expertly executed by the Vikings? Damn it! I need some answers.*

"Okay, it's time for our huddle, Sarah, Zane; where are we?" I asked with my best poker face.

"Sir, Sarah defined our position just before the tow ship showed up right here," Zane said, pointing at a location on the Holo Map display. "The analysis is based on the reference location of Sirius as compared to the Orion constellation. As you know sir, Orion and Sirius are the most recognizable constellation/star combination visible in Earth's sky," Zane said, almost too rehearsed. "You can see here, Orion's three belt stars pointing to Sirius, only the angle is twenty-three degrees off, and its magnitude is measurably off."

Hmmm...I was not liking where this was heading. "Okay Sarah, Zane, give it to me, how far away from our solar system does it appear we are located?"

"We are in the vicinity of Alpha Aquilae, approximately seventeen light years from Earth, based upon the analysis Zane's already provided, sir,"

Sarah choked out as if she did not believe it herself.

I was stunned and not sure how to react, but I realized we could really be in the presence of an alien species... at the mercy of an alien species to be more accurate. I swallowed, glanced sternly around at my crew, thought about those watching via video intercom, and realized all were waiting on me to do or say something inspirational. My stomach started to twist as panic rose in the back of my mind.

"Okay, things are under control folks. Let's just take it slow here...So we've traveled seventeen light years in six days?"

"Yes sir, we traveled at a rate of 2.83 light years per day, presumably while enveloped within the bluish-brown...stuff or field?" Sarah quietly responded.

"Roger that; thank you Sarah; any idea how we managed to achieve that velocity?"

"Sir, the XO and I have a theory on this... as you know, Cherenkov radiation is typically produced when particles are noted traveling faster than what particles of light can travel through the same medium. We noted a ton of the bluish-brown radiation during those six days. Perhaps the *Algonquin* was traveling through some medium. The rate of travel in whatever it was works out to be two point eight-three times the speed of light, presumably for the six days we were in the bluish-brown medium. Whatever this medium was, it seems like it enabled us to uh...travel *faster* than the speed of light."

I looked at Sarah. She'd obviously put a ton of effort into this analysis. I was stunned, and the anxiety was starting to rise from the twisting pit of my stomach. I had to get control of myself. "Any suggestions as to what this medium consists of or what caused us to start or stop our passage through it?" I asked.

"Unfortunately sir, we don't know what the medium could be or what initiated our entry into it; there were zero reactor fluctuations or any other emissions that we assess could have initiated any field effects, let alone field effects of this magnitude," Sarah said.

Well, this is going nowhere, I thought. *Okay. Time to change the beat.* "Roger that, understood. Good rundown. Sarah, Zane, team—this is good; we've got something to work with now." I started thinking about the next steps and how to be as prepared as possible for whatever came next.

I snapped at the team, "Okay. We've got to get ready for next steps with this tow ship, *now*. Zane, I want the crew and ship to prepped for Condition Red in forty minutes."

Condition Red is a status that no one liked as everyone was required to be positioned at their duty workstation wearing their bulky, hard-shell, intra-ship space suits with their helmets on. Wearing that suit was uncomfortable and it made it difficult to work. Also, Condition Red means the crew pairs up and begins a four-hour work and sleep pattern to help extend critical functions for long periods of time. All intra-ship wireless communication is also turned off, which, most notably, affects each individual's wrist computer and accompanying earpiece.

The wrist computer is a femto-sized computer or "FemtoCom" as we called it. FemtoComs connect, via various wireless networks thousands of times per day to the ship's computer.

Without access to the ship-wide wireless mesh network, the FemtoCom connects to the suit via near-field while the suit is hard wired into the ship. Additionally, bulkheads are manually closed, and the reactor is placed into a reserve mode where it produces virtually no output. Yep...we'd be running off the battery/capacitor supply again. A shield is lowered over the reactor core's housing to prevent leaks in the event the ship is struck in a collision or some other type of disruption. All other non-critical ship functions are placed into a standby mode as well, so it's easier to keep track of small changes in the ship's overall status by manipulating the ship's services individually, as needed. It was no small thing I was asking everyone to do.

"Will do sir," Zane replied immediately as he typed the order into his computer, which would then update the ship and everyone else's FemtoCom with the latest directive.

"Gina, I need you, Riley, and Abby to put Chuck into a hard-shell med suit then pack the main infirmary for deployment," I said.

"Yes Captain, I'm here in the MedBay with Riley and Abby," Gina responded.

"Understood sir; we've acknowledged the Condition Red order and will get to work on the suit," Gina replied probably wondering where we'd be deploying the infirmary to.

Not only does the *Algonquin* have a world-class medical bay, part of it is deployable, so we can conduct medical treatments and surgical events on the various moons and space stations throughout the solar system. It essentially allows us to bring a mobile medical health unit to where it's needed. *A very expensive mobile medical health unit.*

"Thank you Gina," I said. It had been a long time since we'd actually had to be in Condition Red, not simply a drill, so I was glad to see everyone moving quickly.

Mickey, the ship's Co-Chief Engineer, chimed in over the intercom, "Roger Captain, we're getting squared away now as well. Also, I've got the Gold Record ready to go, I just need you to swing by and sign it."

Every agency ship has a Gold Record, which, these days, is a really small digital memory cube with multiple built-in communication modes that contains information that should help facilitate communication with pirates, or aliens, in the event any agency ship should ever encounter any. The name "Gold Record" inherits from the record that was sent out with the Voyager Spacecraft back in the 1970s. They were designed to educate aliens about humans and Earth in case Voyager ever came into contact with an alien species. This newer variant has the same "Hello alien, we are humans" type information embedded in it in twenty-eight different ways with five different interfaces including a picture-based interface on top of the unit. For example, if a specific radio frequency is detected, it would transmit data in binary encoding, then in decimal, then in hex, and many other encoding types. The encoded data is designed to form the basis of a rudimentary information exchange. The transmissions begin by establishing familiar terms like low, high, hot, cold, dark, bright and then build on them to create compound messages.

It transmits all this data periodically to help the device get noticed and hopefully begin the first step of communication with someone else or in this case, aliens. Since the Gold Record is very costly, each one is keyed to the commanding officer's signature which is required to validate the need for a deployment. "Captain to Lock 3, captain to Lock 3," said the ship's computer voice from a ceiling-mounted speaker.

What? Who the hell was down in Lock 3? That was the eight-way airlock that interconnected all the externally joined cargo bays to the primary cargo bay. "Person at Lock 3, identify yourself!"

"Sir it's Maria; I'm here in Lock 3 with Sasha; she made the page request, but I happened to be working on the keel conduit, but, bottom line, I think I found part of her cargo."

Well this just keeps getting better and better, I thought. "I'll be right down," I said, anxious to put a conclusive end to Sasha's continuous cargo discussion.

Before I could jump off the flight deck, Zane pulled me aside by my arm with notable stress in his eyes and said, "Dave, I think we should launch the emergency buoy; I'm getting a queasy feeling about this situation."

Well, I suppose launching our buoy would be smart as our captors might just as well pull off our wings pretty soon, I thought. "No, let's hold on to it, Zane, If Sarah's correct about our location, I doubt anyone will ever find it." I said calmly as my stomach continued to twist into knots. Zane nodded in agreement, and I took off to meet Maria and Sasha in Lock 3.

I float-walked down to Lock 3 and saw that Mickey had beat me to the location and was waving me in hurriedly as Maria was plucking away at the log-comp keyboard. The logistics computer was essentially part of the ship's computer except it had its own, independent connection to the agency logistics network, another redundancy.

"Hi Mick," I said with the warmest possible smile I could muster given the circumstances.

"Sir, we need you to take a look at this," Mickey said as a concerned look washed over his face. "Some of Sasha's ore is located in several of the internal cargo bays; it seems like we've misplaced where some of the cargo is located in our hurry to get on the road to Earth—"

Mickey was cut off by Sasha, "An obvious testament to your accounting accuracy, but I'm quite happy some of the ore is still on board."

"Roger that Mickey; I got it; thank you Sasha. Why is the contamination alert going off?"

"Sir, it's residual radiation, probably the cargo reacting to that bluish-brown area we flew through," Mickey said.

I nodded in acknowledgment and said, "Sasha, how much ore are you missing?"

"About eighty percent," Sasha said flatly.

"Mick, Maria, any danger of radiation poisoning?"

"Nominal at this point, but the ship's alarms will alert us to higher trending levels or if the situation is getting unsafe," Maria said.

I nodded back at her approvingly. "Okay, let's get back to business; we've got lots of work to do. Mickey, let me follow you back to the Gold Record so we can get it deployed."

Mickey grinned as he led the way back to the engineering bay where the Gold Record was being held by a grasping mechanism attached to a table. The Gold Record has a sliding mount that pushes it through a portal and extends it six inches from the ship, into space, ensuring it possesses the widest possible field of view for its various methods of signal transmission.

"This thing is so sophisticated; I never got to tinker with one of these for real," Mickey said.

I digitally signed the golden record and signed the deployment order. Then Mickey took off to install it on the quarterdeck.

From there, the crew spent the next several minutes getting ready for Condition Red, a status which I would keep us in until I felt we were not in danger from the aliens or pirates who had been pulling our ship so quickly through space. While the crew readied Condition Red, I spent a lot of time updating the captain's log to capture all that had occurred. I researched agency policy in the area of encountering alien species, but did not find much more than philosophical viewpoints, which I found to be useless given the situation.

I donned my intra-ship suit, grabbed a handful of gear from my quarters, and headed to the MedBay. I checked on Doc's condition, and it had not really changed too much. He was in a heavier suit now with extra medical sensors that enabled the medical staff to perform simple procedures.

I ordered him into the heavier suit because if we were attacked and boarded,

I didn't want Doc to be an easy target. Gina, Riley, and Abby appeared to have everything well under control, so I went up to the bridge to plug in and get to the business of evaluating our situation and moving the ball forward. Hopefully we would be able to develop a couple of smart courses of action to deal with whatever situation was awaiting us.

About an hour later I began receiving reports that the ship was squared away and there were no loose ends...except my friend, Doc. "We're slowing rapidly sir," Zane commented.

"Roger that, thanks," I replied as I made another entry in the ship's log. As we neared what appeared to be a massive space station, I could sense the collective stress of my crew, or perhaps I was just tapping in more fully to my own.

I periodically floated up to stick my head into the observation portal at the top of the bridge and manually opened the blast shields to see what was happening. It was a little clearer than using the ship's external camera system that had taken some damage over the past few days.

"Everybody, listen carefully," I began to say over the ship's intercom system, "the best minds on Earth indicate interaction with an intelligent alien species is dangerous business. We obviously must be cautious to avoid miscommunication, so please don't make any sudden movements, don't do anything that could be misperceived as hostile, and think clearly before taking any action. Most importantly, I want everyone to keep their personal tablet computer with them and document your experiences. Later we may need everyone's perspective to work through next steps. If, I mean, *when* we get back to our own solar system, different perspectives are critical to aid situational comprehension." *That's about as good of a public service announcement as I can muster right now*, I thought.

Two hours later, we approached the station as Sarah, Zane, and Alex were discussing their analysis of the space station...apparently, its mass was about half of Earth's moon. The sensor readings were high as well but the array was so damaged it was difficult to get a good reading.

The alien tow ship slowly turned and used its robotic arms to place the *Algonquin* into what appeared to be a massive cargo bay. *And I mean massive.*

It was the size of a modern football stadium. The *Algonquin* bounced off the far wall and struck the bay floor with a horrendous crash. Some type of anchoring claws grabbed the *Algonquin* from the bay floor.

We were pretty well shaken up. It took thirty minutes of troubleshooting to arrest all the systems issues these collisions caused as the *Algonquin* was not really designed to sit on the floor on its ass. I could sense the light gravity as items that were floating around the bridge clunked their way to the floor.

We won't even need our mag boots to walk around here, I thought. It was good to feel some gravity again as the normal float-walking with mag boots throughout the ship was always an awkward way to get around, but the circumstances could have been better.

My private comms channel light blinked a few times, and I punched the accept button on the suit.

"Dave," Abby broke in, "your heart rate is pretty high; recommend you take a second to relax if you can."

Yes, I suppose it is, I thought. *Kind of Abby to reach out.* I thought about it for just a few seconds and replied, "Thank you Abby, good recommendation...I'll do a few breathing exercises."

Abby was quick to reply, "Since Doc is out right now, I figured I'd try to help where I can."

I smiled and replied, "Really appreciate you doing that Abby. We need everyone on point today, this will probably be a ten-WTFs-per-hour day." I heard Abby snicker just a little bit as she thanked me for injecting some levity into a stressful situation.

Zane and I worked through the list of issues. We contended with all the minor concerns that sprang up, electrical system malfunctions and the like, but I could see the look in Zane's eyes: he wished we'd have fired the emergency beacon before we became imprisoned in this alien tomb.

"Sir, any idea why they strapped us onto the floor?" Zane gently nudged.

I turned and looked at him, "Right. I'm not sure why they did that...I don't know what's going on..." I said, stammering through my words before Alex broke in.

"Sir, I'm seeing those RF signals again."

I could imagine him furiously manipulating the controls at his station as he tried to figure out what was going on.

"Sir, check the forward camera feed...some kind of weird looking screen is displaying an animated three dimensional projection. Looks like the screens came up through the floor...*there*, you can see it from the aft camera as well, so it appears there are two separate screens."

I checked out the camera feed for a few seconds, then I stuck my head up into the portal and saw what the cameras were feeding us.

Hmmm...well this was interesting. I could just see an outline of the thick display unit. It showed a series of bright, tiny neon thread-looking things forming pictures and simple movies. The display apparently used tiny threads instead of pixels, like we'd see on a conventional display. The threads seemed able to flex into any position. Then they started moving together to depict scenes and simple animations comprised of different shapes, motions, and actions. Alex was furiously attempting to make sense of the transmissions with the help of Zane and Sarah. I periodically asked them for a sitrep but received nothing substantial, so I continued to peer out the main deck view portal; in case I could see something out of the camera's field of view.

Minutes ticked by as we tried to figure out what the screens were trying to say. About ninety minutes later, Abby interrupted my train of thought with her broadcast. "Sir, Doc's condition is getting really bad...I believe it has something to do with his body starting to reject his implants; I may need to remove them."

Well crap.

"Uh, Abby, please do your best to stabilize Dr. Roth; we are in an extreme situation right now..." I said, making notes.

"Roger sir, I'll do my best," Abby replied sullenly.

Doc's condition seemed to be worsening, and I had no idea what was going on with our "friends" out there, and it would probably take at least another hour to bring the ship's primary reactors back online fully, which would be necessary to conduct a complex operation such as surgery. We were in an untenable situation.

Chapter 7: Plan A

I replayed the situation in my mind's eye, trying to focus on the biggest problems first. Stress was mounting in the crew as we sat in Condition Red, and the ship continued to sit awkwardly on its hull in an alien cargo bay. I didn't know what to do next except sit tight and try and communicate somehow with the aliens. I could have benefited from a strong pouch of coffee. Unfortunately, as crazy as it seems, coffee is not possible in Condition Red. I shook my head, hoping the motion would give me what I was wishing for from caffeine.

About fifteen minutes later I noted that Sarah, Alex, and Zane were together working on something, but I did not inquire as I was still working out the surgery mechanics with Mickey.

"Sir, I think we've got it," Alex broke in. "We think the RF transmissions and the display projections are related."

I stopped what I was working on and looked over at Alex who was displaying information on his workstation so I could see it. "Okay good, give me the lowdown," I said, trying to make the mental switch in priorities.

I moved over to Huang's cube to look over his shoulder as Sarah began speaking and pointing at places on Huang's screen, "We think the aliens have received the output from the Gold Record at least a thousand times by now, and perhaps that has shaped how the aliens have tried to contact us. We assess they are trying to teach us a common symbology. Symbols to count, and some other basic symbols for syntax; look at these three looping animations: these are electromagnetic waves; there's the magnetic component, and here is the electric component of the wave. Now here we begin to see the relationship between RF transmissions and the animation, as the cycles ramp up in frequency. There, that's a single wave and presumably the symbol for one; there's two waves and the symbol for two, then ten, then twenty, forty, eighty, etc., all in groups of twenty. Each of the loops ends up morphing somehow into icosidodecahedron-shaped objects, which we don't completely understand yet. It does not make sense, but it seems important to them to show it repeatedly."

Alex chimed in, "Here they continue to show animated scenes of physical things in the universe, distant things with many wave symbols between them. Here's a solar system with fifteen planets: some distant and some planets near one another. Here are some close things with just a few units between them. I believe these reinforce the syntax of these symbols. Some things are hot, like stars, showing these symbols and apparently numbers related to temperature or radiation. Others are associated with these symbols and are apparently cold, such as space itself, marked by this symbol. Here we have symbols that fit into what look like basic equations for mass and density. This icosidodecahedron thing is strange though. Several of the loop segments end with a transition to the shape."

I perked up in the hope department as I noted the smart folks on our team making progress. Thank God for Sarah, Alex, and Zane. Sarah is positively brilliant. "Very good work! What do you make of this sequence here in the last series of animation?"

Before I could get a response, Abby loudly interjected over the ship's intercom, "Dave, something is killing the doctor, and I think it's that radiation. His condition is becoming unstable, and I need to remove those implants as soon as possible."

Gina broke in to support Abby's comment saying, "Captain, Abby is right, if we don't remove the implants in his skull, he could die soon; his body is starting to actively reject the implants there, and along his spine."

Well crap.

"Okay. Roger ladies. Abby, are you sure that you know how to remove them? We are not in a good position to set up a surgical session. Are you sure?" I queried, hoping for any crack of a conciliatory response from her.

Don't get me wrong, I really trusted Abby, she is the best: a highly paid agency surgeon broadly trained to deal with various situations that might be encountered on long, space flights, but this type of surgery is very complex. It requires special equipment, monitors and most of all—expertise.

"Dave, he is dying; vital signs are failing. I, I do think I can remove his skull implants. I can't replace them, so he'll be without those sensor feeds and I'm not sure what it will do to his nervous system, but at least he'll be alive," Abby replied, with grave concern in her voice.

Okay, I thought, *how do we best do this?* "Mick, can you set up a stable power feed for the surgery room?" I asked.

"We can sir; it will take about an hour," Mickey replied with a detectable strain in his voice.

"That's fine; I'll need time to setup and run through the procedures," Abby jumped in.

"Okay Mick, but can the ObjectForge make new implant sensor stems for Abby to install?"

"Sir, I don't think so. I don't know; it's possible, but I'd guess it's unlikely given our lack of energy and most importantly we'd need a good, radiation-free particle map of each existing device, and a lot of time. At least hours."

The ObjectForge was a fantastic invention that enabled deep space crews to create, or replicate existing things, provided there was time, power, and an accurate particle map of the original object. The *Algonquin*'s ObjectForge is pretty new tech, like a 3D printer on steroids. Mickey had to use several multi-staged transformers to get the massive, consistent power it required from the *Algonquin*'s older, but still potent, power system.

"Okay, regardless...he's dying, so let's try surgery to at least remove his implants. I realize it will be difficult under Condition Red, but we must try something. Let's get the surgical cell powered up in one of the MedBay surgical rooms, no unnecessary equipment in the room," I replied. My gut was beyond twisted as I started to feel the heat from stomach acid creeping up my throat. I was getting a sinking feeling about this situation as I reviewed Mick's plan to isolate the surgical room with multiple redundant batteries and capacitor banks to ensure nothing would affect the flow of needed power. Suddenly, the bright, alien displays outside the *Algonquin* increased in brightness and the pace of display accelerated.

The color changed from a light-blue neon-threaded display to a green-threaded display. The display depicted a stick figure outline of the *Algonquin* complete with a small, single vertical line in each location of our ship that happened to coincide with the location of each one of my crew. Several in the command deck area, a few in the engineering deck area, and presumably Abby, Gina, Riley, and Doc in the vicinity of the medical bay.

Zane blurted, "Oh hell! They are showing us that they see us inside the *Algonquin*'s hull; sir, I am concerned that they'll be attacking soon!"

"Look, I think they are highlighting the doctor, down in the MedBay," Alex said with disbelief clear in his voice. One of the vertical bars in the MedBay started to slowly disintegrate from top to bottom, then turned into a red, segmented vertical line, then transformed back into a whole line, then slowly disintegrated again. Text symbols appeared across the top and bottom of the display.

"Anybody able to make out what those characters are saying?" I said. "Zane, are you seeing that? Is that representing Doc?" I yelled into my helmet microphone a little louder than I intended.

Zane and Sarah both looked back at me as Zane replied, "It looks that way sir…" Just after Zane's confirmation the animation continued to progress forward with one of the other vertical lines representing some other crew member and the segmented line presumably representing the Doctor, moving out of the stick figure diagram of the *Algonquin*.

Then, several icosidodecahedron figures appeared and escorted the two *Algonquin* stick figures to a nearby location where the icosidodecahedron apparently made the vertical line representing Doc return to its previous, un-segmented design and color. Finally, both crew symbols returned to the *Algonquin*.

"Sir, it appears the aliens think they can help Doctor Roth," Sarah said.

"Roger sir, that's what it looks like to me," Zane chimed in.

I was wishing I knew what to do, and wondering if this was a trick. How the heck could the aliens discern Doc's condition, or any of our conditions, for that matter? "Zane, how in the hell could they understand human biology enough to help Dr Roth?"

Zane looked back at me with that puzzled "Hell if I know" look. "Sir, I'm not sure of many facts right now; it's hard to tell what's really going on," Zane quietly responded.

"Abby, what's Doc's condition? Can we move him around?" I queried over the comms link.

"What? No, sir I'm about to prep him for surgery, he's—"

I cut her off, "Abby, please look at the situation display on Camera 1. Alex pipe that looping feed of the *Algonquin* and the stick figures to all ship's comms panels."

Seconds later, "What is this?" Abby asked, obviously not keeping up with the situation as she'd been focused on Doc's condition.

"Abby, this is one of the later projections from the aliens; it can be seen forward and aft outside the ship and possibly transmitted via basic radio comms, but we've not worked that part out yet. Bottom line, it looks like they are aware of the Doctor's worsening condition, and think they can help. What's your take on that?"

The line was silent for a really long thirty seconds. During that thirty-second period, I made my decision.

Chapter 8: Plan B

I cut Abby off just as she was beginning to speak, "Abby, change in plans… Everyone listen up. I am taking Doctor Roth out to the aliens; I know it sounds like an irrational thing to do, but I've weighed the facts and assess the aliens could have attacked, boarded, and killed us all by now if that was their intent. Abby, put the doctor back in his external suit; remove everything that he won't be needing, like the jetpack fuel injectors and camera assemblies." I stopped to breathe in after making that statement, but just before I was ready to start my next order, Abby broke in.

"Dave, I'm going too. You'll never get him out there yourself, and I can help whoever they are treat the Doctor; I'll start working the suit now."

"Sir, we don't know anything about these beings—" Zane started before I waved him off.

"I understand Zane…but unless you see a better course of action to help Doc, we are doing this."

Zane considered my words and replied, "Roger sir, we'll get postured for this engagement to take place. Sarah, Alex, get the remaining sensors back online and get the backup comms array tuned for this cargo bay, I want to maintain comms to the Commander and Abby. Make it our highest priority."

"Thanks Zane. Okay, I'm running to my quarters to change into my external suit; can you think of a way to get Doc out of the ship? Since we're sitting on our belly, we are basically laying on the best hatches with no way to easily open and close them."

"Roger sir, I've got an idea; we might be able to use that bell hatch on the port side. Go get changed, we'll work it out."

I nodded back at Zane and unplugged from my command station. I walked back to my quarters. *Walking is nice, thank you gravity, I really missed you!* I thought.

I peeled out of my internal, wired suit, and jumped into my external space suit.

That suit is bulkier, but it's also got a three-hundred-hour, self-contained supply of oxygen.

Zane's voice came over the intercom, "Abby, I'm sending Riley to fetch a gator gurney and bring it down; put the Doctor on it, and please use the engineering elevator to bring him up to Deck 15." Gator gurneys, modular with knobby wheels, and able to be connected together to form a longer gurney for moving cargo, were used all over the ship. Using one for Doc was a genius idea.

I finally finished getting suited up, performed my ops checks on the suit, and glanced around the room to see if there was anything else I needed to bring. It was a surreal moment: I felt I would never see this room again.

And I suppose that's why I grabbed so much crap and stuffed it into my pockets: pens, extra cables, chewing gum, tablet computer... *Gotta get moving.* It was no time to feel sentimental about my own tenuous life.

I beat everyone except Zane to the port-side hatchway. He was furiously clearing a path wide enough to get Doc and his gurney through. "Crap, Dave, it should be me going; you are the man with the plan around here," Zane said in between heavy breaths.

I could sense the worry in his voice, so I touched him on the shoulder, pausing his work, and looked him right in the eye as I said, "Zane, this *is* going to work out... and I'm going to stay in video communications the entire time. You keep things under control back here and we'll be back in a jiffy. Hopefully with some knowledge of how to cure Doc. Besides, I'll probably run into a bunch of hot female aliens, and you know how much of a slow starter you are."

Zane smiled as we resumed moving boxes and equipment to clear a path to the Hatch.

"Zane, you are the best XO in the fleet, and nobody knows this ship as well as you. We just need to work through this situation a little at a time," I said as I moved a few final boxes out of the way.

Zane smiled but I could see the worry in his eyes. He tried to make light of the situation and said, "I suppose sir; by the way, I don't need to mention that if you do meet some hot aliens, well, don't do anything crazy or overly romantic. I can see it now; our first intergalactic accord will focus strictly on alien sexual harassment." Zane stood up and looked over at me, smiling gingerly as we both took a moment to exchange glances.

"Good point Zane, and what's your estimate for WTFs per hour on this little endeavor? I'm thinking at least two."

Zane grinned widely and said, "That's a conservative estimate, I'm pretty sure we'll be setting records on this one."

I could hear the engineering elevator getting closer to our floor. "Okay, here they come," I said, thankful Zane and I had a light moment together to reassure one another.

I didn't really have time to consider it, but one of the reasons I felt okay at all in the situation was because of Zane. Zane is one of those guys that's got courage. He'll do anything he senses is necessary for the team; he's courageous, and a man that I'm thankful to have on the team.

The tiny engineering elevator stopped in front of me, opened, and I could see Doc's legs hanging off the front of the gurney while the rest of his trunk was lying flat.

Once off the tiny elevator, Zane expanded the articulating joint on the gurney to provide sufficient length to hold Doc's legs as well. Zane prodded me with a gesture, and I quickly noticed what Zane had already recognized. Doc's son, Riley, looked distraught, worn down, and terrified, all at once. Such a bright young man but his last several days had been tough dealing with his father's deteriorating condition as he tried hard to treat him.

Looking purposefully into Riley's eyes I said, as officially as possible, "XO, I may need some medical expertise during this operation, please arrange for Riley to be available up in the command center in case Abby or I require his assistance."

Zane gently grabbed Riley's shoulder and said, "No sweat sir, I'll have him connected and situationally aware ASAP."

"Riley, believe me...we are going to make this happen, I'm confident that your father is going to make it, and once more, I think he's going to be the bond between humanity and whoever the hell that is out there. They want him to live too." I glanced at Abby who had just arrived with Doc, and noticed her serious expression before a slight smile began to form as I looked in her direction, making eye contact.

Steady Dave I thought.

"Okay, Zane...what's the plan?" I shifted gears quickly.

Zane went over the strategy with us, and since this was a colonial hatch, it was designed for connections to the old-style colonial ships with bell housings that sealed around the hatch. The steep path down the hull was a staircase ramp combo with short segments of each designed for foot access. The narrow wheels of the gator gurney would fit between the step rails and segments of ramp but gravity was going to make the trip down clumsy and dangerous.

Gator gurney, excellent thinking Zane.

So Abby and I pulled on our helmets, opened the hatch, and started making our way down.

I went out first to connect Doc's gurney to the winch Zane strapped into place, and I was followed by Doc's gurney.

Then Abby followed up behind the gurney...the winch only had one speed and it was *real* slow, but that pace was preferable, as I was nervously looking around for our friends, or some identifying features of this cage we were in. As I looked down, it was clear that a fall from this height would likely hurt all of us so I tried not to think about how far it was to the floor while holding on for dear life.

What was that you were saying about gravity a few minutes ago jackass? I thought.

The entire way down to the floor, I kept talking to Abby while pestering Zane and Sarah with questions and queries about mundane topics. I'm sure they sensed my apprehension as they continued to conduct official small talk with me about various sensor readings and comms anomalies. Thank goodness for small talk. We finally made it down to the cargo bay floor and unhooked Doc's gurney from the winch cable. I checked with Abby, and she indicated Doc was no worse given the descent. A few minutes later, I cautiously looked around and saw no movement. Taking a knee, I looked closely at the deck, almost a soft, plastic, corrugated surface that was not considerably dissimilar to our own cargo bay deck plates except it gave in to pressure like a soft skin.

I was discussing this with Zane when Abby broke in with, "Sir, do we walk somewhere in particular?"

Thinking back to the stick figure animations I replied, "No, we'll sit tight right here. I recall the icosidodecahedron figures in the display coming to meet us and leading us to the appropriate exit."

Zane piped in that he spotted some movement near the furthest edge of the bay, but I used all camera enhancement modes and couldn't see much.

Finally, I saw the floor splitting in a distant area with a soft blue, neon-colored glow emanating from what appeared to be a ramp being raised in between the separating floor plates.

Chapter 9: Contact

"Zane, I think they are coming...nine o'clock from the ship's nose as 12 o'clock," I stated.

Zane replied immediately, "Roger sir, looks like a bunch of them; they are approaching the ship in groups of two."

I took a few steps forward, in front of the gurney as if to protect it in case the aliens intended to do something devious, but reminded myself that we were pretty much at their mercy. As the aliens slowly approached me, I could sense my heart-rate increase; sweat started running down my back, and I started to tremble slightly. I briefly instructed Zane to record everything possible, but not to do anything sudden that could be misinterpreted as a violent act. "They are bipeds," I stated over the comms link to Zane.

The aliens slowly fanned out around the lead alien as they approached, as if that one was the focus of engagement.

The aliens appeared to be about the same shape and size as me, but as they drew nearer, I could see that they were all slightly smaller, wearing some type of suit like Abby and I were wearing. The lead alien stopped moving forward and stood before me, about four feet away, and slowly raised its upper two appendages. As it performed this motion, the rest of the aliens shifted their posture into a single knee, kneeling position. Not sure what to do, I remembered the agency training that indicated to calmly reply in kind, but not in a mocking way...*whatever the hell that meant.*

Slowly, I raised my right arm and positioned it directly in between the alien's two extended appendages.

Just then, another one of those neon-threaded, stick animations appeared projected from the alien's right shoulder just to the right of its helmet. It showed the icosidodecahedron symbols reversing direction and moving back down the ramp with the two vertical lines and one horizontal line following behind and two icosidodecahedrons bringing up the rear of the miniature caravan.

I turned slowly and took a step back toward the gurney and grabbed a handle, "Abby, we are going to take Doc down that ramp; I don't know how steep it is, so please help me keep it under control," I said, gulping heartily from the worry of creating an incident from something silly like tripping on an exposed cable.

"Okay, Dave, I understand," Abby replied calmly as she reached out and grabbed a hold of the rear of the gurney where Doc's head and the control systems were located.

Damn, it was nice to have her brilliant medical mind and six-foot, muscled frame on this particular mission! I had a lot of respect for her because she never backed down from a challenge. Despite Chuck being virtually riddled with implants, Abby was ready; hell, she was demanding to perform surgery to save his life. I've known plenty of agency surgeons in my time, and they all avoided surgery like it was a cold bath, mostly because of experience, complexity, and risks involved in surgery performed during spaceflight. That's primarily why the agency went toward a contract model for surgeons, the few agency surgeons with real skills were few and far between. Believe me, six months between stops is a long time if you need something other than tonsils or an occasional appendix removed.

The aliens began slowly walking back toward the ramp while the lead alien never turned to see if I was following, so I figured their helmets were fitted with rear-view optics similar to ours. I was watching Abby and the two aliens behind her in *my rear-view cameras* and trying to control my anxiety.

We slowly headed down the ramp, and I could see faintly bright lights at eye level extending at least fifty feet down some sort of corridor where there was an obvious surge of light being emitted. I figured it was a room of sorts. As we approached the light source, I informed Zane about the strange walls, ceilings, and floors that all appeared to be made of the same soft-ish, corrugated skin like the floor in the landing bay that housed the *Algonquin*. As we walked, I could see bright lines of light emitted from layers a few centimeters below the surface of the wall. As we slowly descended another short ramp and entered a room, my helmet optical shield immediately covered my eyes as the lights were suddenly very bright.

"Abby, use your low-res camera for visuals until we can establish these lights won't damage our eyes," I stated with very little saliva left in my mouth. As I entered the room my optical shield layers slowly dissolved allowing my eyes to adapt to all the lights, and to clearly see all the aliens in this room.

"Zane, we just entered a room about fifty feet by two hundred feet with at least thirty aliens standing around all sorts of equipment. They are all humanoid-looking with comparable height if not a bit shorter than humans; do you copy? Are you seeing this?" I said with a gravelly, dry voice.

"Roger sir," Zane replied. "Your audio is clear, but video is a bit swamped with light; you are sending low-res optical data. Probably not enough bandwidth for the hi-res cameras. No problems here sir."

Okay, I thought, *provided we get out of here, our suits will spool several hours of the hi-res optical data.* Just as I was finalizing my adjustment to the room, the lead alien slowly approached me and gently touched my right wrist, startling me a bit as I turned to see that familiar projected, stick figure animation showing what I believed to be Abby and I following the alien icosidodecahedron figure a short distance away. The alien pointed to lights along the floor that matched the track depicted by the animation.

"Sir, should we leave Doctor Roth with them?" Abby asked, obviously watching the transaction.

I thought about it for a second and figured at this point, we were all in, "Roger Abby, let's move very carefully and follow the alien."

Two other aliens slowly pulled Doc away from us as we moved into an area that looked like a control center of some sort. It was the only area in the room that had many items that resembled computer-style monitors and probable control equipment. The door to the entrance ramp closed with a translucent door that emitted a bluish neon hue. I could see the sensors on my suit registering an atmosphere forming. Abby and I stood in between the lead alien and several other aliens at what appeared to be a console of sorts.

"Sir, it looks like an oxygen-rich atmosphere is forming in here at about 14.9 PSI...perhaps they know us pretty well?" Abby noted.

"Roger, it seems they are trying to get Doc out of his suit," I replied pointing toward the location where Doc was moved off the gurney into a smaller cell, about a foot lower in elevation, which housed a table, many aliens, and equipment.

It was difficult to see Doc clearly as there were so many aliens around him.

The lead alien standing to my right suddenly removed its gloves, revealing two blue arms that had three very long, strong-looking appendages at the end of each: kind of like super-fingers. The alien placed each group of super-fingers over two ball-like control structures and began expertly manipulating them. I immediately recognized the two control structures.

"Abby look, those control panel structures are shaped like the icosido-decahedron we've been seeing everywhere! It's like their version of a sophisticated keyboard!" I exclaimed as if I'd split the atom for the first time.

"Wow, look how efficiently they can move them around and manipulate them with those long tentacle-like fingers; it looks as if the edges, surfaces, and speed are all part of the control?!" Abby replied.

Abby was right, the alien moved the cube-like icosidodecahedrons around as though they were a natural attachment to the end of their arms, as natural looking as a steering wheel held by a human race car driver.

I could see various screens illuminate and flicker as the lead alien manipulated the cubes. Finally, several images appeared on a screen in front of Abby and I showing what was going on with Doc. The aliens worked on Doc for a while, and I could see what was going on in most areas although I did not understand it.

Abby didn't totally understand either, but she did give me a play-by-play whenever the aliens were focused on a particular implant or doing something she recognized.

"Thanks Abby. Please help me stay on top of this, okay? I'm not following this too well," I said as the stress from the meeting began to come down on me.

"I think they've figured out how to treat the areas around the implants to stop the inflammation and rejection. Also, they appear to be testing inputs and responses between implants and the supporting computers. Beyond that I can't really tell what they are doing," Abby replied. Abby and I watched uncomfortably for what seemed like hours as the aliens poked and prodded Doc using various instruments and lasers.

Two hours had passed when Zane piped in, "Sir, you doing okay? Stay frosty, it seems fatigue is wearing you down a bit according to your suit bio monitor." Abby stepped over to me and pointed to the monitors to explain what she thought was going on, but I did not understand it all unfortunately.

Suddenly, I could see Doc's body lurch abruptly as if someone struck him. "Sir, they are killing him!" Abby exclaimed as she ran out of the control room.

Two aliens intercepted her en route to the doctor's little translucent cell, and I yelled, "Abby, please calm down; don't fight these guys. Calm down. What did you see?"

I could see the lead alien spin the icosidodecahedron control cubes, and the interdicting aliens stopped, and then they allowed Abby to pass. Unfortunately, Abby did not know how to get by the translucent cell walls that housed both Doc and the aliens that were operating on him a level lower than she stood.

"Sir, I saw Doc's body jump as if they injured him," Abby said in terror.

"Calm down; we can't be aggressive here; the lead alien called off those other two aliens that intercepted you, so they appear to be emotionally observant. Please compose yourself; can you tell me what's going on down there?" I responded, trying to get Abby to pull herself together. The next several minutes went by with Abby explaining to me what she thought was occurring. Then another alien gently touched Abby's wrist, and I could see a projected animation of those neon-looking threads showing two aliens escorting Abby back to my position. "Abby, perhaps you should come back up here," I stated firmly.

"Yes, I think they are done with whatever they were doing; I've got a hunch, but not sure. I'm on my way back to you," she responded, moving slowly.

Abby deliberately followed the alien back to my side with another alien in tow. Abby spent the next fifteen minutes giving me a high-level overview of how the neural implants worked, interpreting physical responses in the environment, and converting that data into nerve impulses like our ears, eyes, and skin do. Several hours after we began this visit, the lead alien gently touched my arm, and I noticed it had put its gloves back on. It then showed me an animation of us returning to the *Algonquin* with Dr. Roth in tow in the same type of formation as we had formed into to arrive here. I informed Zane we would be returning soon, and he jokingly said he'd roll out the red carpet in case the aliens wanted to join us for tea.

The aliens brought Doc back up the short ramp to our location, and we shifted back into the caravan positions we were in when moving to this underground area. The lead alien was situated in front of me with its lead aliens in front of it.

I pulled Doc's gurney back through the passageway, up the final ramp to our ship with Abby pushing the gurney from the rear as before. The aliens stopped and moved away from us as we approached the *Algonquin*, right where they'd found us. They all raised both their arms, and I did not know exactly what to do except raise my right arm again, hoping that was the proper protocol.

No sooner did I make that motion, when all but the lead alien took a knee again, just as they did when they arrived. *Crap, maybe I had actually guessed right!* All the aliens except the lead alien turned and began disappearing down the ramp, slowly and methodically. I didn't really know what to do as the lead alien stood in front of me. I thought of the agency protocols and what might be a good fit here. I reached into my right-side cargo pocket and pulled out my tablet computer, and then slowly extended it in my hand out to the alien.

The lead alien seemed to cock its head slightly to the left in the universal WTF gesture. It then gently grabbed the tablet computer from my outreached hand.

"Kneel, Dave," Sarah said quietly over the radio. *Good point, a universal symbol of submission.* I slowly brought myself down onto one knee. After a few seconds, I stood back up and looked at the lead alien. Abruptly, the lead alien turned and disappeared down the ramp in a direct, but controlled fashion.

Chapter 10: Recovery

When the ramp disappeared and the cargo bay floor closed, we all broke out into several asynchronous threads of chatter as I hooked Doc's gurney back up to the winch cable. Abby indicated Doc's vital signs had stabilized some hours ago, and we all anticipated the opportunity to get together and discuss this first meeting with the aliens. Sarah could see the alien's three super-fingers and wanted to ask Gina and Abby for details about how they could have evolved. More chatter occurred, but I was laser focused on getting Doc's gurney safely up the hull and into the hatch.

Abby and I talked quite a bit on our own private channel as we ascended up the hull, and I think this experience bonded us together in an unlikely way.

As soon as we entered the colonial hatch, I realized how much time had actually transpired and collapsed against the wall in the hatch-room in exhaustion. Zane verified the room's air pressure and gave me a bear hug, and I smiled back at him while removing my helmet. "I want everyone in the main conference room in thirty minutes, Abby you try and attend too, mission dependent of course. I want everyone's perspective on the events that just occurred, so think about things—See you in thirty minutes," I finished. I slowly walked side-by-side with Abby towards our respective quarters and we talked about some of the most interesting aspects of the engagement. I stopped at Abby's door and faced her, looking at her eye-to-eye.

Abby smiled back at me with a twinkle in her eye and said, "Maybe later you can stop by and we can have a pouch of coffee and discuss our experience some more?"

I smiled and noticed I suddenly had a burst of energy. "Absolutely. That would be fantastic!" I said as I smiled so hard, I thought my nose might pop off my face. Abby went into her room, and I shot down the corridor to my quarters and dumped my suit.

I felt like I'd sweated 100 pounds of perspiration in that thing in just a few hours. I showered quickly to avoid becoming too comfortable; at this point, I felt I could sleep for hours! I glanced over at my internal hard suit and thought I should change the uniform at this point given what we'd seen thus far from our alien friends.

"Listen up, this is your refreshed captain. I'm initiating Alert Condition Green as of 1709 hours—that's now folks; get out of those hard shells. See you in ten mikes."

Just before the conference-room meeting, Zane pulled me aside to show the latest alien animation. Apparently, the aliens wanted us to understand the previous activity as it began to project a replay of what had just occurred, with Abby and I both being issued a unique, dash-dot patterned vertical line of our own like Doc's.

I thought about it critically for a moment then appreciated it.… *So that's my alien name*, I thought, *cool!* Later, in the conference room, I was pretty happy to see each one of my crew as they piled in, each smiling with positive energy.

We gleefully began discussing our alien encounter with small talk that highlighted various viewpoints. I looked around for Abby and noted she was missing.

Everyone continued their discussions and about five minutes later Abby walked into the room and apologized for being a few minutes late, as she was working on Doc with Gina.

Abby then initiated a takeover of the discussion by stating how she had initially overreacted to the alien's treatment of Doctor Roth. Apparently, when treating the area around Doc's cybernetic sensor leads for radiation, they inadvertently created some kind of feedback on one of the cranial nerves that connected to his brain inductively. Doc was wearing a gauze-looking bandage over his skull to help heal parts where radiation damage was the worst. Abby explained how many of Doc's sensors inductively or directly fed one or more of his twelve cranial nerves. The bandage appeared to be some type of organic material combined with a fabric.

When I asked Abby for details related to Doc's sudden reaction to the alien's treatment, Abby explained that after reviewing the camera feeds and discussing with Nurse Gina, she theorized the aliens accidentally connected a hearing sensor with his two optical nerves which resulted in Doc's abrupt reaction because the signals were too dissimilar. Abby said the aliens figured it out, and Doc appeared to be no worse for the wear. She reported that Doc was recovering down in the MedBay.

Ninety minutes after our meeting began, we recorded a summary *After Action Review* of the first alien contact ever in the history of humanity.

I issued orders for everyone to try and tag their personal experiences in the database as readable to all crew members. The more inputs everyone had from differing perspectives the better we'd problem solve along the way.

Just as I was about to adjourn the meeting, Huang publicly paged my FemtoCom with an alert that the aliens had begun transmitting another neon thread projection on the screens just outside the ship's hull.

I adjourned the meeting, and then asked Zane and Sarah to join me on the bridge. Alex was already there and said, "Sir, it's looping already. It's a short message that appears as if they want a meeting with us in six.... Ah, I think, 6.1 hours," he said, sounding pretty pleased with himself.

"Really good stuff Alex, but how do you know it's 6.1 hours?"

"Sir, have a look at the upper left corner of the projected animation... those are the timing symbols that I showed you before, associated with measuring distant locations and events. Well, actually, they are slightly different symbols, but they lie in between these two key distance symbols, and when used in this context, it's most likely a very basic timing countdown. Note how everything else in the loop repeats, yet the timing signals continue to descend. They'd apparently like to meet you again, judging by the symbols, there, that's the Captain Dave symbol again. They want to meet you down below in 6.1 hours. Actually, they want to meet with four of us in 6.1 hours. They don't want Doctor Roth or Abby to come this time, at least they don't specify their specific symbols. Here are what I assess as their time increments based on the data exchanges we've seen thus far, and they look to be pretty simple, all based on twenty-second intervals," Alex finished.

I pondered this for a minute as I evaluated the animation. "Okay, thanks Alex; makes good sense. You've done a wonderful job on this. Zane, you will go this time. Sarah, you'll stay back as commander. Alex, you and Crystal will make the trip too, so get it worked out on the schedule and meet me at the hatch in T-minus five hours for a pre-mission brief. Crystal, it's important that we have our act together, so please be ready for whatever you think may provide us an opportunity to communicate more effectively." Crystal was our ship's psychologist, and in the meeting, she had been enthusiastically running around the room talking to the crew and annotating items in her tablet computer. I really admired her, she had an absolutely dreadful mission; she was responsible for the crew's mental health. I felt good about taking her to the meeting as her perspective would be extremely valuable.

We discussed a few other logistics items for the next step of our operation; everyone nodded as I walked away, and I could hear Zane in the background synching things up with the crew. I quietly tapped out a message to Zane on my FemtoCom that said, "SLEEP 3 HRS." He'd know what that meant. So I darted back to my quarters, stopping by MedBay along the way to see how Doc was doing. He really was doing better, actually—awake, sitting up, and reviewing details of the engagement. I looked him over carefully and his dark skin was scarred as the implanted sensors had apparently burned the tissue around them. I was so glad he was feeling better. I finally broke off the visit, then made my way back to my quarters to get some rest.

I jumped into bed, hoping to get three full hours of sleep before the next encounter, and I realized I had been up for over sixty-five hours and was beginning to become ineffective, despite chemical enhancements. I initially had a difficult time getting to sleep, and when I woke up, three full hours later, I felt pretty rough and needed something hot to drink, so I stopped by the galley on my way to check in on Doc in MedBay.

"Hi Abby, how goes things?" I mentioned as casually as possible upon entering MedBay.

"Hi sir, things here are better than expected," Abby smiled.

Doc stepped out of one of the treatment rooms with a pretty big grin on his face, "Howdy Dave!" Doc slurred his speech a bit as he waved at me.

I had a broad smile plastered all over my face, "Doc, how the hell are you feeling?" I broke down and gave the old man a bear hug.

"I'm doing better, thanks to Abby, Gina, and Riley," Chuck replied, pointing in their direction.

I looked over at each of them and probably paused a little too long looking at Abby. I thought about earlier events and a brewing, special bond we shared after experiencing first contact with the aliens together. I had long thought Abby was stunningly beautiful, but she was also much more. I smiled knowingly at her and said, "You said it Doc, we are quite grateful to have such a gifted, talented, and committed team aboard the mighty *Algonquin*."

Abby smiled and chimed in, "The aliens saved your skin Doc; we theorized the radiation was the issue, but did not have a good way to proceed. Apparently, this type of radiation poisoning is familiar to these aliens; they sensed it from pretty far away and recognized the symptoms despite not being very familiar with human physiology."

Whoa. I thought about that for a second. *How did the aliens know how to treat that specific type of radiation sickness. They must have seen it before. I wonder if...if the aliens somehow had something to do with bringing us here?* We spent the next twenty minutes discussing various aspects of Doc's recovery, and I felt a tear in my eye as I departed the MedBay. I glanced at Abby as I exited and noticed she was looking at me. Was it weird that I could smell her soft blonde hair from across the room? I didn't know. But despite her ruffled, worn-down look after all she'd been through the last few days, she was still beautiful. I smiled back at her, then caught myself thinking a little too much about her. I had to snap out of it. "All right people back to work. Doc, give me twenty push ups."

I smirked and walked out of the MedBay, knowing that he was probably snickering at my "order."

Chapter 11: Round 2

I went up to the bridge to review the current situation with Zane, Sarah, Alex, and also Crystal. Nothing significant had changed, and Zane had a plan of action for this visit which we discussed at length. We all put on our external suits and made our way down the ship to meet the aliens.

This time there were only four aliens that rose from the floor to meet us. We followed them through the familiar passageway into the translucent walled room.

The room held a large rectangular table with no chairs. The translucent walled operating room was gone. Four of us stood on one side of the table while the four aliens positioned themselves on the opposite side. I noticed the gifted tablet computer connected to various computer-looking systems using many unusual looking cables on the table. I also noticed eight, small bulb-shaped devices connected to the mess of systems on the table. *Hmmm, maybe microphones, maybe they want to record the session,* I thought.

My suit sensors indicated that an oxygen-rich but safe pressurized atmosphere was being detected in this room. A few minutes later, the aliens began to remove their gloves and helmets revealing their physical appearance to the four of us. "We should remove our helmets folks, I'll go first, and each of you follow provided I give you a thumbs up. Remember, move slow, take your time, and don't overreact to anything," I stated calmly. I removed my helmet and suddenly realized there was a lot more oxygen in the room than I was ready for.

I became a bit dizzy, but eventually adapted to an increased level of oxygen concentration as best as possible given the situation. I stood across from what seemed like the lead alien. We peered at one another for the first time with our un-aided vision and without our helmets on. It was a bluish, humanoid creature, a full head shorter than me but possessed two rather large, almost compound-looking eyes, a tiny nose, a huge mouth. It had what looked like at least two ears on its heavily defined skull. The lead alien was continuously manipulating the icosidodecahedron controls on the table in front of us.

The mouth was really striking as it seemed to be shaped in a protruding way resembling a mouth like a cat. The lead alien began by typing onto its computer using the icosidodecahedron controller. Instantly, words began hitting my ears from the device's output speaker: "Relaxed...longed-for exposure," was the repeated audio output as the lead alien gestured to an animation that popped to life just above the center of the table. It was the same neon-looking threaded display of the *Algonquin*. I couldn't figure out how it wanted me to respond so I just looked at my team to see if they had any ideas. After two minutes of non-action on our part, the lead blue alien started making sounds like squeals, chirps, and tones from its mouth into the nearest bulb device, obviously a microphone, which resulted in the same words being generated by the speaker, "Relaxed...longed-for exposure."

I started to grasp what they were trying to do, and it was not working out so well, so I thought I'd try a different tact. "Dave," I said speaking into the nearest bulb device while pointing to myself with both hands, then, "Zane," as I pointed to Zane, and, "Crystal," pointing to our psychologist, and finally, "Alex," pointing to my second pilot and resident computer expert. The system on the table converted that into high- and low-pitched tones, squeaks and chirps, presumably the language of the blue creatures.

The main alien followed that lead by pointing at each of us in sequence issuing a series of sounds from its language into the translator system which resulted in an audible statement saying "Dave, Zane, Crystal, Alex,".

The lead alien then pointed at itself and said something that sounded like a squeaky, chirp-filled language which was translated by the systems on the table into: "Isolde," then at its remaining aliens with "Bowendi," "Freishe," "Trudeezic."

"Sir," Alex said quietly.

"What?" I responded calmly without taking my eyes off of those standing at the table.

"Sir, they've somehow jumpered your tablet computer into the other computer-looking box sitting there and I'm guessing it is providing some vocabulary stabilization." Alex said calmly.

"Thanks Alex. I agree. But hold on to that analysis for now unless you have something critical to tell me. I want to stay focused on the engagement here." I quietly replied while continuing to remain poised and calm in front of Isolde.

"Sir, I've accessed the maintenance port on the tablet computer and there is a *lot* of data exchanging between the tablet and that alien system," Alex said with a bit of urgency.

"Welcome traveler. Welcome traveler," stated the home brew translator the aliens had wired up.

I held my head still and whispered, "Alex, don't do anything else without my approval, and that includes scans and the like; I don't want to accidentally cause a problem," I finished, maintaining my poker face.

I knew Alex would comply, and the information he shared did give me something to work with, so I parroted some of the alien greeting back at them to try and gauge a reaction. "Welcome friends. Welcome friends," I stated as cleanly and slowly as possible.

The aliens liked that, and the lead alien then said, "Dave, we are happy you trans-communicated to us."

Okay, I thought, *this is a great start. Need to take baby steps here to avoid miscommunication.* From there we began to trade rudimentary statements to one another. Apparently, Isolde liked talking, or was really focused on figuring us out, so we all began to create conversations with the alien standing opposite of us. Communicating through the rudimentary translator was seriously tedious as I caught myself making mistakes that I'm sure were confusing the blue aliens. I have no idea how, but the microphone devices did a really good job of separating all the voices, squeals, chirps and sounds. We started to make positive progress though, mostly thanks to Alex and his alien counterpart as they used a sort of digitized whiteboard to establish common concepts based on Alex's existing understanding of the communications symbology they'd already shared. Alex figured out some basic word symbol combinations, and we all leveraged their successes. Five hours into this meeting, Isolde apparently ordered the cargo bay to be pressurized, as that's what Sarah and Huang relayed to the crew and me. Although Isolde indicated that at first, she was worried that we carried some type of infectious disease, its people ruled out the potential of infection before engaging with us.

"So, we are compatible organically?" I asked in a calm way pointing at Isolde then myself.

"Compatible, yes," Isolde slowly stated, "but at lowest levels of coding we are too different to be interoperable."

I think they would have spoken to us all night, but finally I decided to end things as we were all exhausted and needed to pull ourselves together. "Isolde, our journey was difficult, my crew is very tired and needs rest, can we meet again in ten hours?"

Isolde seemed happy to confirm the break.

I found their eyes to be the most intriguing aspect of the aliens' biology. Later, ships life sciences expert, Gina would teach me that they are compound eyes mounted below a normal rod and cone: a simple eye that occasionally glowed with a cyan hue probably due to a physical or emotional response. Very Curious indeed.

Isolde informed me that we would no longer need the suits as she had ordered the cargo bay, the passageway, and this meeting room/medical facility to be pressurized and oxygenated, "Eternally," which I found to be a wonderful break from the Condition-Red suits. It would benefit our further interaction, so I thought it was a good decision. Isolde indicated the gravity would increase over the next several hours to a slightly higher level.

The gravity, well, I wasn't sure how increasing it would work, but I decided I would add it to the next engagement's list of topics. Before we left, Isolde said one last thing, "Here is gift between leaders. It will help us be together." I looked down to see a strange-looking device that resembled a computer: a small screen and strange-looking input icosidodecahedron globe. I grasped it with my left hand as I looked back into Isolde's eyes, nodding positively and smiling gently.

The team made its way back to the *Algonquin,* and we immediately met in the main conference room to conduct our typical after-action review.

We all discussed topics we felt were significant to our current disposition, and the topic of alien eyes was a hot button item. Complex and simple eyes was an unusual combination and immediately noticed by all of the crew. Also, the diminutive size of our bipedal friends was not what was expected.

I guess everyone thought alien life would be large, angry-looking monstrosities with massive claws and teeth. *Well, they definitely have the teeth*, I thought, *but they really weren't too different from humans. So much for expectations.* I met with my key staff, including Sarah, Zane, Huang, Mickey, Maria, Crystal, and Gina filling in for Chuck.

We huddled in the conference room and shut the door to discuss several more critical topics finishing with the, "How the heck do we get home?" question followed closely by the, "How the hell did we get here?" question.

Mickey talked to us about Sasha's ore, and how he'd noticed some of its unique properties as he tried to place a magnetic isolation field around the area of the ship that contained the ore, and a sudden burst of radiation was emitted. That was something I needed to take up with Sasha as I had a sense there was something she was hiding regarding that ore.

Zane mentioned that full power had been restored to the *Algonquin,* and the alien oxygen pressurization of the cargo bay had already taken place with sufficient nitrogen but also an oddly high amount of argon and helium gas. "Zane are those levels of argon and helium poisonous to us?"

Zane responded, "Not really. I checked with Gina and Doc, and they indicated at the current levels they are not toxic, and Abby noted much higher concentrations inside their facilities during visits. Abby thinks the aliens may need higher levels of these gases. "I've got the engineering team putting some rudimentary jacks under the right spots of the *Algonquin* to ensure its structure is properly supported. Sitting on her ass impacts the structural integrity of the outer hull, and it's causing damage."

"Jacks, where in the heck did you guys get jacks?"

"We printed them with the ObjectForge. They are made from high-density plastic and aluminum; it's not terribly sophisticated, but sufficient to do the job until we get out of here," Zane said with that smile he gets when he's done something cool for the team. He gets that smile a lot.

I directed everyone to team up and get four hours of sleep as soon as possible. We had only a few hours available before the next meeting, so we needed to take advantage of it and get some rest. I spent some of my spare time in Mickey's office trying to figure out my puzzling gift from Isolde, to no avail.

Mick and I managed to turn it on and off a few times using the tiny icosi-dodecahedron on its front panel, but I could not figure out its functionality. *Great, another freaking puzzle, just what I need*, I thought, and I hoped there would be no test from Isolde on it at the next engagement.

The next meeting with the aliens was the most productive, possibly because we were much more rested and better prepared, and they managed to improve the common vocabulary we used to communicate.

On that trip, I took Zane, Sarah, Mickey, and a very nervous Riley, to meet with the aliens. We all wore our external suits but carried our helmets in our arms just as a precaution. In general, the helmets collapsed neatly, except for the camera and comms gear that protruded outwards in more of a telescoping way.

I carried the gift from Isolde with me, just in case she brought it up, but did not divulge that I could not operate it. Isolde, Bowen, Trudezic, Freishe, and another alien, met us this time and we noted the translation effectiveness of the combination alien and human computers was significantly improved. We also noticed each of the aliens had a device on their arm and head that apparently performed the translations for them as my old tablet computer was no longer present in the room.

Early into this meeting about a dozen aliens entered the room and were introduced, one at a time, by Isolde. Alien engineers, scientists, language specialists, and those with other specialties, were introduced to us, and the meeting devolved somewhat into more of a campus-mixer environment: everyone talking to everyone as the aliens came and went at will.

We managed to find out the aliens called themselves the "Veeniri," as

89

interpreted by our new translation system, and they were in some sort of coalition with two other major species known as the "Higlian" and the "Grojiel."

All right, now we're getting somewhere; three alien species, I thought, taking a moment to think about this historic meeting.

Isolde told us that the Veeniri and the Grojiel both originated from planets in this solar system, which was huge by any standard with dozens of planets, moons, and two broad asteroid fields all surrounding a rather old star. The Grojiel originated from the fourth planet and the Veeniri from the sixth. The Veeniri, apparently, matured more quickly and began colonizing the system, which somehow agitated the Grojiel, as they did not have the same technology as the Veeniri. Eventually, the Grojiel pushed into space too, which caused fighting between the two species to break out.

Though some on both sides tried to keep the peace, a millennium of war ensued, and a serious disease broke out that decimated a quarter of the Veeniri population. At nearly the same time, the Grojiel figured out how to travel faster than light (FTL) and discovered a new species called Higlian in a nearby system. Isolde said the Veeniri are not certain which came first, the Higlian discovery or FTL travel.

"Wow, that's incredible, how does FTL work?" I said to Isolde excitedly. All I could think about in that moment was somehow getting back home to Earth. And I was not the only one. Everyone in the room was quiet now; all eyes were focused on Isolde.

"Yes, incredible, and the Grojiel now outnumbered us with their new allies, controlled access to the coveted resources found in the Higlian system and used that control to keep us from really having command of the FTL travel," Isolde said with some sadness. "We know how it works, but we do not possess enough of the needed raw materials to use it consistently ourselves. We are missing a key component and the Grojiel are working hard to keep this advantage away from us. This has prevented us from exploring with the same speed and agility the Grojiel enjoy, and is why you humans are so important to us: your partnership balances the equation." Isolde said. Shifting back to the story, "Eventually we entered into a peace treaty and made a place for diplomacy, on a moon of the fifth planet. The moon is called Bradea, and each of our people has political representation on Bradea, and we formed a neutral security force to protect the trade activities from being overtaken by any of the three individual societies. This is where your people can help us," Isolde spoke through the translator.

That caught me off guard and I responded, "How can we help you Isolde; there's only a handful of us."

"We want you to commit your species to being an ally to the Veeniri. Commit to a formal alliance that includes mutual defense and exclusive trade. This must be done soon and can only occur at the Council on Bradea."

I actually scratched my head I was so stunned by what she had so quietly asked. "Umm, Isolde, I cannot enter into agreements for all of my species; that's a pretty big deal." I continued, "If there was some way to use the FTL travel, I could return to Earth, then gather and return with the right people who could make such a commitment."

Isolde looked at me without blinking or even moving. Now I'm no judge of alien bodily expression but the increasing cyan hue in her skin led me to think she was pissed. "By statute, we are required to report our discovery of your species to the Council on Bradea within ten days. You must choose, Veeniri, Grojiel, or Higlian alliance."

Now I'm not certain but it looked like Isolde was starting to sweat a little. "Okay, okay Isolde, let me talk through this with our crew, and we'll figure out how to work through this issue. It might help if you can tell me a little more about the history and differences between yourselves, the Grojiel, and Higlian?"

Once more, all eyes and ears were on Isolde as she laid out more of the history and physical attributes related to the three species.

I found one tidbit of information particularly useful as Isolde showed us a rough, three-dimensional display of the Veeniri, Higlian, and Grojiel anatomy. Not that I was curious, but I finally understood how to determine the difference between Veeniri males and females. Huh, not all that different from humans aside from the patterns of white, blue, and green skin that runs from foot to skull on the Veeniri. One pattern for males and another for females. Anyhow, the Grojiel seemed remarkably similar except that they were a bit more skinny, narrow-framed bipeds with skulls that very much resembled the Veeniri except for the green and red skin that similarly ran from head to toe. They were both about the same size, perhaps a little less than the average human from my perspective. The Higlian on the other hand were totally different, which led me to guess that the Veeniri and Grojiel were descendants of the same ancestor.

The Higlian, well, they were weird looking. They looked like a four-foot-tall monkey with four arms and two legs, and were, apparently, an extremely old species that was dying out. Isolde indicated that they had very highly evolved technology though.

The Higlian torso contained a strange-looking, almost jellyfish-like section, which had about the same tint to it as their six eyes that dotted across their skulls. And fins...man, they had short, stubby fins all over their skulls. Like I said, very strange.

"The Higlian are a significantly older species," Isolde said. "We are pretty sure they are responsible for figuring out the Faster than Light Travel and sharing the tech with the Grojiel, although we do not know what the Higlian received in return."

About thirty minutes later, we decided to break for the day as we'd received quite a bit of data to digest. Standing in the corridor I towered over Isolde, and found myself looking down at her and smiling. Isolde asked if she could accompany me to the ship for a brief tour. *Hmmm*, I thought, *I suppose that would work.* I smiled and said, "That would be great Isolde; I will notify my ship to be prepared for a visitor," as I nodded to Zane who covertly radioed a warning message back to the *Algonquin*.

Chapter 12: Misunderstanding

And so, a little later, we all headed back to the *Algonquin*. Isolde and I stopped outside the primary-hull staircase leading to the old-fashioned colonial hatch, and I tried to explain how the ascent would work. She just nodded ambiguously as if she either did not care, or already knew quite conclusively how the process worked. I still did not understand how to read her body expressions well just yet. Regardless, I remained as gentlemanly as possible, and she seemed fine with it, and held my right arm the entire way up to the hatch.

If I didn't know better, I'd say she was laughing part way up. She never let go of me as we moved throughout a brief tour of the *Algonquin*, and some of the crew members gawked a little but smiled and bowed gracefully as Isolde and I walked carefully through the primary portions of the ship while I pointed out interesting things that I thought she might like more details on.

I could tell she was nervous as we encountered crew members along the path as her three-pronged grip on my arm grew intense. Finally, we entered my quarters that were filled with, umm, well, junk. Junk from my decades of visiting the colonies, moons, and space stations. I watched quietly as Isolde took it all in...looking thoroughly at my quarters in an obvious attempt to learn about me and possibly decide if she could trust me with her species' private business.

Finally, she settled on the gift she'd given me. Isolde grabbed the device off my desk, then grabbed my right hand, and she showed me, in slow motion, how to perform basic functions with it. It lit up with many soft colors and vibrations; *man*, it was beautiful. It sprang to life with an amazingly elegant combination of soft humming and crisp color flashes. I finally caught on to how it worked a bit better. I manipulated it successfully with her expert instruction. When I used the device as she had taught, I saw an image of Isolde appear on the device's screen. *Ahhh...* I thought, *it's a fancy radio, I get it.* I showed her how we greet one another using a handshake, which was similar to their raising of the arms.

She found the handshake to be quite natural, yet expressed concerns that the Grojiel did not like touching other species, so I should be careful in future engagements, but she would spread word of this gesture to ensure her people were cognizant.

Our conversation drifted from handshakes and the communications device into a more serious direction. Isolde restated how she must report our encounter to the Council of Civilization as the peace accord stipulates any new intelligent life forms must not be hidden from the other members of the Council. To hide any species is a treasonous act that would have significant repercussions, and Isolde did not wish to risk further confrontation with the Grojiel. I was beginning to truly understand the big picture now, she wanted us to partner with the Veeniri to offset the threat of war. I tried to explain to Isolde that I'm not the right person to speak on behalf of my entire civilization, but she did not understand, or perhaps it was that she did not care; I'm not sure which. Isolde was in a bad spot; if they failed to report us per their agreement...it could lead to war: if I didn't choose to side with the Veeniri it could lead to war. War. What a colossal waste of life.

Apparently, Isolde missed or did not fully understand the point that we did not navigate here on our own, so I tried explaining how we arrived, and she simply replied that our meeting could not be a coincidence, and that we must hurry to the Council as soon as possible, and that I must make the right decision. *Well crap.*

Isolde asked me about the name of our ship, the *Algonquin,* and I told her the name represented an honored and wonderfully rich, complex civilization that Earth's governments wanted to memorialize as we reached into the stars. She nodded in understanding and turned the conversation to early societies on her home world named Kaveralle.

I knew it was important that we not get off track, so I tried explaining how we arrived at this area in space, and how governments worked on Earth. I finally agreed to testify at the Council, but clearly explained to Isolde that I did not have the authority to sign any treaties or declarations. I looked at her solemnly and asked her how the process of testifying would work.

Isolde startled me by looking into my eyes for nearly a minute, and then she gently raised her arm and touched my face with what was, basically, her left hand, and said, "You have a very heavy weight; you must equally represent an entire civilization with precision, honesty, and a clear identity. I do understand this is a mission you were not specifically launched to achieve."

Whoa.

Maybe she was paying attention. Hmmm, what to do. I thought for a moment and slowly, gently, reached out to Isolde's face with my right hand. "I only want my crew to get home safely. I have no idea how we got here. I'm terrified that I'll commit my people to something we cannot deliver on or shouldn't. We want to help you; those of us in this ship especially are moved by your plight, and we want to partner with your people." Her eyes gently glowed in that soft, cyan hue. I was beginning to think she could see right through me. I felt strangely connected to Isolde in this moment. Her scent was...oddly appealing.

Isolde and I continued our philosophical discussion for about an hour which yielded more insight into their leadership and relationships with the Grojiel and the Higlian. Finally, I sensed she was ready to go, so I took her back to the descending ramp, which enabled her to meet back up with her apparent guards. She turned to me and sharply stated, "Our timeline is tight, we must meet again in four hours; you must complete repairs to your ship so that we can depart in another twenty hours."

She always talks like she's in charge; Isolde must be some type of royalty, I thought as I replied calmly and with a warm smile, "Yes Isolde, we will be there in four hours."

Isolde walked away at a rapid clip.

I headed back to the command deck and briefed the XO and team on what I had learned. I let the crew know we'd be heading back to visit in four hours, and hoped Mickey and Maria had a good estimate on ship repairs, but it was pretty clear that we would not meet the newly established deadline. Mick and Alex figured out a way to communicate with the Veeniri comms center using a simple FM radio modulation scheme which worked well. It was too slow though, and eventually they provided us with a sort of space radio connector that was apparently designed as a backup system for their own fleet. It worked well, once we finally got it wired into our emergency comms array. I didn't want it directly wired into the main comms system, and since the emergency comms array is self-contained, we were able to use it from the bridge by connecting a full-sized computer terminal to it. "Zane, is that thing secure?"

He responded that it was mostly for video and audio signal transport with some limited packetized text data exchange, and said that Alex had put several security controls into place, and we should be safe.

"Sarah, you have command. I'm taking Zane to the Veeniri for the next meeting; can you please finalize our departure checklist? I don't want to accidentally rip open the hull by striking one of those claw things."

"Roger captain; I'm on it," Sarah replied.

I headed back to my quarters to get a little sleep. Very little as it turned out. My stomach was twisting up again with all the thoughts rushing through my mind about making a commitment for all of humanity. I tried, but I just couldn't get all the unfinished business out of my head, which always disrupts my sleep. I had to figure out how to navigate this council engagement.

A few hours later Zane and I chewed on some small talk as we made our way back to the Veeniri. He brought me up to speed on some of the ship's problems and let me know we might be fully operational by the deadline thanks to repair help from the Veeniri engineers. I grinned and thought how great it would be to meet our first Veeniri deadline, as each little success seemed really important to our burgeoning, interstellar relationship.

I was still feeling pretty refreshed and positive as we strode proudly into the meeting room and noted a larger than normal volume of Veeniri waiting for us there.

After some greetings and pleasantries, Isolde and her team showed us a three-dimensional star chart of sorts depicting our present location, local planets, stars and moons, and the apparent flight trajectory needed to reach the council planet.

I was stunned when I saw the distance. If I was reading it right, it would take the *Algonquin* at least fifteen days to make that journey under perfect conditions. Yet the Veeniri seemed to think we could cover it in hours.

Isolde then discussed the reception and acceptance procedure for us after we'd arrived and entered the virtual council, and then the live council engagements. Overall, it seemed pretty simple, we just sort of pledged an allegiance to the Council and further disclosed our alliance with the Veeniri. It was apparently some sort of distributed, federalized government system.

I glanced at Zane as he gave me a furrowed brow, a look of disagreement. The kind of look he'd give me before starting up a conversation with some pretty ladies in a remote space port. Didn't matter, I'd already decided to let the air out of the room: "Isolde, we won't be able to make that trip with your ships. Our ship cannot travel that fast."

A stunned Veeniri crowd glanced around at one another and finally: "What is this? How can you mean this?" Isolde choked out.

"I've been telling you this for some time; we don't know how we arrived at this location in space, and we really don't know how to get back home," I said with more than a little stress in my voice.

The Veeniri began what looked like old fashioned bickering amongst themselves. Finally one of the smaller Veeniri jumped up, pointed at Zane and I, then shouted in their language. It sounded something like, "Shock-Zem-Swui." Apparently the translator could not determine which of the Veeniri to translate, as it came across as "Incarcerate them." Or maybe it did, because a security detail came bursting into the room and forcibly ushered us to a prison-like room with no windows and no way to get a signal out to the ship.

Well crap!

"Dave, we could have resisted, even a little; they are tiny; we could have made our way back to the damned ship! Plus I didn't see any sign of serious looking weapons—"

"Hell Zane, no way. There's no way we could successfully battle these guys for any sustained length of time from the *Algonquin*; by the way, remind me to have Mick dig out my 1911 when I get back; I want us to be armed from now on. We are clearly not as sure about our friends here as we'd like to be."

"Clearly," said Zane, as he gestured to our cell.

We sat alone in the little cell while Zane bitched at me about my handling of that situation.

"You could have been a bit more diplomatic with that information, Dave. I mean, *crap*! I think these guys are really counting on us to save their bacon. You—"

"Zane, I get it; you are right, I could have done better. I was just pissed because I have been telling Isolde this all along and not getting much of an acknowledgment from her about our concerns."

"Well you got one now. And I understand, sir, but think of the language barrier and, hell, we just showed up one day in their back yard. I'm sure it seems like a minor detail to them."

I nodded in agreement as we tried to figure out our next step.

Before planning could get too far along, another Veeniri came to the room and began speaking, "I will take you back to the tribal chambers, do not anger/fight or you will become painfully harmed."

I looked over at Zane who was looking back at me. "And me without my trusty pistol," I murmured to Zane who reacted with that familiar grin. We'd been through some tough spots before, suffice it to say. We figured we'd make it here too.

The neon door dissolved, allowing Zane and me to slowly walk through the pathways that eventually led us back to the room where the original meeting occurred before all the excitement happened.

Once back in the room, I noted Isolde's skin was darker blue with what I assessed to be anger, and apparently there were a few soldiers or security personnel, with what appeared to be weapons, and I took note of a decidedly older-looking Veeniri in the room.

He raised his arm to quiet the crowd and began speaking. "Why are you here? Why have you deceived us? What can this be that you are achieving?

There is much about you that we don't know—you might not really want to be our allies. Perhaps you are in league with the Grojiel?"

I looked around the room carefully and said, "Errr, uh, we do want to join an alliance with you, but our space travel technology is not as advanced as yours. That trip is millions of kilometers; it will take us a number of days to reach Bradea."

The discussion went a little better from there. Their engineers appeared to confirm our story as the Veeniri worked up a new plan to tow the *Algonquin* within range, and then detach for us to fly in unassisted. Apparently, they felt it would not send a strong message if their newest ally had to be hauled helplessly to the council. They also wanted to make a few changes to the *Algonquin*: for one, they needed to add a couple of compatible external docks so we could connect in space to other Veeniri ships.

Zane and I took some notes, made some last-minute calculations, and then were off to the *Algonquin* for a few meetings and to get a lot of work done.

Isolde asked that Bowendi and two other Veeniri be authorized to fly on the *Algonquin* with us humans. She also mentioned how appreciative she would be if I would see to their security personally. I ack'd her request, a shorter way of saying "acknowledged" and motioned Bowendi to follow Zane and me. Bowendi was a female engineer, and was one of the most helpful Veeniri so far according to Mick, so it would be nice to have her and her associates on board for the voyage, as I was sure we'd learn a lot from them.

Once we were back on our ship, Sarah, who'd been waiting for us, smiled and said, "Wow, you guys have been gone for quite a while, everything okay?"

I looked over at Zane then glanced back at Sarah, "Yep, everything went swimmingly, although Zane did get a bit mouthy over there with their leadership, so of course we were taken prisoner for a little while and sat in their version of a jail cell."

Sarah turned her head and glared at Zane. Zane rolled his eyes and said, "Oh please. Hey, it wasn't me; it was him!"

I decided to rescue Zane, so I said, "Well it was a confusing situation, and we were only released back to the ship after we talked our way through the miscommunication. Zane will update everyone shortly. I've got to track down Mick and get the ObjectForge to create me something for the trip; talk with you two later."

I smiled and fist bumped Sarah and Zane, then started walking to the engineering section to find Mickey.

Chapter 13: Off to the Council

The rather smallish moon housing the Council of Civilizations was about five days of travel away. Four days being towed by a Veeniri ship so we could travel at their incredibly fast pace, and one day on our own, escorted by the Veeniri flagship.

Apparently the escort was as much security-related as political because of the rather large volume of shipping, trading and commerce occurring from the heavily mixed population on the planet. *I guess crime is common everywhere.* "Sarah, please ask Bowendi to join us for the staff meeting, I'm tracking four hours from now we'll be departing the Veeniri station; is that right?"

"Yes, Bowendi's over here teaching me the departure protocol, and how we'll connect to their ship for the initial towing."

Sarah continued, "Basically they will reach into the bay and hook onto us the same way they placed us in here, and then they will tow us to the decoupling point, and we'll fly the rest of the way together."

"Okay, that's perfect, thank you. When you are done, please let me know as I want your unvarnished opinion on a couple of backup plans I've been working through. Specifically, I want to discuss the rules of engagement with you and Zane. You know, in case things go in an unplanned direction." Sarah smiled with an uncomfortable grin and gave me a thumbs up gesture with her left hand as a response.

Sarah completed her work with Bowendi, and we all sat down to conduct a brief sync session to get our next steps organized. The meeting went pretty quick: we went through our checklist, conducted a fast desktop rehearsal with everyone chiming in with their responsible actions, and ended up with Bowendi going over the procedure for traveling down to the planet after both ships docked at the Council station.

As the session broke up, I had a sidebar conversation with Zane and Sarah where I laid out a couple of generic courses of action to take advantage of any opportunity to grab the faster than light travel hardware. We also talked about self-defense and even a little about offense. I wanted to have a common view of where the line should be drawn.

Mick showed up with a long, flat box and sat down next to Zane on the left side of the table. Sarah and Bowendi stopped on their way out of the staff room. Sarah frowned slightly at the box and said, "Captain, I don't think that is a good idea; we all have our agency-issued electrical shock batons; as I mentioned I think we should avoid conflict as much as possible."

Just in front of Sarah, Bowendi stopped and looked right at me and then gave me a thumbs down gesture with her left hand as she walked out of the room. Sarah's frown dissolved into a wide smile. "I'll... uh... fix that, I believe there might have been a ... misunderstanding." Sarah snickered as she stepped out of the room directly behind Bowendi.

Zane and Mick just stared at me quizzically. "What the hell was that about?" Zane said, calmly but loudly across the table.

"Knowing Dave it's probably some kind of alien mating ritual," Mick quietly stated for the record.

I just smirked and said, "She's mimicking Sarah's behavior from an earlier conversation; it's nothing. Really!" There were wry grins all around as they looked about.

Doc came fumbling into the room and plopped down into the chair that Sarah had just vacated. "Dave, I've been catching up with what's going on and wanted to get five minutes with you after we get going—it's important."

"Sure thing, Doc, what's the topic?"

"The topic is that tedious 'Geologist,' Sasha," Doc said.

"Got it; she can be irritating," I said.

"She's more than that. I did some digging; she's not a Geologist, she's a physicist, an Agency manager, and well connected, and there's more," Doc said, without blinking.

I looked at Doc as I pondered his words. "Okay, Doc, I'll come down to the Medical Bay shortly, and we can discuss it in private. Mick, what do you have for me? I hope its initials are 1-9-1-1," I smiled.

"Right you are, captain, I printed eight, M1911 .45 caliber semi-automatic pistols with specialized types of ammunition in the ObjectForge. I tested them all for accuracy and triple checked the ammo, so it's too weak to penetrate the hull, but strong enough to hurt someone or something."

I ended up with six reliably working models with holsters for the crew going down to the Council. Each person would get four clips of seven rounds each. Two clips were a mix of ball and rock-salt rounds, the latter of which are painful but harmless, unless they hit you in the eye or somewhere really soft. There was also a clip of only rock salt and only ball rounds.

"Outstanding Mick, I really appreciate this. Zane, hand them out will you? And tell folks to get down and practice a bit; I don't want any issues to crop up with our new personnel protection equipment."

"No sweat, sir. I recommend we don't start an intergalactic war with these. I've got to get back to finish the systems check since we are about to break free," Mick said, as he smiled and walked out of the conference room.

"Hey, I'm not starting a war, just want some personal protection after that last little episode with the Veeniri," I said, with my voice trailing off after Mickey left earshot.

Over the next few hours, we ran through checks and finally the *Algonquin* was gently pulled out of the bay by an even larger spider ship's arm. It was the Veeniri fleet admiral's flagship with none other than Isolde aboard. Bowendi was instrumental in making the whole departure happen with as few WTFs as possible.

Bowendi was a brilliant engineer; I saw her helping Mickey, Sarah and Zane sort out some kind of plasma manifold problem which resulted in Mickey building a bunch of new pieces in the ObjectForge, which he promptly put into place in the engine and reactor throttle linkage.

After staring out the portal window for what seemed to be an hour, I turned my head back toward Bowendi and Sarah and asked, "Bowendi, are all the Veeniri ships designed this way? That thing is massive, and I don't understand why it looks like there are engines everywhere."

Bowendi looked at me for a long moment, no doubt waiting for the translation to finish so she could form a response.

Finally, she replied, "All our modern ships possess the G-Ring design with multi-port plasma exhaust; it makes them look like engines are everywhere, but there is only one engine and a capillary distributed plasma exhaust system. There are also many uses for the exhaust ports, including weapons firing."

"Okay, what is the G-Ring part for?"

"It's to generate the field effect for FTL travel; I cannot really tell you much more about it; it is hidden from me."

Bowendi finished as she turned her head back toward the shared computer screen that she and Sarah were focused on. Sarah looked at me with that polite "please buzz off" look that she gets when I'm bothering her.

Message received, okay, let me go down and talk with Doc, in all the action, I forgot to discuss Sasha and the Agency issues he mentioned earlier. As I made my way down to the Medical Bay, I noticed the gift that Isolde gave me was glowing in a pulsing, cyan hue so I pulled it out of my left cargo pocket and tried to remember how to manipulate the darn thing. After about the third try, I managed to correctly perform the authentication sequence and thumb my way over to the triangle that was blinking.

The screen crackled to life and there was Isolde on a split screen with another, older-looking Veeniri. "Captain Dave," said the older Veeniri through a translation, "I am Kjino, the Ambassador to the Council. I would like to offer a session to meet and discuss the current and future situation. Please join us for a collaboration session in eleven hours on our ship.

"We will make arrangements to hold you. We would like to discuss the Council procedures and ensure that we have a common view of the process and outcomes."

"Well alright, Ambassador Kjino, sir, I'd be honored to join you, but the ships are moving very fast, I'm not sure how to get over there to your ship," I said, with as friendly of a smile as I could muster.

The ambassador responded quickly, "Yes, yes, it is no problem, we will extend a tunnel to your bottom hatch. I understand it's been properly modified to accept our auto-tunneler. Do you accept?"

Interesting, I thought. Okay, right to the point, I was beginning to like this little blue fellow. "Yes sir, Mr. Ambassador, we'd be honored to collaborate. Do you mind if I bring an additional person? It helps me to think through hard problems when there's more than just myself to do the thinking."

I could see Isolde's cyan hue increase, I'd learned that happens when she gets irritated. "Yes, yes, bring another human as well—ten hours and fifty-seven minutes from now. We will coordinate."

With that last bit the Ambassador's image disappeared from the space radio that Isolde gave me. "Dave, it is important that you arrive prepared so I'm sending you some documents to review," Isolde said.

"Uh, Isolde this screen is pretty small, not sure how many items you are sending me but—" I was cut off by an apparently annoyed Isolde.

"Dave, I will send them through this device. Let Bowendi know to expect files, she will show you how to transfer the documents to your computer system in a safe way so you can study them."

"Uhh, thank you, Isolde, I will do that. Say, the Ambassador fellow didn't seem to want to talk very much, is he okay?" I asked.

Isolde looked around to her left and then to her right and finally back toward me. "He thinks you are in league with the Grojiel and the engagement at the Council will greatly embarrass him. We have been discussing the matter.

"I agree with him that it's important that we avoid making a mistake, so we need to spend the next hour periods coordinating. You should get ready for a lot of questions Dave.

"I believe that you are the key to making everything work... I have to go now, I will see you soon, Bowendi will ensure the tunnel is in place so you can visit us safely."

I nodded approvingly yet respectfully saying, "Thank you, Isolde, I'll read the documents and be ready."

She gave me a minimal but noticeable smile as she nodded and broke the comms channel. *Wow*, I thought, *I think she really trusts me.* She must be vouching for us with this Ambassador fellow. Only good can come from a relationship like that.

I went back up to the bridge and talked with Zane, Bowendi, Alex and Sarah about getting the documents. Bowendi called the device something that the translator choked on and so she said it again, and the translator finally spit out, "RexCom."

Alex spoke up quickly, "Sir, let's connect it to one of the maintenance tablet computers, they have special protections from differing types of malware and operate as standalone systems with controlled access to isolated maintenance networks."

"Okay Alex, please work with Bowendi to get the documents, we need to be very careful to never allow any of these devices to directly connect to our ship's computer. It would be best to setup three or four maintenance tablets networked together so we can review, make notes, and record events down at the Council."

"Roger, sir, I'll get it done," Alex replied as he turned and float-walked off with Bowendi.

"Sarah, I'll need your help to review the documents."

Sarah nodded, smiled confidently, and said, "No problem, Dave; I also have some thoughts on the Council and how we should handle this alliance situation."

I smiled at Sarah and discussed a few ship issues with Zane. "You know Dave, I'm getting to know the XO of that ship, he, or uh, she, well, I'm not sure but whoever they are well, they are damned smart. We are working pretty well together. It is taking some time, but I think allying with them is the right thing."

Turning to verify that Bowendi had walked away, I started a new, quieter conversation with Zane. "Roger Zane, right now I'm thinking we need to evaluate the other alien species without spooking the Veeniri. We need to try to get our hands on that Faster than Light transport system so we can get the hell back home." I said, with a confidence-building grin to my deputy commander.

Sarah sidled up and said, "It's so curious that the Veeniri do not possess whatever the technological solution is, but the other two aliens do; making me wonder if we are partnering with the wrong species. Especially if we want to use this faster than light capability to actually get home."

"Roger that Sarah. Believe me, that thought has passed through my mind multiple times, however my plan right now is to get our hands on that FTL travel capability during engagements at the Council without creating a stir or problems for the Veeniri," I said.

Zane piped in, "Agreed, but if the Higlian originated the tech I think we need to focus some energy on collaborating with them. Perhaps join the Council as a member. Uh, allied to the Veeniri and Higlian while excluding the Grojiel."

"Good point Zane. Sarah, I want you to visit the ambassador's ship with me—we need to learn how this process works and figure out a way to exploit the situation for humanity and get us home."

Over the next several hours the crew got into a rhythm of eating, sleeping, and working. The ship was in better shape than I'd seen *Big Al* in a long time. I also learned that the modifications Bowendi recommended to Zane significantly improved both maximum speed and the efficiency of our engines, which built my trust in her and my confidence in our collective ability to work together to solve hard problems. That was essential to our long-term success.

Sarah, Zane, Alex, hell nearly the entire crew, and I spent several hours reading through all of the Council documents. It seemed I was essentially signing humanity up to ally with the Veeniri, *and just the Veeniri.*

The Veeniri clearly wanted to exclusively control trade and private access to all of humanity's systems. *Wow, there was going to be a lot of discussion at this meeting.* I told Sarah to make sure she brought an extra maintenance tablet with a microphone that was networked back to *Algonquin* so Zane and the rest of the crew could pay attention to what was going on. This situation was going to take a lot of analysis to make sure we made as few mistakes as possible. I wanted this visit to the Council to be a zero WTFs per hour event.

Just as the ambassador had stated, a massive corridor was extended from the ambassador's ship and connected to the bottom hatch of the *Algonquin*.

"Wow that's a big tunnel Zane."

Zane chuckled and said "Man you said it, their tech is truly amazing."

"Agreed, I did not expect such a large tunnel; hell, I could fly *Ranger-1* through that thing," I replied.

Zane gave me a grin and said, "You two better get a move on; you don't want to be late for your first engagement with the ambassador."

"Thank you, Zane, keep the lights on for us; we won't be too long," I quipped as I stepped into the hatch housing connected to the tunnel with Sarah in tow. Several Veeniri escorted us across the tunnel to the ambassador's massive ship.

When we finally got to the ship, walking to the conference room proved to be a bit intimidating as we saw hundreds of Veeniri along the way. *Hmmm, gravity*, I thought as I noticed we started to sink toward the floor as we float-walked toward the ship's core.

We even saw a few different species that did not look Veeniri at all, and I could not place them. Finally, we made it into the chamber where the admiral, ambassador, Isolde, and a few other dignitaries stood, waiting for us to enter the room apparently. As we entered the room we gave the Veeniri greeting to each of them one at a time, placing our arm extended and between theirs, and smiling as graciously as possible. The walls in the room were adorned with what looked like Veeniri art and digital screens mixed together with the cyan hue of lighting, which softly emanated from symmetrically organized points in the ceiling and walls.

The ambassador said, "Please be seated, there is much to discuss," and the Veeniri all sat down at a long, rectangular table.

As Sarah and I sat down, I noticed a ton of electronic equipment, holographic projectors, and control interfaces resembling the one on the RexCom. "It's very nice of you to host us Mr. Ambassador, sir," I said, with as much gratitude as I could fit into one sentence-smile combination.

"Yes, yes Captain Dave, today we must isolate the intent, and document our agreement, so that when we arrive at the Council there will be no miscommunications," the ambassador said, with very little bodily movement or posture change to judge his disposition by.

"Yes sir, we are prepared to discuss the terms of an alliance, and as we have mentioned we do wish to ally with the Veeniri, but we have a need for the FTL travel so we can return home; is that something we can partner together on?" I said with a smile as big as day.

The ambassador responded in a rather long-winded way. "Yes, Isolde had mentioned your interest in the FTL travel. We too find this mode of transportation to be critical. The challenge lies in gaining access to the block."

Anytime the translator could not translate a word with sufficient precision, it would pause or say, "Block," for each individual syllable that it was trying to convert to English. Sometimes that made the conversation part gibberish. As it came out, "... block block," I noticed a couple of the Veeniri engineers working feverishly on what looked like a computer, and a few seconds later the words, "living rock or graviscopic ore," were spoken by the translator device.

Living Rock? What the heck does that mean?

The ambassador turned to look at the engineers and appeared to nod in a positive way toward them as though he was pleased with their ability to reconcile the translation gap.

"Mr. Ambassador, sir, so am I to understand that you possess the machinery, but don't possess this living rock, or graviscopic ore that is needed to power the system?" I said as quietly and humbly as possible remembering what Isolde had told me about the ambassador's mistrust of us.

The ambassador nodded to an engineer on the other end of the table, and the engineer stood and then touched his computer controller. That's when a massive holographic screen appeared over the table between us showing the local star system and the neighboring star system where several small red dots pulsed slowly.

The Veeniri engineer spoke, "Those points of light depict where the graviscopic ore has been detected; as you can see, most of it lies in the Higlian system, and we are not authorized to travel to that system by Council agreement. All access to that system is controlled by the Grojiel."

Turning my head back to the ambassador I asked another carefully worded question. "Mr. Ambassador, sir, why would you agree to such terms in the Council?" I saw all the Veeniri except the ambassador start to glow with that irritated cyan hue.

The ambassador stood up and put his hands on the table, looking at me with a stern expression. "The Grojiel dealt in dishonor by offering us the technology to employ FTL travel, but did not disclose the necessary means by which to propel the process."

OK, I get it now, I thought as I turned my head to look at an excited Sarah. It seems the Grojiel pulled a fast one and offered the mechanism but not the fuel.

The ambassador sat back down and said, "Since we are asking hard questions, it is difficult to understand how you are here without FTL travel ability. My people are masters of medical technology and nanotechnology, and we analyzed to determine that each of your crew are non-cloned beings and could not have traveled far through space without appropriate sleep stasis capabilities. We have scanned and not found this capability on your ship. Nor have we found the G-Ring field modulator or the Gravitron necessary for FTL travel. Because of these incongruencies, I am genuinely concerned that you are in league with the Grojiel as there is little conceivable way you could have penetrated so deeply into Veeniri space undetected."

Okay, I thought, *this is good, they've laid their cards on the table about being worried that we are in league with the Grojiel, and we've laid our cards on the table concerning interest in FTL travel.*

Once again, I laid out the highlights of how we'd gotten there. How we were returning to our home world from a neighboring planet when we were struck by the bluish-brown field effect. As I continued, I could see activity at the far end of the table where a couple of Veeniri engineers were becoming quite antsy, drawing the attention of the ambassador.

The ambassador looked over at the admiral, who got up and walked down to them and talked to them without any translation being emitted. I tried not to notice as the admiral walked back to his chair and sat down. He continued using his RexCom with great speed as though he was sending thousands of text messages to his staff and reading responses. After two hours of discussion, a small creature, about the dimensions of a medium-sized dog, entered the room and offered drinks to all the Veeniri. Some took a small cup, and I could see a thick, cyan-colored liquid being poured into their cups by the strange little creature's one arm.

"Captain Dave, would you like to try some Veeniri tea? It will not harm you, as many of its properties are not bioavailable to your human bodies, and you may like the taste," Isolde said, with a glance toward the serving-being. I remember the scientists talking with Chuck about how our systems were so different there were very few organic biological properties shared between us, so eating nearly anything from the Veeniri planet would be inert to our biology from a nutrition perspective.

I get it, the tea can't hurt me, and it's good bonding. "Absolutely, I love drinking tea, most kind of you to offer."

The smaller being brought the tea over to Sarah and me. It then poured the tea into two cups and handed one to each of us. The handleless cup was tiny in my big hands, but I tipped it up to my lips and took a swig gingerly, as all the Veeniri eyes were on me at that point.

Wow, it was spicy, almost a cinnamon flavor, not too bad overall; not something I could do a lot of though. "This is really tasty tea, thank you for sharing it with us," I lied as I watched Sarah carefully take a sip. It was funny watching her try to fake a smile after taking a drink of that stuff. She had the look of someone who'd needed to take a huge crap about six hours ago. I guessed she wouldn't be hungry for quite a while.

I smiled at her and raised my cup to take another, very small sip. *Wow, the spiciness seems to be accumulating quickly*, I thought. A couple of times during the conversation Zane sent me messages on the FemtoCom that I wore on my wrist. He indicated that Bowendi was confirming many of the details concerning FTL travel and the graviscopic Ore or crystals. Apparently, this was filling in some gaps in her own knowledge as well. This told me that much of the information must be highly classified in the Veeniri society. The conversation continued for another two hours as we worked our way toward an agreeable position.

Realizing this was going to take a while, the ambassador and I agreed to part ways for another eleven hours, allowing time for us to work through issues and find places where we could agree, and identify possible solutions to areas where we did not.

Sarah and I headed back down the tunnel, and I joked with her about the tea and the funny look she had on her face after drinking just a little. We couldn't help but notice all the Veeniri looking at us as we strode through the tunnel back to the *Algonquin.*

Small talk ensued at zero WTFs per hour on the way back. "At six-foot-four Dave, you are a whole person taller than many of them. How'd they create gravity on their ship, and what was that little thing serving tea?" Sarah said as we walked.

"I have no idea, but it didn't seem particularly sentient to me, almost like it was designed to do that job of serving tea and not much else. I watched it carefully, and it seemed like some sort of organic robot. I'll ask Isolde about it the next time we link up."

Sarah and I took a little time to catch some sleep, and then jumped into the next operations update where we discussed in great detail how to achieve the objective of gaining access to the FTL travel capability while also supporting the Veeniri.

Everyone agreed that there was significant risk to only pursuing the FTL capability, as from the Veeniri perspective it made us look like disingenuous partners. We needed a convincing way of making the Veeniri understand we did want to be their partner, but it was problematic for us to try and make an agreement for all of humanity. The more I thought about it the more I was convinced that us arriving there, at this particular moment in time, right when the Veeniri needed us, was not a coincidence. Somehow, I think we'd been extracted from our solar system and brought there. I mentioned this to the crew and several people agreed, including Sarah, so I knew I was onto something, because typically she thinks I'm overly obsessed with conspiracy theories. If I thought about why we were moved, I guessed it was for bargaining with the Grojiel. But how had they been able to move us from one location to the other?

The move was quite dramatic; it almost killed Doc, and made several other crewmen extremely sick, including me. I told the crew we had to mentally background this topic for the moment and focus on getting the FTL capability. We also had to convince the Veeniri we would be partners, and figure out how to commit humanity, but in a legally reversible way.

The crew and I worked on this nonstop for several hours and came up with a pretty good proposal.

"Okay, thank you team, this is a pretty good document. Sarah can you please ask Bowendi to review it, and, if she doesn't see any deal breakers, to go ahead and transmit it over to the ambassador? We have about an hour and a half before we need to be there for the next meeting. I want to get cleaned up a little. And this time I'll take a gift to share with them as a token of our appreciation during this engagement," I smiled.

"Roger Dave, Bowendi and I will go through it again." Sarah said brightly.

Zane sidled up to me as the meeting broke up, "Say Dave, do you mind sharing with me what this gift is that you're going to bestow upon our partners over there?" Zane motioned over his shoulder with his thumb pointing at the ship towing us at nearly light speed through space. I could see that wry grin on his face that he gets when he thinks I'm going to do something awkward. Zane knew me very well, and he has seen me do multiple awkward things that had near catastrophic results, so I appreciated his engagement on the plan.

"Don't worry Zane; I'm only taking a brewed thermos of our best Hawaiian coffee over to share with them. I'll leave them with some ground coffee as a gift. You heard their bio-engineer comment that we are not biologically compatible, so there's little chance it will hurt them. Besides, eventually, when they get to Earth, they will know that we shared an important gift with them at the earliest possible sign of agreement between our two worlds."

Zane looked reflective for a moment and replied, "Good idea, although some of our green tea might be better. Recommend you don't get tipsy on that Veeniri tea as we don't want to report that we sold Earth to the Veeniri for a bottle of cyan tea and a big blue smile," Zane quipped with a wry grin as he turned to join Sarah in analyzing the documents.

When it was time to go back, Sarah and I made our way across to the conference room. This time I noticed far fewer Veeniri along the path. When Sarah and I entered the room, there were also far fewer Veeniri than before. We stood around and talked a little before getting started, and I could tell the ambassador seemed more energetic than before: hopefully this meant he was in a better mood. "Hello Mr. Ambassador, sir, I have brought you a small gift from our crew. It's a bottle of our best brewed coffee, something that we drink often and on momentous occasions. I'm hoping today can be one of those occasions as we deliberate and agree to a course that benefits both our peoples," I said.

The ambassador's aide took the bottle of coffee, looked at it, and then walked back over to the ambassador delivering it into his tiny hands. "Yes, yes, thank you Captain Dave, this is a kind and generous gift, and I, on behalf of my people, humbly accept it," the ambassador said, in a very calm, even tone, at least it was calm according to the translator device.

Then we got down to business. We discussed our proposal with granular focus on the FTL capability. The Veeniri proposed adjustments here and there. Many of the adjustments made a lot of sense, and I could tell their team had reviewed things thoroughly. In the end the Veeniri said that they would provide us with an FTL capability sufficient for a single trip back home to Earth but warned us that we needed them as much as they needed us.

We were elated to understand that they would provide us a trip home and an agreement to trade with other sentient species in the galaxy. When I asked the ambassador how he intended to provide this FTL capability, he said that they had a limited supply of the needed components, but trading some of it for our partnership was worth the investment to the Veeniri. Then he broached another topic that made us a little less comfortable.

"Captain Dave, if what you say is true, and you do not possess the ability to return home, you need protection, our protection. The protection that can only come from a formal defensive alliance with the Veeniri."

I squirmed uncomfortably in my seat at this last comment. Finally, I replied, "Yes sir, we intend to form an alliance with the Veeniri, but if I could draw on what you just said to get a little more explanation?"

"Yes, yes, allow me to explain. As you know, we are forced to report you to the Council within a specified length of time. We are going to do that tomorrow on schedule so there will be no violation of our treaty terms with the Grojiel and Higlian. As documented in these agreements you must provide the location of your home world to the others, and it is possible they will try and immediately sprint to your home world to ... coordinate, directly... or perhaps violently."

Those words struck like a lightning bolt from space. We could be jeopardizing all the lives on Earth. Sort of damned if we do, and damned if we don't. *We've got to get the wording of this agreement just right,* I thought.

Sarah and I looked at each other, and I asked the admiral and ambassador if I could take a short break to confer with my team. The ambassador agreed and we stepped into a side room to discuss this new perspective and its increased risk to Earth. "Well, I'd say this situation has officially risen to a five-WTFs-per-hour event and a damned complicated mess to boot," I said into the tablet as calmly as possible. I could see Zane's and the others' faces on the screen from the remote end nodding up and down. "Anyone have any ideas?" Seconds ticked by.

"Dave, I think it's critical that we get it written into the Council treaty that no other species may visit Earth except through the Veeniri; this is consistent with how the Grojiel control access to the Higlian domain," Sarah said, in a hoarse, whispery voice.

"Yes, and how do the Veeniri now suddenly have access to a functioning FTL apparatus? Clearly the Veeniri are keeping the truth about this FTL and apparently related gravity technology closely guarded," Zane piped in, and again everyone's heads could be seen bobbing up and down in agreement. From there we discussed it for about an hour and agreed that Sarah's plan was about right with a few minor adjustments. Then we made the changes to the agreement documents and went back in to talk to the ambassador and the rest of the crew.

I presented our changes and asked, "Mr. Ambassador, sir, do you approve of the changes we've made to the agreements?"

"Yes, yes, your requested changes are acceptable. So, you realize the situation you are in," the Ambassador responded very quickly.

"Sir, can you help us understand what has changed and how you will now help us get home using the FTL capability?" I asked as gingerly as I could muster.

It was the ambassador's turn to turn and look at his staff, and finally at Isolde. She leaned over to him and said something that did not get translated to us. He turned his head back to me and shifted slightly in his seat. "Captain Dave, in the previous meeting when you described to us what happened to you and your crew. Well, that didn't make sense, so we analyzed data from many sensor buoys and noticed a massive graviscopic event occurring near the location where we found you. Those signatures and events coupled with other details such as the bluish-brown field effect confirmed many of our suppositions."

I nodded and said, "Yes sir, what does that mean? What are your suppositions?" I tried to remain calm, but I couldn't help but think that he was about to spring something critical on us. My gut began to twist with apprehension.

The ambassador continued, "It means that you were somehow brought here using known FTL capabilities. We do not understand exactly how. But our engineers assess your ship was probably towed through some sort of graviscopic tunnel. Your ship does not have any graviscopic shielding, which is why your crew members got very sick. This convinced us you were probably brought here, against your will—and, possibly, to help us."

My stomach twisted as I started putting pieces of the puzzle together. "Well then, who brought us here? Do you know who could have done this to us? Is this the effect of some powerful Veeniri weapon?" I caught myself saying these words with more angst than I'd liked.

The Ambassador was quick to respond. "No, no, the Veeniri did not do this. We do not have a ship capable of generating the necessary effect to open a tunnel and hold it open for ships to travel through other layers of spacetime. To travel through the Graviscape a ship must have the graviscopic ring modulator to protect the passengers and basically hold the tunnel open which requires enormous energy and specialized crystals."

My eyes bulged as Sarah gently touched my forearm. "Well, if it was not the Veeniri then who did this to us? Who created this Graviscape? Perhaps the Grojiel did this," I replied, focusing hard on calming myself down.

"We do not know for sure who did this to you, but we are working on it. It will take some time to confirm, but we are pretty sure it was *not* the Grojiel or the Higlian as their FTL ships emit a distinctive signature during FTL travel, and navigation signals are broadcasted during flight that cannot be spoofed and are easily tracked. The signatures we detected near your location when you arrived were much different, and our scientists described them as a 'natural phenomenon.' Regardless, it's important that we strengthen our partnership and use this opportunity to balance the power in our shared sector of the galaxy. We must not allow the Grojiel or Higlian to find out that your species does not have the capability for FTL," the ambassador said.

I thought about his comments, then looked over at Sarah who seemed strangely calm as she peered back at me. I turned my head back toward the ambassador and said, with a slight smile, "Yes sir, agreed. One last question, how is it that you are now able to conduct FTL travel when you said before that you were lacking a crucial component?"

"Yes, yes, forgive me but we are still working to trust you fully, so until we can it's unlikely we'll share all our secrets with you. As I said before, our ships are capable, but we only possess minimal amounts of the graviscopic crystals that are used in our ships' Gravitron to generate the field effect. This is what enables FTL communications and limited transportation. Since our meeting yesterday, Isolde and her team managed to find just enough extra crystals to get you back to Earth aboard one of our smallest but most capable ships. We will then formalize and refine the details of our partnership with your world's leaders. We will do this in secret, while remaining true to our Council agreements. After all, you did travel here using FTL means, whether you understood it or not—so it is not a complete fabrication." I nodded back in agreement as the ambassador continued. "There's one last matter for agreement. I'm asking you to agree to act as the Human Keretzon to help strategically stabilize our relationship and promote diplomacy between the Veeniri and Human worlds."

I looked around at my team and back to the ambassador saying, "Sir, what is a 'Keretzon?' That word didn't translate very well." The Ambassador looked over at Isolde then back to me. He took a short sip of his drink and said, "It is like a formal liaison position. You are bound to assist Isolde in interacting with your people as Isolde works to help you interact effectively with the Veeniri people."

I looked at the ambassador and then back to Isolde. I rubbed my chin with my right hand as I needed to think through this a couple of times. I whispered a message to Sarah and hammered out a few text messages to Zane and Chuck. We conferred privately, but everyone agreed this was a pretty good deal if we could pull it off. Everyone wanted to get home, and if the Veeniri could help us, I supposed I could be this Acting Keretzon person. "Yes sir, Mr. Ambassador, you've got yourselves a deal, count us in. We are very grateful for your kindness and happy that you understand our situation better now," I said with a positive lilt in my voice. I could see Isolde turn the brightest hue of cyan I'd seen yet. This effort must be very important to her career. Hell, I'd expect it was important as it's not every day that you broker a treaty with another civilization that lives on a planet light-years away.

"Yes, yes, very good, now let us rehearse the council proceedings and terminate this session as we have many things to do before we meet the Council tomorrow. Remember, there's a physical council meeting followed by the very important, virtual council meeting. Technicians, bring the G-HUD equipment and ensure our new partners' brains are appropriately mapped."

Hmmm, I thought, *mapped for what?* The ambassador stood up and just walked out of the damn room while several technicians came into the room pushing lots of technical-looking equipment on carts. They stopped just in front of us.

"We will first re-scan your body and brain and then fit you with the G-HUD," the lead technician said through its sophisticated-looking translator.

One at a time the technicians took us to a side room where we took metallic portions of our clothes off and were scanned in some kind of noisy system. We later found out that the Veeniri already had good scans of us from previous visits, but wanted new scans that lined up with required Council reporting timelines. The other techs attached massively large helmets to our heads, which made all sorts of noise, and then, finally, we were finished with all their fitting work. I still did not truly understand all that occurred there, but a few minutes later, a tech walked into the room with a set of large goggles for each of us.

The techs walked us through how they worked, and I was amazed as I looked at Sarah. "The spectacle devices are called G-HUDs," the lead technician stated calmly. "They have been designed to connect to your brains, allowing you to inductively perceive communications transactions occurring through the Graviscape. You need to learn how to communicate with them now as conversations during Council proceedings are very critical; there must be no miscommunications."

The technicians asked us to stay seated as the first session would likely cause mild disorientation as the system adapted to our unique cognitive processing configuration. Apparently the system had been used for thousands of years by thousands of species, and would adapt quickly. According to the technicians, the vast majority of neural networks found in the brains of intelligent species generally worked the same way with a few measurable differences, such as physical distribution across a body. Some brains had more sensory inputs than others, but apparently human brains were about average in terms of sensor inputs and neuron count. I put the G-HUD on my head and face, the way a person would slide on a hat with built in sunglasses. I sat quietly for several minutes as the technicians asked me questions, apparently for tuning purposes. Kind of all at once, my eyeballs felt hot and irritated.

They started to feel a little sticky too as though I had been around a cat. As a person who is super allergic to cats, I have experienced this feeling often, but not recently. I also felt a little tickling in my ear, which quickly evolved to heavy pressure, not painful per se but uncomfortable. Just as I was starting to calm down, I felt as if someone had just smacked me in the face with a baseball bat—POW! All I could see were stars, and millions of brilliant colors, dots, and waves. I was really starting to panic when I started hearing crazy sounds. The technicians tried to calm me as the high-pitched sounds and low-pitched tones boomed into my perception, like being at a rock concert as the artists belted out the music.

All the visual and audio levels fluctuated as I could sense the G-HUD system somehow trying to adjust itself to me. This went on for several minutes, and I even detected smells, foul smells and good smells, hell, *all sorts of smells.* It was hard to handle at first, but I managed to hold on by trying to relax as the technician recommended. Finally, all the activity subsided as my sweat-drenched face and torso started to unwind a little.

I immediately turned my head toward Sarah, but I could not see her as the lenses in the headset had transitioned into a solid black color over my eyes. I turned my head back toward the front, where I expected the ambassador's technicians to be when suddenly my vision—my brain—showed me a crystal-clear view of a vast chamber with a round table prominently featured in the middle of the room. The table had what looked like fifteen or twenty Veeniri seated around it.

I could hear the lead technician's translated voice inside of my skull softly say, "By now you should be able to perceive the test environment we've generated; this is how the Council meeting will appear tomorrow. You must learn to move around and communicate within this environment. The first step is to 'think' your body movements while 'feeling' your communications. It's important to avoid letting all of your thoughts flood into open communications as you do not want to reveal your true thoughts inadvertently. Now, let's start by trying to 'think' that you are standing up and walking toward the table."

I considered this for a moment and tried hard to "think" about moving. Nothing happened. With no result, I responded to the technician, "I'm trying to think stand up, walk toward the table but nothing is happening."

The technician responded, "You must try to think harder then."

A few moments later I saw Sarah walk in the environment toward the table.

I could hear her faint footsteps; I could smell Sarah's perfumed scent as she moved toward the table. She suddenly bumped into the table and then found a chair with her hand and sat down at the table. *Wow, Sarah is picking this up really well.* I was starting to get a little antsy, so I thought *really* hard about walking toward the table. This resulted in me apparently sprinting toward the table followed by me crashing into, and then flipping over, the table, putting my body into the center of the circular table area. *Oww! That freaking hurt! They are not kidding, actions in here have a cognitively generated physical effect.* I started feeling very woozy and ended up vomiting all over myself in physical space on the Veeniri ship.

"You must not think emotionally; it's critical that you control how you think about moving your body. Emotion leads to irrationality which can result in real damage to you over time. The events you experience in this virtual environment are very real. They can cause similar physical manifestations of pain, stress, and nausea."

The technician continued, "This process is different for everyone and every type of being. You humans are exceedingly difficult to configure for, despite the advanced AI running in the G-HUD. You have so many different entities living within a single body, and you have neurons within your food digestion tract that are confusing the G-HUD with overlapping yet different neural activity than what is occurring in your skull. We have also experienced challenges compensating for all of the bacterial creatures living in or on your bodies. Your biome is exceedingly complex and even the smallest of beings in your body affect your cognition in unpredictable ways."

Okay, I thought, *this is like virtual or extended reality on steroids. Need to focus here.* Virtual Reality (VR) plus real time connectivity across the universe to any other being—this was definitely going to take some getting used to. What an advantage though, an advantage for any civilization to have the ability to collaborate infinitively with other species. I didn't know what it would be like, but I couldn't wait to virtually see other aliens.

We spent hour after nauseating hour rehearsing how to maneuver in the environment. We also rehearsed how to act and behave during the Council proceedings in the Virtual Environment (VE), and while I think I understood the process and how to move using the G-HUD, it still made me feel a little queasy inside.

Finally, we removed our G-HUDs and the prolonged rehearsal session mercifully ended. Sarah and I looked at each other in our sweat-soaked uniforms with our emotionally drained, reddened eyes. "My ears are ringing," I said to the technician.

The technician replied, "Please understand, your minds and bodies will adapt to this mode of communication. It will take time, but it is important to do so successfully because this is the Galactic standard means of communication and has been used for thousands if not millions of years."

After a few short conversations with the technicians and the remaining staff, Sarah and I departed back down the tunnel to the *Algonquin,* which seemed to take forever as we were both emotionally exhausted. When we reached the ship, I started float-walking my way toward the bridge, and collapsed in the first *Algonquin* passageway.

A firm arm grabbed me and steadied me. "Sir, recommend you and Sarah get some sleep; there's a few hours before our arrival at the Council, and you need to be rested," Zane said calmly with a tired smile.

I looked at him sullenly and nodded in agreement saying, "Roger Zane, let's huddle first and make sure we understand the process, roles and responsibilities for tomorrow then I'll catch some sleep."

Something about wearing the G-HUD visor made me want to drink coffee, so I stopped and grabbed a cup from the autodrink machine and sat down to work through the key issues during the short staff huddle. We discussed all the new events and how we were going to play the Council meeting. I wanted to be sure that we did not accidentally create problems during the event because we lacked a common view of what we were trying to do. I asked Dr. Roth to research the G-HUD technology and reach out to Bowendi as needed, as I was concerned about the safety of using it. I doubted it was a Veeniri weapon, but it didn't hurt to understand the capability better. After all, Dr. Roth was a nanotech implant expert, and he was bound to figure out how it worked and if it was truly safe for humans. It was certainly a stunning capability, sort of like virtual reality but connected to the brain while also real-time networked to apparently any being in the Graviscape-connected universe.

Holy crap. This is stunning. All this time there's been an intergalactic communications medium right under humanity's nose, buried in gravity. All we had to do was open the right door.

Anyhow, Zane was working with the Veeniri executive officer to have all our personnel fitted for G-HUDs so they could participate in Council meetings or other engagements. It would take some time, but they would all benefit from having the ability to communicate in that way; I was certain of that.

Finally, I made it back to my quarters and collapsed in my bed. Out like a freaking light, snoring in seconds. *What a day.* When I could take a moment to reflect on what had occurred, I was flabbergasted. Such a fantastic journey. *Aliens, new worlds, and thanks to technology we seemed to communicate pretty well. Whew!*

Chapter 14: Earthlings at the Council of Civilization

I woke up from a nap feeling pretty solid, and showered up. A good hot shower always seemed to perk a fella up in terms of mood boosting. I started in on my second pouch of coffee and wrapped up a conversation with Isolde over the RexCom.

She was trying to reassure me that the procedure was going to be fine, and that I needed to stand firm as the Grojiel are an aggressive species that do not act in "just ways," which I'd gathered based on our previous conversations. Just as I'd started on the latest ship status report the comms panel crackled with, "Sir, you need to get up here; its nearly Council time and we've got a few issues to sort out." It was Zane calling from the command deck.

"Roger that Zane, I'll be there in a few minutes." It was time to proclaim our partnership with the Veeniri at the Council and figure out a way to get home.

I felt pretty good about the situation. I knew the Council proceedings were going to be complicated, and although I didn't fully understand the processes, I thought we'd work our way through it. *Yep, I'm feeling pretty good about things*, I thought as I gathered my G-HUD, RexCom, 1911 model pistol, and a few other items before heading for the bridge.

"Okay people, it's showtime." I smiled with the budding confidence of the old Captain Dave as I made my way onto the bridge.

"Sir, we've just disconnected from the Veeniri tow ship and are now on path to Bradea, we should be docking at the Bradea station facility in... forty-nine minutes," Zane said as he continued enumerating item statuses from the checklist we'd worked out the night before.

Docking at the Bradea station was turning out to be an amazing experience. Huang piloted the *Algonquin* flawlessly into the assigned docking zone and docked the *Algonquin* to the designated contact point next to the massive Veeniri ship. It was an amazing experience because Bradea station was massive, lit up and brilliantly detailed with hundreds of different types of ships all docked at various points spanning the station. The station was so massive, it nearly surrounded the moon. I could see layers where they'd built the station up over time.

Zane and Sarah coordinated with the ambassador's staff while I had another private comms session with Isolde to confirm her thoughts on our plan to steer clear of the Grojiel while on the ground at the Council. Finally, Zane, Sarah, Huang, and I headed for *Ranger-1*, got strapped in the little shuttle, and gently backed away from the Algonquin as Ranger-1 sits in a docking slip that covers the entire front of the little ship, like a half garage.

As Huang slowly turned the nose of *Ranger-1* toward the moon's surface, we slowly moved forward eventually clearing Bradea station. "Holy Cow," I quietly said, followed by a low whistle from Zane. We were stunned at the number of ships transiting between the moon's surface and the station: there must have been hundreds of them.

Different sizes and shapes all moving in what looked to be a carefully choreographed traffic scheme. "Hold here Huang," Zane said with a finger on his FemtoCom's earpiece, "We are waiting for the Ambassador's shuttle; they want us to follow them down to the space port."

"Roger, sir," Huang replied as he took the opportunity to get a better view of the mass transit of ships between the spaceport on Bradea's surface and the station.

I detached the camera element from my wrist-borne FemtoCom and snapped several short videos; I wanted to be sure and record as much of this as possible. Just then the Ambassador's shuttle swooped over top of us catching us all by surprise.

"Crap, even their shuttles are huge," Huang said, trying to shake off the surprise of suddenly being overflown by a much larger ship. Huang looked back at me and said "I think that counts as one."

I broke in, shaking my head from left to right before Huang could complete his thought "Nope, no way, that doesn't count" and I looked over at Zane. He quickly responded with "I don't think so Huang, it doesn't fit."

Huang looked over at Zane and then back to me "Sir, I was definitely thinking WTF when that shuttle flew over."

"I don't think so Huang," I said as we all looked over at Sarah to mediate if this event should count as a WTF.

Sarah glared back at us and said "okay gentlemen, lets don't fall into a juvenile argument about something like this."

I smiled at Huang, and he shook his head and started engaging the controls to follow the ambassador's ship. We entered the main traffic pattern and saw dozens of ships passing nearby, going in both directions. We were again surprised as halfway down to the surface we were once more overflown and surrounded by a dozen smaller, single person ships blinking bright cyan-blue colored lights. "Holy crap" Huang murmured as my RexCom beeped; it was Isolde, "These ships are our escorts, Dave; they and their crews are here to protect you throughout the process. Please do not incite violence with them."

Whew, I thought, *we need to relax a little*. I looked around as Zane, Sarah and Huang where shaking out the tension in their bodies, obviously caught off guard by the event. "Thank you Isolde, so these are like police then, sort of protection for everyone."

"Yes, that is right; very much like the authority figures you described on your planet. It seems another thing our societies have in common is police," Isolde replied with a familiar-looking expression on her face that I estimated was a smile.

Sarah looked over at Huang, Zane and I and with a twinkle in her eye said "Okay, that plus the previous event definitely counts as one." Huang looked back at Zane and I and we all started snickering at ourselves. "Roger that Sarah, that's one" I said as my snicker evolved into a full fledged chuckle.

Finally, *Ranger-1* landed at the spaceport about one hundred meters away from the ambassador's shuttle, and both were completely surrounded by the smaller, blue-colored police vehicles. We exited the shuttle and walked toward Isolde and the ambassador as they strode toward us.

"Okay Huang, lock up the ship and hold onto the keys," I said smiling at Huang, Zane, and Sarah, as we all knew there was no real way to lock the ship.

"Yes, yes, Captain Dave, we are on the right path together you and me. Let us go below and make our way to the Council," the ambassador said as he bounced along. Heck we all seemed to bounce along a little as we walked as the gravity on Bradea was a bit less than that we were used to back on Earth.

We walked into a small elevator surrounded by the Veeniri police. The elevator moved us very quickly below the surface into what appeared to be a rather large waiting area. I saw the ambassador talking to someone on his RexCom and about a minute later, a wall opened into a much larger room.

Before I could ask any questions, a large vehicle rolled up in front of the doorway and opened its sliding doors. We followed the ambassador, Isolde, and staff onto the vehicle, and the police boarded as well just before the door closed.

Before the vehicle started moving, padded rails and protrusions that seemed to be chairs appeared from the vehicle's floor, and I noticed the ambassador, Isolde, and their staff partially sit or lean on them, so my crew and I braced ourselves too, as the vehicle began moving.

"Yes, yes, Captain Dave we are nearly to the Council; there will be many people looking at you when we depart the vehicle. Please prepare yourselves for this."

"Thank you, Mr. Ambassador, sir; we'll be okay," I said as calmly as possible while nodding affirmatively.

The vehicle stopped and the door slid open, and to our surprise the police hopped out immediately and created some space in the throngs of aliens waiting outside the vehicle. "Holy crap!" I caught myself saying under my breath.

The ambassador and his staff were the first to step out of the vehicle. Sarah seemed paralyzed as we all looked out of the vehicle's door. I gently grabbed her by the arm, and we stepped carefully out of the vehicle together. We started walking along the police-enforced path as we looked at crowds of aliens standing nearby making squeaks, sounds, and gestures toward us. There were thousands of aliens here. Grojiel, Higlian, Veeniri, and even a few others that I did not recognize. "Sarah, you doing okay?" I asked as Sarah stopped walking. It looked like her neck and face was a little flushed as if though she was getting stressed.

"Dave, there are so many beings here, it's a little unnerving."

"I get it; its freaking me out too. Hey, look at me. We are okay, I promise."

Sarah looked up at me as I smiled wide at her. "I'm okay Dave," Sarah said. I offered her a fist to bump. Sarah looked at it for a second, and then back up to me and we bumped fists. The slightest smile came over Sarah's face.

"C'mon guys, let's get going, we don't want to get too far behind the ambassador," Zane said as he touched us on our backs, gently pressing us forward.

Now I don't mind telling you, at my height, I was at least a whole Veeniri taller than most Veeniri people, but the Grojiel were noticeably bigger, and several were nearly my height. Except for the color differences the Grojiel looked very similar to the Veeniri. One could see a resemblance indicating a common ancestor as Isolde had told me during our first biology lesson. They were different, but one could see by the look in their eyes that they were quite sentient. The Higlian, on the other hand, well we only saw a couple of them, and they were strange-looking little beings. Like a hairless, six-eyed, four-armed, five-foot-tall chimpanzee with fins all over its skull. The Higlian's abdomen had clear, jellyfish-looking innards: very weird. *These guys are definitely not related, or at least I don't see any resemblance,* I thought. We finally made our way to the ambassador's chambers, where we had a little time to try and calm down a bit and collect our thoughts.

"Yes, yes, Captain Dave, this must be a very interesting experience for you; I hope you are enjoying the attention," the ambassador stated flatly through the translator.

"Well sir, the word 'interesting' is a bit of an understatement. But we are handling the situation well so far. I do not really like too much attention, but I suppose it's important to be seen," I replied. I wanted to say that I was freaking out inside, but I was trying to promote a calm, positive demeanor for everyone's sake, including mine.

Huang was looking a little green around the gills, so I decided to try and provide a little comfort. "Huang, you feeling okay? I know this is a lot but just hold on, we'll get through it together. Recommend you make a lot of log entries to record how you feel today. That goes for everyone," I glanced at Sarah and Zane.

"Yes, yes, Captain Dave, it is time, we must enter the Chamber and complete the proceedings. Remember, be careful answering too many questions directly from the other species as they will try to force a relationship. It's best to be somewhat ambiguous in early questioning so you do not lock your species into agreements you cannot survive. Also, be very careful in moving about within the virtual chamber. Your behaviors, movements, and responses provide the Federal Council with the means by which they judge and vote."

"Yes sir, Mr. Ambassador, I got it; we should be fine," I replied as confidently as possible. The side door opened to the larger Council chamber where a few hundred Grojiel, Veeniri, and Higlian were seated. We followed the ambassador to the central portion of the room and the large round table opened a small path for us to be seated in the center.

I sat next to the ambassador; Isolde sat on the other side of me with Sarah, Zane and Huang following suit. I looked around in awe as there were a dozen rings of seated beings in the chamber spanning the floor to the ceiling. *Boom, Boom, Boom.* A loud, low-pitched booming sound, and other noises that I think were some sort of music, came from the floor and walls like some sort of speaker system. We also noticed several large display screens come to life all around the Council chamber with lots of funny-looking characters scrolling across them. I noticed two of the larger sets of characters looked like clocks counting down in something resembling seconds. Finally, all the noise, or um, music stopped blaring and the area surrounding us began to glow with that familiar cyan hue. Lighting in the Council chamber decreased somewhat as the Veeniri ambassador stood and began slowly walking while speaking.

He walked through the narrow space between where we were seated and the rest of the circular table. It was strange as my translator was giving me the translated version into my earpiece while I also faintly heard other versions from what I presumed were speakers placed around the chamber.

"Fellow citizens of Bradea Province, we bring a new species and partner to the Council. This species calls themselves Humans, from a system millions of miles away from Council Prime, our great state of Bradea."

At the conclusion of these words, loud squeaks, purrs, and other noises broke out that I supposed passed for cheers in the Council. The formal Veeniri, Grojiel, and Higlian council members and staff were seated at the table just in front of us while the staff seated behind us appeared to be running the proceedings. The formal Council members peered at us with great intensity making only modest squeaks and noises. I smiled at Zane as I could tell he was wondering how long this irritating noise would continue. The ambassador continued talking about their responsibility and bringing us to the Council on time and how they met their obligation, adhering to Council policy. Finally came my part.

I stood and read the lines we'd prepared, approved by the ambassador and his staff. "Kind beings of the Federal Republic of Bradea. We are grateful to be hosted by this special and wonderful Council today. As a representative of my species, I have decided to join in a formal alliance with the Veeniri for exclusive trade and security assurances." As I finished those words the floor became bright blue and the noise... um cheers, I suppose, started again.

All the Veeniri in the room seemed to go crazy, waving their hands standing and patting each other on the back. The cheers continued as music started playing again, only this time, I knew the music: it was the Veeniri hymn of solace that Isolde played for me several times. *Not my taste in music but not terrible either,* I thought.

The ambassador took over from there and continued discussing the high-level terms of our arrangement as required by the Council rules, and just like that, the Federal Republic of Bradea voted to add the government of Earth as a full member of the Republic.

From there the questions began. First, from the Grojiel. They demanded immediate access to our home planet's exact location, population, number of planets settled, and number of patron species we possessed.

I answered all their questions the way we rehearsed on the ambassador's ship: giving some specifics but promising more details as the Veeniri and Earth governments finalized details of our formal relationship. We answered just enough to keep ourselves safe until we sorted out how this relationship would unfold. Oddly, the Higlian ambassador only asked a single question, "How long did it take you humans to travel to this system?"

I glanced back at the ambassador, and he abruptly stood and said, "Kind Ambassador Revus of Tok, it took them mere days to travel here using their powerful ship. We are still having some challenges coordinating the precise measurement of time with our new friends, but will provide the Council a full report soon."

"Yes, I imagine you will, probably just after the Exclusive Trade and Security agreement is completed," the Grojiel Ambassador said in what seemed like a tone of derision.

Perhaps I should offer the grouchy ambassador a spoonful of peanut butter?

I was getting nervous and when I get nervous, I start thinking about peanut butter which, in turn, makes me hungry.

Okay, okay, stay focused, I thought. *We can jump into a pool of peanut butter later, let's just get through this darn session without screwing the Veeniri ... or you know, the future of humanity.* I kept quiet as I struggled to control my inner monologue while the ambassadors traded verbal barbs and postured themselves into a political frenzy. Finally, all the bureaucratic boxes had apparently been checked and the Council session ended.

I noticed the first clock-like counter displayed on the Council screens had stopped incrementing. Interestingly the clock just below it continued to run. All of the beings in the Council chamber stood and started milling around as they waited for the big show, the intergalactic session. They did not move far from their stools, seats, and such, but they did move to contact with one another, and made what looked like small talk between different species. I also noticed several of the Veeniri drink robots passing by delivering what I guessed was Veeniri tea to beings that requested it. *I think the Algonquin could use a peanut butter robot,* I internally mused.

Whew, I felt like a large burden had been lifted from my shoulders. I stood and stepped toward Zane, Sarah, and Huang. "OK, first step is done; now we go virtual. Are you guys doing okay?" I asked.

"Great job sir, that looks like it went over pretty well if the translations were accurate," Huang said,

"I agree with Huang, this is a huge moment for all of humanity, Dave. I think we're doing pretty good despite all of our challenges," Sarah chimed in.

"I agree we are on the right path: so far so good. Dave, remember during the next session to calmly think and do not move around too much. It's important that we don't appear irrational. Just a reminder," Zane said with a wide, thin smile.

"Roger that, so far the situation has been smooth. I suppose I'd measure it at zero WTFs per hour but there was a moment or two there..." I replied, smiling back at all three of them. A few minutes later the familiar sounding "music" began again. *Boom, boom, boom.* The squeaks were crazy loud this time, but everybody made their way back to the seats throughout the Council floor and around the table.

The Ambassador stood up and walked over to all of us, "Yes, yes, now is the time for the big Council meeting; this one is critically important." For the first time the ambassador seemed to look at all of us while he talked, and we watched him put the G-HUD on his head and activate it as he moved back to his seat. We all followed suit, putting on and activating our G-HUDs.

And there it was, a beautiful image in my mind's eye of the Council room with all the beings we had previously seen. The music started slowing down and finally ended. An older Veeniri stood at the front of the Council table and said, "Fellow citizens of Bradea province, I ask you now to be seated and join the Federal Republic as we humbly request ratification of our new species' admission." *Boom, Boom, Boom,* a little bit more music played as I accessed the appropriate G-link channel directed by the ambassador's staff, and prepared myself for what awaited.

I grabbed my chair to steady myself as the full Federal Council came into view. It was breathtaking. Millions of small Council tables popped into view surrounding a massive Council table and the center of this virtual scene. Near the center of the massive Council table was our smaller virtual Council tabletop.

I could see, hear, smell, and, somehow, feel the voices, squeaks, and sounds of millions of other beings. Some were skinny, some were tall, some were huge, and some looked like they were underwater. I had no idea there were this many living beings in the universe, let alone living beings with technology advanced enough to figure out how to access the Graviscape and thus communicate *and* perhaps travel faster than the speed of light allows. An odd-looking, rather huge creature, stood and began walking toward our Council table. My G-HUD display automatically showed a tag just above the being's head depicting an identification: "Key Minister Olath – Intergalactic Federal Council Chief." The Council Chief walked right up to our table and asked, "Bradea province, what business do you have with the Federal Council in your timeslot today?"

Wow, that was a boomingly powerful voice even through the translator, I thought. One of the Bradea Council Chiefs was an older-looking Veeniri seated at our table.

He stood and replied, "Kind minister, Bradea province requests admittance of a new species. This species has requested a trade and security alliance with the Veeniri and admission to Bradea Province. The lead human has pledged the oath of Keretzon."

The Council Chief looked directly at me. *Well crap. Was this the liaison role I agreed to? Pledge, what Pledge?* After staring at me for several uncomfortable seconds it peered at Sarah, Zane, and Huang. Minister Olath 'walked' around in an odd way, even for the virtual world, sort of slow hop-stepping like a three-legged horse while peering at us from many angles.

Then its booming translated voice spoke again, "Which of the Veeniri is the Keretzon?"

Isolde stood and said, "I am the Veeniri Keretzon, I have pledged."

The truly strange creature called Minister Olaf continued slowly hop-stepping along, looking at all of the Bradea representatives assembled and said, "Bradea province, Higlian Ambassador, representative of Tok, do you agree to the proceedings?"

The Higlian Council Chief stood, and we heard its translated voice reply, "Affirmed. we agree to the proceedings."

The Federal Council Chief Olaf then strode over toward the Grojiel Council member and said, "Bradea province Grojiel Council Chief, representative of Cission, do you agree to the proceedings?"

The Grojiel Council member stood and said, "Affirmed. We agree to the proceedings with comment."

The Federal Council Chief then suddenly stopped and looked at the Grojiel Council member and asked, "What is your comment, Grojiel Council Chief of Bradea province?"

The Grojiel Council Chief replied with, "We want to verify that this new species does not already lie within the jurisdiction of Grojiel."

The Veeniri ambassador quickly jumped up and stated, "Yes, yes, Council Chief, we are aware of the stipulation—there is no evidence to indicate overlapping jurisdiction."

The Council Chief walked over to the Veeniri ambassador, stopped, and then peered back toward the Grojiel representative to the Bradea Council. "All Intergalactic Federal Republic procedures must be followed properly. We will revisit this admission to the Bradea province in one galactic block. This is how long you have to resolve the stipulation."

How the hell long is a galactic block? I wondered as the translation did not convert to anything I could understand. I looked at the ambassador, he did not look back, but I received a private G-HUD message from Isolde saying, "Dave, remain calm, there is a sufficient period of time to resolve the issue favorably."

The Council Chief continued, "In the meantime, I move the Federal Council provisionally approves adding the new species of 'Human' to the province of Bradea. Let the deliberation period begin." There were many questions, squeaks, noises, and translated dialogue fragments heard.

I 'moved' in the virtual environment to answer questions by 'walking' in the virtual space to each of the Council tables that had requested a visit. This deliberation period went mostly as planned with questions and visitation. Lots of visitation with numerous intelligent species, it was exhilarating. All this went on for quite some time. There were millions of Council tables, and I didn't think we would ever get to the next part. It was definitely an overwhelming and stressful experience. The vast array of species characteristics, brilliant colors and sounds, were mesmerizing. Even a few light smells shifted past me as we moved about the virtual space. It was very cool interacting with so many different types of beings.

I have a lot to write about tonight in my mission logs.

Thankfully, the Veeniri ambassador and Isolde accompanied me to each table. I could see a digital display in the distance with a checkerboard lattice that began filling in with blue and white squares, apparently indicating which provinces voted yes or no. Like a sort of virtual scoreboard that stayed in focus no matter which direction I looked.

Suddenly pounding drum-like sounds rang out: *Bong, Bong, Bong.* The freakishly large Council Chief appeared from nowhere right in front of me and said, "The deliberation period has ended, please return to your Council chamber to view official voting results."

The Ambassador, Isolde, and I moved back to take our seats. It looked to me like the voting went pretty well, as there were not very many "no" votes. Suddenly, the Federal Council Chief turned toward the Veeniri Council seated at the front of our table and said in that incredibly deep translated voice, "The matter is approved. Congratulations to Bradea Province. Adding an additional species to your federal province is momentous progress for both the region and the Republic. On behalf of the Intergalactic Federal Republic, we look forward to adding Human experiences, knowledge, and contributions to our own for the greater good of all." And just like that we were, apparently, on the team.

The Council meeting broke up, and we were moved back to the ambassador's chambers where we visited privately with the Veeniri's closest allies through our G-HUDs.

They were an astonishingly varied group of species from various parts of the Milky Way Galaxy, and some were from other galaxies as well. It was truly amazing to think that we now possessed this communications capability. When the session was over, we all removed our G-HUDs and took a break together.

I could not help but notice that the Ambassador's cyan color looked brighter, stronger and he appeared to walk a bit taller. "Isolde, the Ambassador seems very happy compared to yesterday."

Isolde turned her head and looked at the ambassador, replying, "Yes Dave, he's the first Veeniri to ever bring a new species to the Council, and no doubt will be remembered in the annals of Veeniri history."

"That's true but I think Isolde deserves a lot of credit as well," I replied, smiling broadly at her.

I noticed her cyan color brighten a bit for a moment, then she appeared to catch herself, and her color returned to its normal hue. She replied, "Perhaps you are right Dave, still one more mystery to solve, and we must broker an exclusive deal with your people before any further success can be enjoyed."

She caught me by surprise by reaching out with her three-fingered hand and placing it on top of mine, giving me a gentle but firm hand hold.

I put my other hand on top of hers and gently squeezed back. Turning suddenly, I noticed Sarah trying not to notice me holding hands with Isolde. *Okay, we'll have to talk about this later*, I thought.

Looking back towards Isolde, I started in on a new line of questions. "How does trade work between the members of the Federal Council?"

Isolde replied, "It's primarily an information economy. Much of the trade consists of data purchases between provinces and sometimes between individual species. Most transactions are data describing knowledge, technologies, or history that some provinces lack, things like that. There are many types of data exchanges and corresponding taxes. There are sometimes unauthorized exchanges of data. These are criminal offenses that each province must root out and eliminate."

"I see then, the more species in a province, the better their relationships with the rest of the Federal Council," I replied.

"Yes, and the more opportunity to rule within the Intergalactic Federal Council structure, this is where the advantage truly exists," Isolde said matter-of-factly.

Sarah asked, "Isolde, are things or materials ever exchanged between provinces using physical graviscopic travel?"

"Yes, but not as frequently as data transactions. Graviscopic modulation was discovered eons ago and subsequent networks were overlaid and optimized for transporting data. However, scientists have figured out how to transport small chunks of matter, including ship-sized pieces, through the Graviscape but it's very dangerous and it requires enormous amounts of energy and special crystals, making it too costly for everyday transport or travel. The crystals needed for material transport must be large, specially shaped, and of high integrity. These types of crystals are difficult to find, and manufacturing them is impossible because there are quantum field interactions and energy inter-dependencies that we cannot replicate using engineered crystals." Isolde looked slightly skyward, as if though she was contemplating something important and said, "Our best scientists think these crystals are somehow, *alive.*"

Holy crap! Well that certainly got everybody's attention. Sarah, Zane, Huang, and I stared, mouths open with surprise at the calm way Isolde articulated such a critical piece of information. "Wow Isolde, that's pretty amazing, a crystalline form of life? How would that work?" I said, trying to keep my view of the situation high level.

Isolde started in, "The crystals exhibit lifelike behavior when they are in certain regions of spacetime; we don't fully understand it ourselves, but we cannot look past the amazing capabilities these crystals exhibit. It's as if they are part of a distributed organism when the crystal structure is just right and located in the right parts of space—they are otherwise dormant. We have much to discuss in this area, however, now is not the time best suited for this. We need to get moving soon so we can get you home aboard the one ship we can afford to use to take you back to your planet.

"You must take representatives with you and a graviscopic access point so that your people can connect directly to higher space time and communicate with the Council. Time is short, the Grojiel have most likely planned to send a recon force to your home system. Now that they know where it is, the risk of catastrophic violence is high." Just as Isolde finished her sentence, the chamber's massive doors opened and Ambassador Revus, the unusual-looking Higlian representative to the Bradea Council, stepped through the door and walked right up to Ambassador Kjino, who appeared bluer and brighter than ever.

The Higlian were truly a strange-looking species. "Kjino, it is good to see you successful in this endeavor. Please accept my compliments on a job well done."

"Thank you Revus; such kind words from you honors my people greatly," Kjino replied. The two walked off together, talking and displaying what seemed like jovial gestures and pleasant dialogue. If I didn't know better, I'd have said that they were professional peers but also maybe friends. It was difficult to reconcile how weird-looking the Higlian were. Isolde and her aid sped off to take part in the dialogue between the two ambassadors, so I took the opportunity to make notes about the crystals Isolde mentioned, so I could discuss with the crew later that night.

I was stowing my gear in a travel bag while making small talk with Sarah when the chamber's massive doors opened again, and this time a large procession of Grojiel entered, escorted by what looked like Veeniri security. Ambassador Revus and Ambassador Kjino appeared from behind us walking with speed to greet the Grojiel delegation with Isolde in tow.

When the two groups got about ten feet away from one another the guards swarmed around in a very antsy way. I swear, I thought they were going to draw weapons and duel or something. Stepping forward a few more feet, Ambassador Revus spoke first, "Ambassador Geone, Admiral Parakto, it's a surprise to see you but welcome nonetheless. How may we be of assistance?"

The Grojiel Ambassador, Ambassador Geone, and Space Fleet's Commanding Officer, Admiral Parakto, were imposing figures, nearly as tall as me, and I'm six-foot-four. They had wiry bodies that appeared to have many patches of scar like skin.

Each one had to weigh at least 180 lbs. They stood imposingly over a much smaller Ambassador Revus, but Revus didn't flinch; he seemed undaunted.

Geone turned his head toward Ambassador Kjino and said, "We've come to... congratulate you Kjino... on bringing a new species to the Council, and we wanted to see this species for ourselves up close. Although, officially, I must also warn you that my government asserts these beings are within the Grojiel Federal District and any technology or data they export is partial property of the Grojiel and must be openly shared and taxed."

"Now, now Ambassador," Kjino interrupted as he stepped closer to Geone, "we've plenty of time to sort out the details of our new friends' precise background," Kjino said looking over at me.

Now I've seen this behavior before, this guy was a freaking bully. A big, intimidating bully, especially compared to the other two species. I don't like bullies, so I decided to walk over and introduce myself. I took three large strides and was standing a couple of feet away from Ambassador Geone and the Fleet Admiral. They and I took a moment to look at each other from head to toe. *These aliens definitely look tough,* I thought. They were sinewy creatures with knife-like weapons adorning what could pass for forearms and calves. After thinking about it a bit, I realized that they really were pretty imposing creatures. I couldn't imagine how they appeared to the other two, smaller, Veeniri and Higlian beings. I spoke through my translator, "Ambassador Geone, very nice to make your acquaintance; my name is Captain Dave—" before I could finish my sentence, Ambassador Geone broke in and stepped toward me, closing the distance between us to about twelve very uncomfortable inches.

"Captain Dave, such a pleasure to make your acquaintance." His tone shifted to a threatening pitch. "Hear me now on this topic of your treaty with the Veeniri. You must inform the government of your planet that we are the rightful brokers of any technologies or information you possess.

"We have legal, federally approved claims to sixty-four quadrants of space known as the Grojiel extended Kingdom. According to federal law you are our subjects and will submit to our rule."

Well hell, I really am starting to dislike this jackass.

"Ambassador Geone, it's extremely unlikely that my people will subjugate themselves to your rule just because you claim to have staked out sixty-four quadrants of space as your backyard," I said as Ambassador Revus stepped forward and broke in, seeming to sense the escalating tension.

"Captain Dave, the federal law must be respected. It is unlikely the Grojiel claims will be substantiated, but we must not interpret federal law to mean whatever we want it to mean. You have rightfully obligated your species to follow federal law, and we will sort this out."

Craaaap! This is starting to turn into at least a five WTFs per hour event. Did I really commit all of humanity to an agreement that could subject every human being to enslavement by these Grojiel creatures? Humanity takes a pretty dim view of slavery; anything like that won't go over well.

Ambassador Geone looked toward Ambassador Revus and Ambassador Kjino and said, "Revus, I understand that you will be accompanying the humans back to their planet. I too will travel with the humans to make sure that all of our agreements are adhered to. We are also sending an immediate reconnaissance force to assess your home system, which is within our right. This will be followed by a visit by our royal fleet who will be prepared to... negotiate with your home world's leadership."

The way the translation of the word "agreements" came out was very strange, almost as if Ambassador Geone was threatening Ambassador Revus. "I am traveling to the human planet personally, Ambassador Geone; I wish to ensure a fair and honest adherence to federal law."

Ambassador Geone quipped, "Yes, I suppose you are interested in ensuring federal law is followed to the letter. Remember where you come from Revus, and don't forget your people's agreements with the Grojiel. I wouldn't want anything bad to happen to the few colonies your people have left in the galaxy."

What? What the heck did that mean? There must be a lot more to these relationships than I've picked up on so far. We've got to get more background, I thought.

The ambassadors chit-chatted a bit more, then the Grojiel delegation turned and departed the chambers leaving us humans looking at one another thinking, *What the hell is going on with these guys?*

Ambassador Kjino looked at me and said, "Yes, yes, Captain Dave, we must move quickly; Ambassador Geone and Ambassador Revus will be accompanying you back to Earth; we must act swiftly to stall violence and federal embarrassment, which would lead to oversight by the Council. Unwanted oversight, or worse... the Council could punish us, and that would not be good for any of our societies."

From there we made our way back to our ships and started planning the next step, going home. Hmmm, I didn't like the sound of what I had heard: *Oversight? Punishment? I wonder what forms of punishment and oversight we'd be facing.*

In a different space-time dimension, the being known as Harker731 made a short statement to the group: "The humans are now in play; there's a high probability our plan will be successful."

June77 responded: "The timing is...well, the general timing works in all existence planes; however, the humans must act swiftly or—"

"Yes, I'm aware of the stakes," Harker731 interrupted impatiently, "existence itself is in peril. There isn't much more we can do from here."

June77 calmly responded, "Agreed, let's move to the next junction."

We headed back to the *Algonquin*, with Ambassadors Revus and Kjino chattering about *who knows what* while I made audible notes and engaged in small talk with Isolde.

Isolde indicated she would not be traveling with us to the graviscopic departure point as she had many issues to get sorted out with the tiny ship they were outfitting for our trip home. She did ask if we could stay in contact during the travel, and I agreed to do so.

The walk gave me time to think about things and reflect on the amazing events we'd experienced so far. *Folks back home on Earth have no idea how big the universe is about to get.* Back on the *Algonquin*, I gave orders for departure and chaired a short staff huddle where Revus and Kjino joined us as Bowendi provided details about what steps we'd need to take to the departure point. "Ambassador Geone is not joining us?" I asked Zane who'd been working to coordinate our departure with the station command and control facility.

"Sorry sir, at the last minute, the ambassador's staff informed us that he may join us at the graviscopic departure point, but it's not for certain. They didn't say why." I nodded at Zane, and he turned to work on the next task on his list. Bowendi provided details on how long it would take to arrive at the departure point—about seventy hours was what I gathered.

The specialized Veeniri ship was not yet ready, as traveling through the Graviscape apparently required a very complex preparation process to ensure we ended up at the right location and in one piece. After the staff sync meeting, I walked Ambassador Kjino and Revus around the ship, giving them both a tour. This seemed very exciting to Revus as he asked a ton of questions at every stopping point. I suppose Kjino had seen scans and was probably briefed in great detail on the *Algonquin* while we were in their early custody. Meanwhile, Bowendi and the ambassadors' aids were busy organizing the guest quarters so the ambassadors could travel as comfortably as possible.

Over the next few days, we spent a great deal of time talking with the ambassadors and learning how the federal system worked. It was an extremely old republic system based on communicating through this Graviscape thing which I also learned more about. Technically the word "Graviscape" is the computer's translation of the alien word for gravity field or something like that. Inside our current universe, light's velocity was the speed limit, but when you tunneled through the Graviscape there would be different speed limits. That was the magic of the Gravitron reactor. It enabled the modulation of data over the Graviscape as a transport medium or tunneling of small things through the Graviscape which apparently is the only field that uniformly traversed all layers of space time and thus all universes.

Sarah was really excited by this and spent a lot of time working with Bowendi and Alex to understand the Graviscape and how the G-HUDs worked with it. I also learned that Ambassador Revus was one of the Higlian's greatest scientists-turned-statesmen, and was over a thousand years old. Yes, a thousand years old. *Holy crap*, I couldn't conceive of living ten human life spans. During the slow travel, the Ambassadors analyzed, plotted, and discussed tons of different courses of action and how to work with humanity to get the greatest possible outcomes from our relationship. After hours of conversations with them, I got the sense they were creatures of excellent character. They truly wished to foster goodwill and focus on the greater good of our societies.

I also came to understand that the Grojiel were difficult to deal with, and were much more violent than the Veeniri or the Higlian. When I asked about the relationship between the Higlian and the Grojiel, Revus replied, "The Higlian home world is a large moon to the third planet in the Tok system. We are a very old, declining society where violence has long since been eschewed. When the Grojiel species discovered us, they issued multiple threats, and then to prove their true intent, they destroyed our colony on Septis Six, which is a small moon around the fourth planet in our system. We lost thousands of Higlian as they bombarded the colony from space, and we knew they could have easily destroyed cities on our home planet or other colonies. In fact, they could have damaged or destroyed all our colonies across our home system before we could have mounted an effective, conventional defense. We have far superior technology, but the Grojiel possessed a large military space fleet, and behaved like a very young erratic species. They repeatedly threatened us in a very belligerent way. So, we quickly entered into an agreement with them so we would not have to fight yet another war. My people are weary of war: both internal and external."

I nodded my head in understanding as Revus continued to talk about how they'd allowed the Grojiel to become brokers to their technology and their existence. It was a bad deal, but it's how the system worked. I got the sense that the Higlians still had a few tricks up their sleeve or in their pockets that hadn't yet been used. I took a note to get more details on the Grojiel.

A few hours later we were getting pretty close to the departure point, and everything seemed to be going pretty well. The crew was still a little depressed and increasingly worried about Earth, especially with the thought of the Grojiel visiting unannounced and potentially attacking. *Who could blame them?* Collectively, though, their mood was gaining positive momentum and they were getting into a groove, heck, I like it when things are going just as smooth as butter. *Peanut butter that is.*

Chapter 15: Pirates, Again

Ambassador Revus and I were walking through the cargo bays of the *Algonquin,* and I was explaining how things functioned. I asked him details of how the graviscopic transportation worked. He gave me a lot of details and even drew helpful diagrams on my tablet to help me understand. It was really beyond my grasp, but his diagrams helped. I enjoyed spending time with Ambassador Revus, he seemed like a true person of character, and he had a lot of energy for an old man. He really wanted to understand how everything worked, every button, every circuit. His curiosity was ravenous. As we float-walked along the walkway toward the bridge, a sudden, loud, metal-on-metal crashing sound rang out as something clearly had struck the *Algonquin. Hard.*

It was a vicious-sounding strike, knocking Revus' and my magnetic boots off the floor, and we spun out of control, banging off the various ship's structures.

The lights dropped to emergency levels and alarms started going off, seemingly everywhere at once. An especially bad alarm pulsed through my ears with high chirps indicating there was a nearby hull breach. Panic set in as I looked around and realized it must be behind us, in the neighborhood of the new docking apparatus that was installed by the Veeniri so we could dock with their ships.

I whipped my head around to look back in that direction, and I could see every floating piece of ship's equipment, fragments and debris being drawn backwards quickly toward the new dock area. I suddenly realized I was being pulled backwards to that area along with all the air in the room. I tried to grab onto a couple of protruding pieces of the ship, but couldn't maintain a decent grip. *Crap, we are going to get sucked out into space!*

I turned forward to face the ambassador, hoping he'd made it through to the next hatchway. Nope, there he was, about three feet ahead of me. *Yep, he's getting pulled toward the leak with me.* Breathing was suddenly becoming very difficult.

That was the moment that I realized that Revus and I were going to die.

Suddenly, the air started to repressurize in the chamber, as four figures started floating into the bay from the direction we were being pulled toward. Correction, two of the figures started moving quickly toward Revus and me.

I called out, "Mick, is that you?" It was hard to see in the low light, and there were a ton of loose items floating around. *Had Mick fixed the hole?* A few seconds later they were up close and personal—unrecognizable aliens in suits that I'd never seen before. Two of them had small devices in their hands and wielded them like some kind of simple handheld weapons, and just as I was about to say something nice to highlight how welcome they were, the figure closest to me shot in our direction with his hand weapon.

Three very loud popping sounds erupted from the weapon: *Pop, Pop, Pop.* I pushed off the railing to protect Revus by putting myself in the way between the aliens and him. My leg and foot were hit by some sort of projectile. "*Ow, Crap!*" *What the hell was that?* My leg started to bleed, with droplets spraying into space around me, but my boot apparently protected my foot. I faced the aliens and moved backwards to sandwich Revus between my back and the wall behind us in order to protect him.

The two figures that had shot me didn't move forward anymore; they lowered their weapons and started moving cargo boxes toward the door.

"Crap," I said under my breath. I reached over to the wall and clicked on the wired intercom, "I need some help down in Cargo Main 3, stern side, we've got four intruders here in the bay."

Zane's trusty voice crackled over the speaker, "Roger, on it sir; be there in a moment. Sir, we've got four ships just outside our hull."

Okay so someone is attacking us and boarding the Algonquin, we need to get away from these guys. After thinking about options, I finally settled on one particular course of action. "Huang, Mick, I want max pulses from our maneuvering thrusters at thirty-eight degrees X plane and nine degrees Y plane for two minutes, and then punch the mains full out until we get away from these guys."

Ambassador Revus shook me gently and said, "Calm Captain Dave, you must calm yourself; you are leaking fluids at an alarming rate; I presume if I hold pressure.... here, this will slow it down?" Two of Revus' four arms put their hand-like things over the hole in my leg where the projectile hit me, trying to stop the bleeding.

"Thank you, Ambassador; yes, that will help."

"Captain, we must get out of here; they will not close the door behind them if you take my meaning," Revus stated calmly.

Just as Revus finished his statement I suddenly understood what he meant: the pirates would not bother closing the door or repressurizing the bay; we would likely get sucked out into space in a couple of seconds. Suddenly the ship lurched abruptly, probably following the maneuver Zane directed Huang to execute, and everything shifted around.

Revus held onto me and I held onto the only piece of the ship I could grab, trying to get back toward the pressure door so that we could escape being sucked out into space. The *Algonquin*'s power flickered back to life as we could see the lights from various displays brighten but the main lighting in the bay was still less than normal. I kept my eyes on the intruders as I warned, "Zane, the Ambassador and I cannot get the door open behind us because the air pressure in here is mismatched."

"Dave, turn around," Zane said over the intercom.

I turned and saw Zane's face through the tiny window in the pressure door. *Thank God.*

"I'm about to open the door, and I'll pull you both in and then go after the bad guys," Zane said.

Zane didn't realize that the bad guys would probably rip off the docking door resulting in him being sucked out into space. I couldn't let that happen. "Zane, no—" just then, the door whooshed open and there was Zane, in a full pressure suit with a .45 caliber model 1911 pistol in his hand. *Hot damn! Zane must have thought through it on his own. He's the best.*

Revus and I held onto the rail as Zane passed by us as he was sucked into the Cargo Bay by the difference in pressure. He quickly stabilized himself by grabbing a handrail, attached his metallic boots onto the walkway, and started shooting at the intruders. *Blam, Blam, Blam, Blam.* Zane's pistol barked fire a foot long out of the muzzle as he fired shots at the bad guys.

The .45 was damned loud. Zane clearly hit one of them as we saw it stumble and spin out of control, but the others dragged it along as they all turned to apparently flee with the remaining bits of cargo in their grasp. Two of the bad guys returned fire, missing wildly while the others spent their energy taking the last bits of cargo, presumably toward their ship. I think the fire leaping out of the muzzle of Zane's gun coupled well with the loud belching sound to unnerve the attackers.

As the air balanced, Zane turned and pushed us forward into the next chamber, then pulled himself in as well and finally closed the door behind us. We were safe for the moment. Despite Revus' effort to hold my wound closed, blood was floating back toward the door, indicating our ship was starting to move fast now, adding about a half a G of force. "Let's get to the bridge and strap in; we'll have to try and outrun these guys," Zane said with a grin.

I looked over at Zane and said, "You liked shooting that thing didn't you Zane?" I smiled as I saw a hint of youthful energy spike in Zane's eyes.

"Hey, just doing my job, sir. Let's go." Zane gently pushed Ambassador Revus toward the bridge as they exchanged thoughts on the intruders.

We climbed our way up to the bridge and strapped in just as Riley showed up to try and patch my leg. "Thank you, Riley, what do you see?"

"Looks like some kind of flechette round. In through the front and apparently went through clean and out the back of your leg. There you go sir, that should hold you; I've stopped the bleeding, and we'll take a closer look after you get us out of this mess we're in," Riley smiled with enthusiastic energy. I smiled back and asked Riley what we were looking at in terms of WTFs per hour. "Looking to be about three to five WTFs per hour at this point, sir," he smiled.

I was working to keep Riley calm and confident in the team, as that's what we needed at that moment. The *Algonquin* started to pull away from the attackers. I looked over at Zane, "Zane, let's calculate solutions to fire one round each at the two closest pursuing ships."

Zane gave me a thumbs up and turned to work a control panel, I could hear him talking to Mickey and Maria down in engineering. "Sir," Zane said, "we've got enough juice for three rail shots over the next thirty minutes, two immediate via capacitor surge, and then we'll have to recharge the rail gun, that will take about thirty minutes."

They were not gaining on us much, so we'd have to be careful expending rounds as they consumed a lot of electricity. Each round cost about 600 kilowatts of juice, which was a lot. We had emergency chemical rechargers, but they took about thirty minutes to recharge the capacitor array. Normal charging took hours—again, we were in a space RV, not a military destroyer.

"Okay, Huang, Sarah, Alex, we can use one shot, maybe two if it's critical. We need to make it count." I pulled up the events holo feed and noticed that three of the ships had slowed down, while the biggest one kept after us.

Sarah and Alex conferred with Huang and Zane for a minute or two, then Zane said, "Sir, despite our evasive maneuvers, their largest ship is not deviating from the current fairly straight-line course. I don't think they are worried about us shooting at them."

Ambassador Revus piped in with, "Not all pirate ships are well equipped; it's possible this larger vessel lacks the needed AI controllers to execute sophisticated evasive maneuvers. A common procedure is to use smaller more agile ships to disable targets while the larger ships focus on boarding and cargo theft."

"Okay," I replied, "tee up the first shot focused on the big ship, fire when ready." The communicator on Ambassador Kjino's belt lit up and he grabbed the device, manipulating it with his fingers. I could hear audible communications occurring but no translation.

Kjino handed me his communicator, and it began translating Isolde's voice to me. "Captain Dave, what is happening?" Isolde said through the translator.

"We were attacked by four pirate ships, and we are trying to get away," I said.

Isolde's voice became agitated as she said, "Get to the departure point as quickly as possible; I'll send ships to meet you and help with security. You are dangerously off course. There's much to discuss, other, simultaneous attacks and events are occurring."

"Okay, we are on our way with as much speed as we can muster." I handed the device back to Kjino.

As I handed the communications device back to him, I heard an apparent inadvertent voice translation fragment where Isolde said, "Father, please be careful ...."

"Father." *What the heck? Is Kjino Isolde's father?*

I peered over at Zane who was looking back at me with a, "What the hell is going on around here?" look on his face.

Crap.

We would have to deal with that later, so I mentally backgrounded the Isolde-Ambassador Kjino, father-daughter issue. Turning my head back to my panel, I looked at the displays and said, "Alex, where are we at with that shot?"

"Ready... in eighteen seconds, seventeen, sixteen..." Alex continued to count down as he adjusted the firing controls.

Shooting in space is really difficult, as the rail gun rounds are devastating, but hitting a moving target in space is hard. Now, in this case, the bad guys weren't maneuvering at all, so I felt pretty good about this first shot.

"Fire, Fire, Fire," Alex said as he pressed the firing button on his panel. I later found out that the round had hit the bad guys' ship and torn a jagged, nine-foot hole in its starboard engine housing, right where it attached to the main part of the ship, not only disabling the ship but causing the other pirates to tow the ship back to their base.

Ouch. Anyhow, the bad guys fell back to lick their wounds.

We focused our sensors in their direction, and they appeared to be heading away from us. Looked like we were safe for now, so we went into damage assessment mode as we slowly corrected our course back toward the launch point.

"All right people, let's keep an eye out for these guys. Aside from me there's been no injuries that I'm aware of so let's assess our disposition in fifteen minutes, main conference room. Need to know about ship's damage, cargo, passengers, the works. Also need to know how they snuck up on us; Sarah let's figure this out. Doc, I'm coming down to get patched up, need to discuss a few issues." I meandered around the ship on my way to Doc's office just to check on the crew, Abby, and check the hull. I knew they were rattled and so was I. To the humans aboard the mighty *Algonquin*, the universe just got a lot more complicated, wonderful, and frightening, all at once.

Looked like damage to the ship was repairable, although they did take quite a few cargo handling tools in the cargo bay near one of the new docking locks the Veeniri installed. As I privately reflected on this situation, the distrustful part of my mind started to wonder if installing those Veeniri locks aided the pirates' ability to get in, and if so...

Chapter 16: Stuck

Ninety minutes later, the key staff started shuffling into the *Algonquin*'s main conference room. I walked in and shifted a few folks around to ensure Ambassadors Revus and Kjino had seats at the table near me.

"Okay sir, I realize you are tracking much of this, but for the rest of the staff, here's the rundown: we'll be arriving at the departure point in about twenty minutes; we've got Veeniri ships inbound to provide security overwatch the rest of the way, and Isolde's transport should be docking with us anytime," Zane said. "Engines are fine, life support, reactors, electrical, and C2 systems are all unaffected by the attackers' activity. The hull and starboard dock did sustain some damage that we'll need the Veeniri's help to repair."

"Roger XO, thank you. I've been thinking about this for a while, and I'm not sure what the pirates would have found from us that is valuable. Do we have a read on what was taken?"

Zane replied with a list of minor ship tools, pressure hoses, and, interestingly, several emergency med kits. Before Zane could finish, Sasha butted in with, "Captain, they took nearly all of my cargo! Months of work on Mars for nothing. Earth was counting on us; we've got to track that cargo down, work with the Veeniri or something."

Everyone stopped and looked at Sasha, then back at me. "Sasha. I understand, however, we are in no position to pursue the pirates," I started, "our priority is to get back to Earth before the Grojiel do."

Isolde float-walked into the conference room and interrupted us, "Captain Dave, we need to talk—it's urgent."

Holy crap, Isolde's sudden appearance was unexpected.

"Isolde. Welcome aboard," I said with a surprised look but a genuine, growing smile. It was good to see her, and I was hoping she could help us figure out what the heck was going on. Isolde looked at me and then scanned the room for her father.

Her blue color deepened as she spotted Ambassador Kjino.

She stared at him for a few seconds as if to verify his physical integrity, then looked back to me. "The graviscopic jump ship has been severely damaged in what appears to be a coordinated attack. Someone attacked your ship, the jump ship, and four other Veeniri outposts, all occurring at nearly the same time, and stole goods from all."

I tried to adjust the dumbfounded look on my face as I said, "Isolde, do we know what was taken?"

"Yes, Captain Dave, we have a good understanding of the items that were taken: mechanical equipment such as power regulators and other expensive pieces that will be easy to sell on the black market. We also have some interesting thoughts to share concerning the attack on your ship, the *Algonquin*. Our intelligence sources report that some of the ore your ship was carrying has special properties that were detected by Bradea station sensors while we were docked at the Council. That information was sold on the market to three high-profile, anonymous buyers. We've studied our sensor readings from when you were first captured, and when your ship was held in our station's dry dock facility. We think at least some of the ore you were carrying possessed graviscopic properties, just like the crystals we use to access the Graviscape. This is why we think the pirates came after your ship."

The announcement soon had everyone talking in sidebars. I made a few notes before asking everyone to quiet down so Isolde could continue.

"If your ship possessed hundreds of pounds of graviscopic material, it would be such a lucrative target that pirates or governments would risk almost anything to get their hands on it. Also, the attacks seemed well coordinated with your presence and the urgently planned graviscopic jump back to your planet Earth. There's mounting evidence the Grojiel may be involved as they are known to work with the pirates in this sector of space.

Also, we assess Ambassador Geone's last-minute schedule change indicates he did not want to be aboard your ship for the return travel. We think the attackers intended to disrupt or stop your return while stealing the highly valuable ore."

As she paused, I thought about what Isolde had said. I looked at the Ambassadors, then back to Isolde. "Isolde, are we going to be able to get home using that ship now?"

"No, Captain Dave, the ship was heavily damaged in the internal power conduits, navigation controls and other key systems. It's not flight capable for space travel, let alone graviscopic travel of that significant distance."

Crap, okay, maintain composure here. Have to make something work and get us home. I made a few notes in my notebook and pondered a new plan as Isolde continued.

"We are moving a mobile space dock here to effect repairs, but it will be weeks before the ship can survive a graviscopic hop," Isolde continued.

I wanted to be clear about the situation as miscommunications due to the auto translators occurred frequently so I asked, "Isolde, what is our plan then, should we wait until the ship is repaired, or should we pursue other courses of action?"

"Captain Dave, as your ship is incapable of jumping back to Earth using the Graviscape jump capability, I don't know how we can do anything except wait until this ship is repaired. A jump of that distance requires a small ship to minimize the size of needed crystals and power consumption."

The room fell silent for a moment and then multiple sidebar conversations ensued.

I analyzed my notes and then I looked at Zane and we chatted about other possibilities. Essentially, there were no other options for us to get back to Earth quickly. I noted Ambassador Revus, Ambassador Kjino, and Isolde all talking and pointing at charts or something on the display of the tablet they were passing around.

Finally, I broke up the sidebar conversations and in sheer desperation, I said, "Ambassador Revus, can you help us?"

Ambassador Revus looked around the room and then directly at me.

"Captain Dave, I have analyzed the details shared by my esteemed colleague Ambassador Kjino, and the Veeniri intelligence groups. I think there is a way forward here. According to the jump ship's damage report the graviscopic components were not affected, only the ship's internal systems. I think this indicates we could move the graviscopic components to the *Algonquin*, do a test run to ensure it works, and then use the *Algonquin* to get you home. I've studied your ship and its design, and while many aspects of your technology are not sophisticated, your power systems, reactor, propulsion, and hull design are modern and strong. Also, the ObjectForge system can accurately produce many things that our own scientists cannot reproduce with the same speed and effectiveness. With a few modifications, I think the ObjectForge can generate the capabilities we need. This ship is so well structured that I'm certain that with modifications, it could easily withstand transitions through the Graviscape while the g-ring modulator provides sufficient radiation insulation. Please give me one more moment."

Okay, that's a shot in the arm, high praise coming from such an esteemed figure. Also feels pretty good that the lowly humans got a few things right.

Isolde, Kjino, and Revus continued to collaborate over the tablet's screen, and after a few more minutes of collaboration and sidebar discussions Ambassador Revus said, "Captain Dave, even if we attach the components to enable a ship of this size to traverse the Graviscape, there's still the matter of the graviscopic crystals, which we do not have. The crystals intended for use in this effort were stolen during the coordinated attack on the jump ship."

I felt my stomach sink because I knew that I'd just heard something super bad. Okay, so technically we could figure out how to make the *Algonquin* jump through the Graviscape by attaching the external hull components and wiring it into the *Algonquin*'s systems, but we didn't have the crystals to power the jump. "Thank you ambassador; is there any place in this part of the Galaxy where we could find some crystals, or can we make a substitute in our ObjectForge replication device?" That question got a synchronized, hearty chuckle from Bowendi, Ambassador Kjino and Revus, as Isolde focused on the tablet and making calculations of some sort with Sarah paying close attention.

I saw from my peripheral vision where Sarah was pointing at items on the tablet, but Isolde seemed to be doing all the talking. "Captain Dave it is a very low probability that we will find these crystals nearby or within light years. I don't say that to be pejorative; it's just that in the last one hundred years we have found enough raw material to generate fewer than ten total pounds of crystals. And that's searching throughout the galaxy using long range exploration ships and graviscopic jumps. There is just very little of this ore in existence."

I frowned in my mind's eye but kept a straight face and said, "OK, let me ask a few more questions here; I have a theory brewing. Ambassador Kjino, if it's possible that the ore that was stolen from the *Algonquin* was in fact graviscopic crystals, or perhaps precursors to crystals, can we use them to power the *Algonquin*'s jump back to Earth?" To my left, I noticed Sasha's eyes light up as she realized I had, in fact, read her report concerning the ore's special properties back on Mars.

Ambassador Kjino's posture shifted into what I guessed was a speculative position and said, "Yes, yes, Captain Dave, I do believe it's possible, but we'd need to conduct many tests. Again, we no longer have the crystals or the ore; how do you propose that we test this? Surely the Pirates have transferred the material they stole from your ship by now."

"Just leave that part to me: I think I know where we can get some ore to process and test." As I said this I smiled broadly and looked over at Sarah who was looking at me like I had three hands growing out of my nose, as she was trying to figure out where I was going to get the crystals.

"Zane, Sarah, you remember when we first dropped into this part of the galaxy? One of our super large cargo bays snapped off?" And that's when the memory hit everyone.

The largest single load of Sasha's Martian ore was in the external cargo hold attached to the outside of the ship. It was thousands of pounds of ore. There had to be either crystals or sufficient precursor materials in that container to get us home. At least that was my thought. I talked to Isolde, and she agreed to take a Veeniri ship back to the original location of our first encounter. Sarah volunteered to go with them, and though I did not like the idea of splitting up with the pirates out there, this was an opportunity for Sarah to lead and do something revolutionary for the team. It's poor leadership to take away those opportunities, and we had to have that ore, so I let her go with them. Ambassador Kjino indicated their fleet was at a heightened state of readiness so further surprise pirate attacks would be unlikely.

We ended the meeting and split the crew into small teams to prep the *Algonquin* for modifications.

I could see Mickey's and Maria's eyes light up. They sensed some serious engineering was about to go down. And on *their* ship.

There was just enough time for a team meal in the *Algonquin*'s galley followed by a short nap before the Veeniri mobile dock arrived. That dock was massive, and it slowly wrapped itself around the *Algonquin* on one side and the Veeniri graviscopic jump ship on the other.

The next forty-eight hours were very stressful as we worked to outfit the ship hoping that Sarah and the Veeniri would be successful at finding our cargo bay. Maria and Mickey came to me several times and vented about the modifications to their reactor and power conduits. "Dammit Dave, I don't understand half the crap these guys are wiring into my systems," Mickey said.

"Okay Mick, I understand; is there a way to combine them, but yet keep them separate?"

"Yes, that is what we are doing but it still seems risky. Think of it like a tiered pipe or a pipe inside another pipe, and I'm using computer APIs to modulate how much power is going through the innermost pipe which are *Algonquin*'s original pipes."

"Wow, that's a lot of pipes," I smirked in a hopefully congenial way in a poor attempt to divert his anxiety just a bit.

Without missing a beat, he threw off my comment and continued with a slight smile budding on his face as he nodded his head up and down gently. "Right, but the risky part is because the outer pipes are... well, huge. If something cracks one open with the intended volumes of power traversing them, I'm pretty sure we'll all be dead in seconds. No alarm, no warning just terawatts of phased energy and plasma being expelled."

What? Terrawatts? Yikes, need to discuss this with Isolde. Terrawatts, that's a lot of energy. Steady Dave. "Okay Mick, do you want me to put a stop to the transition?" I watched Mickey's face as he thought about it, then looked at the floor and finally looked back up at me.

"No boss, there's no way for us to get home unless we do this ourselves. I'll just try to put in as many safety measures and controls as possible."

I looked at Mickey solemnly. "Okay Mick, that makes sense. Say, you are looking a little rough, why don't you take an hour or two to get some shuteye?"

Mickey looked back at me and said, "I should be done in about two hours, and then I've got six glorious hours of sleep planned as Maria takes over the conduit upgrades and control panel configurations. She's way better at that than I am anyway, so I'll be of limited value during that part of the process. Also, the Veeniri engineers are getting a better understanding of our systems and are really becoming critical to getting this ship patched back together. The Veeniri have even generated needed parts using the ObjectForge, and I'm telling you Dave, those circuit designs are slick. They've shown us how to amplify our reactor's output with increased overall efficiency. Computer chips embedded everywhere, smart conduits, smart switching, it's like every inch of this hardware is all computer controlled with multiple edge-based redundancies. We are learning a great deal," Mick said with a smile forming on his face.

I could see that Mick was feeling better about our situation. I think he was just worried about taking on too much risk and letting something stupid happen to us all. I got that. I reached out and grabbed Mickey's shoulder gave him a soft shake and said, "Hey Mick, you're the best engineer in the universe. We're going to get home together; I'm certain of this. I realize we're taking on a lot of risk here, but if the Grojiel get to Earth before us it's likely they will treat us humans the same way that they treated the Higlians, or worse."

"Dave, I'm also worried that if they think the Earth is rich with this ore, they will shoot first and ask questions later to get at it."

Now that is one hell of a great point, I'll have to consider that. "Good thinking

Mick, I will add that into the planning calculus for the return trip; we'll need a good strategic narrative to engage with the leaders of Earth." I looked Mickey in the eye and as slowly and calmly as I could I said, "Mick, it's about Earth and all of humanity. This thing could go sideways at any time. I'm not sure who we can trust." I waited a moment, taking a sip of coffee, then continued, "I know we can trust *us*, and with all of Earth at stake, I'm happy to take on the additional responsibility." Mickey looked at me solemnly. He got it.

Mickey upended his coffee pouch to swallow the last bit of go juice, and set the container onto the table between us. He smiled and said, "Thanks for taking time to listen to me captain; I appreciate your counsel. I'm going to head back to get after this installation. I agree, we've got to trust ourselves as much as possible." We both straightened up and shook hands, and he turned and float-walked out of the room, apparently feeling much better about his and our situation. Hell, he probably just needed a little time to vent. Everyone needs a little time to vent once in a while, and I think that adding perspective to every contentious situation is one of my key responsibilities as captain.

"Sir," Zane broke in over ships comms, "Sarah just contacted us and indicated they found the cargo bay right where we left it."

"Excellent Zane, good news. What's the ETA for their return?" I said with energy in my voice.

"She said about seven hours. Also, she said when they tuned the Veeniri sensors to look for a wider range of graviscopic crystal structures, the cargo hull lit up like a freaking North Star. I wonder if that's how the *Algonquin* looked to the pirates, or whoever it was that hit us."

"Roger Zane, I've been thinking about that. Perhaps there are different types of these crystals. Also, if our cargo was so visible, why did it take so long for anyone to target us? I'm thinking that the ore was not processed enough or something, so it was not recognizable to the Veeniri sensors."

"I'm not sure, sir, but one thing is certain, we need to be ready for future attacks once that cargo gets back to us. I'll bet that volume of such prized material will cause even friends to look at us twice. I'll move our cargo around so we can get all of Sasha's ore moved to the internal cargo bays when she gets here."

"Agreed Zane, good thinking. Let's run an internal tabletop exercise next opportunity to game out how we handle friends or enemies that are a little too interested. Then later, when we have time, let's exercise a few response scenarios to ensure we've not gotten too far out of shape for conducting emergency response or repelling intruders."

"Acknowledged sir," Zane finished with a grin.

I took the opportunity to stop by and visit Abby as talking with her always seemed to brighten my mood no matter how complex the day had been. I think she enjoyed my company as well, as our visit ended with a wonderfully enticing hug, not a handshake. Our visits were becoming more intimate, and man was that fine with me.

Okay, refocus Dave, I thought as I headed back to the bridge. *There's still a lot of work to do.*

Chapter 17: Complete Disappearance

Back at the Agency's crisis-action team conference room on Earth, Logan, the current operations watch officer worked his way around the room getting details from each department head.

"Okay folks, this is turning out to be a much more difficult and complex problem than we originally anticipated. The evidence that we have indicates the *Algonquin* simply disappeared without a trace. There's a trail leading up to a point where everything just seems to stop or vanish."

Jake, the senior astrophysicist from the research directorate spoke up hesitantly. "Sir, we are seeing similar energy bursts and surges out near Uranus station. They are similar to the energy bursts we saw when the *Algonquin* disappeared. There's been no other associated activity or TGLEs though so it's possible we've got a sensor error now that we are looking for these types of signatures throughout the system."

Logan considered this in the context of the other events and decided to aim more sensors toward Uranus. "Sensor Chief, let's get the Feynman array pointed out toward the source location of those energy bursts."

"Roger, sir, we'll get some better data if the events occur again, and I'll task the Jupiter station team to look at the spectral recordings to see if we have any better data incidentally captured from their location."

"Thank you for highlighting this, Jake, it could be something we should be looking for system-wide, so we'll need to consider how to search across all our own and partner sensors to find clues."

Chapter 18: Building the Team

While we waited for Sarah to return with the ore, I had a great session with Ambassador Revus where I asked him to partner with us, formally if possible, but I also hinted that a covert relationship would work too.

Earth needed allies, so partnering with an experienced species like the Higlian could help us navigate in the new, much more populated universe. It was clear his species was formally allied to the Grojiel by treaty, but I had hoped they would consider partnering with us. He told me he'd think about it and let me know later. He was leery of starting a conflict with the Grojiel, but I could tell that he was excited about somehow partnering with Humans and Veeniri on this expedition to Earth. Perhaps he was thinking this trio could defeat the Grojiel if a war broke out, or that an alliance could simply help with improving the current Tok political position in the galaxy.

I wasn't really sure what he was thinking, but if they helped us, they'd no doubt realize the advantage of the relationship, especially since we possessed so much of the graviscopic ore. That would give us an immediate strategic advantage in every way if a conflict did break out. It was becoming very clear how having access to the ore, the Graviscape, and the speedy data exchanges with other species were such significant advantages in a universe that required partnerships and near constant collaboration.

After stopping in to check on Doc and some of the other crew, I was happy to bump into Sarah, who had just returned from the trip to retrieve the ore. She smiled broadly as she talked about the experience with the Veeniri on their ship, which was vastly larger and more sophisticated than the *Algonquin*. It was wonderful to see her so happy and fulfilled. She said that she learned a lot about navigation and ship's business processes that would help us optimize our ship procedures while better understanding the Veeniri culture.

That was followed by a meeting with the Veeniri science and engineering team who indicated the ore needed pre-processing to be converted into the appropriately configured crystals before being used in the Gravitron reactor. We discussed lots of issues and challenges but thankfully, there were no showstoppers. The thought was to take the *Algonquin* on a test run after the ore was processed into crystals. During the afternoon staff meeting we received welcome news that our crystal pre-processing was completed ahead of time, and all tests indicated a successful conversion process.

That was excellent news, but the most interesting bit was that Ambassador Revus revealed he'd secretly summoned a few trusted Higlian engineers to partner with us.

"Captain Dave, I'd like to introduce you to our private Higlian Envoy to Humanity."

Ambassador Revus introduced my staff and me to the envoy group via his tablet's view screen.

The three primarily visible on screen were definitely younger than Ambassador Revus, and they looked larger in height, but the jellyfish-like central area of their stomach was smaller and glowed with a slight bluish hue.

Revus seemed proud to provide their background as he appeared to stand a little straighter. There was a significant propagation delay which made the conversation a little awkward but it was fascinating none the less. "The taller one to the left, that's Jimmex, he's an engineer and graviscopic researcher, the one in the center is Elainex, and she's a Higlian evolutionary anthropologist."

Holy crap, the translator computers are kicking ass today, I thought. *I can't imagine what Evolutionary Anthropologist must have translated from in the Higlian language.*

"...and on the right, that's Clarad; she's one of our finest quantum mechanical engineers. And don't let their youthful images deceive you; they are all over 500 of your Earth years old, and are experts in their respective fields. Most importantly, they can be trusted."

"Sir, I'm honored to meet this amazing cadre of professionals; we're grateful that they can join the team," I said as I looked around the room, and I realized I hadn't told anyone else about the clandestine request I'd made to Revus. *I need to fix that,* I thought. *Wow, 500 years old? Damn, what would it be like to live that long?* I wondered.

"They will arrive just in time to make the test jump. They'll be instrumental in helping us configure and refit the *Algonquin* as needed and bring trusted expertise to this..." he looked around at *Big Al* "... engineering challenge," he finally finished, smiling in what I thought might have been a forced smile. "Captain Dave, we must keep this relationship very, very quiet."

From there the introductory small talk settled, and we started refocusing on the test flight strategy: outlining the most important steps and documenting the functional configuration of many of the ships systems so we could make adjustments later as needed. We covered much of the test flight timeline and finally directed that most everyone evacuate to the Veeniri flagship during the test. It would be just me, Zane, Doc, Huang, Alex, Sarah, Maria, Mickey, Veeniri and Higlian engineers, Bowendi and Trudezic and oddly, Ambassador Revus. He was fighting with his staff something fierce to join us.

We'd bonded a bit, and I think he felt somewhat responsible for how the test turned out as it was sort of his idea to outfit the *Algonquin* with the Veeniri jump ship's graviscopic jump apparatus. Of course, now that Revus was coming, Ambassador Kjino decided that he too must come. And that brought a lot of drama with Isolde. *Okay, we'll need to work through it,* I thought.

The meeting was long enough to cover all the core tasks and functions we needed to focus on during the test. The envoy would be arriving within the next few hours, and I thought that having them aboard for the test would be great, as the Higlian are a wise, older species, and might be able to help us if something went wrong during the test.

Chapter 19: First Jump

I bounced around the ship for a while talking to members of the crew about how they were doing, and asking if they had concerns about anything specific or if they had an issue they wanted me to address. Most of the crew felt pretty good about things, so I headed up to the bridge to check in with Huang and Sarah.

"Okay Huang, how are the new systems looking? You got this under control?" I asked in a polite but direct way.

"Sir, it's taking some getting used to, but I think I've got it. Sarah's got the difficult task with navigation. Those new Nav computers, if you want to call them that, are exceedingly complex."

"Got it, thanks Huang, I feel better knowing that you've got a good grip on this: it's a historic moment. Sarah, how are we looking over on the navigation side of things?" I shifted my gaze to Sarah, who was presently surrounded by keyboards and electronic equipment with wires and pieces of electrical conduit strewn across her lap.

It really looked like she was wearing a computer *or three*. She looked around, gently touched keys on a few keyboards and looked at the screen to verify the appropriate responses and then shifted her gaze up to me. "Well, I think so Captain... it's very complicated, but I think I've got it about right. I don't fully understand how the navigation works, which is disconcerting, but I've got the rules coded into the navigation computer that I'm using to connect to the Veeniri system, which will handle the heavy lifting."

I looked at the mess of spaghetti-like wiring, keyboards, written notes, and became more concerned as I thought about the complexity that we were implementing here. *Okay, time for confidence building, Dave*, I thought. I smiled at Sarah, being sure to make eye contact the whole time and calmly said, "Great, good to hear Sarah, I'm confident we'll make this jump happen without incident. Err, uhh, by the way, why so many keyboards? I should think that would cause a bit of unwanted complexity."

Sarah looked at me in a humorously exasperated way and said, "I completely agree, but given the short time we've had to integrate the *Algonquin* and Veeniri components, well, they are essentially still separate systems with specific functional integration points for now. I'll have to integrate them more fully later, when I have time to better understand their interfaces. I can manage the navigation controls—well, at least I've managed to succeed during the simulation tests so far. There are fail-safe functions that helpfully prevent me from making a catastrophic mistake but I don't like trusting those functions with our lives."

As she finished her sentence, she held her chin high and looked directly into my eyes with a clear look of confidence. Sarah always added exceptions to her comments, and I've found, over the years, that it seemed to help her ensure that she never provided incorrect information about something. She was a conscientious leader and technician, never wanting to mislead someone. "I understand Sarah," I beamed back with a confident smile.

We all wanted to go home, that was for sure, but this opportunity was so amazing. Despite the stress of our situation, the things we'd seen, and the places we'd gone... well, it was like hitting a bottom of the ninth inning, grand slam home run, and winning a Nobel prize, and saving ten children from a burning school bus—all at once.

I peered around the room and decided to move on, giving everyone a little space to get work done without me hovering over them.

We were about four hours out from the first actual jump test, and I learned that the Higlian Envoy to Humanity would not be arriving in time, so we disembarked everyone from the *Algonquin* onto the Veeniri ships, and met to conduct the last pre-jump sync meeting to verify we had a common view of what was going to occur, and what backups we'd have in place to help us recover if something were to go wrong. I started the meeting with my patented, "Humor is suave for any situation," methodology.

"Okay folks, this will be an amazing test that we can build upon to get home, and to hopefully get ahead of the Grojiel. Huang, what are we looking at here, two or three?"

Huang looked up, as he was not expecting to be the target of my initial comments, so he looked at me and said with a voice that trailed off into silence, "Well sir, I think that's the right ballpark..."

I looked over at the ever-patient XO and said, "XO, what do you think?" Zane opened his mouth to speak, then paused, looked around the room at the other faces and finally said, "That seems about right, sir. We'll handle this mission and flatten out the bumps along the way, no problem."

To my right, I heard Mickey say something under his breath, and so I swung my eyes over to Mickey and said, "Alright Mick, out with it, do you have an estimate?"

Mickey looked around the room and then back at me and said, "Sir, I think we're going to get run-ruled by WTFs today..."

I smiled and looked over at Sarah, Ambassador Revus and the rest of the team and burst out into a hearty laugh. "Well, I guess you could be right Mick, but no matter what happens, we are not giving up," I said, shifting from humor to a more pragmatic demeanor. "We will get home, and we will help our families, friends—hell, we'll help all of humanity to step into the universe that we now know is not so quiet or disconnected. It's wonderful to know that we are not alone, and that thousands of other species exist, collaborate, and even barter with one another each day."

It was jump time, and as a precaution, the *Algonquin* slowly sauntered away from the surrounding Veeniri support ships and structures for the purpose of giving us all a little buffer if something went terribly wrong.

I was on the bridge with Ambassador Kjino and Revus seated near me in a specially designed cube. Sarah, Zane, Huang, and the rest of the bridge crew sat in their normal positions just forward and a meter or so lower than my seat with Sarah looking like she was wearing a computer suit, fraught with all sorts of wires, fibers, and meshes of junction cables. "Zane, my checklist looks pretty good, how does yours look?" I said through the microphone of my bulky, intraship space suit. I'd ordered everyone into the bulky suits to ensure we had the best chance at survival if something went wrong. We verified we all could communicate with the ambassadors and proceeded to work next steps for the jump.

"I'm all green on this end sir, Sarah and Huang just confirmed they are all green as well." Zane replied.

I gave Zane a thumbs up signal and called Mickey, "Mick, what's the story down in engineering?" Mickey responded just as I'd hoped.

"Well sir, our punch list is green and I'm feeling pretty good about the readings we are seeing down here."

"Thank you, Mick," I stated automatically as I turned my head to look at the ambassadors, who were both wearing the equivalent heavy space suit from each of their organizations. "Ambassador Revus, Ambassador Kjino, are you both okay and ready for the test jump?"

"Yes, Captain Dave, I'm ready and all of the calculations seem to check out," said Revus patiently as he manipulated his tablet computer.

"Yes, yes, I too am prepared for the event. This will be an historic achievement as we've never grafted Veeniri technology as complex as this onto an alien platform," replied Kjino.

"Excellent!" was all I could muster as a response as I was working through my own gargantuan checklist with my hands trembling under the stress of anxiety. *Looks like everything checks out so I guess... well, I guess there's no time like now to forever change the status and trajectory of humanity.* "Okay Sarah, on the count of three it will be on your mark," I said looking over at Sarah.

She gave me a single thumbs-up and responded, "Acknowledged Captain, going in three, two, one—Executing."

Lights all over the bridge flashed, then went out for a second as emergency lighting flickered on then turned back off when the normal bridge lighting returned.

Zane started, "I'm getting some weird readings here sir..." and then a massive Ker-Woompf! sound occurred as *Big Al* shook with tremors.

It felt like the *Algonquin* stepped into a big hole in the road, just as before, only this time I was feeling, well... *Unpleasant.* My stomach felt like it was twisting into a pretzel as my vision blurred into a fused smear of fantastically bright lights and all sounds simply meshed together into a cacophony of flat trumpet-like sounds. I could hear Sarah's faint voice overlapping with Zane's, but I couldn't make out what they were saying. "Zane," I tried to say, "Zane!"

The light began to fade into a paisley blue-green color as the noise receded to a low roar. My gut untwisted just a bit as I jumped out of my seat, moving quickly toward Zane. I glanced at the ambassadors and noted that Kjino was looking around, seemingly okay, as Revus was furiously manipulating his tablet which projected some sort of sophisticated holographic display out of the top of the tablet, and he was manipulating the holograph like it was some type of user interface. Not quite a keyboard but definitely moving structures around with his fingers.

Interesting tablet, I thought, *the Tok must have been more advanced technically than they've let on.* The light continued to fade into an ambient, but still brownish blue-green, hue.

I grabbed Zane and turned him around; I could see through his faceplate that he was barely conscious, so I put him back into his chair and moved over to Sarah, bent over and grabbed her by the shoulder. "Sarah, are you okay?" I said, touching my helmet to hers which invoked the person-to-person emergency comms direct link.

Her eyes slowly focused as she looked at me and said, "Sir, I feel terrible."

"Roger that Sarah, we are stuck in the wrong place, or something, do all the readings check out?"

Sarah gathered herself mentally like the tough superhero that she was and started clicking commands onto the keyboards while periodically scanning across several of the displays with her eyes. "Sir, something is wrong with the signals coming from engineering: they don't make sense," Sarah said. Mickey, Maria. Crap. I threw my head around facing the bridge door which caused enormous nausea and pain in my gut.

I forced myself to float-walk in a sprint through the door, down the passageway toward engineering. I only made it about ten meters before noticing the blinding patch of brownish green and blue light emanating from

CHAPTER 19: FIRST JUMP

the corridor directly ahead. It was like there was a giant hole made of light in the center of the walkway and the back end of the *Algonquin* was just gone.

I was reeling and thinking to myself that we were not ready for this, *Nope, we humans are just not ready for this.* I was bumped from behind, so I turned my head and saw Zane standing behind me, looking past me at the light as he moved his helmet around. I could see that he was looking for the missing part of the ship.

Zane bounced his helmet off mine to invoke the direct link comms and said, "Holy crap, we broke the damned ship in half! Dave what are we going to do?"

I looked at Zane, and I turned to look back at the missing half of the ship. "Steady Zane, I'm thinking. Actually, I was thinking about jumping into the light…"

"Hell no, Dave! We don't know what that is or where it goes; we're just not that sure of our facts right now," Zane replied.

"I know but Maria and Mick are back there…"

"Test it first, use this fire extinguishing probe," Zane said as he pulled a 3-foot-long piece of stiff, fire extinguisher extension hosing off the wall.

So I grabbed the hose and started moving forward to plunge the tip of the hose into the brightly lit chasm where the back of our ship should be. Closer… Closer

"Stop! Stop Dave!"

Out of nowhere, Revus leaped into view above my head then pushed his way down onto the walkway, grabbing my arm.

"You must not do this, quickly back to the bridge; we must balance the phase synchronization, or we'll be lost forever here."

"But my friends are lost wherever that leads to, where is the rest of the ship?" I said incredulously.

"Dave, I will explain later; it's not *where* is it. It's *when* is it," Revus said with extreme urgency in his translated voice.

Well crap.

"Okay, everyone back to the Bridge," I said. We all frantically made our way back to the bridge and Revus bolted for Sarah's position. He started talking to her, apparently explaining how to balance the Gravitron's phase synchronization. Sarah tapped away at the keyboards, and then, just like before, there was a loud Ker-Woompf! sound as the *Algonquin* felt like it drove over a giant mud hole in the highway with nearly the same explosion of blinding, twisting, overlapping light and sound.

I don't know how much time elapsed, but I opened my eyes and saw the ceiling of the bridge.

That's odd, I feel tugs of gravity, I thought. Then I rolled over and realized my suit's auto tether had fired, indicating I must have been out, motionless, for at least a minute or two.

Slowly pulling myself together I attached my feet to the floor and raised myself up, scanning around the bridge. It looked like the crew was coming around, and like they were floating, but auto tethered to their last conscious positions. Revus and Kjino were floating and bumping throughout the bridge, so I moved to grab Kjino and place him in the seat we'd engineered for him, then doing the same for Revus.

Mickey and Maria, I suddenly thought with a flood of memories rushing back into my mind's eye. I bolted through the bridge door, float-walking my way to the engineering section of the ship.

The back of the ship was intact, and I was elated as I continued my way to Mickey and Maria's likely position. As I rounded the corner to Mickey's workstation, I looked in, and my anxiety rose a meter, as he was not there. I looked around the engineering area and did not see either of them. Intra-ship comms started to flutter with coordination and chatter. *Crap, where are they?*

I had horrible mind's-eye-generated images of Mickey and Maria being destroyed by *whatever that was. Where would they go in an emergency?* I thought.

The reactor. I bounded back out the door, turned left toward the reactor compartment as I moved along, and I heard Zane taking charge of things on the bridge as Sarah and the Ambassadors came online making comments and discussing details.

The reactor room door was open, and both Maria and Mickey were there, auto tethered to the reactor control panel next to the Veeniri control system.

I grabbed Mickey's body and twisted him so I could see through his faceplate. He was conscious and looked at me as I invoked the direct comms link. "Mickey, can you hear me? Are you okay?"

Mickey focused his eyes and looked at me, then glancing around the room apparently gathering himself mentally. "Sir... I... feel like I was stepped on by a particularly angry elephant or something." He removed his tether and attached his feet to the deck. "Dave, holy crap, that was weird...."

"Weird indeed my friend, what happened down here?" I asked as I checked Maria's condition.

Mickey pointed back and forth between the Veeniri computers, panels, cables, and junctions. "This stuff, that's what happened... just after we jumped, I realized something was wired up incorrectly, so we bolted back here and took a look. That's when we realized something had gone terribly wrong, and I started feeling bad. I mean bad, like my stomach twisted up, and I thought my head was going to explode it hurt so badly. We saw that something was wired-up wrong, but it was too late for either of us to unplug or move anything—way too much energy going through that thing," Mickey said as he pointed beside *Big Al*'s reactor at the Gravitron. Maria was recovering now and nodded in agreement as Mickey continued, "Man, that thing was bright. I mean when it finally lit up all the way, I couldn't see anything. I must have just passed out!"

"Come on, let's get to the bridge and see if we can figure out what happened." Mickey and Maria gave me the thumbs up and so we made our way back to the bridge.

"Zane, team, gather data and let's meet in five minutes to figure out what the hell just happened." I looked over at Huang who seemed to be recovering pretty quickly. "Huang, you doing okay?"

Huang looked at me and smiled, "Yes Sir, I'm good, I've flown in much worse situations than whatever the heck that was."

I talked to Huang for a few more minutes to make sure he was really okay, and it seemed like he was doing better than the rest of us. I gave the condition green signal via FemtoCom, and everyone slowly started removing their helmets.

Grabbing my tablet computer, I headed for the conference room a little ahead of schedule because I wanted to review the events prior to the official sync meeting.

I started the meeting with a question, "Okay folks, let's begin with location. Where exactly are we? Sarah?"

"Sir," Sarah started, "we are 0.357 light years from the departure point and only slightly off our target distance of 0.4 light years." Trudezic elbowed Sarah's arm and pointed at her tablet as Sarah responded to her, nodding her head up and down. "We are off course according to Trudezic's calculations by about three degrees," Sarah said.

"Okay what happened Sarah, Trudezic, anyone have a good idea what went wrong? Is that the way jumps are supposed to occur?" I started.

Sarah indicated they had a good idea of what happened, but we likely would not get all our questions answered until we returned to the Veeniri dock so we could compare notes with other experts.

"Sir, bottom line it looks like we made a minor configuration error when we wired the Gravitron into the command-and-control data plane. With help from Trudezic and Ambassador Revus, we've managed to adjust the command-and-control software so there's no need to modify the hardware down in engineering. It's probably my fault, if that's the sort of thing we need to get documented..." Sarah said with a trailing remorseful voice.

I looked over at Zane and Mickey to see if they had any comments, but they both passed by raising an ungloved hand to the middle of their chest and shaking their heads from left to right. "Sarah, there's not going to be any blame handed out on this—we all want to get home, and we are exceptionally grateful that you were able to wire all this together and make the systems compatible enough for us to get this far," I said looking right at Sarah. "Does anyone know how the ship seemed to be broken into two parts and what happened there? Ambassador Revus, what was it you said down below, it's not where is the back half of the ship it's when? What did you mean?"

Ambassador Revus didn't look away or down at his tablet, he looked right at me and said, "We must all remember certain features about the Graviscape. For example, when properly activated it acts as a fast transport medium, enabling us to transmit information faster than light speed across large distances. Some species have even learned to manipulate that activation feature by opening a large hole and transporting entire ships through it while the ship generates a precisely organized field of energy, replicating field effects from this universe to protect it. The *Algonquin* entered the Graviscape, but a polarity misalignment in the Gravitron configuration created an emitted protection field that covered only half the ship properly. This resulted in the other half being exposed to overlapping field effects emanating from multiple dimensions, which pummeled the back half of the ship in incalculable subatomic ways."

Holy crap.

I looked at Sarah, Mickey and finally over to Zane. "So, we got lucky then, is that right?" I said in response to Revus's informative comments.

Revus looked slowly around the room and in a solemn translated voice said, "I don't know how we... or the ship, survived this. I've seen similar measurements and events during probe tests and during operations. All with the same type of light emissions and visual effects, and in every case the situation ultimately resulted in a catastrophic nuclear-fission-sourced explosion. No Captain Dave... Luck, does not adequately describe the incredulity of our survival in this situation."

The room fell very quiet as we all pondered the events a bit deeper. *I need to get us moving. We can't dwell on the mistakes, but we also can't stick around here.* "Is there a way to test the configuration, perhaps using a low power simulation, to verify the system?" I asked as I looked over at Sarah then over to Mickey.

They conferred for a second, and then Mickey replied, "Yes captain, we've been working on a way to validate the configuration, and we'll need about three hours, and we'll have to use the ObjectForge to build a test harness."

"Okay, what else? We've confirmed our people and ship are okay. There don't seem to be any threats around. We've got a plan to resolve the configuration issue and patches for the software. What are we missing folks?" I said as I pointed to each person going around the table, ensuring I gave every person the opportunity to say something or make a comment.

There were a few comments, but it was clear everyone was ready to get back to it. "All right, let's get after it, team, next huddle here in three hours—condition green until then."

Far off in another dimension:

"Did you see that? How did it do that? I've never seen that type of interaction before," said Harker731 to June77.

"Quickly, we must assist Lance001; its signals are weakening," replied June77. "Lance001, we are here, let us assist you—" June77 started but was cut off by Lance001.

"Stop. Stay back, I'm... I'm damaged... I need time to recover."

"Your signals are weakening; we are concerned. How did you do that? You, you saved them. The beings in that ship, how did you do that?" said Harker731.

"I can't explain it right now; I need to rest. I had to try and save them; the risk to me was worth it. We put the humans there; we *must* help them."

"Can you show me how to do that?" asked Harker731.

"No... Yes, when I have recovered, yes," replied Lance001 as he faded from contact.

"The old ones are indeed powerful," Harker731 stated to no one in particular.

June77 agreed and said, "I think we've just witnessed the most powerful demonstration of interdimensional energy being wielded by any being that's ever existed."

"Yes," agreed Harker731, "indeed, a powerful, yet curious display of strength and compassion for those beings."

Three hours later, back in the commander's conference room, we met again, with the ambassadors and other alien partners all seated or standing around the conference room table. "XO, team, everything on the punch list looks good from my view, what am I missing?"

Zane, Sarah, Mickey, and everyone else nodded in agreement as they prepared their portion of the discussion using their notes and tablets.

Clarad and Jimmex rewired Sarah's propulsion and navigation computer to reduce complexity, enabling the pilot to have more direct control over both navigation and propulsion. The thought was that this would help us make fewer mistakes operating the super complex Gravitron and enable two-person integrity of certain tasks.

We started walking through the procedures, and things seemed like they were generally in order with no challenges cropping up in the sequence of events that would lead to us jumping back to our origin point. The team members had really done their homework on this one, thankfully; based on Revus's comments concerning the previous jump, we didn't want to push our luck. As the session ended, I scanned the faces of folks around the table as they spoke or listened and noted some very weary looks. When I was convinced that we were ready and had implemented controls at the risky steps of the jump sequence, I made an adjustment to our timeline on my tablet.

"Okay team, we are ready. We are going to take a break for four hours. I want everyone to get some rest—that's an order. Meet back here for final checks with condition-red gear and ready to execute." Most of the people around the table perked up a beat, and everyone started chatting with one another as they filtered out of the room.

"Dave, a moment please," Revus said as he and Kjino moved to sit on either side of me at the table.

"Gentlemen, what can I do for you?" I said, smiling at each of the ambassadors one at a time.

"Yes, yes, Captain Dave, we need to check in. This jump has taken much longer than we anticipated," said Kjino as he looked up at me then over to Revus.

"Roger, Alex just reminded me that if we jumped back soon, we would beat any message back to the origin point because our jump would be FTL, and our message would not."

Revus reached over to place one of his four hands on my forearm and said, "We can use the Graviscape to send and receive FTL text-based messages Dave."

175

"I thought we could only use our G-HUDs on Bradea because of the amount of power needed to sustain the full duplex graviscopic transport session data?"

Kjino replied, "Yes, yes, Captain Dave, to use full virtual engagement we must use a facility like the one on Bradea, because its large-scale reactors can sustainably power that sophisticated signal consistently over time. Also, Bradea creates a gravity well that can be shaped to provide some assistance to the modulation process. Nevertheless, we can also use the *Algonquin*'s Gravitron as a graviscopic access point for raw, lightweight messaging."

Then Revus broke in, "I spoke with Jimmex and Bowendi to share the proper parameters with your engineering team. To use the Graviscape as a raw transport medium, turn on the ship's transport Gravitron, level two, power rating of 23.7% and adjust a few configuration variables, and we should be able to use the RexCom that Isolde gave you to send and receive messages. It contains a specially designed modem that can transmit simple text messages if it's close enough to a strong transport medium. Accessing the Bradea messaging servers through the Graviscape should work."

"*Holy crap, the RexCom can be used to send and receive raw FTL messages?*" I was blown away by the thought that, all that time, I'd had a super powerful comms device in my possession. Now I was getting pretty excited. "Outstanding, roger, yes, I'll get it working. One question though, if we fire up the Gravitron, will it affect the ship's position or cause any out-of-phase damage like we experienced before on the jump?"

Revus replied, "No, at that power level the ship cannot jump through, but the RexCom can use it to send and receive FTL messages and the radiation risk should be minimal."

Perfect, I thought.

Typing out the message on my wrist computer, I asked Mickey to fire up the Gravitron when he or Maria woke up. This elicited a rather immediate voice teleconference started by Mickey, which made me chuckle.

"You want to do what? After what just happened to us in that jump, you want to run up the Gravitron reactor?" said a surprised sounding Mickey, as Maria, Zane and Sarah jumped onto the call.

"I know, I know, it seems crazy, but this will work, according to the ambassadors. Besides, I thought you guys were sleeping?"

"Not sleeping yet, but you know the old saying, mission before men," Zane said.

"Or women," Sarah added with a snappy lilt in her voice.

Okay, I get it, they all want to be involved in anything we do. Hell, they deserve to be, we'd be nowhere without their efforts. "Roger that, let's meet by the Gravitron in fifteen minutes; I'll grab the RexCom and see you all there." Everyone acknowledged, and we split up to gather a few items, and, for me, to hit the latrine prior to meeting down in the engineering section.

Chapter 20: Messaging

"Okay, Captain, we've reached 23.7% output on the Gravitron, the field configuration is exactly as specified, power and field effect seems..." Mickey said, "stable," as he looked between several console screens around the makeshift Gravitron control panel.

"Dave," Revus started, "activate the RexCom and select ALT NET."

"Roger, I see it. Okay, its connecting... still connecting...."

Revus jumped back into the conversation, stepping closer to look at the screen as I manipulated the controls. "The display will briefly fill with plus symbols when it completely connects."

"*Bingo!*" I said excitedly as both Revus and Kjino leaped backwards in an urgent, self-protective way with their hands and arms covering their faces. Then they looked over at each other quizzically.

"Is it connecting Dave?" asked Revus.

"Oh, yes, I'm sorry; it's connected. I didn't mean to startle you," I said as I sheepishly looked over at Maria, Mick, Zane, and Sarah who were looking at each other trying not to laugh, softly snickering at the bingo reference.

Apparently, that wasn't translated well. "Ah, well, Bingo is a game, you see," I fumbled trying to explain the concept to Revus and Kjino. "And, when certain circumstances occur, a person is supposed to say 'Bingo!' indicating that they've met the winning conditions."

Kjino looked from me back to Revus and then back to me and said, "Yes, yes Captain Dave; that's utterly fascinating, please proceed."

I refocused back on the RexCom, flipping through the screens looking for something that I should connect the device to as a message server. "I don't understand how to connect or what to connect to," I said.

That's when Kjino moved forward, peering over my shoulder and said, "Yes, yes, Captain Dave, I'll show you. Slide the keyboard to the home position. Yes, that's it, now click on the transport selector icon, and yes, that's it. Then select raw graviscopic access point. Now slide it up and over, up, and over, until you reach the Veeniri domain zone hosted from the Bradea servers. It's a raw connection so you will not get an indicator light depicting a solid channel lock. You will only see a green indicator showing carrier pings resolve to the desired domain servers. Yes, that's it. There should be a channel descriptor for you; Isolde made three for you when she configured the device."

"Okay, any idea what she may have called them?" I asked.

"Yes, yes, it will be in the Veeniri consulate or ambassador channels."

"Got it," I replied. "I found one in Veeniri -> Ambassador -> Consulate -> *Algonquin* -> Message ->Queue."

I looked up at everyone, and noted Sarah talking quietly with Zane, and I heard Zane say, "Well at least he didn't say *BINGO*...."

I snickered internally, then looked over to ask Kjino, "I think I'm in the right spot, but I don't see any messages."

"Yes, yes, give it some moments, they must be decrypted and loaded—graviscopic transport is slow but reliable for text. The master messaging server is hosted on Bradea because of its planet scale reactors for power and natural ability to sustain a graviscopic access point signal. Be sure to use the audio feature so we can all hear the messages through our translators."

Sure enough, messages started appearing, although they looked encrypted, so I clicked on the first one and a computerized voice orated the message from Isolde.

"Hello, Dave, this is a communications check please reply when you receive this." I looked at the message queue and noted numerous messages rolling in. Another message from Isolde: "Dave, please acknowledge receipt of my message if you've received it." There were at least twenty messages in here from Isolde sent at about the same time. The last message said, "Dave, are you ignoring these messages to purposely irritate me? Because it is working."

Well crap. I guess I should have been paying attention to this darn thing. "Kjino, how was Isolde sending me messages? Was it connecting to the Graviscape back when she first gave me the device?" I asked, trying to piece together how the messaging back-end must work.

"Yes, yes, Captain Dave—the RexCom can connect using multiple network modes for transport. It looks like you never connected the RexCom to any station networks when your ship was held in our cargo bay as Isolde expected. It's a very capable system. In fact, Isolde's team used its translation technology to accelerate our ability to communicate with you when we first met."

I looked at Kjino and said, "Huh. She came on board and trained me on using it many times, I wonder why she did not connect it?"

Kjino responded, "When you first connect it, it makes you discoverable... by everyone, if you take my meaning. Even the Grojiel would be aware of a new point of presence aligned to the Veeniri consulate."

"I see, she probably was just trying to protect me," I said smiling and nodding up and down back at Kjino and the rest of the folks standing around the small circle.

We started listening to the messages, which were all basically verbal pings from Isolde. I clicked on the last message, which had no subject descriptor and a really large message size, and it started playing some weird sounds like it was some kind of sound file instead of text. "What's this message?" I asked.

Kjino pulled my hand with the RexCom in it up to his face, apparently to get a better view. He shook his head in what I thought was a puzzled motion, and then moved my hand over to Revus. They both looked at each other and finally Kjino responded with, "Not sure Captain Dave, very strange. Some messages can encode and encapsulate images and videos for transport, which is what this looks like, but the formatting isn't quite correct, so your RexCom is having a difficult time rendering the content. Recommend you send Isolde a message stating that all is well on this end, and that we will return in five hours. It's great that your system is working now. After you send your message, may we use it to check our messages?"

"Yes, of course, but how can you access your messages, as I thought this system was only accessible to me?"

"Yes, yes, Captain Dave, it is very secure and operates off of a combination of your passcode and biometric security factors, but you can simply log out, and then both Revus and I can log in to the device as guests and access guest accounts that will enable emergency access to special, hidden accounts used for this sort of situation."

"Oh, okay, I get it. Thank you Kjino." I smiled, "That's a pretty versatile feature."

I created a message for Isolde letting her know that we were okay and a few other details, and then waited to confirm it left my send queue before handing the device to Kjino. Zane, Sarah, Maria, Mickey, and I stood around talking as the ambassadors took turns using the device. We noticed that they'd turned off the audio as they worked through their messaging queue so we could not hear any translated messages audibly. Nothing sinister from my view, as I was sure they had a lot more going on from a messaging perspective than we did. I looked over at Mickey, and he was lightly chuckling.

"Bingo!?!" Mickey said smiling from ear to ear shaking his head lightly from side to side. "You scared the crap out of those guys Dave."

Of course Zane had to chime in with his comment picking up where Mickey left off, "Oh man was that funny, Dave; you should save that sort of thing for that ambassador from Grojiel."

Sarah and Maria wouldn't be left out as they picked up where Zane left off, "I swear, next thing ya' know, you'll be offering them peanut butter which will get stuck in the roof of their mouths." Sarah grinned as she softly giggled.

Finally, Maria chimed in with, "Yes, and the peanut butter will turn out to be like an alien aphrodisiac that leads to some kind of monster-mash-inspired intergalactic crisis."

I smiled at each of them, shaking my head innocently from side to side and quietly responded, "Oh, come on guys; it wasn't that bad..." they continued giggling. "Was it?" I trailed off.

Suddenly Kjino broke in, "Yes, yes, Captain Dave, we are finished with our message review. Interesting details regarding the attackers at the origin site.

It appears they were a Grojiel criminal affiliate. Come with me and I will explain it to you as we return to our cabins."

Thank God.

"Okay team." I grinned at my officers. "Let's get things tidied up and get some rest." Maria and Mickey moved over to the control panel to turn off the Gravitron, giggling and snickering as Kjino, Revus and I walked the other way toward the cabins.

"Yes, yes Captain Dave, why were they behaving that way?"

I smiled down at my light blue friend and simply said, "No big deal; they were just complimenting your expertise using the RexCom and highlighting how my performance was.... Less adroit."

The three of us took a few more steps and then closed the bulkhead door leaving the smart-ass funny crew behind. Man, I love those four. "Busting chops," as we call it, is a healthy pastime amongst crews that must serve together for long periods of time in close quarters like a spaceship. Because it can help us address issues before they grow to become concerning, as well as build incrementally thicker skins in the crew over time.

After Kjino briefed me on the threat, we parted ways to get minor tasks knocked out. I grabbed a peanut butter sandwich from the galley on the way back to my quarters, and promptly wolfed it down. *Damn, there's just something magical about peanut butter. It goes perfectly on anything, apples, fish, bananas, and even desserts!* After knocking out a few report entries and triple checking our punch list for departure, I finally crashed into bed hoping to get a few hours of blissful sleep.

Chapter 21: Second Jump

A few hours later I dragged myself out of bed and sipped a wonderfully warm pouch-cup of black coffee while I pondered if the Grojiel recon party had made it to our home solar system yet. Urgency crawled up from my gut, twisting it as I thought about how Earth would react to well-armed, if small, recon ships entering the system. They'd blame me for leading them to Earth. They would be correct.

My anxiety flared a bit as I considered all the possible future scenarios.

I didn't like any of those thoughts. *Okay, let's perk up, keep some optimism. If all goes well, we'll jump back to the origin point. Collect up the rest of our crew, and sprint back to Earth.* Yet my inner monologue continued to taunt me. *The Grojiel recon party must be near Earth by now. Gotta get moving and acting with urgency. Earth is counting on you and the crew. This is a can't-fail mission, but we have to be smart, because acting rash almost got us killed on the first jump.* I stewed through my thoughts and decisions, thinking about what we could, and should, do next. *Let's get back to the bridge and get ourselves home*, I thought.

Back on the bridge we were all sitting in our condition-red space suits. Everyone seemed a lot more refreshed, and as a result, mentally sharper.

No mistakes this time, I told myself. "Okay team, here's the deal, we are ready to execute humanity's second jump through the Graviscape. I know everyone is thinking about home, our families, and getting back there to help, but for now we need everyone focused on this jump. Senior crew, please confirm readiness level. We are doing this one by the book." I arranged my tablet checklist to sit at eye level while I clicked away on my small captain's computer attached as a side car to my chair. "Navigation—" I started.

Sarah broke in to say, "Navigation is green, graviscopic waypoints are plotted, Nav computers have dual power, and systems are locked."

"C2," I said.

Huang replied, "Pilot is ready, risk assessment is green, propulsion is green, all comms and controls are responsive, all gauges are green."

"Roger, engineering," I said.

Mickey replied, "Roger sir, Gravitron power is stable, and, thanks to Clarad, power is triple buffered..." Mickey continued on a bit as we steadily progressed through the punch list finally ending with Ambassador Revus, Dr. Roth, and Zane.

"XO, are we ready?" I asked Zane, as he and I were supposed to parse the same checklist to ensure two-person integrity whenever the checklist contained over forty items.

"Roger sir, we are ready."

I made a quick annotation in my personal log that said simply, "Today we see if humanity, with help from its partners, can master the Graviscape."

Finally, I said, "Execute the jump Huang. Now! Now! Now!" And we jumped.

This time the jump seemed uneventful. The ship lurched downward a bit like it had hit a small pothole in the road and there was an audible ZZPOOF! sound, but otherwise there were no other effects to feel—the jump was flawless. I could see the familiar soft bluish-brown hue of the field effect surrounding the ship.

When the Gravitron powerfully fired up and generated its protective field that also opened access to the Graviscape, the friction between our ship and the Graviscape manifested itself in the form of this oddly colored radiation. Revus said something about the field effect using enormous amounts of the right kind of energy to open the access, and then hold the ship safely in a protective field until it pops back out at the pre-coordinated location.

I needed to learn more about how this worked, as apparently there are places in space where it works, and others where it does not or is inconsistent. A few minutes later we felt the familiar pothole-like bump, and the view of normal space could be seen through the portholes.

Everyone on the bridge looked over at me curiously, wondering if the jump had completed. *Crap. I'm not sure myself but the radiation is gone and all the sensors that typically go offline during a jump are back online. The Gravitron gauges were... pulsing but low yield and nominal.*

"Huang, Sarah, are we back where we started? Jump complete?" I said with a bit of uncertainty in my voice. Sarah looked over at Huang, and he nodded approvingly that we were good on his end.

Sarah looked at her panel and performed a few calculations. "Yes, sir, we are 2,000 kilometers from the origin point, so our jump back was pretty accurate..." she said with a measure of confidence building as her voice trailed off. She and Huang turned to look at me and Zane.

Then Zane turned to look at me saying, "Sir, we are good. Jump was successful. No issues to report."

I looked from Zane to my panel, trying to understand if everything was good. *Yep, the SITREP looks great.* "Okay team, fantastic work—I do mean fantastic. Well done, Huang, Sarah—looks like we are almost back where we started. Huang, move us over to the space pier and get the docking sequence underway. I want to be on our way back to Earth as soon as feasible. The people of Earth are counting on us and they don't even know it yet. Okay, condition green as of the current timestamp, everyone get out of those suits for now but don't put them too far away."

Folks high-fived one another as they peeled off their condition-red, thick space suits. I reached out to Maria, Mickey, Sarah, and Zane on a private channel. "I want all four of you to start thinking about weapons. Not this instant but very soon. If we can seriously jump as desired and we do manage to get home, we are going to need some type of weapon to defend Earth from the Grojiel fleet. Let's face it. We've got no real defense system, and these Grojiel have a vast fleet of warships. If we get back to Earth in time to make a difference, I'm pretty sure we're going to need to shoot things and be able to move."

Maria replied first, "Yes sir, I've got a couple of ideas. Concepts really, but I'm pretty sure we can come up with something. Would be great to understand the Grojiel weapons though."

Sarah chimed in as well, "Sir, let me work with Bowendi, Clarad, and Jimmex to see what I can dig up on that."

Zane closed out the conversation with a smile and a short comment. "Sir, if there's one thing that humans tend to get right, it's guns and ammo."

I smiled at them giving them a thumbs up saying, "For humanity."

The ambassadors and I migrated over to the command conference room and discussed how the second jump looked from the sensor perspective. "Appreciate your thoughts on this experience. Thank you both; we would not have been successful without your help. Any final concerns before we break gentlemen?" I said, starting to wind down our conversation.

Kjino didn't have any comments, but Revus mentioned again how lucky we'd been on the first jump. I doubt I'll ever forget how close we came to certain death. "Dave, this jumping through space has to be done carefully *every single time* you do it. Sometimes the Graviscape will just spit your ship back out without any warning, or travel unexpectedly takes triple the normal length of time for no apparent reason. Normally it does so safely, but the Gravitron reactor must be running properly. It's really important to watch the Gravitron sensors for anomalous behavior, as they can be an indicator that something is dangerous in the region or dimension of space time the ship is in at a given moment."

I considered his words for a moment and asked, "I don't fully understand what the Graviscape is. How would regions of space spit us back out? Is our perception or measurements of reality different across parts of the Graviscape?"

"Dave, we don't fully understand this technology or the nature of existence ourselves, but think of the Gravitron as a device that modulates the Graviscape to enable travel through it as a transportation medium. The Graviscape is like gravity's shadow. It is the only field that traverses all dimensions of space-time and reality. We can propel ourselves within the Graviscape through the galactic substrate that underpins all dimensions and universes as we understand them. In that substrate, normal laws of physics don't apply. Using probes and test ships we've learned that there are limits to how fast we can safely travel."

"Okay, I'm starting to get it. Do we know how many realities there are?"

Revus looked over at Kjino and he turned back to me saying, "Dave, I don't think reality means what you think it does. But we have some very detailed analysis that covers the Graviscape and I'd like to share it with you at a future point, if we can learn to truly trust one another as partners. Much of the technology we use has been shared or purchased from aliens through the Intergalactic Federal Council. This technology is very old and has been used for millions of years. Thankfully, a certain maturity is achieved by the time most species discover the Graviscape. We discovered the Graviscape and eventually learned to communicate through it to exchange data and build the messaging architecture that's centralized on Bradea. We do have to follow the Intergalactic Federal Council rules."

Wow, this is going to be complicated, I thought. "Right, that makes good sense. This has been helpful. Thank you Revus, Kjino; I will work hard to ensure that my people respect yours, and hopefully we get off to a good start. I wanted to broach another topic with you. Something I've been thinking about quite a bit since we started the jump trials. Weapons. Can either of you help me understand what weapons the Grojiel have and would be likely to use against our ship or my home world?"

Kjino looked at Revus and then started talking in his predictably kind way. "Yes, yes, Captain Dave. We can share some of this, but Revus is technically prohibited from having this conversation with you," he said, gesturing to our friendly ambassador from Tok. "Dave, the Grojiel are a very violent species. They outnumber both Veeniri and Higlian hundreds to one, with numerous outposts, colonies, and unfortunately, weapons. It is likely they will engage with weapons first, and ask to bond later if you follow me."

"Yes, you've mentioned that before, but I have... well I have the basis for a plan, but we'd need to have some better weapons than we have now," I said, which provoked a response from Kjino.

"Okay Captain Dave, let's meet on my ship an hour after docking, I'll need a little time to assemble the right people and information. We'll hold a small group discussion about weapons, defense..." he looked over at Revus and continued, "and offense. You'll need to help us understand how well protected your home planet is."

Well, that won't take long, I thought, in my internal monologue's pessimistic voice.

"Good thinking, okay, one hour after docking, that should give us time to get ourselves organized for the jump home. Then I want to get home. It's taking us too long," I responded wearily. We stood up and I shook what passed for hands on both ambassadors.

"Yes, yes, Captain Dave, one additional thing," Kjino started as we proceeded out of the conference room back into the main bridge.

I stopped and turned around, looking back at Kjino.

"I recommend you keep the RexCom with you at all times, and please select the 'any available network' mode from now on. You need to stay in comms with all available species. I'll explain more, but since you are now intergalactically addressable, you will be... a *popular* target for conversation," he smiled as he looked over at Revus. He put an odd emphasis on the word *popular*.

REXCOM: Public Queue -> Message 5150 -> "Hello, my name is Honorable Prince Ixnariach Raolzhens of the Sation of Ramarchis Three. I would like to ask you to please help me. It's critically important that I receive 540000000000 pletos so I can post bond and be released from imprisonment. If you help me today, when I return to Ramarchis Three I will pay you back one hundred-fold for your kind assistance. I am of course very rich and famous, which is why I can afford to pay a one-hundred-fold reward. If you cannot fund the entire bond amount, I can use smaller volumes of pletos over time to gain release."

Man, Kjino wasn't kidding. My RexCom's public message queue was full of spam message after spam message. It's unbelievably ironic that we've got the ability to communicate intergalactically with thousands of aliens and I'm getting alien spam. Intergalactic alien spam, but spam nonetheless. I created a few message handling rules, and several more queues for messages to better organize and leverage the RexCom's ability to sort on originator, topic, date/time received and such, which helped me keep things organized much better.

I exchanged a few messages with Isolde and couldn't help but notice that overall, our engagement was evolving to be... well, more personal as we started sharing feelings about the situation and ourselves. She was in a tough position as she was viewed as being responsible for finding us, getting our buy-in to a security agreement, and helping us fit into the culture of the Intergalactic Federal System. Just as I decided to start overthinking all that, I received a message from Kjino that indicated it was time to meet, so I gathered some documents, corralled Sarah and Zane, and then headed for Kjino's ship. It was docked at the origin point's massive space station, where the original jump ship was attacked. There were several Veeniri ships here now, no doubt acting as protection while repairs to the station were completed.

Apparently, these types of shipbuilding and maintenance stations were extremely expensive to build and sustain, which is why they were repairing it—so it could be towed back into service at a different location. Mickey asked to stay back on our ship as he, Maria, and the Veeniri engineers were working with Jimmex, Clarad, and Bowendi to permanently install the graviscopic jump apparatus and power lines into the *Algonquin* while making a few configuration adjustments along the way.

Fifteen minutes later we walked into the conference room, sat down, and strapped into the seats around the long, super-skinny table. Kjino introduced me to Commander Timlet of the Veeniri Attack Fleet. He was the Senior Operations Commander and had a lot of combat experience in fighting the Grojiel in open combat and in skirmishes at various sites across the region. "Very nice to meet you," I said as I raised my arm so the commander could complete the Veeniri handshake by raising his arms outside mine. Surprisingly, he reached out and grabbed my hand and started shaking it furiously. *Holy crap this guy has a strong grip!* My hand was cramping under the pressure from his three-fingered grasp.

"I am Timlet, it is a great honor to meet such a wonderful partner," he replied through a facial expression that looked like an overzealous Veeniri smile.

"Oh, great handshake, that's quite kind of you," I replied as I realized he was trying to do a handshake but getting it a little wrong by over squeezing and over shaking. Timlet looked rough, with lots of dark cyan patchiness to his skin. He was by far the most sinewy Veeniri I'd seen, with serious veins and muscles bulging everywhere where his skin was exposed. Finally, he released his grip, and I looked down the table at Isolde who was smiling, I think. Yes, it looked like she was happy, as her cyan hue increased in brightness a bit. Isolde was no doubt proud that she'd taught her people to shake hands the way humans did as a gesture of kindness.

I introduced Sarah and Zane, who both introduced themselves a little more fully. We exchanged documents through the Veeniri network file exchanger, and I noted Revus started reviewing our files as well. We provided a high-level outline of Earth's system defense, which honestly wasn't much besides defenses against pirates or marauders.

I noticed that Kjino and Timlet seemed to be exchanging messages on their tablets. "Unfortunately, we have a very rudimentary defensive system. What can we expect from the Grojiel?" I asked.

Timlet replied, "Based on what you've shared about your home system's defenses, I'm afraid your situation is quite bleak. By now, I'm fairly sure a recon party has been sent to your system to assess security and look for resources or places they could potentially take over and hold at risk to compel your government into compliance. They've probably already arrived or will arrive very soon. The recon party would typically be one of their smallest ships with a small crew consisting of two to six personnel and lightly armed with a focus on stealth and speed." Timlet moved his hand-like appendages around as he spoke.

Good to know that aliens use that type of feedback to help them articulate concepts just like humans. *He's a hands talker,* my inner monologue smirked as I considered what he said and asked, "What kind of weapons do the recon ships have?"

"The Grojiel recon ships have twenty-five missiles. Fifteen short-range missiles and ten long-range missiles with explosive-tipped payloads designed to rupture an armored ship's hull. At short ranges, they do have pulsed microwave weapons designed to target a ship's computer infrastructure, and basic rail guns that are designed to puncture a target's hull. Defensively, these ships are lightly armored and designed for speed and agility. They are definitely not designed to stand ship-to-ship with an armored battleship which is how we have staved off defeat in numerous skirmishes. We have low numbers of very large, powerful vessels."

"Okay, we have some rail gun capability, but they are low energy in general, so I doubt we'll have any advantage there," I replied, skimming through my tablet computer.

"Timlet," Sarah started, "if we think recon ships have made it to Earth, would they return to Grojiel space to report their findings?"

Timlet looked at Kjino and Revus, and then over to Sarah stating, "It's unlikely. Intelligence indicates they would stay in your home world's system waiting for part or all of a Grojiel battle group to arrive. I think that would take about two weeks to complete, as the Grojiel don't have a complete battle fleet set aside for this sort of thing, it's just too costly. You can probably count on at least one Grojiel battleship eventually arriving to conduct combat or engagement with your government's leadership. Their battleships are huge and have more powerful missiles possessing longer effective ranges, and a much larger crew complement that includes spacer infantry soldiers for holding territory after an initial attack."

I looked at Sarah and Zane, then started thinking out loud, "Okay so we don't have any advantage at all. Kjino, can you help us? Can you give us some missiles that we can use to fight their recon or main fleet? Perhaps launched from the *Algonquin*?"

"Yes, yes, Captain Dave. The situation is not good, but we are working now to provide you with missiles. It is taking some time to generate them, but the station's engineers are working furiously to build them."

Timlet looked from Kjino to me and said, "Our missiles are powerful, explosively, but the Grojiel battleship missiles have a much greater range, giving them a significant stand-off advantage if you engage them. You must employ a combination of erratic movement and countermeasures to confuse their missile tracking systems. In space combat, possessing a longer stand-off effective missile range is critical to success unless one is extremely maneuverable with a combination of sophisticated countermeasures, sprint speed and agility."

"I certainly see how that could be important," I replied.

Timlet continued. "We'll provide you with several of our best missiles and some experimental designs at the request of your engineer, Maria. The experimental missile housings, explosive tips, and trackers are modifiable and our teams will assist you in making the desired modifications while enroute back to your home world. Time is getting short, and you certainly want to get there before the Grojiel battle fleet, if at all possible. Perhaps there's something your people can do with this information to supplement your defense." Timlet motioned to the tablet as he shared technical files concerning the Grojiel weapons and Veeniri missiles with us. I asked Timlet for combat scheme of maneuver recommendations and tactical strategy ideas as we are not a military crew so we are not trained in the art of space combat. He and two of his crew laid out several recommended maneuvers that we could use to seize opportunities and smartly fall back to regroup as needed. Sarah and Zane made a ton of notes during this part of our session. I could see the lights going on in Sarah's eyes as she seemed enlightened by the discussion. "You will do well if you keep your movements randomized and your overall scheme of maneuver simple. Stay focused on using your jump advantage." Timlet finished.

"Thank you Timlet, you've been extremely helpful," I said, looking at the documents and diagrams as they loaded on our tablets.

"Captain Dave," Timlet said as he placed what passed for hands on the table looking straight at me, "the Grojiel are deceptive, but also truthful in that they will do what they say. If they threaten to destroy your moons or a whole outpost to prove a point, they will do it and not be concerned at all about the welfare of your people. They claim to own major parts of this galaxy. They do not want peace. If they don't get what they want legitimately, they will create a false provocation, then skirmish with you, wear you down and beat you with mass, maneuverability, and firepower, over time."

I looked at Zane and Sarah with a solemn stare. This just didn't seem right. How did we get here? Why was all of this happening to us? *Steady Dave*, I told myself as I tried to fake my way back to confidence and a useful conversation with Timlet and the other Veeniri at the table. "I understand that our chances of defeating the Grojiel in space combat are very poor. I'm not sure what to do but we will try to protect our people," I said looking back at Timlet. Man, he was a rough-looking soldier, but, somehow, I think he could sense my desperation.

Timlet responded before I could continue, "Yes, very poor. But that only means you must wield the few advantages that you have exceptionally well." *What? What possible advantages do we have?*

Zane chimed in, "We've got the Gravitron, and that gives us mobility."

I looked down at Zane and nodded my head approvingly as I turned my head to look back at Timlet.

"You have much more than that," said Revus.

Everyone's heads turned to look down the table to Revus. He'd been silent up until now.

"You have more graviscopic ore than has ever existed in our systems in your cargo bay. This means you likely have vast amounts back in your system. Yes, we are very grateful for the amount of ore that you shared with us, but it must be kept secret, as this is one resource the Grojiel would willingly destroy your entire species to control. We will keep the ore you shared with us secret, and we will use it judiciously. You must use this ore to your advantage knowing that the Grojiel have very little of it. This means that sending numerous ships to your system is very costly to them and I suspect they will not send a large fleet initially, which gives you an advantage. Also, your ObjectForge is capable of rapidly manufacturing complex apparatuses in short periods of time. This print-things technology is something we do not have at the same level of sophistication. Use that against the Grojiel too."

I rubbed my temples with my forefingers and replied, "Yes, those are good Revus, but I'm not sure how it helps us against a Grojiel battle group if one shows up," I said, perhaps a little too melodramatically. *Whoa, Dave, you are overthinking this*, I thought to myself. *Need to push the panic-induced anxiety back down a notch.*

"Dave, you also have the ability to communicate with thousands of other species throughout the galaxy. Seek new partnerships and use that against the Grojiel within the Federal system. You have the ability to pursue support and other perspectives that can help you in ways that you can't possibly understand today. That is the Grojiel's weakness. They do not collaborate with others; they only barter for technology that gives them an immediate advantage. They choose not to partner, learn from others, and think in innovative ways."

I considered what Revus said, turning it over again and again in my mind's eye. "You are right Ambassador Revus. There's got to be a pathway to success here, we just need to do the work and find it."

Revus smiled back at me and said, "Now you are holding it right Dave."

Revus often would tell me that I was not holding it correctly. It's an expression they have that I learned means that if a person can't overcome the challenge, it's because the person is not thinking hard enough about the issue at hand or holding the problem in the mind's eye clearly enough to see it from all perspectives.

Sarah and Zane were quietly chatting about something. "Timlet, are the pulsed microwave weapons effective against the Grojiel ships?" Sarah asked excitedly.

"Yes, they are effective against virtually any hardware, but they require a dangerously close employment range to be effective," Timlet replied.

Sarah looked at Zane, and then over to me and replied, "Timlet, can we possibly get one of those pulsed microwave weapons?"

Timlet looked from Sarah to Kjino. Kjino replied, "Yes, yes Sarah, we can give you one, but as they only work at very short ranges, I'm not sure how you would wield such a weapon. The lack of armor on the majority of the *Algonquin*'s hull doesn't set up well for successful close-quarters fighting with a Grojiel battleship."

"Yes, sir, but I have a plan. I think we can make very good use of one of those systems if it's feasible to install onto the *Algonquin*."

I saw Kjino quietly conversing with Timlet. Finally, Timlet looked at Sarah,

"Yes, it will be done. The weapon itself is very small, but the volume of power required is significant, yet should be no problem for the improved *Algonquin*."

Okay, I thought, *this is what we need. Innovation, tactics, thinking outside the box just as Revus said.* I looked down at Isolde as she was typing away on her RexCom. Our conversations continued to focus on how we could best handle the impending engagement with the Grojiel back home and some last-minute logistics issues. I took down a ton of notes and requested Timlet's RexCom address. He happily provided it to me. I pulled the RexCom out of my freshly made leg holster and manipulated the messaging queues to survey new messages. *Huh?* I thought, as a message popped up, *will this be yet another wealthy Prince that just needs a little money today for a big payday later?* You can't make this stuff up. The message that popped up showed up in my Isolde queue. I looked down at her, smiling. Then looked back at the RexCom. "As you know, I'm coming with you. We are bonded as Keretzon," the message said. *Whoa. No that's not good. I thought I was the 'Acting Keretzon' until we found the actual back on Earth. I can't handle more responsibility. She's Kjino's daughter.* So I messaged back to say how kind of an offer that was, but I would have to politely decline, as she's so important on her world, and I didn't want to disrupt any of that. Her response was swift.

"Sorry Dave, *not a request.* I'm going with you. Too much invested, the risk of the Grojiel taking this out on my people is high."

Well crap.

This was looking like a five or six WTFs per hour situation.

The Voyage Home:

Four hours later, we were back on the *Algonquin*, and making final preparations to depart from the Veeniri space dock for the voyage home.

We had two dozen of the Veeniri's best missiles loaded into our main cargo bay with extra seeker units that could steer new missiles once we built them with the ObjectForge. The Veeniri engineers grafted the pulsed microwave weapon's tube array onto the hull and wired it into the direct powerline ring that traversed the ship's keel. It wasn't pretty, but it would do. *Still not completely sure what the plan is there,* I thought to myself, *but I trust Sarah.*

With some positive zeal in my voice, I opened a ship-wide broadcast comms link and said, "Okay team, everyone not going to Earth needs to depart in fifteen minutes. We are launching in thirty minutes rain or shine," I noted the Veeniri engineers looking back at me as Sarah smiled and told them that it was just a colloquialism and that everything was fine. I turned to go back to my quarters to pick up a couple of items when I stopped and looked down at Kjino float-standing right in my path. He looked up at me, slowly extending his three-fingered hand-like appendage.

"Captain Dave, I'm departing as I'm needed back on Bradea." Kjino looked at me with a strange look that I'd never seen before. "Please, please bring my daughter back to me. She is all that I have left in my family. I'm not certain how humans define this feeling called love but I want you to understand I love my daughter a great deal and when you depart, my spirit will sting with fear that something terrible could happen to her. If humans feel the same way about their closest friends and family, then you understand what my translated words are trying to convey. You may have realized this by now, but she truly believes in you. You are the Keretzon for humanity."

Love. It's a complicated thing, that's for sure no matter what species one is. I can feel how earnest Kjino is being with me, and it is a lot to think through in the moment. Steady Dave. I looked down at his hand, gently grasped it and shook it lightly up and down three times. Looking Kjino in the eyes, I carefully released the grip as I said, "Kjino, I'll bring her back. You have my word on this." Kjino looked sad and released my hand.

He simply turned and float-walked out of the bridge. He was tearful. I turned my head to see Bowendi looking at me while standing by Sarah. "He's a great leader in our society. She is a kind yet strong leader but there is a concern by our people that she's leading the Veeniri to certain war with the Grojiel. We can't handle another war. We lost millions of Veeniri, and the cost to our society was incalculable on many other levels."

I looked at Bowendi's face and thought about Isolde.

"He will no doubt return to the Council and tell the story of our recent activities to strengthen our partnerships and political ties. But ultimately the people will viciously judge Ambassador Kjino and Honorable Isolde if these events lead us to another war with the Grojiel," finished Bowendi.

Okay. I need to add that back to the list of things to get right. Fulfill our promise to the Veeniri so they can take over as Council Chair while avoiding all out war.. "Thank you Bowendi," I said.

She smiled at me and said, "Anything for the Keretzon."

I smiled back at her and then turned to float-walk down the passageway to my quarters. *Damn, I've got to be sure we don't start another war between the Veeniri and the Grojiel.* My gut started twisting up again. *The stress of all of this is making me crazy. Gotta think positive, get some space from all these stressors for a few minutes.*

I float-walked into my quarters planning to throw up from all the anxiety but was stunned to see Isolde moving my things around to apparently make room for her things in my closet. *What the...* "Umm, Hi Isolde," I said with my best poker face.

She turned to look at me and said, "I did not know where to stay on the ship as there were no other quarters available."

I stood there stunned. *There has to be a ton of other quarters. WTFs are ratcheting up here all of the sudden. Most of our military complement is not on the ship; we left them on Mars to assist with the Snale Pox outbreak at the request of Agency leadership.* Then, out of nowhere, Zane and Mickey walked into my room as they were allowed to because the door was open, and well, that's the protocol. If the door's open, anyone is welcome.

They both looked over at Isolde, then looked at me, then back to Isolde. "Uh, hi Isolde," Zane said gingerly as he looked over at Mickey then over to me again. "It's great to see you. Are you uh, going to Earth with us?" Zane said with a voice little too highly pitched at the end of his sentence.

"Yes, I am going to Earth with you," she said as she looked over toward me. I noted her cyan color was deadening a bit to become more of a darker hue, which if I was reading it right, meant she was angry or embarrassed.

"Okay gents what can I do for you?" I asked impatiently.

"Well, we uh, thought that you should know that the microwave pulsar thing is uh... well its wired up and ready for a test shot. The uhh, well the Veeniri engineers recommended we do that before jumping to get some... uh, test data."

Now I could see these two were trying to figure out what the hell was going on here. "Yes, yes," I said. *Crap! I sound like Isolde's father.* "Yes, please test it out, get the aiming and tests knocked out. Okay both of you get the hell outta here," I said.

Mickey smiled at me and elbowed Zane, "C'mon XO let's give these two some space."

"Oh, it's not like that Mick..." I said without trying to draw too much attention to Isolde. They departed my quarters, leaving me to negotiate this engagement with Isolde alone.

Well crap.

It was taking longer than anticipated to finish all the modifications and cargo loading. Some two hours later I was back on the bridge going through the punch list for making the graviscopic jump. Everything seemed in order, so I guess we are ready to jump.

Several Veeniri had worked on our systems until the very last moment and had then departed via the tiny space dock trolly with Ambassador Revus and his aid onboard. It's essentially a small shuttle used for moving people and attached tools around while working on ships in the space drydock.

The trolley was taking the last group back to their ships near the dock station, which had been reconfigured for towing as most of the support ships had already undocked and departed. Isolde was sitting in Kjino's old seat with her full space suit on looking nervous as hell. She was making me nervous as I was terrified something would happen to her on my watch and her father would kill me. *Okay, whatever. Gotta stay focused.* "Ready to jump Huang?" I said nonchalantly, as I had already received a thumbs up from Sarah, Mickey, and Zane. I felt emotionally exhausted, and I counted down from five to ensure everyone had a common view of when, exactly when, we'd jump. In fact, I intended to conduct important activities while broadcasting ship-wide for a little while. "Okay folks, jumping in five, four—" I didn't get four fully out of my mouth before the mobile space dock detonated in a violent, exceptionally bright explosion. *Holy crap,* I thought. "Zane, what the hell was that?"

"Checking Sir," was the response from Zane.

Sarah removed her hard-shell helmet, and looked at Huang then back toward Zane and me. "Sir, the attackers are hitting the space dock. We have to help the Veeniri in the trolley shuttle."

What? I considered her statement and started trying to do the math but failed. Somebody attacked the dock because most of the Veeniri ships had already departed. All the security they provided was gone. "Sarah, how far away is the shuttle?" I snapped, getting back into the flow.

Huang responded first, "Sir, the shuttle is less than one hundred kilometers from us."

Okay, I thought. *We have less than a second of margin in which to act.* "Sarah, plot a graviscopic jump one kilometer in front of the shuttle's path—Huang, hit it as soon as she's done." I could see Sarah working furiously to plot something that was so unplanned, I was not sure it would work.

"Got it sir, short jumps are easy to plot. Okay, course plott—" Sarah didn't finish before Huang hit it. ZZPOOF! In a blink we were on top of the shuttle.

"Get that shuttle into cargo bay..." I glanced at my Ops-COP, the ship's common operating picture, looking for a cargo bay with some empty space. "... Cargo Bay 9," finally finishing my own sentence as I opened the bay doors to Cargo Bay 9. It wasn't empty but I knew it should have enough room to hold a good chunk of the shuttle securely until we could maneuver away.

"Sir, moving target indicators heading directly for us," Zane said. "Marking one through three auto tagging," the computer marked the MTI's and projected them on the Holo Map so we could see their course and trajectory.

Isolde floated over to grab my arm which distracted me a bit. "Sarah—" I started before she cut me off.

"Plotting a new jump now," she said.

"Sarah," I said, "it doesn't have to be a long jump, just a safe one to get us away." Huang maneuvered *Big Al* like a champ, but it was not working; he couldn't get the shuttle lined up for Cargo Bay 9's door.

"Uhh, I'm getting a crapload of new radar signals focused in our direction. Yes, heading right for us," Zane said, working off the front sensor array dashboard.

Bowendi chimed in, "They've fired at us, multiple missiles coming in fast with radar trackers—I'm launching countermeasures—pilot, please move the ship."

Move the ship?

I could see Huang working the controls furiously trying to simultaneously set up a shuttle dock while taking evasive action against the missiles. "Sir, I can't get them into the cargo bay. They are off course and navigating away, apparently, they don't see the bay door open and don't understand what we are trying to do."

Craaaaap. "How far away are they?"

"Thirty-three meters," said Sarah.

"Okay, new plan. Maria, get over to the starboard robotic arm and grab them, stuff them as best as possible into Cargo Bay 9 so we can jump. Huang, fly Maria's arm toward the ship, quickly."

Down in engineering, Zane looked over at Maria. She replied, "I've got it," then launched herself at *Algonquin*'s robotic arm control panel. She reached it just in time to slide her helmet off, then slipped her head into the VR headset and grabbed the robotic controls while her left hand hit the power button to turn on the arm. She was disoriented and accidentally swung the arm out wildly toward the shuttle, nearly striking the *Algonquin*. Finally, she regained her perspective in the headset. "Huang," Maria said, with more than a little urgency, "starboard thrust, there, a little more, spin me clockwise about 30 degrees. Okay, closer. Closer. Got It!" Huang executed the thrusts and Maria grabbed the tiny shuttle by firing the wire snare, which wrapped around its hull, and then she deftly maneuvered the arm to put most of the shuttle into Cargo Bay 9. "That's as far as I can get the shuttle into the bay, sir," Maria yelled over the comms link. "I'll hold it in place with the arm as best I can."

"Bay doors closing, sir," Zane said as he closed Cargo Bay 9's doors to fifty percent, which would be good enough to keep most everything inside.

"Mick, Bowendi, will the Gravitron reactor field cover the part of the shuttle that's sticking out of the cargo bay?" I asked as I had flashbacks of our first jump.

"Its good Sir, I've maxed out the reactor's coverage envelope as far as it will go, we have a meter or so to spare" Mickey said.

"Huang, go! Go! Go!" I said as Huang jumped the *Algonquin*. ZZPOOF!

I blinked a couple of times and looked around. "Sarah—" I started but was cut off.

"Sir, we are about one light hour from our previous location. We jumped behind the ships, so despite this being a short jump, it will take them a while to slow down and turn to head back in this direction. That was a tactic Timlet taught us. Bowendi and I estimate we've got about six hours before they could travel to this location, and three hours before missiles could feasibly reach us," Sarah responded. "We need to reset the Gravitron for the next jump."

"Roger, good thinking to jump behind them. Let's keep our sensors focused on looking for any other attackers. Using their momentum against them was really smart Sarah," I responded.

Bowendi broke into my train of thought, "The shuttle is damaged; we've got to get them out of there."

I considered the situation and said, "Maria, fantastic effort—thank you! Mickey, can you get them out of that shuttle?"

"Roger, we're on it. I've got an idea—Huang. Don't move the ship if you can help it, I need a few minutes to make this work," Mickey replied. Mickey and a couple of other crewmen tethered the cargo together and then pushed it all out of Bay 9. Then Maria moved the shuttle into the bay allowing Mickey to pressurize the bay and get the Veeniri out of the shuttle. Maria pulled the damaged shuttle out into space and released it. Finally, Mickey pulled the tethered cargo back into bay 9 and closed the cargo bay doors. *Man, these robotic arms are problem solvers*, I thought as Mickey, Maria the engineering and logistics staff deftly handled the situation.

Ninety minutes later we were once again ready to jump to Earth. Only now we had extra passengers. Revus was on the shuttle with the Veeniri engineers, and man was he happy to be back aboard *Big Al*.

As soon as possible he was back in his seat, clicking through various items on his tablet trying to get caught up. We made room for the Veeniri engineers in the MedBay as some of them did not have hard suits to wear as we jumped, and the MedBay was able to retain pressurization quite well, even when other failures occurred across the ship.

We probably wouldn't always need to be in the condition-red suits, but I thought it was a good idea to wear them for the first few jumps.

As we readied to jump again, I was hopeful everything would go smoothly this time. I looked down at Sarah and opened a private channel. "That was some fantastic navigation, Sarah. Your quick thinking saved our butts back there."

"Thank you," she smiled back at me and said, "You know, I think we have a pretty interesting advantage in using the Gravitron. Just like Revus said, most of the ships either don't have a Gravitron, or it's too costly for them to use it. We can use ours all the time given the amount of ore we've got."

"I agree," I said, giving her a thumbs up. *It's the decisive advantage,* I thought, running through some scenarios in my mind.

"Okay Huang, let's get out of here—our own world needs our help," I said, looking around the bridge at all the differing species, "and we are bringing the alien cavalry... Ready in 5, 4, 3, 2, 1, jump!" I said. And ZZPOOF! We jumped.

Chapter 22: The Odyssey Home

Graviscopic jumps didn't mean we were instantaneously transported across light years. Just like the travel from our solar system to where the Veeniri found us, it took several days of traveling through the Graviscape to get there.

This jump was going well so far and after about four hours with no discernible signs of radiation, I ordered everyone out of Condition Red and back to Condition Green, which meant everything was back to normal.

I wanted everyone to get into as normal a rhythm as possible, so I held a staff huddle and outlined the key tasks we needed to get done, putting some folks on a rest break in order to start twenty-four-hour operations. "First priority is scheme of maneuver, second priority is missiles, and pulse microwave weapon, third priority is armor, and fourth priority is countermeasures. Alex, I need you to start generating a message that we can broadly disseminate as soon as we reach our home system. A message that covers the key points of our little adventure up to now." Everyone discussed their subtasks, providing a timeline of what they thought they could get done over the next twenty-four to forty-eight hours.

Mickey was pretty proud of his work to modify the ObjectForge and vastly accelerate how fast it could generate parts and pieces using some of the tech the Veeniri engineers had given him.

The staff meeting broke up and everyone went in their own directions. I noticed a high-priority message alert light blinking on my RexCom, so I opened it up, logged in, and breezed through a few messages from Isolde's father, Kjino. Then, in my private queue, I noticed a message with flash priority but no originating address. I clicked the message and read it. *What?*

I need to re-read this.

"You need help. So I'm going to give you a push in the right direction."

I decided to reply as my RexCom was connected to the Gravitron's field effect indicating it could send and receive messages using the raw modulation mode. *This must be some kind of spam message,* I thought.

I typed out the message, "Who is this? What do you mean?" and hit send.

Before I could shut down the RexCom, another message appeared nearly instantly in the same private queue:

"I am a friend."

Another message filed in:

"You are not ready for the engagement that awaits—you need help. I will assist you to find help."

I responded with another message: "Who are you?"

Another message popped into the queue:

"A friend."

I responded with: "How do you know we need help? Who are you? I am Captain Dave Murray."

No response.

Well this stinks, probably another spam message.

After a long day of getting caught up on numerous tasks, I decided it was time for some peanut butter. I pulled a peanut butter sandwich out of a wrapper and strapped into the table to savor its flavor. Talking with Zane and Isolde, I showed them both the messages that magically appeared in my RexCom. Zane was the first to offer some insight.

"A friend. Great. Well at least it didn't say it's an enemy," he said with a wry grin on his face. "Maybe it's another spam message," he said as I looked at him to gauge how serious he was.

"I don't think its spam; the way I have this thing configured, unsolicited messages from people not in my contacts should not populate the top-level queues.

"That's right Dave," Isolde said, looking closely at the device in my hand. "It doesn't make sense, there's no way for a message to obfuscate its sender's address; it must be some kind of malfunction."

Zane yawned which caused Isolde to push away from the table in fear. "It's okay Isolde, that's a human body's way of saying that it's tired. It's just an indicator."

Isolde pulled herself back to the table and said, "It looks very aggressive," turning a slightly darker shade of cyan.

Man, these Veeniri are not very good at hiding their emotions, I thought.

"I'm going to check on Bowendi's and Jimmex's work on the missiles. I'll see you later," she said, unstrapping from the table and heading out of the galley.

I sat there for a minute and realized how tired I was.

"I gotta go. Time to get some rest," Zane said as he unbuckled from the table. "Sir, I've got watch in four hours, and you are back in six, you might want to grab some sleep too."

I rubbed my eyes with my fingers, agreeing vociferously in my inner monologue. "Yea, you said it Zane, I'm emotionally exhausted." We both departed the galley, and I went back to my quarters. It didn't take long, and it was like someone flipped my light switch to the off position: out like a light.

I woke up with a little tickle in my nose. I felt so good I didn't want to move. I didn't want to open my eyes or even think about anything. My alarm hadn't gone off yet, so that meant I could just lay there. *That's odd though, I don't get tickles in my nose often*, I thought.

I moved around a little, and then I noticed my bed sort of *squirmed* in an unnatural way. It sort of smelled funny. Not bad. Just different. That's when I opened my eyes, and there she was. Isolde was strapped into bed with me along the front of my body with her back to my front. She was sleeping pretty hard herself.

What the hell is going on here.

I immediately looked at my door, and thankfully it was closed. *What the hell did I do?* Isolde started squirming, and I saw her exotic, oversized eyes flutter a bit then open, looking back at me.

"Dave, are you awake?" she asked.

Uhh, yes, I'm in bed with a freaking alien so, yes, I'm awake, my inner monologue screamed.

"Uhh, yes, I'm awake. When did, *uhh*, you join me?" I asked quietly.

"You said I could '...bunk with you,' and I looked at the meaning of that, and your intent to keep me protected, so I thought this was appropriate. Did I misunderstand? You and I are Keretzon," she said, looking back up at me with those big cyan eyes.

I didn't know what to say, so I just said, "Well it's a little bit unusual for us to sleep together, but I suppose it's okay for now." I carefully pulled myself out of the bed leaving her in it.

She grabbed my hand as I was about to go and said, "Dave, these are important times. Thank you for helping my people as we are helping yours."

I smiled back at her with a furrowed brow and said, "You are right; these are critical moments in our history. We've got to stick together."

She smiled and said something strange. Well maybe not super strange but definitely out of character for her and the moment, "Dave, we have learned that only love can persevere through the tyranny of hate, distance, and greed. Life is so important. Do your people share this philosophy?"

I stared at her, carefully considering what she had said and finally nodded affirmatively saying "Yes Isolde, we share that viewpoint for certain." Her cyan hue brightened briefly, then she let go of my hand and nestled back into the sleeping bag-like bed.

I need a shower, I thought, *yes that's it, a shower.*

That day went really well. We had several missiles built and a plan to install launchers at the right locations on the ship and from the cargo bays. Sarah was working with Mickey, Maria, and the Veeniri engineers to build a longer, larger missile based on the original Veeniri design. Sarah called it the Skip Missile. It was designed with a small Gravitron on board enabling it to jump toward its target and give us a significant standoff range. The Veeniri engineers were amazed that we had so much of the graviscopic ore that we could afford to use it in this fashion.

"This is outstanding," Bowendi said as we stood around the freshly printed first run of missile body Gravitron's.

I decided to ask a couple of questions, "So will this make our missiles strike even faster and harder?"

"No," Bowendi replied, "traveling through the Graviscape doesn't really propel the missile faster; it just allows us to increase our reach by a factor of ten million." She smiled as she continued, "They are very costly in terms of using navigation, and of course the graviscopic ore, so we can't afford to build many of them, but we think we have enough material to build about four missiles."

Sarah said, "We actually have plenty of ore, it's the complex Nav gear that needs to be simple to program and function semi-autonomously; that's the bottleneck."

I nodded looking at all the smart folks collaborating on this effort. "This is excellent work, very clever Sarah."

Huang called over the ship-wide broadcast, "Captain to the bridge, captain to the bridge."

I walked over to the nearest comms panel and asked, "Huang, this is the captain, what's going on?"

Huang's voice came through the panel speaker, "Sir, we are getting some strange readings on the Gravitron's instrument suite. Ambassador Revus recommends you get up here to take a look and discuss the issue."

I looked over at the team working hard on the missile. "Roger, I'm on my way," I said, clicking the comms link off.

"It's exceptionally curious," said Jimmex as he, Revus, and I looked over Huang's shoulder at the Gravitron's instrument dashboard.

"Yes, it's erratic. I agree. What do you recommend?"

"I don't know Captain. I think we should make some more restrictive thresholds. If the activity continues beyond these new thresholds..." Jimmex said as he manipulated the dashboard to create some new settings, "... we should abort the jump and perform some tests and possibly maintenance. Maybe we hurt the system with those super-short jumps that occurred within minutes of one another."

"Agreed. Huang, did you get some rest?"

"Yes, sir, I did. I just relieved Alex about forty minutes ago."

"Okay, let's keep an eye on this, and please let me know if the situation worsens," I said. I spent a few minutes messaging Kjino and updating him on our current status while working through some reports. I strongly suspected that our reports would be reviewed by every government on Earth someday.

I went up to the medical bay to check on Doctor Roth, Abby and the team. "Doc... how are things up this way?" I asked with a grin while shaking hands with him. I noticed Dr. Lindfield and Elainex in the room, so I looked their way with a big smile and said, "Crystal, Elainex it's good to see you as well."

Doc said, "Dave, Crystal's been doing some amazing work with Elainex. Apparently the Veeniri and the Grojiel have a common ancestor."

"Yes, I'm tracking that part Doc."

"Well, the part you may not be tracking is the similarities between Veeniri and human genetic code. Crystal, can you give us a high-level view?"

"Captain, let me draw your attention to this screen where Elainex has converted the code sequences from the Veeniri and Grojiel into a common intermediate language," Crystal pointed to the display on the wall. "Using this language, *here, here* and *here,* you see significant overlapping sequences indicating very similar protein structures between the Veeniri and the Grojiel, with the Grojiel being significantly older as a species," she said pointing to a second screen to the right of the main screen.

Crystal changed the diagram on the main screen and overlayed human genetic code in a translucent layer hovering above the other two code examples. "Now here's the interesting part—Elainex showed me how to extract and encode human DNA using the same intermediate language, and here is what that looks like," she said changing to the next page in the presentation. "Using the intermediate language as a guide we are able to extract the same twelve encoded features."

WTF? This was turning into a two-WTFs-per-hour visit already. "So, what does this mean Crystal?"

Crystal beamed with pride as she smiled and said, "Sir, we think it may mean that Humans, Veeniri, and Grojiel have a few common biological functions, perhaps indicating a biological compatibility, maybe even a distant relationship. We still aren't sure, but evidence is mounting that would indicate this is the case."

"Okay Crystal, this is... well I'm stunned. I thought we had really good evidence of evolution: that life on Earth evolved from slimy water millions of years ago, independent of any seeding effect." Doc chimed in at this point, as he seemed to get that I was about to come cognitively unglued.

"Dave, it's just a hunch, but a good hunch backed by some splendid analysis by Crystal and Elainex. I wouldn't get too worked up about it just yet. You are quite right, the fossil record of Earth clearly depicts a long evolutionary path, but it's hard to say if something wasn't injected at some point along the way, possibly by an asteroid hitting Earth or some other event. That's what they are alluding to."

Elainex jumped in as well, "That's right Captain; we see similarities in the intermediate language, but, as of yet, no direct sequence overlap like we can now see between the Grojiel and Veeniri."

I was stunned into silence as I considered the possibilities that there could be some relationship between our species.

It just seems very unlikely, I thought, *given how far away we are.* "Whoa, this is very interesting. Please keep working on this Crystal; I'd like to hear more," I said, smiling at the group of them. "Crystal, I didn't realize you had a genetics background?"

Crystal replied, "I minored in genetic studies, and I've been getting tutored by Dr. Roth, and he's a pretty good teacher."

My RexCom beeped with an alert signal that I set up to notify me when messages arrived from my anonymous friend.

"Hold on a second, I need to check something," I said as I pulled the device out of my leg holster.

Message from Unknown at Unknown:

"Get ready, it's time to find allies."

That sinking feeling in the pit of my stomach appeared again. I must have frowned.

"Bad news Dave?" Doc said as he read my facial expression.

"Uhh, not sure, just got another message from my anonymous friend that's, well, a bit ambiguous." I said, "I'd better head back to the bridge. Fantastic work team, please keep working to understand any relationships or features we can use to help us on our mission. We need allies so it's great that you are working together to solve problems."

On my way back to the bridge I pondered the potential meanings of this message. Alex was strapped into the pilot's chair, and Zane welcomed me with a puzzled grin. "Captain, you aren't due back here for a couple of hours...."

I looked at Zane and said, "is everything okay? Is the Gravitron working..." *BOOM! CRASH!* Suddenly I felt that all too familiar feeling of the *Algonquin* hitting a major pothole along the road. Unfortunately for me, I wasn't strapped into my seat yet, which resulted in me clunking my head against the edge of one of the dashboard displays.

"Emergency! Emergency!" I heard Zane say over the ship-wide comms system.

I looked out the portal windows and it looked like we were back in normal space. "Zane, are we near Earth?" I said quietly nursing my bruised forehead.

"I don't think so, sir. Checking now," Zane replied with a bit of curiosity in his voice. "No, nowhere close," Zane finally replied.

Revus pushed his way onto the bridge, strapping into his seat near my station. "Dr Roth said you received a message from the anonymous messenger. What did it say?"

I went back through the message content with Revus, Zane, and Alex. We discussed the situation, and Mickey joined the conversation via the comms panel saying that apparently, the Gravitron overloaded and was in auto shutdown mode. It would not be able to be restarted for about thirty hours. "Well..." I started as I looked around the bridge, "crap. Revus, has this sort of thing happened to your people before?" I asked looking at the old Higlian Ambassador.

Revus looked at each of us, and saw, I'm sure, us looking to him for some type of sage advice. "Yes. These types of anomalies have occurred many times, although there is one very distinct difference."

"The message," I said to no one in particular.

"Yes, that's right. It would seem someone or something wants us to look around this area for weapons or help of some sort."

I punched the broadcast button on the comms panel. "Primary staff meet in the main conference room in twenty minutes. It looks like we've been pushed out of the Graviscape back into normal space. The Gravitron is resetting, and we'll be able to try and jump again, if that's the decision, in about thirty hours. Everyone take a look around and see if there was some sort of indicator or ship failure that might have initiated this event." I released the broadcast button and looked around at the team. "Zane, try to figure out where we are; Alex, get us ready to move. Don't go anywhere, but test out the controls—I want to understand what else is broken." I moved over toward Revus and asked him to join me in the conference room.

I pulled out the RexCom and showed him the messages, including the most recent one that he had not seen. He flipped through the different settings, seemingly looking for some type of anomaly that could explain the peculiar traffic.

"Dave, there's nothing wrong here. These messages are very strange, it doesn't make sense, even in raw transport mode there must be an originator, the Federal System requires it." Revus said, handing the RexCom back to me.

"Okay Revus," I replied, putting the RexCom back in its leg holster. "How come you don't carry one of these? I mean your people have had this technology for a long time."

"My people have been using the Graviscape and its technology for thousands of years."

Whoa, I thought. *That's a really long time to have had this tech.*

"We learned that being too connected is not healthy. It's better to put controls on it. You'll see what I mean. Besides, it's the strength of connections not the number. Our best allies were willing to risk their livelihood to help us in our short war with the Grojiel. But we would never allow them to be at risk as there are better opportunities for reconciling our situation in the future. The Grojiel are a young, inexperienced species trying hard to colonize far and wide. Colonization is costly, and it will take time before their culture rebalances. Then perhaps we can have another conversation with them."

People started flowing into the conference room as Revus and I continued to chat. The staff meeting was quick because we didn't really know anything, so we synchronized what we collectively knew, and went about fixing the Gravitron and testing every system on the ship, which took about five hours.

I asked Zane and Sarah to help the sensor crew search for anything relevant in the area. *Maybe there is an "Intergalactic Buy-Ur-Guns-Here" store nearby,* smirked my inner monologue.

I spent a couple of hours working with Isolde on reading and responding to certain messages on the RexCom. The messages would just spool until transport became available. I did enjoy spending time with her. I found her very... interesting.

"It's important that you act and communicate like an ambassador Dave," she said as we worked through the list of the top species to establish communications with. She kept touching my hands with her soft, cyan-colored three-fingered hands.

I looked at her smiling and said, "Isolde, I'm not an ambassador; hell, I'm barely a ship's captain on most days, and definitely a poor communicator on the other days."

She laughed at me softly in the funny squeaking sound the Veeniri some-times produced. She reached over to grab my face between her two hands and touched her soft little nose to my comparatively ginormous nose. *It's funny,* I thought, *she doesn't look quite as alien to me anymore...almost....*

Bam! Bam! Bam! Bam! Several loud pounding sounds struck the hull of the *Algonquin. What the...* I thought. I raced to the bridge, leaving Isolde in my quarters.

Arriving on the bridge a minute later. "Zane, what is pounding our hull!" I yelled as I looked over his shoulder and saw a crap-load of moving target indicators.

"Captain, these, these ball-like things, they are all over us." Bam, Bam, Bam. It was like the *Algonquin* was in some sort of hailstorm only the hail was sticking to the ship's hull. "Huang, get us outta here," I barked as I strapped myself into my seat. "Can't sir, we seem to be surrounded," Huang responded. "Sir, pick up the Holo Map, there's hundreds of the damn things all around us, there's nowhere to go."

I turned on my workstation's power and my eyes got oriented to the data displayed on the screens. *Holy crap, 558 MTI's what the hell is this?* "Zane any ideas?"

"No Captain these things just appeared out of nowhere," Zane replied as Sarah, Bowendi, Revus, and Isolde entered the bridge and strapped themselves in. Bam! Bam! Bam! More and more of these things hit the hull and stuck.

About thirty seconds later Revus said, "They've stopped."

"He's right Captain," Zane said. "From a quick survey, it looks like there are several hundred of those things attached to our hull."

Huang looked back at me and said, "Sir, I'm going with at least a ten here." Revus looked over at me, puzzled by the comment.

"Noted Huang. Noted." The ship's power started blinking off and on. "Oh crap," I said under my breath.

"Dave," Revus said, "these are weapons. They're going to kill our power; best to get everyone into suits if possible."

Roger that, I thought hitting the broadcast button on the Comms panel, "Condition Red, everyone get into a suit, Now! Now! Now! I need reports from all sections when your people are secure." A series of sounds gently popped and snapped like popcorn cooking: Pop! Zriiing! Pop! The ship's power kept flickering on and off.

"Sir, I think these orbs are somehow inductively affecting our power couplings and forcing them to shut down," said Maria.

Mickey jumped in as well, "The orbs have some sort of dampening mechanism; I can't quite make out what they are, but they are wreaking havoc with our power system. I'm going to have to shut down some systems and reduce the reactor output."

A few minutes later Huang turned to look at me and said, "Sir, there's a ship headed this way from behind us. Uhh, it's a big freaking ship."

I hit the optical zoom on the external cameras. *Whoa.* "That doesn't look like a ship," I said showing the image to Revus who was floating over by me. As the ship approached *Big Al*, we could see its mammoth size. It looked like a huge, well, like a huge bubble with some sort of control station mounted on a ring that encircled the bubble.

"It looks like some kind of a probe or perhaps a capture vessel," Revus said.

"Well, it's big whatever it is. Looks like we are going to get frisked again," Zane said incredulously.

"A probe makes sense as these orbs are designed to weaken its prey so the probe can... analyze it," Revus replied.

As the ship approached, our power continued to diminish. In seconds that felt like hours, the gelatinous probe started to attach itself to the *Algonquin*.

As it pressed against *Big Al*'s hull, I could see the probe engulfing an entire half of our ship by pressing its gelatinous body around the ship, almost like it was trying to ingest the *Algonquin*. "Now what?"

"Sir, you better get down here, they just ripped the port side main docking door off," barked Mickey over the comms link.

"On my way," I replied unstrapping myself and bolting out of the bridge. I made it down to the corridor, and as I approached the hatch, well, *former hatch*, there was a very bright greenish-white light bursting towards us through the gelatinous material the alien ship seemed to be made from. I looked over at Mickey and Doc, and they both had sidearms in their gloved hands: .45 caliber pistols. I had nothing, and I turned to see Revus moving in behind me. I stepped closer to the hatch. It had been torn off its hinges by the gelatinous probe covering the hatchway. I was fascinated by the amazing, dazzling lights emanating from somewhere inside the probe's gelatinous body. I stepped into the hatchway, and I noticed a small indentation occurred as I approached the doorway. I stopped. Moved backwards and then forward. The indentation grew deeper as I approached it. "Apparently it wants us to go in there," I said as I glanced back at Doc.

"Here, Dave, take my pistol," said Mickey.

Uhh, me first? I thought. *Steady Dave, Okay, what the hell.*

I took the pistol from his hand and started moving towards the opening in the probe's gelatinous body. As I moved toward it a perfectly spherical passageway with multiple handle-like edges opened like a shallow tunnel. I had to put the pistol into my left leg cargo pocket because I needed my hands to pull myself through the gelatinous passageway. And because I was so scared, I was afraid my trembling hand might accidentally shoot this thing. After several seconds of pulling, I turned my head to look back toward my ship, and I realized I'd gone pretty far: about fifty meters. I was following the path created for me that led to the source of the bright lights. I was getting that sinking sensation in the pit of my stomach as I looked all around and realized that I could be some kind of food for some type of massive creature that eats by swallowing its prey in space. *Keep it cool Dave, stay calm.*

Finally, I could see the colors changing and pulsing in a new way. *Damn, I thought, I hope they aren't trying to communicate with flashing colors or something.* I caught a glimpse of movement and turned to see Revus, Doc, and Mickey floating in the gelatinous passageway right behind me.

"Anything new, Dave?" asked Doc.

"Well, the colors emitted there have changed, and they are pulsing and flashing, but that's about it. Otherwise, it seems that the path stops here at this smooth, clear wall that looks a little different than the rest of this thing. I'm not sure what this means," I replied.

"*I AM NOT SURE WHAT THIS MEANS,*" came a rather loud acoustic broadcast that seemed to be coming from the lights at the end of the passageway.

"Hello there," I said, "I am Dave."

"*HELLO THERE ... I AM DAVE,*" came the immediate reply.

I turned to look at Mickey and Doc to see if they had any ideas, and then Doc pointed back toward the big wall, and I could see a strange translucent shape getting closer to the clear wall. It looked like some sort of round, mechanized floating thing with a couple of projectors attached. Sounds appeared from the wall. Lots of sounds. Clicking, whirling, and irritating screeches.

There, it repeated itself, I thought.

Revus tapped me on the shoulder and said, "Use the RexCom, Dave." I looked at Revus and then fiddled with my space suit to pull it out of my right cargo pocket. I opened the controls and Revus grabbed the hand that I was using to hold the RexCom while he spun the controller into a new sequence of positions that I had not seen before.

The clicking, screeching, and horn-like sounds repeated two more times. Revus replied, "There, it looks like a base ten signaling system. Try sending this..." Revus tapped out a message in Higlian, which automatically converted to English as I flipped the selector to user Dave. The RexCom spat out a bunch of audio clicks and screeches that sounded similar to, but not quite like, the ones emitted from the wall. New sounds were emitted from the wall, and it sounded roughly similar to what we'd just sent with the RexCom. "Dave, did the RexCom decipher it?"

"No, not quite," I replied.

Revus took the RexCom, making some adjustments to linguistic weights in the system just as the strange sounds repeated. We kept trading acoustic noise messages with Revus making adjustments until finally I looked down at the RexCom screen, and it read:

Hello Stranger, what you called?

Excellent, it worked, I thought. I typed another message into the RexCom.

Hello Friend. We are Human.

It released a long, shrill-sounding group of clicks, squeals, and screech sounds. I could see the computerized machine behind the transparent wall become very active with bright, intense blinking and flashing. About forty-five seconds later a loud and somewhat irritating sounding response came from the wall panel. I bent down onto one knee so Doc, Mickey and Revus could see the tiny screen. The message said:

Hello maybe Friend. We are Kromakiks we no kill yet.

"Okay, I think it's starting to work guys; what do we want to try and say next?" I said.

"Ask them to remove the orbs, Dave; they are screwing up our systems," Mickey said with a little stress detected in his voice.

"Okay, good thinking Mick," I replied. And I tapped out the message.

We continued messaging back in forth with the Kromakiks while Revus used the RexCom's configuration interface to iteratively update the RexCom's translation term space with new word meaning information. This was especially important when we got a word's meaning wrong, and we could tell from context.

The RexCom was an amazing piece of equipment, used for millions of years in different forms by an untold number of species across the universe to communicate. Revus explained that the RexCom software and various hardware designs were essentially available via brokers through the Intergalactic Federal Commerce network.

After about two hours of this, an interesting message appeared in the RexCom:

Commander is near—soon meet you. I must stop communicating—please stop.

What the heck did that mean? I looked back at the trio behind me. They shook their heads in unison and finally Alex said, "Maybe he means he needs to take a break, and we should, you know, stop communicating."

"Okay, that makes sense, good thinking Alex. We've got to stay flexible with all the potential for misinterpreting." So, we basically just sat down in the passageway and waited. We tried messaging our unnamed friend, but he never responded.

Zane's voice came in clear over my headset, "Sir, there's a bunch of ships coming in, ETA about thirty minutes. Looks like about fifteen MTIs."

Well crap. That sinking feeling in my stomach was back and feeling a little worse than normal given how vulnerable we were at that moment. *Well, do we stay here? I guess there's no sense in moving yet. Okay stomach, stay with me; I still need to be thinking through the various courses of action, how to respond to threats and any type of attack.* "Roger, thank you Zane."

Luckily, Revus started talking before my paranoid internal monologue could get going. "These might be other Kromakiks Dave; perhaps not a bad thing, and why our friend has stopped communicating. It's waiting on them for some reason. Perhaps this is an AI driven drone."

I thought through how that could work and replied, "Yes, that makes sense—good thinking Revus. Alex, any thoughts?" Alex, Mickey and I continued chatting, but part of my brain was involved with my internal monologue which had partially taken over my thoughts.

This is turning out to be quite an event. Started out to be about a one or a two and then escalated quickly to about a ten WTFs per hour kind of day.

My inner monologue was interrupted by Mickey and Alex's conversation. "That RexCom is saving our butts Dave," Mickey said.

I nodded in agreement, "Yes, it's a critical piece of technology," I said looking back toward Mickey and Revus as we tried to remain calm by settling into some time-wasting small talk.

About forty minutes later, small, bullet-shaped ships surrounded the *Algonquin* as Zane gave us a bit of a play-by-play, and, finally, we started seeing a lot of motion and movement on the other side of the wall. The bright flashing lights moved to the side, and it got dark behind the wall, and we could see basic motion and lights. Then lights began flashing, and we started hearing the familiar screeching, clicking, and squealing sounds, as my eyes tried to refocus a little, and when they did I realized that I could see a bipedal creature on the other side of the wall, just standing there looking at the three of us seated on the passageway floor.

It was a relatively small, odd-looking creature: about four feet tall and looked like, well, it looked like a strange, brown-colored walking grasshopper, wearing some sort of uniform. How bizarre, it looked creepy, ugly, and dangerous all at once. The screeching, clicking, and popping sounds started again.

You emerge near Kromakiks military base. You lucky machine translates, I gave order to destroy first, talk second. Thinking you trick of our enemy.

Then two more Kromakiks stepped into view. So I typed out a message on the RexCom:

We are on long journey to our home world; ship broke down here as we passed by.

Several more Kromakiks appeared behind the leader, the one we were apparently speaking with.

May I board ship? I want to see you, make sure you not a trick by enemy.

I looked back at Mickey, Revus, and Alex. Mickey shrugged his shoulders questioningly and finally said, "Why not?"

Yes. I typed back via RexCom.

I could see the Kromakiks putting some sort of helmet on over their hideous-looking heads, and without ceremony the transparent wall started opening like an iris: starting from the center and flexing open.

We pushed our way back through the Corridor into *Big Al* as ten of the

Kromakiks followed us. We were now in the large room where, so long ago now, we had packaged Doctor Roth so Abby and I could transport him to the Veeniri for the lifesaving surgery.

I motioned to Mickey to close the inner hatch so that I could try and pressurize the room. As Mickey started to move the hatch door, the little Kromakiks started to raise what looked like weapons. Then the apparent leader stepped toward them motioning to lower their weapons.

"Sarah, keep this room sealed, no one makes it outta here, keep the adjacent doors locked." I said as I hit the controls to pressurize the room.

Without a second's thought, Revus waved a tablet in the air and immediately took his helmet off revealing his hairless, six eyed chimpanzee-looking face and skull. I could see from the motion of the Kromakiks they were caught off guard by his actions. "Mickey, Doc, Alex, keep your helmets on," I said as Doc protested my obvious intention to take my helmet off too.

"*We don't know if these little buggers have some type of parasites that will kill us, Dave!*" Doc screeched as I uncoupled my helmet.

Everyone just stood there for a moment looking at one another. The Kromakiks were looking at one another, obviously communicating incessantly inside their helmets.

Finally, the lead Kromakik took its helmet off, and holy crap, was it bizarre looking. The clicks and screeches started emanating from a device on the lead Kromakik's suit as the corresponding messages came across the RexCom which was in a bit of a death grip in my hands:

This air weak but tolerable.

Me Billee what you?

How far you go to home?

I looked at the messages and messaged back:

Me Dave

We from far, far away

The Kromakiks leader responded:

How you ship travel far?

Oh boy, not sure we've sufficiently developed enough language to have this conversation. Revus, seemingly sensing my concern, took the RexCom and messaged back to the Kromakiks:

My world different and farther away

Me help Dave and his people fight enemy.

The Kromakiks seemed to consider this and replied with two very key messages:

We do war long time, good at war.

You show us how to travel far—we help you fight enemy.

I looked at my team and took the RexCom back from Revus who was already attempting to hand it back to me.

YES.

I typed in another response message, and before sending it, I carefully bent down onto one knee close to the lead Kromakik. It didn't move in fear at all. I looked closely into its face and triggered the message to be sent.

We be friends.

As the message came out, I slowly raised my hand to the little creature who used its gloved hand to reach out and place its hand on top of mine as it typed.

Yes, we be friends.

The leader returned to its ship while a couple of the Kromakiks stayed behind working with Revus, Mickey, and Alex to work out a basic messaging syntax. They also focused on defining a way for us to transmit and receive messages using X band radio signals, as this was the Kromakiks' preferred method for communicating.

I put my helmet back on and went to MedBay for an examination by Doc. In one of the isolation chambers, I exited my suit and Doc scanned the crap out of me while griping at me the whole time. "Dammit Dave, you just can't take chances like that; there's a lot more at stake here than messing with these overgrown grasshoppers."

"Doc, I'm sorry. Yes you are quite right—can you please just scan me to help me understand if I'm riddled with disease, bacteria, or parasites?"

Doc proceeded to go on a rant about these different species and how dangerous it might be to just willy-nilly start rubbing elbows. Doc was just letting off steam, so I tried to ignore his angst. I offered Doc a bribe of sharing my platinum-class peanut butter with him if he would stop griping at me, which made him calm down a little and even smile.

We managed to make good progress over the next twenty-four hours, with everyone leaning into the key tasks. My relationship with Billee improved to the point where he let Doc, Elainex, and Freishe do an examination of him in the MedBay isolation room without his suit on. Freishe was the Veeniri doctor and biologist who helped Doctor Roth get his implants working properly again after the initial major surgery that took place back at the Veeniri station.

A few hours later, as best as the experts could tell, everyone on our ship agreed that there was nothing really toxic or deadly about the Kromakiks or their biome. We were very biologically incompatible, but nothing was preventing us from interacting with one another, so that was good.

On the third day, I was eating my beloved peanut butter sandwich while meeting with the team in engineering. Billee kept floating toward me getting into my personal space. Each time I gently pushed him away.

"Dave, let me try that, its scent is so good."

I smiled at Billee and replied, "Sorry Billee, I don't think so, this peanut butter is a very powerful nutrient; it might make you sick."

Billee seemed agitated and replied, "Dave, you airbags are so frail, you must keep from harshness of space. Kromakiks strong; let me have a try."

"No way grasshopper, the last thing that needs to happen is for me to poison our newest friend and ally."

I quickly finished the sandwich to avoid further friction and looked over at Doc who was grinning at me after Billee called me an airbag. I mouthed the word "Airbag" without saying it over towards Doc. He chuckled and replied, "Yea, they call us Airbags because we use lungs to breathe in and out and they don't." Doc then gestured toward one of the Kromakiks that he'd been working with, one named "Angel," who had been helping Doc to sort out all the biological differences. Elainex, the wise old Higlian anthropologist, helped Doctor Roth and Angel figure out how safe it was to interact, and Angel turned its back to show me the holes in its body that Doc was referring to.

Wow, no lungs, that is weird, I thought. "Doc, how the hell do they breathe then?"

Doc looked back at me and smiled, "They breathe very much like insects back on Earth: they have breathing holes where air passes through these areas here and here," pointing to the holes in the back part of his new friend Angel. "They can sort of fan the air across their holes using these internal fan-shaped protrusions. It's quite ingenious as because of it they can survive a wide variety of environments."

Absolutely astounding, I thought. It would take us years to fully comprehend these other species. Hell, we didn't really even understand our own bodies with significant detail.

Later in the day, I talked with Billee and Zane about how we could enable some of their ships with Gravitrons so they could travel back to Earth and help us fight the Grojiel if they started a confrontation. You know, build a partnership.

Earlier, Zane had privately discussed with me his concerns about equipping a warlike species with the capability to jump into our home system.

A valid concern to be sure, but I told him that we'd carefully control the amount of crystals we gave them to prevent them from attacking us themselves. Zane still was not comfortable, but he accepted the answer and moved on as I had begun discussing the orb technology that Billee's people had used against the *Algonquin*: apparently it takes a large number of orbs to disrupt and overwhelm power systems, but only a few to attach and then roll toward a weak point or part of the ship and explode. Billee said he could have destroyed the *Algonquin* with only three orbs because of the lack of defensive shielding, but bleeding and disrupting power was always better as it typically pushed enemies to negotiate rather than fight.

The orb technology was critical in the war with their enemy. We talked about our species' respective cultures and problems, and I found that Billee was insightful in both wisdom and compassion. Billee hated war and shifted our discussion to talk about unique forms of life on his home planet. He described what I imagined to be beautiful flowers or trees. These flowers were an important part of their culture and important to their physiology somehow. Overall, my impression was that the Kromakiks were an odd yet amazing species. Well, at least from this limited perspective.

###

"Damn it, I do not understand why this isn't working!" exclaimed Mickey to Maria as she nodded in agreement with a frustrated look on her face. We'd been trying to build the Kromakiks their own ship-sized Gravitron reactor, but every prototype had failed in testing. Despite the Kromakiks' ships being much smaller, the proportionately scaled reactors still didn't function properly. Mickey and Maria were getting very frustrated. "I can't figure this out, Dave," complained Mickey, "we've generated several of the really small Gravitrons that appear to work once or twice for the advanced missiles we are building but making a Kromakik-ship-sized reactor isn't working, and I don't know why. The *Algonquin*'s Gravitron isn't strong enough to bring their ships through to our solar system, and these prototypes are not even close to working right and the clock is ticking."

Jimmex commented that building the slightly larger Gravitron was problematic when the ObjectForge got to the part where it generated the sixteen-way quantum-grav-magnetic chamber. The chamber wasn't tuned correctly for the power and size of the field effect, and just didn't work and would need to be reshaped, which would take days of modeling and testing. Days that we could not afford to spend sitting idly by while the Grojiel engaged humanity without us.

After another day of trying, Zane and Maria held a sync session down in engineering near the ObjectForge test harness that we'd been using to test the newer ship-sized Gravitrons. Mid conversation, Zane leaned over toward me. "Sir, we've been here for nearly four days; we really need to get home. We have no idea how long it will take for the Grojiel's battle fleet to reach Earth. Besides, a single, well-armed ship like the Grojiel recon vessel could wreak havoc across our relatively defenseless system. I'm guessing that ship's been there for several days by now."

Zane had a solemn, serious look on his face. Then, I looked across the room at Isolde, Mickey, Maria, Doctor Roth, Billee, Elainex, Angel, and finally over at Revus.

I thought about options and the best path forward. That sinking feeling in the pit of my gut was back. Everyone appeared to have heard Zane's comment and were stone quiet. I looked back to Zane. Then while scanning across the faces peering back at me, I said out loud to no one in particular, "If we can help the Kromakiks by building Gravitrons for their ships, they can come with us back to Earth and help us fight against the Grojiel." I kept the public conversation with myself going, "Without them we have limited advantages. But we can't wait too much longer. We have to at least help the leaders on Earth understand what's going on, with the background that perhaps there's something they can do that we aren't aware of." I focused my gaze on Revus. "Revus, what do you think? Should we leave immediately or try to equip the Kromakiks' ships?"

Revus looked at me with what I'd come to learn was a slight smile and said, "You know the answer, Dave."

Images of Earth's destruction from orbit flashed through my mind's eye as I felt the weight of humanity's survival bearing down on every decision. "I don't. I don't know if we should stay and try to bring the Kromakiks with us, or just go and hope that the weapons you and the Veeniri provided us will be sufficient."

"If you don't know the answer Dave, you are not holding it right," Revus replied.

This was the same damned irritating answer I'd heard many times from Revus when I'd asked him for his advice.

I'd come to understand that he meant that I was not thinking hard enough about the problem, and I was not holding the whole problem in my mind's eye clearly enough to solve it. *Well crap.*

Isolde floated over to me and touched my face with her long, three-fingered, cyan-blue hand saying softly, "You..." she paused, and it seemed that touching my face caused her eyes to flutter and to pulse brighter in a slight cyan hue that looked oddly beautiful. She continued, "need to leverage your advantages, Dave. Especially the comparatively unlimited amount of graviscopic ore which Maria now knows how to process into crystals to feed the Gravitron reactor. Jumping consumes the crystals quickly, yet your ship can jump often and far thanks to your near endless supply. The Grojiel don't have the same luxury. To them every jump comes at a huge cost in terms of graviscopic material. And they must constantly be concerned about how much crystal it takes them to jump home lest they end up stranded."

Revus jumped back in, "You also have allies. Allies that you can collaborate with," he said pointing to the RexCom. "The Veeniri are your allies; now the Kromakiks are your allies," Revus said pointing at Billee.

Billee looked up at me and inserted a translated sentence, "Yes, we allies with you, oversized airbags."

As he said it, his face shifted into a very broad, tooth-filled smile. At least I hoped that was a smile as his grin was full of razor-sharp-looking teeth.

I recalled how all this went down, the Snale Pox emergency, the drama on Mars, and all the potential for disaster we had overcome. We'd already beat the odds quite a few times.... Pushing it down, controlling it for once, I felt a calm peaceful state come over me. Somehow, I tamed that damned anxiety-ridden, paranoid inner monologue, at least this time. I had a good idea what needed to be done. I looked over into Isolde's eyes and smiled as I scanned the other faces in the room confidently saying, "Thank you. Thank you all, you are of course quite right."

Isolde's cyan hue pulsed a shade brighter as I turned and looked over at Zane with confidence and said, "Zane, get the ship ready; we're going home." I floated over to the intercom and punched the broadcast button. "Okay folks we are going home, *time now*. Pre jump huddle in thirty minutes in the main conference room. We need to do these jumps by the numbers and be sure we don't make a silly mistake. Sarah, I want you and Zane to try and optimize the offensive and defensive scheme of maneuver. Let's leverage the graviscopic jump advantage. Keep it simple but let's have some preplanned maneuvers ready for various situations. We also need the SITREP message to be ready for immediate broadcast as soon as we get into our home system." I felt more confident than ever as I voiced my plan. So this was what it felt like to "hold it" right.

Everyone acknowledged their tasks and Zane bolted back to the bridge to orchestrate the planning and jump.

I turned to Billee and said, "I'm sorry Billee; we have to go. Time is our enemy in this situation. It waits for no one. I give you my word that I will return," then I stuck my hand out for him to touch in the odd sort of half handshake we'd seemed to develop together.

Billee looked at me and again gave me that frightfully aggressive-looking smile and said, "No, Dave, we go with you. We can breathe your air well enough," and he pointed to Angel, and then back to himself. "We need help; you need our help. We allies, Besides, you not soldier, don't know how to fight. I help your crew make tactics." he said as though he'd just added the word allies to his vocabulary.

Ahh, okay, well crap. I don't know how this will work but what the hell, we do need allies.

Billee continued, "I go get supplies from my ship and be back shortly. Your airbag food is disgusting."

I smiled at Billee as we seemed to have developed a directly worded relationship where we could be honest with one another without getting too offended. He always spoke straight to the point compared to the other species we'd met. "Okay Billee," I said, giggling slightly, "I'll ask Mickey and Maria to help you get settled in. Most kind of you to join us. I don't know when we can bring you back home, but you have my word it will be done as soon as I can."

A new thought just struck me as I considered having Billee and Angel aboard the *Algonquin* for the return flight. "Say Billee, I have an idea, what do you think about this?" I said as I asked him a question about his ship.

Billee pondered my question, looked at Angel and exchanged some messages on their tablet computers before looking back at me saying, "Interesting. Okay. We are all in. We trust new ally. The cost of missing this opportunity is great even if we die in your airbag war." Billee reached out what passed for a Kromakik's hand, so I offered my hand again, and this time Billee shook my hand aggressively. "I learn this from others, Kromakiks fast learners," he smiled up at me with that fearsome multi-toothed grin.

Strong handshake from such a small being, I thought. But I felt good about having another ally aboard as we headed home to Earth.

I stopped briefly to pass along some new orders to Maria and Mickey, then headed to MedBay to see Doc and check in on Abby. Talking to Doc relaxes me and increases my self-confidence and talking to Abby is... well, mesmerizing. Abby and I had coffee and talked for a while as I poked at my tablet computer working on small tasks. Our engagement ended in another wonderful hug.

Later, we all met in the bridge conference room, and as I looked around the large table with all the various species strapped to their seats, I couldn't help but think of how amazing the last several weeks had been.

I felt proud of the collective group and all that we'd accomplished, but I also couldn't keep that sinking feeling out of the pit of my gut. What was happening back on Earth? Had the Grojiel attacked our colonies? Had my actions somehow resulted in the destruction or enslavement of humanity?

"Dave," Zane whispered as he nudged me with his hand.

I snapped back into the moment and realized that everyone was looking at me.

Trying to play it off, looking down at my tablet computer, I started speaking to the group in a serious tone. "Okay, let's go over the pre jump punch list," and we began working our way rather quickly through the list as we had started to build up some jump process muscle-memory.

Zane, Sarah and Huang laid out their plans for how we'd jump into our system and try to quickly find a message buoy and upload the SITREP message that we'd generated. The SITREP comprehensively laid out what had happened to us up to now and as much detail as we could provide about the inbound Grojiel ships. The buoy system would then broadcast our message, widely disseminating it to anyone with an agency-compatible comms system—which is pretty much everyone.

"Yes, this is good, Sarah. Brilliant," I said, "and this will ensure the word gets out no matter what happens to us."

Sarah and Huang went on, describing the plan to find the Grojiel ships and figure out how to engage with them via missiles and maneuver if hostilities were initiated. Apparently Billee's tactical combat knowledge was essential to their planning.

It was a good plan. Zane and Mickey chimed in about how we'd use a combination of Veeniri anti-missile countermeasures and decoy emitter drones designed to make the *Algonquin* a difficult target to track and strike.

Looking over at Zane, I asked about our own rail gun and if it was capable of operating.

"Yes, sir, it's ready," Zane said proudly as he glanced over at Mickey.

Mickey chimed in with, "We've upgraded the railgun sir; I think you'll find it packs a punch now despite only being able to fire twice every ten minutes." I took a note to check the specs later, smiled back at the team and dismissed everyone from the meeting.

After the meeting broke up, Revus sidled up to me with Isolde and said, "Dave, if the battle fleet has arrived, your chances of defeating them are low. If that occurs, we must be prepared to change tactics and consider how to engage them politically using the council's authority. You must consider how to use Kjino's position to stall, giving us an opportunity to gain some kind of advantage."

I smiled at Revus and then Isolde and replied, "I've been thinking about that, and I have an idea...."

Chapter 23: Clash of the Airbags

We jumped back into our solar system. "Stars line up, sir, we are home!" Sarah said with excitement as she lightly punched Huang in the arm.

"Good stuff," I replied, "where are we?"

Sarah replied, "Sir, we are about two standard propulsion hours from Mars, and ninety hours to Earth. They happen to be pretty close in their orbits right now."

"Nearest telecommunications buoy?" I replied.

Huang was the first to identify a buoy nearby. "Sir, there's an M-Buoy that we can hit with the comms lasers within about six minutes of travel, will that work?"

"Roger," I replied. M-Buoys are maneuverable, hence the M, and are constantly traveling in a large, slow, circular pattern. They connect to several other buoys resulting in a mesh network to optimize messaging security and transport across our solar system. I looked around the ship at the crew, "Any issues?" Everyone was excitedly chatting on sub channels about at least being back in our own solar system. No one replied so that was a good thing. "Zane, what are the sensors showing us?"

Zane kept shaking his head as he said, "Working on it, sir."

I messaged Kjino via RexCom and noticed a few priority messages from other species that I'd met during our initial Council of Civilization meeting. Six minutes later we laser linked with the M-Buoy to upload our message, only to find about 10,000 messages for download.

"Lots of concerns about our whereabouts, sir," Zane said as he started sifting through the message queue, beginning with the priority messages. I clicked to open the latest priority message about the same time as Zane. He looked back at me and mouthed one word, "Mars."

"Huang increase speed to Mars," I tried to remain calm as we accelerated. Debris struck the *Algonquin* from several directions as we got close enough for ship-to-shore video comms. I punched the direct comms link button on my workstation.

As Huang complained about space debris everywhere in our path, Chief Gerrard's weary face appeared on the comms screen. "Dave, where the hell have you been? What have you gotten us into?"

Whoa. That was very unlike the straight-laced Chief: to use profanity over a semi-public comms link. That sinking feeling in the pit of my stomach started growing. "Chief," I started, "we just returned. We fell into some kind of space anomaly, and it transported us light years away. It took us weeks to figure out how to get back."

He looked at me with an incredulous grimace on his face.

"Are they here, the aliens? The Grojiel?"

He nodded affirmatively and responded, "Yes, they arrived a few days ago we think, or longer, we are just not sure. What the hell happened to your ship, it looks strange?" he said as he barked orders to people behind him.

"Chief, it's a long story, it'd be best if you can tell me where they are or where they went. We'll send you a detailed SITREP to catch you up on the details."

He looked around and signed a document on a tablet that someone thrust into his face. "They showed up and demanded that we surrender and sign an immediate treaty which we declined."

I could see the lines in Gerrard's face tighten as he cognitively relived the shocking experience.

"We told them no and to prove how destructive they could be they destroyed Phobos station with some kind of massive missile attack, and then they fired on our colony killing hundreds. Our water and air generators are damaged and the situation here is critical."

I could feel anger welling up inside my mind and it was not helping my twisting gut. *Tap. Tap. Tap. Tap.* The taps on my shoulder were by Revus.

"We cannot stay still Dave; we must keep moving."

Crap. Of course, we'll be a sitting duck if we sit still. "Huang, evasive maneuvers, execute, now! Now! Zane any sign of the Grojiel ships on the sensors?" I looked back at Gerrard on the screen, "Chief, where are they; do you know where they are?"

He shook a strained and red-eyed face back at me and said, "We think they left for Earth, about ninety hours ago."

Ninety hours ago?! Well crap.

"How many ships were there?"

"Just one as far as we could tell," he responded.

I looked at the camera view of Mars colony: there was smoke, wreckage and damage everywhere. Gerrard's face grew sullen as he continued, "The only success came from a brave act of heroism. One of the skylark pilots rammed the ship." Gerrard started to stiffen as he raised his chin. "That ship outmaneuvered our rail-gun rounds, and the pilot gave his life to hit the ship with his skylark out of sheer desperation."

Zane tapped my leg to get my attention and whispered, "If that ship departed that long ago, they'd be getting close to Earth or at least Earth station by now."

I nodded to Zane, "Chief, we gotta go; I just sent you the SITREP message. It's the same one we uploaded to the telecommunications buoys so everyone should have the story soon."

Sarah chimed in quietly, "I retransmitted the whole message to the Mars colony directly—they all should have it."

I could tell Sarah was heavily impacted at seeing all the death and destruction the cameras depicted below.

"Dave, please be careful, they have some kind of stealth missiles that we couldn't track or see. They took out several of our skylarks in a single volley," Gerrard said as he turned to bark out orders to folks around him.

I squinted my eyes a little as I pondered our future steps. Looking directly into Chief Gerrard's eyes I confidently said. "We'll stop them Chief, and we'll be back to help." Then closed the channel. "Zane, execute a jump to Earth, and bring us in high above Earth Station, furthest away from earth so we can get a lay of the situation."

Earth Station is a massive ring-based spaceport orbiting Earth. We jumped. ZZPOOF! In seconds for us, we were there. 10,000 kilometers below us was Earth Station and planet Earth shone in the distance below the station. Alex was the first to speak, "Sir, we are receiving a flood of communications."

I looked around at my workstation monitors to review various external cameras and sensor feeds. A few kilometers away from the great ringed Space Port, I could see three ships in the tight arrow pattern: the pattern that the Veeniri had described to us.

"That is the battle group, A single battleship with two lightly armored support freighters" Revus said.

Zane piped in, "Sir, SITREPs are coming in from skylarks all over the place. The Grojiel fired on the station. And look, they've blown a massive hole in it."

Zane wasn't kidding. The battle group had punched a huge hole in the station. "Somebody get eyes on that recon ship," I said as I noted a massive load of MTI data reeling into my computer and holographic events display.

I flipped through the comms channels looking for the one that would hail the Grojiel battle group according to the Veeniri experts. There were tons of MTIs, but most had an identification code indicating it was an agency or other known ship or was marked as debris. The three alien ships were depicted as unidentified enemy spacecraft. Revus looked toward Isolde and then tapped my shoulder, drawing my attention. They were both staring at me as Revus said, "Dave, don't contact them just yet. The Grojiel only respect a strong show of force or the sharp edge of an expertly targeted political statement. Right now, you possess the element of surprise, don't waste it." I stared at Revus as I considered his comment.

Good point, the Grojiel are probably not expecting a missile attack using peer-level tech that's been optimized for explosive penetration power. We need to attack while we can. The time for talk is not yet upon us.

I could see the spaceport burning, and I could only imagine the fear and despair that must be rampant on the station and on Earth.

"Huang, ready maneuver Romeo-Mike. Sarah, on order be ready to fire missiles one thru five at the battleship. Fire missiles six through twenty at the freighters. We need to fire at close range so they can't react, that's our only tactical advantage." Huang readied his navigation controls and I could see from his hand movements that he was mentally rehearsing the Romeo-Mike maneuver. It would jump the *Algonquin* in close, closer still, and then immediately jump back out, allowing for the firing of all missiles while distracting the enemy by focusing them on the *Algonquin*'s erratic movements.

Finally, Sarah came back with, "Missiles are armed and tracking their targets. We are ready to jump."

I nodded and replied, "Execute maneuver: now!"

ZZPOOF! Big Al blinked out of normal space and then back after a very short jump. "First five missiles away," Zane said as Huang then executed the second jump. ZZPOOF! *Big Al* blinked out and back again. A different visual perspective was shown on screen of the battle group as we were very close to them after the second jump. "Missiles six through twenty are away," Zane said again as I watched on screen for any damage. There was none yet: power systems blinked for a second, and then again.

"Dave jump, quickly! We are in range of the pulse weapons!" Revus said just as Huang tried to jump.

"I can't jump! I'm maneuvering away!" said Huang. "Power isn't stable enough to jump!"

"Mickey!" I yelled.

"I'm on it!" he replied. Then he said, "Hit it now Huang!" ZZPOOF! We jumped away from the enemy battle fleet.

I had just asked Zane what happened when Alex piped in first, "Sir, based on the sensors, we moved just into range of the enemy's microwave pulse weapons and took a glancing blow which scrambled our power system controllers for a moment. If Huang hadn't maneuvered around immediately, they'd have scored a direct hit and we'd be toast."

Mickey chimed in with, "I tied the emergency capacitor array into the Gravitron power circuits, the way Jimmex designed for emergency use. Jimmex saved our butts. We can't do that trick again for at least thirty minutes, as it takes a while to properly charge the massive capacitor bank."

I looked over at Isolde and she smiled, and I said, "Roger that Mick—Veeniri and Higlians to the rescue once again."

My internal monologue started to dwell on the mistake. *Crap, we didn't plan for them to be so responsive. Well, we can't make that mistake again, after all, they are a professional combat space fleet, and we are a space colonization RV/auxiliary ship.*

Explosions erupted on screen as every single missile hit its target. Both smaller freighters started drifting out of control, but the big one didn't seem to receive any damage. It started maneuvering around sharply.

Oh crap, I thought.

The green signal indicator light at the top of my display screen lit and I clicked the accept session button as the face of Admiral Parakto appeared in the center of the screen. "Captain Murray, you've attacked my fleet, this is an act of war!"

"You attacked us first, admiral; now stand down and jump out of our system or be destroyed. Sarah, arm missiles twenty-one through thirty and prepare to launch on my signal," I called out loudly so the admiral could hear.

"Dave we must keep moving, launching countermeasures and decoy drones," Revus said. "They've surely fired missiles at us by now."

"Huang jump us to Zenith, quickly." Zenith was our coded signal to quick jump far away, at least 200,000 kilometers in a semi-random direction.

Zane suddenly yelled out, "Inbound! Fast movers!" as, *ZZPOOF!* we jumped to the zenith position.

Just. In. Time.

"Holy crap! That was close," Zane said. "Great jump Huang."

Huang replied, "Don't thank me; thank Chief Romero for holding the power on the Gravitron."

I mentally agreed as Alex chimed in, "I've been in comms with Agency leadership for the past few minutes. The situation on the station is... *its bad.* They've lost at least 400 people, and the station is no longer spinning fast enough to create its needed gravity."

Well crap.

"Thanks Alex; did you tell them about our situation?"

"Yes, sir, they've received our SITREP message and have a ton of questions which I'm trying to answer but the current fight has got both of our attention."

I thought about the next steps and said, "Alex, do they have any Skylarks left that can verify those two freighters are out of commission while we focus on the battleship?"

Seconds later, Alex responded, "Roger, they've got a lot of defensive missiles on the protection platforms and a wing of Skylarks plus another wing from the belt are inbound."

Revus cut Alex off, "Dave...."

I looked over at Revus who was tapping me on the shoulder. I immediately turned back toward Huang and said, "Right, time to move again. Huang, jump maneuver rainbow. Execute." Rainbow is a series of zig-zagging jumps like we had been doing, but jumping in a completely randomized pattern of distances and directions. "Alex, tell them to focus on the disabled ships. Tear them a new one, we are going after the big ship. Anybody seen that dammed recon ship?"

Crickets.

The signal light blinked again, and the Grojiel battle fleet admiral's face popped back onto the screen.

"Dave," Revus said to me quietly, "now is a small window to talk but only if you are holding it right."

I watched him push himself back to his seat and strap in. I turned back to the comms screen and said, "Admiral, you are outmatched and out-gunned. Stand down and jump out of our system." I saw the admiral's face contort into an even uglier and more angry looking expression.

"You... have US outgunned, *Human? I think not!*"

My stomach twisted into knots as I looked over at Revus.

He looked back at me and whispered, "You have it in hand, Dave."

I looked over at Zane and Sarah, and they were staring at me along with Isolde. I turned back to the screen, "This is your last chance, Admiral," I said as cool and confidently as I could.

A sudden loud crash occurred; an explosion jerked the *Algonquin* around, and it started to spin nose-over-tail, twisting out of control. We'd been hit.

I banged my head against the computer console as I heard the admiral's words, "I don't think so Human. This system is now subject to the Grojiel Federal Empire as it falls within our legal boundary."

"Huang!" I screamed and then, *ZZPOOF!* We jumped.

This time we jumped our ship while spinning out of control the entire time. I guessed the Graviscape didn't care if we were spinning and twisting or sitting perfectly still as we entered and exited the Graviscape. Slowly and steadily, Huang stopped the spinning and twisting. *Ohh. I'm so nauseous,* I thought to myself.

"Oh crap," Zane said as he unstrapped and bolted out of the bridge.

Oh crap indeed. I saw the damage to the top rear of the ship. I rubbed my eyes to try and push the headache pain out of my skull.

About sixty seconds later Doc called in, "Sir, we've got some injuries down here. We are triaging them now."

Zane said, "Sir, it looks like we took a missile into *Ranger-1*. Sort of lucky, as it was packed with equipment that we've been moving around to make additional room in the cargo holds so it absorbed the brunt of the missile's force." *Ranger-1* was docked in its half-hangar on the top rear of the *Algonquin* when it was struck by the Grojiel missile. *Wow, We were very lucky,* I thought.

"Any critical damage to the hull?" I replied over the comms link.

"Yes sir, the surgical triage bay has several gaping holes as many parts of Ranger-1 ripped holes in the hull. It's serious but I think we can fix them. We've got to keep everyone below the triage deck until we can make repairs. The concussive force of the explosion really shook us up."

I thought about that and considered what to do next. "Doc, Zane, Mickey, evacuate the folks out of there, we'll try to patch later—we've got a fight to finish."

Chapter 24: Holding it Right

A few minutes later, we had *Big Al* back under control, and Doc, Gina and Abby patched folks up as best they could while strapping everyone and everything down in the MedBay.

"Sarah, I thought our jump pattern, would make us an impossible target for the Grojiel battleship's missile systems based on the analysis from Timlet?"

Sarah had started to reply when Revus said, "It was the recon ship, Dave; we must find it and destroy it. One of the large missiles from the Grojiel battleship would have destroyed us. We have to keep moving and using the countermeasures."

"Alex, get on the horn with HQ and see if anyone can track that damn recon ship in all this debris. Huang, are you ready? Sarah, do we have jumps preprogrammed? We need to go back after the admiral as soon as possible. The advantage of our surprise attack is gone, and they are no doubt plotting ways to attack us."

"Give me two more minutes, Sir," Sarah worked furiously to plot jumps and stuff them into the complicated jump sequencer.

Alex's voice was very excited when he said, "HQ found it: the recon ship is painted as MTI 2163. Use the live feed off the logistics autonav array. I'm piping it into the ship's Holo Map."

Excellent. The break we needed. It will be hard for the Recon ship to hide now that the Agency's massive autonav sensor array has its features tagged. I looked at the map and spun it around.

"Okay, here's a new plan people: pick up your Holo Map," I said as everyone flipped over to display a copy of my map. I painted two jump destinations and two missile launches, followed by two more jumps, and three more missile launches, and then an immediate jump back to a distant location like the one we were in. Sarah and Huang acknowledged the changes and started prepping for the jumps.

The green comms indicator lit up again as the admiral's face appeared, "Captain, it looks like you recovered from my punch. Now you must stand down. Jump away and stay away. The more you fight the harder we will be on your people."

Well now that sounds just like a big freaking bully. "Sorry, Admiral, I'm having a few problems here, putting out fires and such, so why don't you just *screw off* for a few minutes?" And this time I cut the comms signal. "Are we ready?"

"Check, Sir," said Sarah.

"Roger sir, ready to go," said Huang.

"Mickey, Maria, are we ready with the missiles?"

Maria answered back, "Sir, we only have four missiles left that check out right now. Mickey's working on the rest, but we only have four that passed preflight checks."

Well crap. "Okay, Sarah, adjust the missile launch, two and two," I said as Sarah gave me a thumbs up. "Okay people we jump in five seconds. Four... three... two... one... *Jump! Now!* ZZPOOF! And just like that we jumped and fired, then jumped and fired again and then jumped back out.

"Direct hit on the Admiral's battleship and solid proximity hit on the recon ship. Firing from such close range really gives us an advantage. They have almost no time to react and launch countermeasures," Zane said.

Alex responded with, "Earth station reports the recon ship is twisting erratically and on fire, but the admiral's flagship sustained minimal damage and is moving toward the station. The concern is it could fire on the station again, or ram it."

Well crap. I didn't count on that last part.

"Sarah, I want you to execute a sequence of jumps," I began, but before I could complete my sentence Mickey broke in.

"Sir, I need to swap out the graviscopic crystals now."

Now? I thought.

"The current crystals are nearly completely disintegrated; I don't know how we made that last jump."

Well, this is rapidly turning into a 150-WTFs-per-hour event. "How long?"

"three or four minutes according to Jimmex's best estimate of doing it quickly."

Crap, that's going to be a really long three or four minutes, I thought.

I looked over at Zane and he gave me a one-word suggestion: "Stall."

I turned back to my comms panel, "Keep us moving Huang: present a harder target to shoot missiles at." I flipped the comms panel back on and the angry face of Admiral Parakto was front and center.

"I will punish your station for your useless attacks on my ship, Captain Dave!" his twisted face growled at me.

I grabbed my RexCom and opened it up, looking for the message thread that I'd been working on when discussing courses of action with Revus. *Yep, that's the one. Stall for time, here we go.* "Okay, Admiral, *listen up*, in accordance with council policy RT-4, paragraph ninety-one, I've formally requested the Skailiens to arbitrate our dispute."

This response caused the admiral to jerk his face back to the camera and it subsequently twisted up into an ugly frown as he appeared to look at a screen to his left scrolling with his hands. A few seconds later, he replied, "We do not accept arbitration by the Skailiens; we already own this sector of the galaxy."

The flagship slowed its movement towards the station slightly.

I continued, "That has not been decided by the Council and its within our right to request immediate arbitration by an outside party. I've contacted the council, and the request has been accepted for arbitration by your ambassador and the council chief." I lied. "Check for yourself, Admiral, any actions you take from here out will be scrutinized, and no doubt result in the Intergalactic Federal Council handing out punishment to the Grojiel Federal Empire. All because of your reckless actions."

The admiral barked several orders that I couldn't make out and waited for a response. Several minutes elapsed when finally he replied, "What was the transaction control number, Human?"

Control number? Well crap. I didn't see that coming. "Well hold one second there, Admiral, let me get that number for you." As I muted, I asked Mickey, "What's the deal with the Gravitron, Mick?"

"You lie Human! I will cut your ship to pieces for this insolent behavior—fire on the station!" said the admiral.

Mickey's voice overlapped the last part of the admiral's words. "Sir, we're ready for a jump."

I didn't like the shaky sound in Mickey's voice as he seemed to specify "a jump." *We can't let them hit the defenseless station again.* "Huang jump!" I said. *ZZPOOF!* Huang executed a programmed jump, and we appeared back in normal space, just below the admiral's flagship, and we started pounding it with everything we had left: a rail gun round, and one missile Maria managed to get working, and Sarah's highly optimized pulse microwave gun.

"Okay, Huang, jump us out of here," I said.

"It's—it's not responding sir!"

"Mickey!" I yelled into the comms panel.

"Working on it, sir. Jimmie thinks something's misaligned; it's not passing safety checks."

"Huang, evasive maneuvers. Keep backing us away erratically, and try to keep us below that ship and away from the big pulse weapon on top. We can't survive a direct hit from that thing. Mickey, get that damn thing fixed!"

Seconds ticked by as the flagship slowly spun around in what seemed like an effort to line up its pulse beam weapon.

Huang spun and twisted us around as we back-pedaled away from that hulking flagship launching decoy drones. Its armor was very thick, and our missiles weren't having a significant enough effect against it. *Holy crap, this maneuvering is nauseating.*

"Four inbound unidentified MTIs, moving very fast," Zane said over the comms link.

I could hear Revus then say, "Missiles... Dave, countermeasures..."

Crap, I fumbled around for the countermeasures panel.

There it is.

In our plan, countermeasures were my responsibility because everyone already had a full plate of duties during the combat session. I launched several countermeasures. "Mickey!" I yelled. A few long seconds later...

"Hit it Huang!" came Mickey's voice.

ZZPOOF!

We jumped, but not far. I spun the Holo Map around to see that it appeared that our countermeasures took out three of the four missiles, while the fourth slowly started to arc around toward our current location. *Well crap. Okay well at least it's not heading for Earth Station....* "Mick, can we jump again?" I asked.

"Roger that, Dave, not far, but we should be able do... *two-ish* more jumps in quick succession. Then I need two minutes to reset, and I think we'll be back to full power after that."

"Got it. Huang, Sarah, let that missile get a little closer, and then jump us out ten thousand kilometers to zenith plus ten degrees to port. We want the missile to follow us if possible."

"Ack, Sir," said Huang.

"Working it now, Sir," said Sarah after him.

ZZPOOF!

I looked at my Holo Map and camera monitors. "Okay, hold... let the missile reacquire...." *Well crap. The missile lost us.* I saw it start to slowly spiral as it turned toward the station. "Huang, give us a strong burn with the main engines, the missile lost us."

"Roger, Sir," came Huang's reply as he artfully manipulated the controls.

As *Big Al* started to maneuver, I noticed the missile stopped spiraling toward the station and seemed to pick up our trail again as it began streaking directly toward our position on what looked like an intercept course. "Mickey we ready for the second jump? No surprises, as we are going to cut this one a little close."

Nothing.

"Mick!" I yelled loudly into the intercom.

"Yes, sir, it should work for one more short, very short, jump," came Mickey's voice.

"Huang, wait..." I said. "Hold... Hold... Jump!"

ZZPOOF!

I looked at my monitors and Holo Map. *Not updated yet!* It always seemed to take a few seconds for them to catch up after a jump, but this time they didn't change or respond at all.

Well crap. What else is going to go wrong here? I thought.

"Sarah, Zane, sensors are not updating..."

"I'm checking it, Sir," replied Sarah.

Where is that missile?

After what seemed like an hour, but was only a few seconds, the Holo Map and the other sensor feeds started updating. The missile was gone but the station, the enemy, and debris were still in the same relative positions. Sarah replied, "Sir, the main sensor compute unit rebooted and failed over to the backup which took a few minutes to cache and catch up."

"Ack, thank you. Anyone see the missile?"

No one replied. Seconds ticked by. "Huang, evasive action, anything, execute now... I'm launching countermeasures," I said as I hit the button to deploy two packets of active countermeasures in hopes that the signature we programmed into it would look like *Big Al* enough to attract the missile.

Then Zane piped in, "I checked with Earth station; that missile struck an unmanned, remotely piloted freighter that was hightailing it out of here—completely destroyed it. Must have been one of the big battleship missiles."

"Roger, thank you Zane. Huang, pause evasive," I said as I prepared mentally for the next steps with the admiral. "What's left? Maria, any missiles?"

Maria responded quickly, "We have two of the super duty skip missiles ready to go, and rail gun rounds that will be effective from close range and if we hit the right spots. The pulse weapon is tied into main power and is ready to go but again only at close quarters."

I walked through options in my head. I didn't immediately see any good ones. *The plan is failing, and this is going to be on me. Crap.*

The green comms signal indicator light came on as Admiral Parakto's face appeared on screen. "It's you or the station, Captain Murray," he said.

"Don't jump again and prepare for boarding."

Those words hit me like a sledgehammer to the stomach. I couldn't breathe. I couldn't move my eyes from the face on screen. I could feel Zane and the others looking at me. A flood of thoughts hit me like a punch in my already twisted gut. I thought about all the souls on the station that had already died and the number to come. I started second-guessing all my decisions. *I should have tried to negotiate differently... I ... I... should have...*

"Dave..." I could hear Zane's words, but I was frozen with fear, anger, and the despair of responsibility all at once. My mind had chosen this precise moment to point out all my perceived decision mistakes in a symphony of events replaying through my mind. *I suppose my psych file was right after all... maybe I am an incompetent coward who can't handle the true stress of leadership or making hard decisions.*

Somewhere deep inside my brain, a loud, confident-sounding glimmer of hope fired brightly saying, *Break out of it, man! You've got to stop letting fear and anxiety paralyze you.*

Lead the team. Lead in success or in failure but lead!

Yes, that's right. There's still a chance, I thought as I remembered an emergency tactic that we had not yet employed. Plus the skip missiles have twice the penetration power of the standard Veeniri missiles.

Finally, I snapped back to the moment and looked at my crew, many of whom were staring at me awkwardly from their current positions.

"We are not out of this yet people—Maria, prepare to fire both of the experimental skip missiles. Huang, line us up for the shot as the skip missiles are not very tactically maneuverable. Then we are going to jump in ultra close and use Sarah's pulse weapon to raze their systems where the missiles strike. Mickey, we'll be firing the rail gun at close range where the missiles detonate," I said with a calm but strong voice. "Yes sir." responded Huang, "Ack" said Maria.

"Dave... the battleship's point defenses are going crazy..." Zane observed.

I rapidly scanned the monitors and sensor feeds looking for the cause of the activity.

I caught a glimpse of what I'd hoped was the cause of all the point defense cannon fire from the admiral's ship. *Hell yes,* I thought!

FINALLY... my stomach untwisted a notch as confidence sparked to life in my mind. After weeks of stress and suffering. After all our emergency planning and risk taking. After all our freezing with no power and desperate collaboration and bartering... we were finally getting the upper hand. The Grojiel were going to get punched right in the throat.

"Smile you asshole," I said to Admiral Parakto on the comms screen.

This comment caused him to snap a stern look back at me as it took a moment for the translation to get through to him.

"Admiral, we are not standing down; you are the illegal aggressor here. If we surrender, you will continue to attack us. We're the only hope we have, and we *will* defeat you, right here, right now," I said with growing confidence.

"Dave. We're receiving an X band signal; it's a comms request," Zane said.

I looked down at him as I hit the green signal acceptance button on the comms panel. My comms screen split into two side-by-side visuals with Admiral Parakto on the left and a new face on the right.

Chapter 25: The Advantage of Allies

"These Airbags your enemy?" said Billee, with his normal snappy voice that always seemed like he was cracking a joke through the translator.

I smiled as I confirmed from the sensor feeds that the admiral's point defenses were shooting at the orbs from Billee's ship. Those damned little orbs.

"Yes Billee, that's our enemy."

"Well, it about to have big problem," Billee replied. "We launched orbs. Maybe you share peanut butter next time, and we get here sooner. You drop us off too far from fight," Billee said with a very toothy grin.

My eyes refocused on the admiral on my comms screen. "Looks like you are... experiencing some problems with your ship there, Admiral," I said, as menacingly as possible.

The admiral inadvertently left his comms link up, and we could hear the panicked staff briefing him on the attacking orbs, as they apparently attached to the hull and rolled into weak points in the ship, and then exploded like an attached microwave pulse weapon, some with high-output payloads and others with energy draining electromagnetic pulses. It was an extremely effective combination, and it was distributed across the admiral's entire ship.

The admiral's link went down.

"Billee get outta there; they still have a pulse weapon and many missiles," I yelled into my comms panel. Billee's face never left the screen as he barked out orders to his crew that didn't get translated. Billee's ship was very close to the Admiral's ship and it looked like they were moving away at high speed.

"No worry, Dave; we battle often. This ship no problem," Billee replied.

Just as Billee said this, four new MTIs appeared on our Holo Map from the flagship arcing toward Billee's bullet-shaped ship, which immediately launched countermeasures and moved swiftly, unlike any maneuver I'd ever seen. Billee's ship seemed to dance and dodged the inbound missiles effortlessly.

Holy crap. How did that ship move like that? I thought.

"Wow," said Huang, "I've never seen a ship maneuver like that before. It just spin-jumped out of the path of the missiles and bounced right back to the same position. And those countermeasures, they seemed to really dazzle the missiles."

"Roger that, I saw it as well. Apparently, their ships have a propulsion type that enables great agility," I replied to Huang.

Zane turned to look back at me and said, "Sir, pick up camera four; looks like they're hitting Billee with that pulse weapon."

I opened camera four's video feed.

"I see it. Looks like Billee's ship has some kind of shielding based on the visual reflections of multicolor energy being dissipated away from their hull."

Billee's in trouble, I thought. "Maria, fire both skip missiles, let's provide some room for Billee to maneuver."

Maria's voice rang loudly through the intercom, "Sir, both missiles launched successfully."

Two very bright explosions bloomed on the battleship as Billee's ship maneuvered away.

"Ack, thank you, Maria, good shooting!" I replied.

Sarah's voice sharply broadcast over the intercom, "Camera seven feed shows *a whole bunch* of explosions on the enemy's ship, a bunch of small explosions. Not sure if it's penetrating their armored hull, but it's certainly causing havoc with their systems, as they've stopped pursuit of the Kromakiks' ship and the battleship has started to reel out of control."

I pivoted to camera seven's feed, and wow, just like Sarah had said, hundreds of explosions. I also saw some fire at sporadic points across the hull. Seconds passed. I couldn't take my eyes off the camera-seven feed. There was so much debris, smoke, and fire: the admiral's mighty flagship was clearly in trouble.

Explosion after brilliant explosion occurred on the hull of the Grojiel flagship. The bridge became eerily quiet as we all looked at the ship listing out of control.

"Bingo!" yelled Revus. He said it with such sharpness and volume I nearly jumped out of my seat. Everyone looked over at Revus, clearly startled as he presented us with a "what did I do wrong?" expression. "Did I misuse that aphorism?"

I smiled at Zane and Sarah, finally back at Isolde and over to Revus saying, "You got it mostly right Revus. It just startled us. We were not expecting such a loud outburst." Huang, Sarah and Zane started chuckling as they shifted back to the mission at hand.

"Sir, I've lost the Kromakiks' ship signal," Alex said. "Checking with Earth Station as their sensors are far superior at this point given all the debris floating around the area."

"Uhh. Billee, are you okay?" I whispered over the X band comms link.

Nothing.

"Billee... comms check," I said cleanly over the X band comms link, forcing a smile to no one in particular.

Seconds later.

"Billee!" I said with a notable amount of stress in my voice.

"Sir, Earth station does not have a good track for the Kromakiks' ship... not saying it was destroyed just not..." Alex was interrupted.

"Hello, Dave," came Billee's voice over the X band transceiver.

It was audio only, which concerned me a bit as I hesitated, trying to temper my optimism.

"We took more punishment than I want, but we seem okay. That ship trash now. Just like I promise." Just as Billee finished his comments the hulking flagship started drifting out of the smokey cloud that surrounded it, clearly drifting out of control.

"Looks like they are launching escape pods, Dave," said Zane as Huang started moving us away from a huge mass of debris.

"Good," said Billee as he must have heard Zane's comment. "Now you

247

have prisoners, hopefully senior prisoners, you can exchange for something useful. That the way this works. Good can come from negotiations. Good can come from peace agreements. Maybe these guys respect you more they live to tell about it."

"Alex, please ask the agency if the Skylarks can intercept those pods," I said as Alex acknowledged.

Alex replied about a minute later, "Umm, sir. Umm. Well, the SCA Director and the President of the United States want to speak to you on the Agency priority alert channel. I tried to encrypt the channel but, well it won't sync so basically everyone on Earth and on the station will hear your conversation. I think."

Well crap.

But for once, I felt a bit more confident and well, less concerned about what I'd say and how it would be perceived. *No more of that anxiety,* I thought to myself. *Just going to be reasonable with what I say and let it fly. I suppose they are going to have a ton of questions, and deservedly so. We transmitted a thorough SITREP upon arriving at the system so I'm hoping that pre-answered many of their questions. If they received it.* I continued trying to remain calm and casual as I'd prepared for this. I pulled out my notes and then, I pushed my anxieties aside, not back down. I said, "Roger Alex, put them on. This is as good of a time as any to clear up the situation as best we can." I looked over at Revus and he looked at me in question, to which I whispered, "Politicians."

Revus caught the translation and nodded knowingly, rubbing both his temples *and* the places between all his eyes, in what looked like a very complex yet effective contemplation move. After all, he's got four arms, four hands, and six eyes, so there's a lot of turf to cover there. I've learned that gesture is Revus's way of physically signaling, *"Well crap."*

"Captain Murray, what is your status? Please acknowledge," came the words from the Space Colonization Agency's director whose face popped into view. I was familiar with him, and he was viewed as a good leader by most accounts but the global responsibilities of his mission made him a bit of a politician.

"Sir, it's a long story but the short version is that we were somehow transported light years away where we were picked up by a society known as the Veeniri...."

The director broke back in, "Okay, yes, we received your rather thorough report. What is the current situation up there from your perspective?"

I thought through the situation and finally responded, "Sir, we owe the Veeniri a huge debt; they have literally saved us all." I let that sink in a minute, and as the director started to nod in agreement as though he was ready for more input, I continued, "regarding the current situation, well, it seems like we've got the upper hand and have managed to disable the Grojiel fleet, thanks to our partners and allies. Without them we'd never have made it back home, nor would we have had any tools to fight with. The Veeniri, Higlian, and the Kromakiks are allies, even though the Higlian are technically subjects to the Grojiel. I've been in contact with numerous other species, like the Skailiens, who would like to establish a partnership with the people of Earth despite being millions of light years away. Bottom line, sir, the Graviscape gives us the ability to communicate in minutes to hours, intergalactically, with thousands, perhaps millions of other species. And, thanks to our friends, we can even shortcut through the Graviscape in small ships to travel faster than light. It's not instant. But it is fast. The key to the technology lies in the graviscopic ore, which has some type of organic properties associated with its unique atomic structure. It can be processed into powerful crystals making the ore extraordinarily valuable as it's quite scarce. It's very confusing. We'll provide you with a thorough briefing, sir."

The director nodded through my verbal report to him, rubbing his chin along the way, and seeming to ponder some of the concepts.

As I tried to answer all his immediate questions, someone drew his attention away, and I got the impression we were done for the moment. After nearly a minute of uncomfortable waiting the director turned back to me and replied, "Good work, Captain; I'm on my way to Earth Station within the hour, and I look forward to discussing this with you personally."

Then, United States President Kelly Lopez's face appeared on screen. And well, she had a crap-load of questions, as we discussed our relationship with the Veeniri, Higlian, and the Kromakiks at length, as well as the background of our agreement with the Veeniri and the Grojiel dynamics. She was very interested in the council of civilization and how all the key bits worked together and understanding the limitations of our Gravitron-powered jump capabilities.

The dialogue went on for about twenty minutes, and, finally, she had to cut off the conversation as she was heading into a global meeting to discuss the situation. "No problem, Ma'am; we'll be available if you have additional questions or concerns. We'll be heading back to Mars now, as we are among the few that can help the people there restore our colony." I gave my word to her that we'd support future engagements but told her that it was important for us to get back to Mars ASAP. She nodded and the comms link went down. I turned my attention back to the link connecting Billee's ship, "Billee, you staying here or going with us back to Mars?" I asked casually as I looked at the detailed damage reports from Mars that had been rolling in over the past couple hours.

"Hey, don't leave us here, you owe me peanut butter, Dave," replied Billee.

"Okay, let's get you strapped back onto the side of our hull. I looked over at Zane, "Zane can you get us out of this area, away from all the debris? Reattaching Billee's ship will take another space walk, and I don't want to get nailed by anything big." I smiled at Zane and followed up with, "Time to get our herd corralled up, so we can head home." Pow. Another cowboy reference!

Zane just smiled and shook his head at me. "Weak Sir, that one was weak."

I could see Sarah and Huang smiling as I looked over at the ambassador, and he gave me four thumbs up. I could see he was starting to get humor, at least my jokes.

As Billee maneuvered his ship toward the port side of *Big Al*, I could see some serious damage to the bottom quarter of his ship. *Damn*, I thought, *they took a few serious hits there. Hopefully they didn't lose any lives.* I was trying hard not to think about the loss of life as I could not dodge the feeling of responsibility for pretty much everything. *Pull it together, Dave*, I thought. "Billee, everyone okay in there? I see a lot of damage from here."

"Yes, we okay. Some shake up but no damage that last. We bring wounded onto your ship help patch them. Doc says yes, bring immediately," replied Billee in a more subdued voice and tenor.

"Yes, that makes sense."

About a minute later he replied again, "Dave, you clean windows there too yes, maybe paint and polish edges?" he replied with his more normal, sarcastically humorous voice.

I laughed a little in response as I said, "Sure Billee, we'll even change the oil."

Mickey and I reattached Billee's ship to the port side of *Big Al* by basically wiring it onto the *Big Al's* robotic arm and hull mounts that we welded into place before departing the Kromakiks' system. Their five person ships are much smaller, mostly because the Kromakiks are a small species and don't require the same size ship as humans or Grojiel. Physically, the Kromakiks were even smaller than the Higlians, who were about two thirds the height of the Veeniri. Billee's ship essentially covered the entire port side of the *Algonquin*, but the overall shape enabled the Gravitron reactor, with a few modifications, to cover its mass sufficiently to enable jumping. If the ship stuck out too much further, well, it would not have been fully protected by the reactor's field effect. "Okay, we're good, its secured," I finally said to Zane and Mickey over the comms link. Mickey and I headed back into the ship to prep for our next jump.

Trudezic and Jimmex had figured out a way to extend the graviscopic field effect just enough so that we could bring a single Kromakik ship with us, since we couldn't figure out how to make Gravitrons for their ships to travel independently, and it had turned out to be the best decision we'd ever made. If not for Billee and his ship, I think we'd have lost the battle. We did bring extra orbs as well. We'd stored them in one of the internal cargo bays as we were not sure how many ships we'd find in the Earth system, so we'd anticipated Billee may have needed to reload.

Meanwhile, Billee and his crew brought his wounded into the *Algonquin*'s MedBay where he and Angel helped Doctor Roth and the Veeniri provide needed care. Zane, Sarah, and Mickey got the ship ready to jump, while I popped into MedBay to visit our collective of injured partners and crew. I float-walked down the row of beds talking with the folks strapped into each one of them and thanked them for their contributions. Fortunately, there were no critical patients in the whole ward.

"Sir, we are ready to jump when you give the word," Zane's voice crackled over the ship-wide broadcast.

I floated over to the nearest comm panel and said, "Go ahead Zane, jump us to Mars."

ZZPOOF!

We arrived near Mars and immediately started working to understand the situation. There were a few additional Agency ships in orbit, likely called in to assist. "Chief," I said over the comms link, "We're back, where can we best assist?" I looked at the news feeds being broadcast from the colony as I waited for my transmission to reach Chief Gerrard and give him time to respond.

A few seconds later, Chief Gerrard replied with video on the comms screen. He was still looking harried, "Captain Murray, thank you for coming back, your arrival is the highlight of our day. If you are here, that must mean you defeated that recon ship and the other enemy vessels?"

I smiled and replied, "Roger Chief, we stopped them. For now."

Gerrard mustered a smile at that and said, "Fantastic, the situation here is improving. We've got water and air generators working and fully operational now along with major electric grid repairs completed." His face grew solemn as he continued, "256 dead, 788 wounded. It could have been much worse as those damned aliens didn't know where our critical population centers were located."

I nodded glumly in agreement. "We'll be ready for them next time. They will be back," I said as I continued skimming through the colony news feeds.

"Dave. My wife, well... if you hadn't moved her when you were here before... " Gerrard let out a shaky breath, then continued, "she probably would have died in the attack." I could see the depths of gratitude in Gerrard's eyes; he was truly grateful to have his wife back.

"Happy it worked out Chief; we wouldn't want to lose her." I smiled in response trying to be respectful but low key on taking credit for anything.

"Chief, my cruiser, *Ranger 1,* took a shot, and I've got no way to get down there to assist, can you send someone up to get us?" Chief Gerrard nodded affirmatively and turned to order a shuttle to our location in orbit.

The shuttle took Doctor Roth, Abby, Maria, and several others down to the Mars colony so they could assist in the appropriate areas such as medical, engineering, and infrastructure repair. In three days, we had the colony back up and functioning almost normally again.

Over the next several days we made several jumps back and forth to Earth Station, which was being repaired and seemed to be functioning somewhat normally again as the Skylarks collected up the disabled Grojiel ships.

Admiral Parakto was in a cell with several other survivors, and was facing a hearing at which the United Nations wanted me to testify. During the multiple trips to Earth Station to meet with Earth's leaders from all nations, I also spent a ton of time with the SCA agency seniors explaining the first contact scenarios. The crew and I were interviewed over, and over, and over again. During one meeting, I addressed a special session of the United Nations where I tried to explain how the Council of Civilization worked, and why I'd committed humanity to partner with the Veeniri, and how the partnership would work according to my role as Keretzon.

Revus was exceptionally helpful as he patiently conveyed the intergalactic business processes that formed the Council and how weighty an advantage our significant supply of graviscopic ore was. He also talked at length about how brave the crew and I were during the entire voyage.

There were still tons of questions surrounding how our original transport occurred, and the crew and I answered them as best we could. They wanted to take my RexCom, but Isolde made an impassioned statement, that was backed by Revus, supporting my retention of the device as this was the expectation of the Veeniri people. They also highlighted how Earth would soon be able to stand up its own permanent graviscopic access point similar to the system on Bradea, then they could maintain constant communication using systems like the G-Huds. I was grateful we were collectively able to convince them that the RexCom was tied to me and my role in representing humanity. Isolde was quite the diplomat, as she knew the right things to say and how to broker a proper relationship with the People of Earth. Like father, like daughter I supposed.

I was very proud of Isolde. However, she did insist that I escort her to every engagement and session, which drew some strange comments and started rumors about us and a romantic relationship. I never knew what to say in those situations as I did not want to mess up in my role as Keretzon. So, I often played it off that if we were in a relationship, it was more of a beauty and the beast situation where I was the beast and Isolde was the beauty. I privately testified, without Isolde, that I did volunteer and commit to the role as Keretzon as I desperately wanted the Veeniri's help in getting home. Regardless, I told them that I am the Keretzon and was committed to fulfilling the role's responsibilities. I mentioned the personal commitment I'd made when I last spoke with Ambassador Kjino. It seemed like there was broad understanding of the situation and the reasons for my actions.

Later, in one of the Earth Station's fantastic galleys, I sat with Zane, Sarah, and Isolde enjoying some warm food and a pouch of green tea. Isolde rather publicly gave me a few more details on the Keretzon role. "What? I'm married to you, Isolde?" I said as my panicked voice escalated to a high screech. Zane and Sarah looked back at me as Revus looked over at us with a touch of alarm.

Isolde looked right at me and said, "Yes, you are my Prince, and I am your Princess. It is a ritual to bond our two worlds together for us to be covenanted by our peoples while we pledge to one another."

I looked back at her and said, "I thought I was acting? You know, until we could find the real Keretzon!?" I said, looking at her soft blue face as she peered back at me.

"Dave, you are the real Keretzon. I've known it since we met. You care so much about your crew. You risked so much to bring us Doctor Roth," she said. She gestured toward Sarah and Zane as she continued, "You risked so much to save the people of your home world. You are so kind and respectful to me. You truly are the Keretzon." She reached out with her odd, three-fingered hand, and gently placed it over my left hand.

I looked over at her smile and then down at her hand on mine. I slowly looked over at Zane and Sarah. They were both smiling too. *Huh*, I thought.

No twisting in my gut. That's... well, that's nice. "Oh, what the hell. I've never been a prince before so I guess I can do the best I can," I said as I smiled at everyone around the table.

We spent weeks engaging with the UN and Earth's other leaders in session after tediously long session, answering questions and providing perspective. Revus was irritated that we never found the recon ship or major chunks of its hull, but Earth's fleet was looking for it.

Overall, Earth's leadership was trying hard to figure out a way ahead, and man was it taking time. I never fully disclosed or discussed the mysterious, anonymous messages, or how we got dumped out in what seemed like a planned diversion into the Kromakiks' territory by someone or something. It had to be some *one.* I think it was the same someone who somehow pulled us from Earth's solar system and dropped us conveniently into Veeniri space.

I've also got a new close friend. Billee hasn't really left my side since we met. He's traveling with me from Mars to Earth Station, and back over several trips, and I've learned about his people and their amazing culture. They've been at war for decades, but have established some formal peace in most areas of their solar system. The contentious areas, where natural resources were abundant, is where their proxy war continued between different political factions. He said fighting gets old, but the political fights cut the deepest wounds in his people. Those wounds take generations to heal.

One morning, after everything had settled down, I was conducting my staff circulation task—where I float-walked around the ship to touch base with the crew—when I got into an interesting discussion with Maria down in engineering. She'd been working with Bowendi, Jimmex, and Clarad and thought they'd narrowed down a way to implement a synthetic gravity field on the *Algonquin* using a special algorithm to manipulate a hyper-fast pulsed mode in the Gravitron reactor. "Wow," I said, "that would be awesome if we could have normal Earth-like gravity all the time. But what would that cost in terms of energy and crystals?" I asked.

Bowendi replied, "It would consume about fifteen percent of energy and ten percent of the amount of Gravimetric crystal that's consumed during a normal jump, per ten-hour period. So, over time it would be costly, but given the volume of ore you humans possess, it makes sense to pursue this. We could even craft a specialized Gravitron used only for generating the synthetic gravity field so it could be optimized over time yet not disrupt transportation usage."

Maria said, "It would really make ship life much more appealing, sir, and the health benefits would be significant. Humans didn't evolve in low gravity, so it takes a pretty solid toll on our health."

I looked at them and internally marveled at their multi-species collaboration. This sort of thing probably hadn't even been considered by the other species since the crystals were in such short supply. "Roger," I said, "walking around the ship with mag boots on is definitely not an effective way to get around. It would be great to walk around like we would on Earth. This is excellent; let's try it as soon as we can. I'm sure it will take some trial and error to get it tuned just right. I'm really proud of you. Maria, Bowendi, Clarad, and Jimmex, you are quite the innovative and dynamic thinking team." I gave them all a broad smile and shook hands with each of them, which really seemed to make them feel good about themselves. And that was the point. I believed in them. Anyhow, off to the galley for some peanut butter. "Talk with you later," I said smiling as I float-walked out of engineering. I'd set aside some time to spend with Abby and I was really looking forward to it.

The next morning, we were on our latest jump back to Earth Station and the trip was taking too much time. We were three hours into it, which was far longer than the seconds or minutes the trip had previously taken. "Mickey, what's going on with the Gravitron; why's it taking so long to get to Earth this time?" I asked with a tiny bit of irritation in my voice as I tried to multitask between several ankle-biter duties.

We were going to be at Earth Station for a while on this trip, so I was trying to get my calendar finalized—given all the interviews, talks, and engagements that had been scheduled for me.

Mickey replied a few seconds later, "Everything is nominal down here, sir; Jimmex and Bowendi indicated there's what amounts to normal resistance in the path, something they cannot adequately explain, predict, or even go around. I'd have to get them to explain the details to you. The Gravitron's gauges are all green and steady."

I looked over at Isolde and then over toward Revus and asked him, "Are you aware of some effect that somehow varies our rate of travel through the Graviscape?"

Isolde looked at me as I spoke, then looked toward Revus as he shifted in his seat and said, "Yes, Dave, over thousands of years of using the Graviscape for messaging and even some physical travel, we noticed certain trends and our scientists think that there's some type of strong field effect that prevents physical paradoxes from occurring."

I looked at him with my mouth hanging open as I tried to piece together how that worked. I managed to get a few thoughts together and replied, "You mean the Graviscape knows when a physical paradox will occur; *how the hell does it do that? How could it possibly understand when a paradox is going to occur?*"

Revus replied, "We are not certain how it works, but we think its related to the quantum entanglement phenomena where entangled particles have properties that remain linked through some sort of field effect across vast distances, and somehow this memory results in an anti-paradoxical field effect. I'll ask Jimmex to explain it to you as he's an expert in this particular area of graviscopic research."

I considered his words and glanced back toward Isolde as she added, "Dave, this is the sort of information that we can barter for using the RexCom and engaging through the Intergalactic Knowledge Market. It's likely the Veeniri have already purchased this information as well, but it may be hidden in a protective enclave because of its cost."

I smiled at her and nodded affirmatively. She'd been providing me with a ton of background about the Council of Civilization, history, and the culture of their societies. Fascinating stuff. I did find her some quarters of her own to live in, and that worked for her for a night or two. She couldn't always sleep well, so she mostly bunked with me. I was worried about what the perception of that was with the crew, but Doc told me it was best to keep her close as her father apparently put a lot of faith in me protecting her, and we did just save

Earth thanks to Isolde, the Veeniri, and her father's faith in my fulfilling the Keretzon role.

"You need to take this Keretzon role seriously, Dave," Doc said, as he asked me if we'd been fooling around.

I gave him a fake, over-acted look of righteous indignation and shock. I told him I was trying to keep it professional, but our bodies do touch. We do sort of... well, she was *sometimes* nice to have around. And she was. After all, she's brilliant, kind, and... well, she believed in me. And still does—I can't let her, her father, or her people down.

The trip to Earth Station took four hours in total. I decided not to dwell on the paradox issue at that time as it was my turn to testify at the United Nations, and I needed to get my testimony right, so I needed some focus there.

The UN had put together a task force and a series of special sessions to sort out the way ahead for how Earth would be represented at the Council, given we didn't exactly have a single, unified planetary government. Since my organization was responsible for this first contact situation, the Space Colonization Agency was tasked to help build additional ships with graviscopic transport capability. We were on path to make that happen as our combined, alien and human, crew worked together and helped create three more Gravitron reactors. The need for a Gravitron was only part of the solution, we also had to create two more of the super complicated JumpNav computer systems, which was mostly work completed by the Higlian and Veeniri engineers. Over the weeks we spent docked at Earth Station, they'd outfitted two other ships with Gravitron reactors and computer systems. They didn't work right out of the gate, and required a ton of testing. Ultimately, they would help us better defend our solar system while we grew the ability to travel and explore the galaxy.

Luckily, Earth's leadership managed to agree on a couple of important things:

One, everyone knew the bad guys would be back, so it was just a matter of time and we had to decide how ready we'd be when they returned. Two, Humanity just stepped, or, actually, stumbled, into a vastly complicated intergalactic society that demanded we reorganize our global leadership and political hierarchy, so that we would have somewhat of a unified voice. Therefore, the leaders of Earth created a forum adjacent to the United Nations designed to specifically interact with and deal with alien civilizations. Their job was to represent all the people of Earth and all the colonies in the system. The body was named The Council of Solis. Three, if the people of Earth were to survive, we'd need partners. So, thanks to Isolde, Revus, and Billee, they finally worked out solid mutual defense, trade, and support agreements with the Veeniri, Kromakiks, and the Higlian. The agreements with the Higlian would be handled separately and quietly according to the agency strategists. We'd trade tons of the graviscopic ore to our partners for their support, as we worked out the formal relationship. Now that we knew what to look for, scans of Mercury, Venus, the Asteroid belt, and Mars showed strong indications that there were high concentrations of the graviscopic ore in all those places. The Higlian and Veeniri engineers were ecstatic.

The rest of the support agreements were very basic as everyone wanted to keep things somewhat high-level until we got our best representatives to the Council of Civilization on Bradea to wheel and deal with the local council in person.

"Well, at least the next five years or so won't be boring," I said to Isolde as I departed in the anteroom after testifying against Admiral Parakto for the last time. This was the last session I was required to attend, and I was looking forward to a break from all the attention, as it was nearly time to take Billee and the Kromakiks back home and fulfill our commitment to them.

The next afternoon I was enjoying some fake gravity as Billee, Zane, and I were walking down to engineering to congratulate Maria on her handiwork. "Dave, I don't mind telling you, this will be awesome if we can cheaply maintain near-Earth gravity aboard the *Algonquin*," Zane said as we walked down the gangway to engineering.

"I agree Zane, this could be a game changer for the agency; we could explore distant worlds and find more of the graviscopic ore to barter with, and really make things happen," I replied with a smile on my face.

Billee looked up at Zane and said, "Ha, we Kromakiks are tough and have no need of such luxuries."

I glanced down at Billee and smiled while saying, "Oh come on Billee, you seriously don't want gravity systems for your ships? I'm sure we can work something out."

Billee looked up at me as we approached engineering and smiled saying, "Okay, we could test systems to see if it make life better, but I don't want crews too comfortable."

I smiled as I looked over at Zane, shaking my head at Billee's projection of a tough guy persona, knowing that it was just a shell around a kind, generous and selfless leader.

We walked into engineering and Mickey greeted us and walked us over into a section of the room where Maria was standing near a display screen. Mickey looked at us with a prideful smile, holding out his fist for a fist bump, and said, "Best decision we ever made bringing Maria onto the *Algonquin*'s team. I told you she would get us to the next level, Dave."

Both Zane and I bumped Mickey's fist. "Maria," I started, "this is fantastic work; feels just like home aboard *Big Al*."

"Well, sir, it's truly been a pretty big team effort," Maria said as she pointed to the Veeniri and Higlian engineers standing nearby. "But the system looks like it's going to hold up pretty well while also consuming less of the graviscopic crystal than we thought. The best part is, we've created four smaller Gravitron reactors that function a little differently, yet provide the fake gravity at the right intensity." I looked at the team and then back to Maria as I smiled broadly. Maria continued, "It's similar to how radios need a certain length of antenna to transmit and receive at certain frequencies. In this case, the four reactors are interconnected to these antenna-like devices, which are built at the proper length to create fake gravity with the right shape and intensity with high energy efficiency."

Jimmex spoke from his position standing at the other end of the graviscopic antenna array, "Sir, this has been a collaborative effort, but the true innovation was all Maria. She's really got a knack for plumbing graviscopic fields."

This high praise caused Maria to blush as she smiled over at Jimmex.

"We'll I'm glad we've got a team of experts that can work together—"

My comments were cut off as Isolde ran into the engineering room yelling, "We have to go, Dave! We have to go!"

I turned my head and looked down at an out of breath Isolde.

As she grabbed both my hands, she said, "They've captured my father, and are holding him for ransom on Bradea, Dave; we must go now; I have to help my father!"

I held her sweating hands as I said, "Whoa now, hold on just a second. What's happened to your father?"

She replied, "Look at your RexCom! The Grojiel have taken him and several others as hostages. They want to trade my father for Admiral Parakto and his officers, and they want an unconditional surrender of you humans."

Well crap. They don't want much, I thought. I looked into her blue eyes and could see Isolde was terribly stressed and emotions had churned up the dark blue hue in her skin. It hurt me to see her like this. She was vulnerable to the loss of her father. I needed to step in and get after this problem as it wasn't going to get better with time; it was only going to get worse. "Okay, I get it," I said, "Let's go up to the conference room and plan a return. I need to bring Earth's leadership into this as I don't have the authority to do anything with Admiral Parakto and his officers." I turned to Zane and said, "XO, let's get supplied up as best as possible and be ready for departure in twelve hours. I'm not saying we'll be able to leave then, but that's the mark on the wall." I slowly moved my head looking at everyone in the room and said, "Everyone, now is the time to strategize. We need everyone to think about how we can be prepared for an encounter on Bradea. Or, heck, anywhere along the way. Thanks again for the great work here; now let's get the *Algonquin* ready for departure."

Chapter 26: Back to the Council

Isolde didn't misread anything. The Veeniri council reached out to both of us with an official, emergency communique requesting we return within the next one hundred hours. That's when the Grojiel intended to start killing one of the ambassador's staff, ending with the ambassador himself, every hour if we didn't show up to meet their demands.

We met with the Council of Solis leadership led by the freshly elected Council Chief, Doctor Timothy Chang, in a large conference room on Earth Station where the Agency and Council staffers had worked out a rough plan to get us back to Veeniri space. The plan included the right people, specialized equipment, and a time buffer in case something went wrong.

The Council Chief's final guidance rang like a bell in my head as we finished the session. "Captain, our best analysts indicate the Grojiel will return within six months to test our resolve. We're going to be ready for them; I'll see to that. We'll be sending senior personnel with you, but in your role as Keretzon, you'll still be in charge overall. I expect you'll be thrust, again... into impossible situations. Please remember, wherever you are, do the best you can in the moment, but... don't forget the big picture. The security of Earth must be factored into everything you do and say. I would say good luck, but you won't need luck, just the right data, purpose and judgment."

I knew what he was getting at.

During the previous mission, I'd dangerously committed Earth to agreements beyond my authority in an effort to get home at all costs. I couldn't do that again. If it comes down to it, we'll sacrifice ourselves to keep Earth in a defensible, equitable position. *Message received.* I'm sure that means there will be armed soldiers aboard with orders to remove me, if the situation demands it.

We would take Admiral Parakto and a few of his officers on the *Algonquin* and sprint back to Bradea to engage with the Grojiel while following our strategy. We'd also take a military special forces team, professional negotiators, and a few other mission specialists to make sure we gave ourselves the best chance to get the Veeniri out of this situation. The *Algonquin* was going to be packed on this trip back to Bradea.

I talked with Zane, as Billee, Revus, Isolde, Sarah and I float-walked back to the ship from Earth Station. Only Zane and I were allowed to attend the session with Earth's senior leaders, strategists and yes, politicians, which irritated Isolde. "The Grojiel want us back on a short timeline, so we do not have time to prepare an effective attack. That damn recon ship must have returned to Grojiel space with news of the fleet's defeat," said Revus.

I looked over at him and back toward Isolde. She was doing better, but was still very stressed out. "Yes, that makes sense. Revus... this time we'll have a few tricks up our own sleeve." I grabbed Isolde's hand and continued, "Isolde, this plan will work. We are going to get your father back safely." I smiled as I was trying to convince myself that we could pull this off.

Isolde took my hand in her large three-digit hand and said, "Dave, I'm grateful for how your people are working so hard to assist us. Unfortunately, I know how treacherous and hateful the Grojiel can be.... I... I'm trying to ready myself for any outcome," she said as she squeezed my hand.

Back on the *Algonquin*, things were... well... things were crowded. The ship was about fifteen people past capacity, and two cargo bays had to be fitted out as quarters. Doc's voice came over the ship's broadcast comms system, "Captain to MedBay, Captain to MedBay."

Acknowledging the signal, I dropped my stuff in my quarters and trotted out, enjoying the fake gravity, and headed to MedBay. When I walked into the room, I saw Doc, and he wordlessly motioned toward one of the isolation rooms. I quietly walked into the room and saw Abby organizing some packed equipment.

"Hey," I said as I walked into the room, "isn't this gravity awesome?" I grinned broadly as I looked her way. She stood up and turned her head to look at me, smiling weakly.

Her smile dissolved as she said, "I'm being ordered to another ship for a while. Zane and Doc thought I should tell you privately..."

I walked over to her, looking into her eyes, our faces inches apart, "I didn't authorize any crew changes—"

Abby cut me off responding, "The Agency leadership doesn't want anything to get in the way of your role as Keretzon. Anything *like me* apparently."

Abby was trying to smile, but she was visibly upset. I got it though; the Agency didn't want me to screw up things with Isolde. "I'll reach out to the Operations Chief directly," I said as Abby shook her head disapprovingly. She really surprised me with her next move. She stepped close to me, so close I could smell the scent of her body and it mesmerized me.

She grabbed my head with her soft hands and kissed me deeply on the lips. Now this was something I'd thought about every day since she'd arrived aboard the mighty *Algonquin,* but the reality far exceeded my dreams.

I wrapped my arms around her and returned the kiss as firmly, but gently, as possible.

Finally, she pulled back and looked into my eyes saying, "Go do your job, Captain Dave Murray. I believe in you." A single tear rolled down her cheek. She looked as though she wanted to say something else.

I said, "Abby..." but before I could continue, she placed an index finger over my lips. Then she stepped back toward the equipment case she'd been packing, grabbed it by the handle and quietly walked out of the room.

I was stunned. I just stood there, frozen in my overwhelmingly emotional thoughts.

Doc walked into the room and said, "Dave, snap out of it. We've got a mission to accomplish. You with me?"

I stood there frozen as thousands of thoughts, thousands of different decision paths, flashed across my mind. No matter how hard I tried, the number of paths always narrowed to a single route. The route where I take the *Algonquin* to Bradea to try and rescue Isolde's father.

I turned slowly to look at Doc with a stupefied expression on my face and

CHAPTER 26: BACK TO THE COUNCIL

said, "Yes, I... I'm okay." Doc and I exchanged glances for several seconds as I could tell he was trying to assess my mental state.

Finally, an understanding smile broke across his face. "Success at love is hard, Dave. It's wonderful when it works, and it's torture when it doesn't. I'm not saying this won't eventually work. But for now, best you pull yourself together and get the team to Bradea. We can talk about it along the way."

I smiled back at Doc and then ran my hand over my face to wipe away the budding tears welling in my eyes. Then I straightened up, looked over toward Doc, and said, "Thanks, Doc. I'll take you up on that. You are right, we need to get after it. We've got a lot of work ahead of us."

I stepped toward Doc and gave him a handshake-hug as he smiled and patted my shoulder a few times with his non-handshake hand.

"Thanks for this, Doc. I really appreciate all your guidance and help over the years." I pushed back to face him, straightened my uniform shirt collar and said, "I'll see you in a little while."

I turned and walked out of MedBay.

Man on a mission.

To be continued...

Request of Author Support

Thank you for reading my book, I truly hope you enjoyed it.

If you could please leave a review and tell a friend how much you enjoyed it, I'd be grateful.

About the Author

M.A. Mollenkopf is a cyberspace security specialist who enjoys writing software and science fiction.

As a boy he was inspired by Robert Heinlein's Space Cadet novel and became an instant, lifelong fan of science fiction.

He is married and lives in Georgia with his wife.

You can reach out to him at **mamollenkopf@graviscape.net**

You can connect with me on:

🌐 https://graviscape.net